Second Chance Under the Mistletoe

Second Chance Under the Mistletoe

Renee McCorry

Dedication

For my husband — my constant source of strength and calm through every late-night draft and rewrite. Your faith in me never wavered, even when mine did. I couldn't have written a single word without your love beside me

Contents

Prologue

Rain whispered against the tall windows, soft but insistent, blurring the lights of the city into streaks of gold and gray. The apartment was mostly dark, lit only by the amber glow of a desk lamp that cast long shadows across the room. Julian sat motionless at his desk, a pen resting between his fingers, a half-finished letter before him.

The ink had dried years ago.

He stared at the page; at the words he'd already written and the ones he couldn't bring himself to. The city beyond the glass hummed with restless energy, taxis slicing through puddles, horns echoing up through the rain. But here, in the quiet, it felt like another world entirely.

The letter wasn't meant for the public, or a food critic, or even a friend from his polished circles. It was personal. Too personal.

He ran a hand through his hair, exhaling slowly. He'd written thousands of words in his life, menus, speeches, thank-you notes, and press statements. But these few sentences felt heavier than all of them.

His gaze drifted to the photo propped on the edge of the desk: a snapshot from the mountain town. The bakery's front window glowed behind them, snow falling in soft spirals, Lani's smile on the faded photograph.

Lani,

Some nights, I still hear the train whistle in my dreams.

The kitchens are louder here, the air thicker, the pace relentless.

They say success tastes sweet, but I've learned it also burns. I've made a name for myself with awards, articles, and cameras. But sometimes, when I'm plating a dish, I still think of you kneading bread by the window, sunlight in your hair. That's what real creation looks like.

I thought leaving would make me more. Instead, I think it just made me... different.

You were right. Home isn't a place you outgrow. It's a heartbeat you carry with you, whether you mean to or not.

If you ever wondered, I didn't leave because I stopped loving you. I left because I was scared that love wasn't enough to build the life I dreamed of. But what I've learned, Lani, is that life means nothing if you can't share it with the person who believed in you first.

He set the pen down next to the envelope, staring at her name. The ink shimmered faintly before smudging under his thumb. He didn't send it. He never did.

Instead, he once again folded it carefully, tucked it into the back of an old recipe book — the one with her handwriting in the margins — and sat in silence as the city lights flickered outside.

{ 1 }

Lani

The biting wind whipped Lani Shepard's hair across her face as she stepped out of the car, the crunch of snow under her boots a familiar, yet jarring, sound. She inhaled a crisp, clean breath that tasted of pine needles and the sharp promise of winter. It had been years since she'd breathed this crisp mountain air, years since the scent of pine and woodsmoke had been a constant, comforting presence. Now, it felt like a ghost, whispering promises and regrets. She'd driven for hours, the landscape gradually transforming from the muted grays of late autumn to the stark, dazzling white of winter.

The ache of her divorce, a constant, dull throb beneath the surface of her everyday life, seemed to recede with each mile she put between herself and the life she had meticulously constructed, only to watch it crumble.

Gone was the acrid bite of gasoline and the cloying sweetness of exhaust. Instead, a sharp, invigorating tang of pine needles pricked her nostrils, followed by the damp, earthy perfume of decaying leaves underfoot. She inhaled deeply, the coolness expanding in her chest, a tangible sigh escaping her lips.

"Finally," she breathed, the word a soft exhalation against the quiet hum of the forest.

Evergreen Hollow. The name itself conjured images of quaint storefronts dusted with snow, of cozy evenings by crackling fires, and the comforting, unwavering rhythm of a town that time seemed to have forgotten. In the best possible way. It was a place where she had learned to ride a bike, skinned her knees on its charmingly uneven sidewalks, and first experienced the dizzying rush of young love. Her hometown, nestled in the embrace of towering, snow-dusted peaks, was a postcard come to life, a place she'd both cherished and fled. Now, she was returning with her daughter, Naomi, in tow.

Unpacking the car was a laborious affair, each box a heavy testament to the life she was momentarily leaving behind, a life that felt increasingly fragile. The movers had deposited the last of them by the porch of her childhood home, a sturdy, welcoming structure that seemed to have weathered time as gracefully as her parents.

Her parents.

The thought brought a pang of guilt mixed with an overwhelming surge of love. They were the anchor that had drawn her back, the reason this temporary haven had been established in her old room.

As she wrestled a particularly stubborn box labeled 'Linens – Fragile,' a small hand tugged at her sleeve. Naomi, her daughter, her bright, inquisitive six-year-old, stood beside her, her eyes wide with wonder as she gazed at the snow-laden branches of the ancient oak tree in the yard.

"Mommy, look!" she exclaimed, her voice a clear bell against the hushed landscape. "It's like a fairy tale!"

Lani forced a smile, her heart aching with tenderness so intense it almost hurt. Naomi, so full of innocent joy, was blissfully unaware of the emotional baggage her mother carried. For Naomi, this was an adventure, a winter wonderland to explore. For Lani, it was a return to a past she'd fought so hard to escape, confronting ghosts she'd hoped had long since faded into obscurity. The weight of her divorce, the uncertainty of her future, the quiet desperation that had led her to this very doorstep. It all felt as tangible as the boxes she was unpacking.

The house itself was a comforting embrace. The scent of cinnamon and something distinctly sweet, something that spoke of flour and sugar and the magic of transformation, wafted from the adjoining building. Shepard's Sweets. Her parents' bakery. It was more than just a business; it was the heart of their lives, the source of their livelihood, and for Lani, a potent symbol of everything she had left behind. The aroma, usually a source of comfort, now felt like a bittersweet anchor, pulling her back to a life she had believed was irrevocably in her rearview mirror. Each breath of that familiar fragrance was a reminder of the woman she had once been, the dreams she had nurtured within these very walls, and the painful reality of how far she had strayed.

Her childhood bedroom, untouched and preserved like a museum exhibit, greeted her with a silent embrace. Dust motes danced in the sliver of sunlight piercing the drawn curtains, illuminating the silent tableau. The air, thick with the scent of aged paper and a faint whisper of lavender, settled around her shoulders like a familiar shawl. Her gaze snagged on the wall, where a riot of faded roses and trailing vines, a younger self's fervent choice, still clung with stubborn cheerfulness. The small bed, its mattress plumped by an unseen hand, wore a quilt of sunshine yellow and sky blue, a stark contrast to the muted tones elsewhere. Beside it, a tower of paperbacks, spines cracked and pages dog-eared, leaned precariously, guarding a galaxy of forgotten treasures, a chipped porcelain bird, a smooth, sea-worn stone, a tarnished silver locket.

"Still looks just the same," she murmured.

She ran a finger along the cool, slightly rough surface of the nightstand, the dust yielding beneath her touch. "Except... everything feels a little smaller. It was a sanctuary, a temporary reprieve, but it also felt like a cage, a gilded prison of memories.

As she opened the first box, a wave of forgotten moments washed over her. A framed photograph, slightly askew, showed a younger Lani, her eyes bright with untamed ambition, standing proudly beside her parents in front of the bakery. She remembered that day. The opening of the new display window, the excitement of fresh inventory, the boundless optimism of a future that seemed limitless. Now, that optimism felt like a distant echo, a faint whisper from a life lived by someone else.

She carefully lifted out a small, intricately carved wooden bird. Her father had made it for her when she was little, a symbol of freedom, he'd said, a reminder that she could always fly. Lani's fingers traced the smooth, worn wood, a lump forming in her throat. She hadn't flown, not in the way he'd intended. She'd simply... moved. And then, she'd fallen. And now, here she was, back in the nest, the wings that had once felt so strong now feeling heavy and uncertain.

Naomi, having exhausted her initial fascination with the snow, had found a stack of Lani's old art supplies. Her small hands, smudged with what Lani suspected was stray flour from the bakery, were already sketching furiously in a discarded notebook. Lani watched her, a fierce protectiveness rising within her. Naomi was the reason she was here. To shield her from the harsh realities of their recent past, to give her the stability and wonder of a childhood, Lani feared she had inadvertently denied her.

This town, this bakery, this return to roots. It was all for Naomi.

The boxes held more than just physical objects; they held emotional artifacts -tangible pieces of a life Lani had meticulously packed away, hoping to leave behind forever. A worn diary, its pages filled with teenage angst and dreams of artistic grandeur. A collection of concert tickets, remnants of youthful abandon. A chipped ceramic mug, a gift from a college friend. Each item was a small explosion of memory, some sweet, some sharp, all contributing to the complex tapestry of her past.

She paused, leaning against the doorframe that separated her temporary room from the bustling heart of the bakery. The rhythmic thud of dough being kneaded, the clatter of baking pans, the cheerful hum of conversation from customers, it was a symphony of normalcy, a stark contrast to the turmoil brewing within her. Her parents, bless them, were enduring pillars of strength and love. They had opened their home and their business to her and Naomi without question, offering solace and a much-needed sense of belonging. But Lani knew their welcome wasn't just about her; it was about Naomi, too. They saw in Naomi the continuation of their legacy, the spark of generations past, and Lani was determined not to let them down.

She picked up another box, heavier this time, labeled 'University – Art.' The contents were a potent reminder of a different path, a future she'd envisioned for herself that had ultimately been rerouted. Galleries, exhibitions, the thrill of creation. These were once her driving forces. But life, as it often does, had intervened, and her artistic aspirations had been set aside, then shelved, and finally, seemingly forgotten.

Now, surrounded by the comforting, yet confining, familiarity of her childhood room, the scent of baking a constant reminder of her parents' craft, Lani felt a pang of regret, a deep yearning for the dreams she had deferred.

As she began to unpack, carefully placing each item in its designated drawer or shelf, a sense of order began to emerge from the chaos. It was a deliberate act, an attempt to impose structure on her life, to create a sense of control in a situation that felt overwhelmingly out of her hands. Each item placed was a small victory, a step towards establishing a temporary foothold in this place she had once called home.

Meanwhile, Naomi had moved on to a box of old Christmas decorations. Her delighted squeals echoed through the house as she pulled out shimmering baubles, tinsel, and strings of fairy lights.

"Mommy, can we decorate the tree now?" she pleaded, her eyes sparkling with anticipation.

Lani's heart softened. "Not yet, sweetheart." The holiday season was fast approaching, and in this town, it was more than just a festive occasion; it was a sacred ritual, a time of profound connection and shared joy.

She looked at the boxes, still scattered around the room, each one a chapter of her life waiting to be reread. The task of unpacking felt monumental, not just physically, but emotionally. It was an excavation, an unearthing of buried feelings, a confrontation with the woman she had been and the woman she was now. The crisp mountain air, once a symbol of freedom, now felt heavy with the weight of her past.

The sweet scent of the bakery, once a beacon of warmth, now served as a bittersweet reminder of a life she had tried to outrun. But as she looked at Naomi, her daughter's innocent excitement, a beacon of pure joy, Lani knew she had to unpack it all, not just for herself, but for her. This was the beginning of a new chapter, whether she was ready for it or not. The past was no longer a foreign country; it was her present, and she had to learn to navigate its familiar, yet treacherous, terrain.

The process of unpacking was slow, deliberate, and deeply emotional. Each item pulled from the cardboard confines served as a catalyst, unlocking a floodgate of memories, both pleasant and painful. Lani found herself pausing more often than not, lost in thought, a faint smile or a wistful sigh escaping her lips. She discovered a stack of letters tied with a faded ribbon, her mother's elegant script adorning the envelopes. Hesitantly, she untied the ribbon, her fingers trembling slightly.

They were letters written to her father during his brief time away for a business conference years ago, filled with mundane details of life at home, interspersed with declarations of love and unwavering support. Reading them, Lani was struck by the quiet strength and resilience of her mother, the bedrock upon which their family and the bakery had been built. It was a testament to a love that endured, a partnership forged not just in shared dreams but in the daily grind of life. This was the kind of strength Lani was beginning to hope she could find within herself again.

Nestled amongst the letters was a small, pressed flower, its petals a delicate, ethereal blue. Lani vaguely remembered picking it from the meadow behind the house during a rare moment of solitude, a fleeting escape from the pressures of her then-unfolding life.

It was a fragile symbol of a time when she still sought solace in nature, a reminder of a connection to the world around her that had been dulled by the complexities of adulthood and the ensuing heartache of her divorce. Its delicate beauty felt like a whisper from her younger self, a gentle reminder of the artist she once was, the dreamer who found inspiration in the simplest of things.

As she continued to sort through the university box, her hands brushed against a collection of charcoal sketches, quick, gestural studies of faces and forms. These were the works of a student brimming with raw talent and eager ambition. She remembered the thrill of those classes, the late nights spent in the studio, the visceral joy of translating emotion onto paper.

But juxtaposed with these vibrant creations were more recent sketches, darker, more abstract pieces, reflecting a period of emotional turmoil. She found herself hesitating, her fingers hovering over the darker works, reluctant to delve too deeply into that painful chapter of her life.

Yet, she knew that confronting these memories, however difficult, was an essential part of her healing process.

The tangle of fairy lights, like captured starlight, now pulsed softly, casting a warm glow on a few chipped baubles nestled amongst them.

Naomi's small hands, dusted with glitter, still clutched a faded teddy bear. Her knees, pressed into the plush rug, formed a soft mound beneath her. The vibrant hum of her earlier energy had evaporated, replaced by a stillness that settled like dust motes in the quiet room.

Outside, the world dissolved into a watercolor wash of white. Fat flakes, like tiny, silent dancers, pirouetted against the frosted glass, blurring the edges of the world beyond. Each descent seemed to carry a whispered secret, a hushed promise of the season. The air itself felt heavy with the scent of pine, a fragrant whisper from the meager tree, mingling with the faint sweetness of gingerbread cookies cooling on a nearby rack.

Suddenly, a small sigh escaped her lips, a puff of warm air misting the glass. She shifted, her elbow nudging the bear, its button eyes staring blankly ahead. A single, stray thread, the color of forgotten dreams, clung to its worn ear.

"It's pretty, isn't it, Mommy?"

Lani didn't turn. Her gaze remained locked on the swirling descent of the snow.

"Mmm," she hummed, a sound like the soft rumble of distant thunder, barely audible above the sigh of the wind.

Lani watched her, her heart clenching. Naomi's quiet moments were often a prelude to deep questions, the kind that Lani sometimes struggled to answer. She knew that her daughter, even at such a young age, possessed a remarkable sensitivity to the feelings around her. Naomi had already sensed the quiet weight in Lani's mood, reading it with the instinctive awareness only a child could have.

Lani picked up a framed photograph of herself and her ex-husband, a relic from a happier time. They were laughing, caught in a candid moment, their eyes full of a love that now felt like a distant mirage. She placed it back in the box, sadness washing over her. It wasn't anger or bitterness that she felt, but a deep sense of loss, not just for the marriage itself, but for the future they had once envisioned together. The dream had soured, leaving behind a bitter aftertaste that lingered even now. She knew she had to let go, truly let go, if she was to embrace the possibilities that lay before her.

The scent of baking, a constant presence, seemed to deepen as her parents moved through their evening preparations. It was a smell that spoke of comfort, of tradition, of generations of culinary passion. It was the smell of home, but also the smell of obligation, a reminder of the role she was expected to play. Lani wondered if she could ever truly reclaim that sense of belonging, that easy comfort, or if she would forever be an outsider, a visitor in her own past.

As she carefully placed a delicate porcelain teacup, a cherished heirloom, into a padded compartment, she caught her reflection in its polished surface. The woman looking back was weary, her eyes holding a depth of experience that belied her relatively young age. But there was also a flicker of something else, a nascent spark of resilience, a quiet determination that had seen her through the darkest of times. The unpacking was more than just organizing possessions; it was an act of self-discovery, a process of rediscovering the pieces of herself that had been scattered and lost.

The boxes, once daunting and overwhelming, were slowly being emptied, their contents finding their place within the familiar walls of her childhood bedroom. The room where one stored the past was gradually transforming into a temporary home. A space where memories and present reality could coexist. The crisp mountain air still bit at her cheeks, and the scent of the bakery still tugged at her heartstrings, but now, mingled with the bittersweet ache, was a faint, yet persistent, note of hope.

The unpacking was far from over, but with each item carefully placed, Lani felt a little closer to understanding where she had been, and perhaps, just perhaps, where she was going. The journey of confronting her past had truly begun, and though the path was uncertain, she was no longer walking it alone. Naomi's presence, a constant reminder of her purpose, and the quiet strength of her parents, offered an anchor in the swirling currents of her emotions. The weight of the boxes was beginning to feel less like a burden and more like the foundation of a new beginning.

As they walked towards the bakery, Lani's gaze swept over the familiar storefront the red awning now a little faded and the window displays were a cheerful testament to the season. The 'Shepard's Sweets' sign, hand-painted by her grandfather decades ago, was still proudly displayed. It was a silent promise of continuity, of a heritage that had weathered storms and celebrated triumphs.

Naomi, a blur of pink snowsuit, was already captivated by the elaborate Christmas display in the window, her small hands pressed against the glass, her breath fogging the pane. Lani watched her, a soft smile gracing her lips. Naomi's unadulterated joy was a constant source of comfort, a reminder of the precious things in life that remained untainted by heartbreak.

As Lani peeked into the bakery's front window, the scent of cinnamon and caramelized sugar, a perfume woven into the town's very fabric clung to the air of Shepard's Sweets. Here, where flour dusted every surface like a benevolent snowfall and the hum of the mixer was a familiar lullaby. This was where Lani's parents reigned.

Her father's apron was still perpetually dusted with a cloud of confectioners' sugar and he still wielded a spatula with the practiced grace of a conductor. Her mother, her movements a gentle ballet behind the counter, her smile a practiced balm for any troubled soul, arranged trays of gleaming pastries.

But a new rhythm had crept into their movements. Her mother's fingers, once so swift and precise, now hesitated, a faint tremor tracing the line of her wrist as she scooped flour. The rhythmic thud of her father's rolling pin had softened, punctuated by the quiet exhalations of weariness that escaped him between tasks. The boisterous rumble of his laugh, a sound that had once echoed through the shop, had thinned to a fragile thread against the cheerful clatter of customers.

"Another batch of the honey spice, dear?" Her father's voice, though softer, still carried the warmth of a hearth. He gestured with a flour-dusted hand towards a cooling rack laden with golden-brown rounds.

Her mother nodded, her gaze lingering on the rows of cupcakes, the vibrant swirls of buttercream suddenly seeming to demand a strength she no longer felt in her fingertips. "They're a favorite," she murmured, her voice barely a whisper above the gentle hiss of the espresso machine.

Lani watched them, the familiar worn comfort of the bakery pressing in. The worn wooden counter, grooved by decades of leaning elbows and eager hands. The bell above the door, its cheerful chime a constant reminder of comings and goings, of celebrations and quiet moments shared over a sweet indulgence. She saw the years etched not just on their faces, but in the slight stoop of their shoulders, the slower shuffle of their steps. They built this place, brick by brick, batter by batter, into a town landmark, a sanctuary where memories were baked in. Now, the foundations, sturdy as they were, were beginning to show cracks. They needed her. Even with the ghost of old anxieties still nipping at her heels, Lani knew the truth: she needed them too.

The lure of the oven, the comforting chaos of the kitchen, pulled at her, a familiar ache in her bones.

Stepping across the threshold felt like stepping into a warm embrace. The air inside was thick with the comforting aroma of cinnamon, nutmeg, and the sweet, unmistakable fragrance of freshly baked gingerbread. It was a stark contrast to the sterile efficiency of her city office, where the only scents were recycled air and the faint metallic tang of toner. Here, the air was alive, infused with the very essence of comfort and home.

"Mom? Dad?" Lani called out, her voice a little unsteady.

A moment later, her mother emerged from the back, wiping her hands on her apron, breaking into a wide, loving smile.

"Oh, Lani, darling," she murmured, her voice a gentle rasp. "It's so good to have you home. And look at you, ladybug!" she exclaimed, scooping up her granddaughter into a hug that Lani knew was filled with all the unspoken love and longing of months apart.

Her father, Thomas, his hands calloused from years of shaping dough and his smile lines deeper than ever, joined the embrace, his gruff affection a solid anchor.

"Look what the cat dragged in!" he boomed, his voice warm and full of its old familiar resonance.

Lani returned their embraces, her own arms feeling awkward and hesitant. She was the prodigal daughter, returned not with fanfare, but with the quiet resignation of necessity. Lani's chest tightened, a mixture of relief and a deep, abiding love washing over her. This was it. This was what she had been missing. This tangible, undeniable connection to her roots, to her family. The bakery wasn't just flour and sugar; it was a repository of memories, a sanctuary from the storm that had been raging in her personal life. It was a place where the anxieties of her current reality, the looming financial implications of her divorce and the uncertainty of her future seemed to melt away with each warm, inviting scent.

Here, among the comforting rhythm of kneading dough and the sweet perfume of baking, she could finally breathe. This was more than just a visit; it was a pilgrimage, a deliberate act of returning to the source, to a place where she knew, without a shadow of a doubt, that she belonged.

As she took in the familiar scene – the gleaming display cases filled with tempting treats, the sturdy wooden counters worn smooth by generations of bakers, the gentle hum of the ovens, a profound sense of peace settled over her.

The bakery, usually humming with a steady stream of customers even on a quiet afternoon, was in a state of festive pre-holiday organized chaos. Large stainless-steel bowls overflowed with dough, waiting to be kneaded. Trays upon trays of intricately decorated sugar cookies, snowflakes and gingerbread men shimmering with edible glitter, were meticulously arranged on cooling racks. The air vibrated with the rhythmic thud of dough being worked, the cheerful clatter of pans, and the murmur of her parents' quiet, efficient instructions to the handful of trusted employees who formed their close-knit bakery family.

"I can help," Lani offered, her voice a little shaky, gesturing towards a large mound of pale, pliant dough. It was an instinct, a deeply ingrained habit from years spent as her parents' shadow, an eager apprentice in this sweet kingdom.

Elenore patted her hand, her touch warm and knowing. "Of course, dear. We can always use an extra pair of hands. Just wash up first. And don't you worry about a thing. We'll get through the Christmas rush together."

Lani headed to the industrial-sized sink, the cool water a welcome sensation on her suddenly clammy hands. As she scrubbed them clean, she watched her mother deftly pipe delicate swirls of white icing onto a gingerbread house, her movements precise and practiced. A pang, sharp and sudden, pierced through Lani's carefully constructed composure. She remembered being that girl, her own small hands often smudged with flour, mirroring her mother's every move, her heart brimming with the ambition to one day be as skilled, as confident.

She dried her hands and approached a large wooden table, its surface worn smooth by decades of kneading and shaping. Thomas had already portioned out a manageable ball of dough for her. He offered a gruff nod.

"Don't be shy, now. Give it a good knead. This one's for the sourdough. Needs a firm hand."

Lani took the dough, its cool elasticity a familiar sensation beneath her palms. She pulled it, folded it, turned it, her body remembering the rhythm even if her mind felt miles away. With each push and fold, she felt a small piece of herself reawakened, a part that had been dormant for too long. The scent of the yeasty dough was intoxicating, a primal scent that spoke of sustenance and creation. It was the smell of her family, of her heritage, of a simpler time.

As she worked, she caught glimpses of her younger self flitting through the bakery. The image of an awkward teenager, her hair perpetually tied back in a messy ponytail, enthusiastically decorating cakes, her brow furrowed in concentration. She saw the girl who dreamed of art school, who spent hours sketching in notebooks, who believed that beauty and creativity were the most important things in the world. That girl felt like a ghost, a whisper from a life that seemed almost impossibly distant. She had traded her paints for spreadsheets, her canvases for client meetings, her creative aspirations for the sterile predictability of corporate life. The divorce had been the final, brutal punctuation mark, leaving her adrift, questioning everything she thought she knew about herself and her path.

"Careful with that," Elenore's voice cut through Lani's reverie. "We don't want to overwork it. Just until it's smooth and elastic." Her mother stood beside her, her gaze gentle. Lani realized she'd been kneading with a little too much force, lost in the storm of her thoughts.

"Right," Lani murmured, consciously easing her pressure. "Sorry, Mom."

"No need to apologize, dear," Elenore said, her eyes crinkling at the corners. "It's good for you to be here. To feel the dough in your hands again. This bakery... it's in your blood, you know."

Lani offered a weak smile, the words hitting a raw nerve. Was it in her blood? Or had she deliberately tried to purge it, to forge a new identity independent of the sweet, comforting, yet ultimately stifling, legacy of Shepard's Sweets?

"I want some too," Naomi piped in.

"Naomi, why don't you go pick out a special treat? We made them just for you," Elenore said, her voice soft.

Naomi, her eyes wide with excitement, didn't need to be told twice. She dashed off towards the display case, her little boots tapping a joyful rhythm on the worn wooden floor.

Lani watched her daughter, then turned back to her parents. "I unpacked a few boxes of our things," she said, "And I've got my laptop. I can help with inventory, online orders, whatever you need."

Her father chuckled. "Don't you worry your pretty head about that. We'll put you to work."

The bakery was a haven for her parents, a source of pride and joy, but for Lani, it had also become a symbol of the life she had felt compelled to escape. The expectation, the quiet assumption that she would follow in their footsteps, had always felt like a gentle, yet unyielding, pressure.

She glanced at the display case, a vibrant kaleidoscope of pastries and breads. The signature snowflake cookies, dusted with pearlized sugar, were arranged in perfect symmetry. Beside them, rustic loaves of sourdough, their crusts a deep, burnished gold, sat proudly. There was an artistry to it, a dedication to quality and tradition that Lani had always admired, even when she was rebelling against it. Her parents had poured their lives into this place, and the results were undeniable. The bakery was more than just a business; it was a testament to their unwavering commitment, their shared passion.

A customer entered, their breath misting in the air as the door chimed its familiar welcome. The warmth of the bakery seemed to embrace them, the aroma of baking a comforting invitation. Lani watched as Elenore greeted them with a bright smile, her attentiveness unwavering. It was this genuine hospitality, this deep connection with their community, that had made Shepard's Sweets a beloved institution. They knew their customers by name, remembered their preferences, and always had a kind word. It was a way of life, a dedication that Lani, in her own pursuit of a different kind of success, had often overlooked.

Later, as she helped arrange a fresh batch of chocolate chip cookies – her personal favorite, a recipe passed down from her grandmother – Lani found herself lost in the scent. The dark, rich chocolate, the hint of vanilla, the satisfying chewiness of the dough. She remembered sneaking them, still warm from the oven, when she was a child, her mother chiding her gently for spoiling her dinner. These were more than just cookies; they were edible memories, each bite a portal to a past filled with simpler joys.

"These look perfect, Mom," Lani said, arranging a row of cookies on a pristine white plate.

Elenore smiled, her eyes twinkling. "Just like you used to make them, darling. You always had a knack for getting the chocolate chips just right."

The compliment, though well-intentioned, landed with a thud. It was a reminder of the girl she had been, the artist who had once found solace and joy in the simple act of baking. Now, her creative impulses were channeled into crafting persuasive marketing campaigns and managing complex budgets. It was a different kind of creation, a different kind of artistry, but it lacked the tangible warmth, the immediate gratification, of a perfectly baked cookie.

The rhythmic kneading continued, a steady beat in the symphony of the bakery. Lani's muscles began to ache, a familiar ache that brought with it a strange sense of accomplishment. She was contributing, she was part of something, even if it was only for a short while.

The pre-holiday rush was a whirlwind, a demanding dance of flour, sugar, and yeast, and Lani found herself, despite her reservations, getting caught up in its momentum. The familiar scent of cinnamon and melting chocolate, once a source of apprehension, was slowly morphing into something else. It was still tinged with nostalgia, with a touch of sadness for the dreams she had deferred, but beneath it, a fragile seed of acceptance was beginning to sprout. This was her past, yes, but it was also a part of her present, and perhaps, just perhaps, a foundation for whatever future lay ahead.

The ghosts of Christmas past were here, in the warm embrace of Shepard's Sweets, and Lani was beginning to realize that they weren't quite as frightening as she had imagined.

They were simply memories, woven into the very fabric of the place, waiting to be acknowledged, and perhaps, even understood. The sweet, comforting scent of the bakery was no longer just a reminder of what she had lost, but a gentle invitation to reconnect with the enduring strength of her roots. It was a subtle shift, a quiet recalibration, but for Lani, it felt like the beginning of something profound. The weight of her past was still there, but now, it felt less like an anchor dragging her down, and more like a warm, familiar quilt, wrapping her in a sense of belonging she hadn't realized she had craved.

{ 2 }

Lani

The crisp winter air, laden with the promise of snow and the sweet scent of pine, was a stark contrast to the polished glass and sterile office buildings Lani had grown accustomed to.

Yet, it was here, in the heart of her picturesque home-town, that a different kind of wonder began to unfurl, not for Lani, but for her daughter, Naomi. The village, nestled like a jewel in the embrace of snow-capped mountains, seemed to have materialized straight from the pages of a storybook.

Lampposts, their ornate ironwork dusted with white, were adorned with garlands of evergreen and twinkling fairy lights, casting a warm, inviting glow onto the already glistening cobblestone streets. The rooftops, draped in a pristine blanket of snow, looked like frosted confectionery, mirroring the very business Lani had left behind but was now immersed in once more.

Naomi, usually a quiet observer, her gaze often fixed on a tablet or a well-worn book, was a revelation. Her shyness, a delicate veil that often concealed her vibrant spirit, seemed to evaporate with each gust of wind that swirled the snowflakes around them. Her eyes, wide and luminous, darted everywhere, taking in the enchanting spectacle with an almost breathless awe. She pointed a small, mitten-clad finger towards the towering, snow-laden peaks that framed the town.

"Mommy, look! It's like a giant fluffy blanket!" Her voice, usually a soft murmur, was filled with an unadulterated delight that was as infectious as the winter chill.

Lani, whose own heart had been a tangled mess of apprehension and reluctant nostalgia, found her gaze drawn to her daughter's unburdened joy. It was a much-needed balm, a gentle reminder of the simple beauty that often got lost in the complexities of adult life.

She knelt beside Naomi, the cold seeping through her jeans, and followed her daughter's pointing finger. "It is, sweetheart," Lani agreed, a genuine smile finally gracing her lips. "This is the mountains. They get a lot of snow here in the winter."

They had arrived just as the first significant snowfall of the season began to grace the landscape, transforming the familiar, yet long-unvisited, streets of Lani's childhood into a magical wonderland. For Naomi, who had only ever experienced snow in fleeting, urban flurries, this was an entirely new world. The sheer abundance of it, the way it softened the edges of everything, the hush it imposed on the world, captivated her.

Making their way back to Shepard's Sweets, they found the bakery was a hive of activity, a stark contrast to the serene beauty outside. The air inside was thick with the comforting aromas of baking and the cheerful chatter of customers seeking refuge from the cold.

Lani's parents were in their element, their faces flushed with the warmth of the ovens and the joy of the festive season. But it was Naomi's involvement in the preparations that truly began to soften Lani's hardened edges.

Elenore, ever observant of her granddaughter's fascination, had enlisted Naomi's help in decorating the bakery windows. Lani felt a lump form in her throat as Naomi, perched precariously on a sturdy stool, meticulously placed small, intricately decorated gingerbread figures onto the large display window. Her brow was furrowed in concentration, her tongue peeking out from the corner of her mouth as she carefully positioned a tiny gingerbread man next to a shimmering sugar snowflake.

"Careful there, sweet pea," Elenore said, her voice a gentle lullaby as she guided Naomi's hand. "We want him to have a good view of all the lovely people walking by, don't we?"

Naomi nodded solemnly, her tiny hands steady. "He wants to see the snow, Grandma."

Lani felt a pang of bittersweet emotion. She remembered being that child, her own small hands once dusted with flour, eager to help, eager to be a part of the magic that emanated from this very bakery. The memories, once sharp and almost painful, were now being softened by the innocent joy radiating from her daughter. Naomi's presence, her unadulterated wonder, was acting as a gentle counterpoint to Lani's own complex feelings of obligation, regret, and the lingering ache of a life she had tried to outrun.

"They look so happy, Mommy," Naomi commented, stepping back to admire their handiwork. The window was now a charming tableau of gingerbread characters peeking out from behind a snowy landscape of piped icing and edible glitter.

Lani joined her daughter, looking at the festive scene with fresh eyes. "They do, don't they? They're ready for Christmas."

Naomi's gaze drifted from the window to the bustling interior of the bakery, then back to the snowy street. Her head tilted, a curious expression on her face.

"Mommy, did you grow up here? When it was all snowy like this?"

The question, simple and direct, caught Lani off guard. It was an opening, an invitation to share a part of herself that she had kept carefully guarded for so long. She hesitated for a moment, then met Naomi's expectant gaze. "Yes, sweetheart. I did. This was my hometown, just like it is for Grandma and Grandpa."

Naomi's eyes widened further. "Really? You lived here? In this town with the big mountains?"

"Yes, I did," Lani confirmed, a soft smile playing on her lips. "And I loved it. Especially in the winter."

"Why didn't we ever come here?" Naomi asked with wide blue eyes.

"It wasn't a place your dad felt comfortable," she explained. Mark thought the town was beneath him and visits with her parents were to be conducted at a luxury apartment where they lived in the city.

She deflected from further explanation and began to tell Naomi about the days when she was a little girl, when the snow was not just a backdrop but a playground. She spoke of building snow forts that rivaled the gingerbread houses, of sledding down hills so steep they made her stomach flip, of catching snowflakes on her tongue and marveling at their intricate designs. She described the warmth of coming inside afterwards, hands and cheeks rosy from the cold, to be greeted by the comforting scent of baking and the promise of hot chocolate.

Naomi listened, captivated, her earlier shyness completely forgotten. She peppered Lani with questions, her curiosity insatiable.

"Did you have a gingerbread man when you were little, Mommy?" "Were the mountains even bigger then?" "Did you help make the cookies for the people?"

Lani found herself answering each question, weaving a tapestry of memories for her daughter. With each story, a piece of her own carefully constructed wall began to crumble. She talked about her favorite sledding spot, a steep, winding hill behind the old general store, and how she and her childhood friends would race each other down it, their laughter echoing through the crisp winter air. She described the thrill of bundling up in layers of wool and flannel, the scratchy sensation of her scarf against her chin, and the way her breath would plume out in white clouds as she ran.

"And the bakery," Lani continued, her voice softening, "it was always so busy during the holidays. It was my favorite time of year. The whole town felt... magical. Like a secret whispered on the wind."

Naomi leaned against Lani's leg, her gaze fixed on her mother. "What was your favorite cookie, Mommy?"

Lani chuckled, a genuine, warm sound. "Oh, that's a tough one. But I always loved the snowflake cookies. They were so delicate, and the pearlized sugar made them sparkle like real snowflakes." She glanced towards the counter, where trays of precisely arranged snowflakes were already a testament to her parents' enduring skill.

"Mine too!" Naomi exclaimed, pointing to the display. "They're so pretty!"

As they spoke, a group of local children, their faces flushed and exhilarated, burst into the bakery, shaking snow from their boots and hats. Their boisterous energy filled the space, their laughter a joyous counterpoint to the gentle hum of conversation. Naomi watched them with wide-eyed fascination, a hint of longing in her gaze.

"Can I go play in the snow, Mommy?" she asked, her voice barely a whisper.

Lani hesitated. Her initial intention had been to keep Naomi close, to focus on helping her parents and navigating her own complicated emotions.

"Maybe later, sweetheart," she said gently. "Right now, we need to help Grandma and Grandpa with the orders."

Naomi nodded, her disappointment palpable but not overwhelming. She understood, Lani knew. But the seed of desire had been planted. And Lani, for the first time since arriving, felt a flicker of something akin to her daughter's enthusiasm for the snowy wonderland outside. Seeing the pure, unadulterated yearning in her daughter's eyes, she couldn't refuse.

"Stay on this side of the street," Lani relented.

"Okay," and in a flash of pink swirl she was out the door.

Later, as Lani helped her mother ice batches of sugar cookies, Elenore gently probed, "Naomi's joy is quite infectious, isn't it?"

Lani nodded, carefully tracing a delicate pattern onto a star-shaped cookie. "She's loving it, Mom. She's never seen snow like this before."

"This town has a way of doing that," Elenore said softly, her gaze distant for a moment, as if recalling her own youth. "It reminds you of what's important. Of the simple pleasures." She paused, then looked at Lani, her eyes kind.

"You spent so much time inside here when you were little, Lani. Always with a smudge of flour on your nose. I remember you telling me you wanted to be a baker, just like me."

The words, meant to be a tender recollection, landed like a soft blow. Lani's hand faltered, the icing brush leaving a wobbly line. "That was a long time ago, Mom."

Elenore sighed, a sound devoid of judgment, filled only with understanding. "I know, dear. And you've built a wonderful life for yourself. A very different life." She reached out and gently wiped a stray speck of flour from Lani's cheek, a gesture that was both maternal and a silent acknowledgment of their shared history. "But a part of you always loved this, didn't you? The creation. The sweetness."

Lani looked at the cookie in her hand, its surface smooth and ready for decoration. She remembered the pride she felt when her own creations were deemed perfect, the sense of accomplishment when a customer's face lit up with delight. It was a different kind of satisfaction than closing a business deal or hitting a sales target. It was tangible, immediate, and deeply rooted in sensory experience. It was part of why she wanted to go to art school.

"It's... it's different now," Lani murmured, her voice barely audible. "Life is... more complicated."

"Of course it is," Elenore agreed. "But complications don't erase the simple joys, Lani. They just... bury them sometimes. Like snow. But the sun always melts it eventually, doesn't it?"

Lani nodded, unable to explain the complex emotions churning within her. She thought of Naomi, her daughter's eyes reflecting the twinkling lights of the village, her heart brimming with joy that Lani herself had long suppressed.

Naomi's innocent questions about her mother's childhood were not just a child's curiosity; they were gentle probes into a past that Lani had actively tried to forget. Each question, each shared memory, was like a tiny icicle melting, revealing glimpses of the girl she used to be, the girl who had loved this town, this bakery, with all her heart.

"Tell me more stories about when you were a little girl here, Mommy," Naomi urged later as they walked through the softly falling snow towards the small park at the edge of town, her small hand tucked into Lani's. The lampposts cast long, dancing shadows, and the silence was broken only by the crunch of their boots on the snow-covered path and the distant jingle of sleigh bells.

Lani looked down at her daughter, her heart swelling with a mixture of tenderness and a newfound resolve. She had come back to this town with trepidation, burdened by the weight of her past and the uncertainty of her future. But in Naomi's bright, inquisitive eyes, she saw a reflection of a simpler, happier self.

The winter wonderland of her mother's hometown was not just a picturesque setting; it was a portal, a chance to reconnect with her roots, and more importantly, to share that connection with her daughter.

"Well," Lani began, her voice gaining a newfound warmth, "when I was your age, we used to come to this very park all the time. Especially when it snowed. We'd build the biggest snowmen you've ever seen..."

As she spoke, the snow continued to fall, a gentle curtain of white, blanketing the world and softening the sharp edges of Lani's own past, allowing the sweet, snow-kissed wonder of Naomi's innocent joy to finally bloom. The festive spirit of the town was indeed infectious, and in its embrace, Lani felt a subtle shift, a thawing within her own carefully guarded heart, a quiet promise of rediscovery.

The scent of pine and baking, once a bittersweet reminder, was now a fragrant invitation to embrace the present, to weave new memories from the threads of her past, and to witness the magic of it all through the wide, wonder-filled eyes of her daughter. The quiet whispers of her mother's youth, once a distant echo, were now becoming a shared narrative, a story unfolding, layer by delicate layer, like the falling snow.

The winter transformation of the small mountain town was nothing short of breathtaking. It was as if the very air had thickened, sweetened, and been dusted with a generous layer of festive cheer. Lani had seen it many times before, in her childhood, but never had it struck her with such potent force as it did now, through Naomi's wide, unblinking eyes.

Christmas began on November 1st in Evergreen Hollow. The main street, usually a quaint thoroughfare of independent shops, had been utterly consumed by the Christmas spirit. Garland, thick and fragrant with pine, cascaded from every lamppost, its dark green boughs adorned with ruby-red ribbons that fluttered gently in the crisp breeze. Each storefront was a miniature masterpiece of holiday decoration. The windows of the little bookstore, "The Page Turner," usually displaying the latest novels, were now framed with shimmering tinsel and featured a meticulously crafted Nativity scene, complete with tiny, hand-painted figures.

Across the street, the hardware store, usually a utilitarian haven of tools and useful gadgets, was festooned with strings of twinkling white lights that snaked around its brick facade like delicate icicles. Even the mundane was rendered magical.

"Mommy, look!" Naomi's voice, a melodic lilt, tugged Lani back from her reverie. She pointed towards a small cart parked near the town square. From it wafted a scent so rich and inviting, Lani's stomach rumbled in response. "What is that yummy smell?"

Lani smiled, a genuine, unforced smile that felt foreign and yet wonderfully familiar on her lips.

"That, sweetheart, is roasted chestnuts. They're a special treat this time of year." She steered Naomi towards the vendor, a jolly man with a beard dusted white, not with snow, but with flour, presumably from his own baking ventures. He greeted them with a booming laugh, his cheeks rosy from the heat of the roaster.

"Well, hello there! And who do we have here? Brought a little ray of sunshine with you, have you?" he asked, his gaze twinkling as he looked at Naomi.

Naomi, initially shy, offered a small, hesitant smile. Lani nudged her gently. "Go on, ask him about the chestnuts."

Emboldened, Naomi piped up, "Are they magic, sir? They smell so good!"

The vendor chuckled, the sound like warm bells. "Well, I reckon they are, little one. They have a bit of Christmas magic in every bite, especially when they come from this town." He scooped a handful of the steaming nuts into a small paper cone, the heat radiating through the thin material. "On the house, for you and your young lady. Enjoy the magic!"

Lani thanked him, her heart feeling a little lighter with each passing moment. As they walked away, Naomi, carefully holding her warm cone, Lani felt a familiar ache in her chest. These were the sights and smells that had once been her everyday reality. The scent of roasted chestnuts, the twinkle of fairy lights, the distant echo of carols – they were the very fabric of her childhood Christmases.

They made their way towards the heart of the town square, where the true centerpiece of the holiday festivities awaited. A magnificent Norway spruce, towering over everything, its branches already laden with the recent snowfall, looking like it had been dipped in confectioner's sugar. It was a tree that had always been the focal point, the silent witness to countless Christmases.

Lani remembered the annual tradition of the tree-lighting ceremony. The entire town would gather, bundled in their warmest layers, the air thick with anticipation. Children would hold sparklers, their small hands creating dazzling arcs of light in the twilight, and then, as the mayor, a kindly man with a booming voice, would count down from ten. Then the tree would erupt in a dazzling cascade of light, banishing the darkness and filling every heart with an incandescent glow.

"Wow," Naomi breathed, her eyes fixed on the majestic tree. "It's so big! Is it going to get all sparkly lights, Mommy?"

Lani nodded, a wistful smile playing on her lips. "Yes, sweetheart. Tonight's the night. They're going to light it up, and the whole town will be here to watch. It's quite a sight." She paused, her gaze sweeping over the square.

The ice rink, nestled in a clearing just beyond the tree, was already alive with activity. Children and adults alike glided across the frozen surface, their laughter mingling with the cheerful, though slightly tinny, strains of Christmas music from the speakers.

Lani remembered learning to skate there, her small, clumsy attempts resulting in more falls than graceful glides, her father's strong hands steadying her, his laughter warm and encouraging.

"Can we go ice skating, Mommy?" Naomi asked, her eyes wide with a desperate plea.

Lani's heart ached. She wanted to say yes, and embrace the simple joy that her daughter was so eager to experience. But the reality of her situation, the constant undercurrent of unease and the looming specter of her parents' financial struggles held her back.

"Maybe tomorrow, sweet pea," she said gently, squeezing Naomi's hand. "Today, we need to focus on helping Grandma and Grandpa with the bakery."

Naomi's shoulders drooped slightly, but she nodded, accepting the compromise with a maturity that always surprised Lani. She was a resilient child, but Lani couldn't shake the feeling that she was also depriving her daughter of so much. The sheer abundance of festive offerings in the town square was almost overwhelming.

Everywhere Lani looked, a memory surfaced, a ghost of Christmases past. The quaint cinema, "The Bijou," where she'd had her first awkward date, sharing a bag of popcorn with a boy whose name she could barely recall now. The small park bench, where she and her best friend Sarah had whispered secrets and dreams under the starlit sky. Each corner turned, each scent inhaled, was a potent reminder of the life she had left behind, a life that felt both intensely familiar and impossibly distant.

The contrast between the vibrant, festive atmosphere of the town and the quiet, worried whispers she'd overheard from her parents the night before was a jarring dissonance. They had spoken of dwindling supplies, of the rising cost of ingredients, of a Christmas season that, if not exceptionally successful, could spell disaster for Shepard's Sweets. Lani had tried to block out the words, to focus on Naomi's happiness, but the underlying anxiety was a persistent hum beneath the cheerful carols.

"Look, Mommy!" Naomi exclaimed again, her attention now drawn to a group of carolers gathered near the base of the towering Christmas tree.

Their voices, clear and strong, rose in a harmonious rendition of "O Come, All Ye Faithful." The sound was pure, unadulterated Christmas magic, the kind that resonated deep within the soul. Lani found herself humming along, a forgotten melody awakening within her.

She watched as the townsfolk gathered around, their faces illuminated by the soft glow of lanterns and the promise of the impending tree-lighting. There was a palpable sense of community, a shared joy that transcended individual worries. It was this very sense of togetherness, this shared experience of festive celebration, that Lani had always cherished about her hometown.

But now, it felt tinged with a new layer of complexity. She was an outsider, a visitor, her life having taken a drastically different path. Her success in the city, measured in boardrooms and profit margins, felt hollow and insignificant in the face of this genuine, heartwarming communal spirit.

"They're singing about Jesus coming," Naomi whispered, her small hand tightening on Lani's.

"Yes, they are," Lani replied, her voice soft. "It's a very old song, and it's about hope and the good news." She knelt beside Naomi, pulling her closer. "And tonight, when they light the tree, it's like a beacon of hope for everyone in town. It tells us that even in the darkest, coldest nights, there's still light and warmth to be found."

As if on cue, a man with a distinguished air, whom Lani recognized as the town's mayor, stepped forward, holding a large, ornate key. A hush fell over the crowd. Even Naomi fell silent, her gaze fixed on the massive tree, her small face alight with wonder. The mayor began to speak, his voice amplified by a microphone, recounting the town's history and the significance of the annual tree-lighting. He spoke of traditions, of community, of the enduring spirit of the holiday season. Lani listened, her heart a complex tapestry of nostalgia and a growing sense of responsibility.

Then, he began the countdown. "Ten! Nine! Eight!"

The crowd joined in, their voices echoing through the crisp air. Lani felt a surge of emotion, a lump forming in her throat. She looked at Naomi, her daughter's face radiant, reflecting the twinkling lights of the surrounding buildings and the anticipation of the moment to come.

This was what Naomi deserved: moments of pure, unadulterated magic, moments that would etch themselves into her memory, shaping her understanding of joy and belonging.

"Three! Two! One!"

With a final, resonant shout, the mayor turned the key. For a breathless moment, nothing happened. Then, with a soft hum, a single string of lights flickered to life at the very top of the tree. Another string joined it, and then another, and another, until the entire colossal spruce was ablaze with a dazzling display of multicolored lights. A collective gasp of delight swept through the crowd, followed by thunderous applause.

Naomi squealed with pure joy, clapping her hands together with unbridled enthusiasm.

Lani watched her daughter, a sense of peace settling over her. The overwhelming festive saturation, the constant barrage of memories, no longer felt like a burden. Instead, they felt like a comforting embrace, a reminder of the enduring magic that this town held. She realized that while her life in the city had been built on ambition and success, it had lacked this deep, intrinsic sense of belonging, this shared celebration of simple pleasures.

The aroma of roasted chestnuts and popcorn, the sweet scent of pine, the distant echo of carols, the dazzling spectacle of the tree lighting. It all merged into an experience that was both deeply personal and universally shared. It was a powerful reminder that despite the difficulties of adult life, the simple joys, the traditions, the shared moments of wonder, were what truly mattered. And in that moment, surrounded by the warm glow of the Christmas tree and the infectious delight of her daughter, Lani felt a profound sense of gratitude, a quiet understanding that perhaps, just perhaps, she had come home.

The town, dressed in its holiday hues, was not just a postcard-perfect scene; it was an invitation, a gentle nudge from the past, urging her to embrace the present, to reconnect with her roots, and to rediscover the magic that had once lived within her, now being so beautifully reawakened through the eyes of her daughter. The sheer amount of festive charm was almost overwhelming, each garland, each twinkling light, each carol sung, a whisper from her past, a stark yet welcome contrast to the sterile efficiency of her urban existence. It was a saturation of joy that seeped into her very being, a potent reminder of what once was, and a subtle invitation to what could be.

{ 3 }

Lani

The air in her parents' home, usually a comforting embrace of cinnamon and old wood, now held a faint, almost imperceptible chill that Lani couldn't attribute to the winter weather. It was the chill of uncertainty, a creeping dread that had begun to insinuate itself into her thoughts the moment she'd agreed to this extended visit.

Looking at Naomi, who was currently engrossed in a puzzle of woodland creatures laid out on the Persian rug in the living room, Lani felt a pang of guilt so sharp it threatened to steal her breath. She was here, in this idyllic mountain town, surrounded by the tangible Christmas displays, and yet, a persistent hum of anxiety vibrated beneath the surface of her carefully constructed composure.

The idyllic setting, the very essence of the quaint, festive charm she'd once taken for granted, now served as a stark contrast to the instability of her current reality. Her parents' home was a sanctuary of her childhood, but it was only a temporary refuge.

Her parents' home was a sanctuary of her childhood, was a only temporary refuge. It offered a warm bed, a ready supply of her favorite tea, and the unwavering love of her mother, who hovered with the quiet efficiency of a seasoned nurse.

Yet, beneath the veneer of familial comfort, Lani felt like an imposter, a visitor who had overstayed her welcome. The city, with all its demanding pace and competitive spirit, had been her battlefield, a place where she had carved out a life for herself, a life that, while currently in flux, was undeniably her own. Now, the quietude of this mountain town, so beloved in memory, felt almost suffocating.

Her thoughts, like fallen snowflakes, swirled and settled, forming intricate patterns of worry. Naomi's adjustment, for one, was a constant source of concern. Her daughter, so accustomed to the structured environment of her city preschool and the vibrant diversity of their urban playground, seemed to be adapting with remarkable grace. But Lani knew that this placid surface hid a deeper reality.

Was Naomi truly thriving, or was she simply mirroring Lani's own attempts at feigned contentment? The constant reassurances Lani offered felt increasingly hollow, even to her own ears.

"It's just for a little while, sweet pea," she'd say, her voice lacking the conviction she wished it possessed. "We're going to have so much fun."

But the unspoken truth, that this "little while" was stretching into an indefinite period, dictated by circumstances beyond her immediate control, hung heavy in the air between them.

And then there were her own career prospects. The thought of re-entering the fiercely competitive corporate world after an extended absence sent a shiver down her spine. Her meticulously crafted resume, her hard-won professional network, her reputation. All of it felt like a fragile construct, susceptible to the harsh realities of economic downturns and the inevitable question: "Why the gap?"

She had excelled in her field, had been on the cusp of significant advancements, and now, through a cruel twist of fate, she found herself contemplating a future that seemed to involve dusting off old recipes and learning to frost cupcakes with unwavering precision. The irony was not lost on her, and it was a bitter pill to swallow.

The close-knit community, with its ingrained traditions and unspoken expectations, added another layer to her growing unease. She was Lani Shepard, daughter of Elenore and Thomas, granddaughter of the legendary Annabelle Shepard, who had built Shepard's Sweets from the ground up.

She was the prodigal daughter, returned from the gilded cage of the city, bringing with her not only her child but also the undeniable weight of her divorce.

The whispers, she knew, would have already begun, soft murmurs carried on the mountain breeze, speculating about the reasons for her return, the disintegration of her marriage, and the future of her own aspirations. She had fought so hard to shed the mantle of small-town girl, to forge an identity independent of her lineage, and now, she was back, seemingly succumbing to the very life she had once yearned to escape.

The divorce itself was a gaping wound that refused to heal cleanly. The legal battles had been long and cruel, each court date peeling back another layer of hurt. When it was finally over, Lani had expected relief. A sense of closure, but instead, there was only emptiness. What cut deepest wasn't the end of the marriage, but the callousness that followed.

Her ex-husband Marc had made it painfully clear that his freedom meant more to him than his role as a father. He'd signed away his visitation rights without hesitation, his lawyer's words cold and matter-of-fact: *"If it saves him from child support, he's willing to let her go."*

That sentence had echoed in Lani's mind for months, bruising something tender inside her every time she looked at Naomi. She could handle losing a husband. What she couldn't comprehend was how anyone could turn away from their own child so easily.

And now, in the quiet aftermath of it all, the necessity of leaning on her parents, of moving back into the house she once left behind, felt like a surrender she hadn't been ready for. But it was also survival. For Naomi's sake, she'd chosen steadiness over pride, love over bitterness. And though the ache of betrayal still lingered, there was also a fragile, growing sense of peace. The kind that comes when a broken heart begins, at last, to mend.

She was a grown woman, a successful professional, and yet, she was back under her parents' roof, a dependent, her financial stability shattered. The shame of it was a constant companion, a gnawing sensation that no amount of festive cheer could fully eradicate. She saw the concern in her mother's eyes, the quiet support in her father's steady presence, and while she was grateful beyond words, a part of her recoiled from the perceived weakness, the vulnerability that her current situation exposed.

Was this a temporary reprieve? A necessary pause to regroup and rebuild, or a permanent surrender to her former life? The questions gnawed at her, a persistent, unwelcome interloper in her thoughts. She had envisioned a different homecoming, one that spoke of triumph and reinvention, not of retreat and reliance. She had dreamt of returning to her parents with stories of continued success, perhaps even with a new, exciting chapter of her own to share.

Instead, she was here, a question mark in her own life. Grappling with the wreckage of her past and the uncertain landscape of her future.

The delicate balance between her ingrained sense of duty and her personal desires felt increasingly precarious. Her parents' bakery was more than just a family business; it was an institution, a cornerstone of this community. And Lani knew, with a certainty that chilled her to the bone, that it was in trouble. The overheard whispers from the night before, snippets of anxious conversations between her parents about dwindling supplies and escalating ingredient costs, had painted a grim picture. A disastrous Christmas season, they had admitted with weary resignation, could spell ruin for the beloved establishment. This knowledge added a heavy layer of responsibility to her already burdened shoulders.

She had always loved baking, the pleasure of kneading dough, the magic of transforming simple ingredients into something delicious. In the city, it had been a cherished hobby, a weekend escape from the demands of her professional life.

But now, the prospect of stepping into the bakery, of facing the demanding rhythms of a commercial kitchen, felt daunting. It was a world away from the sterile efficiency of her office, a world where every cake frosted, every cookie baked, carried the weight of her family's legacy and their financial survival.

Could she truly contribute, or would her presence, with her city-bred habits and her potentially disruptive ideas, do more harm than good?

The weight of these unspoken worries wove a subtle thread of melancholy through the vibrant tapestry of the town's festive preparations. Every twinkling light, every scent of pine and gingerbread, every carol sung, seemed to amplify the dissonance within her. She wanted to immerse herself in the joy, to embrace the spirit of the season, but a part of her remained stubbornly anchored to the anxieties that plagued her. She found herself observing Naomi with an almost forensic intensity, searching for signs of distress, for any indication that her daughter was not coping as well as she outwardly appeared.

"Mommy, look at the sparkly sugar!" Naomi's voice, bright and unburdened, cut through Lani's reverie. She pointed to the cookie decorations laid out on the table for her.

Lani forced a smile, her gaze lingering on the cheerful image before returning to her daughter's expectant face. She always found beauty in the smallest things.

"They are very pretty, sweet pea," Lani replied, her voice softer than she intended. "Are you ready to decorate the cookies?"

Naomi nodded her head with enthusiasm.

Lani smiled softly as she got her daughter started on her next project.

She felt a profound sense of longing, a desire to shield Naomi from the difficulties and uncertainties that were beginning to cloud Lani's own world. She wanted to offer her daughter the uncomplicated joy of childhood, the kind that seemed to blossom so effortlessly in this picturesque setting. But how could she, when her own heart felt like a tangled knot of duty, doubt, and a yearning for stability that had seemingly vanished overnight?

The decision to return had been born out of a desperate need, a temporary escape from the emotional and financial fallout of her divorce. But as the days turned into weeks, the lines between temporary and permanent began to blur. The comfort of her parents' home, the familiarity of the town, the sheer, overwhelming embrace of the holiday season – it all conspired to lull her into a false sense of security.

Yet, beneath the surface, the seeds of doubt continued to sprout, their tendrils reaching for the fragile roots of her resolve. Was she strong enough to reclaim her independence, or was she destined to become a permanent fixture in this quiet mountain town, a ghost of her former self, forever haunted by the life she had left behind?

The answer, she feared, lay somewhere within the twinkling lights of the Christmas tree, a beacon of hope that seemed to cast long, unsettling shadows on her path forward. The weight of her past, a familiar burden, pressed down on her, a constant reminder of the choices she had made and the unexpected turns her life had taken. She was Lani Shepard, yes, but she was also Lani Sutton. And the dissonance between those two identities was a chasm she was still struggling to bridge. The return to her roots had brought clarity, but it had also exposed the raw, unhealed wounds of her present. And as the scent of pine and cinnamon filled the air, Lani knew that the real challenge lay not in surviving the holiday season, but in navigating the uncertain future that lay beyond it, a future she was no longer entirely sure how to shape.

The rhythmic thump of dough being kneaded echoed through the bakery, a familiar heartbeat that usually soothed Lani's frayed nerves. Today, however, it only served to amplify the frantic fluttering in her own chest. She was about to become elbow-deep in a batch of gingerbread dough as the scent of molasses and spice became a comforting blanket against the gnawing anxiety that had become her constant companion.

Naomi, bless her innocent heart, was happily decorating sugar cookies with a sprinkle of edible glitter, her small tongue poking out in concentration. Elenore moved with her usual quiet grace, her hands deftly arranging trays of intricately iced stars and snowflakes. The scene was a tableau of cozy domesticity, a picture-perfect postcard of a pre-Christmas day in their quaint mountain town. Yet, Lani felt a tremor of unease, a premonition that something was about to shatter this carefully constructed peace.

*****

The bell above the bakery door chimed, a cheerful, innocuous sound that usually meant a customer or a delivery. Lani didn't even glance up, assuming it was just Thomas, her father, returning from his morning rounds at the suppliers. Her mother, however, paused mid-frosting, a subtle shift in her posture betraying her own mild surprise.

"Odd," Elenore murmured, her voice barely audible above the gentle hum of the industrial mixer. "Thomas usually calls if he's bringing anyone with him."

Lani continued to focus on her dough, trying to push away the nagging feeling that this was more than just a casual drop-in. The air in the bakery seemed to thicken, to hum with an almost electrical charge. It was the kind of palpable shift that preceded a storm, a sudden stillness before the wind whipped through the trees. She could feel it, a prickling sensation on her skin, a tightening in her throat.

Then a deep, resonant voice cut through the quiet.

"Elenore. Thomas. It's... good to see you both."

That voice. Lani's breath hitched. It was a voice she hadn't heard spoken aloud in... years.

A voice that conjured a kaleidoscope of memories. Hushed conversations in darkened movie theaters, breathless laughter under a canopy of stars, whispered promises exchanged in the back of a beat-up pickup truck. Her hands stilled, then froze entirely, coated in a sticky sheen of gingerbread dough. The rhythmic thump of her own heart escalated to a frantic drum solo against her ribs.

Slowly, painstakingly, she wiped her hands on her apron, her gaze still fixed on the workbench. She could feel the newcomers presence as acutely as if he were standing directly behind her, a phantom limb reaching out from her past.

Naomi, momentarily distracted from her cookie artistry, piped up, "Who is it, Mommy?"

Lani couldn't answer. Her vocal cords seemed to have seized, paralyzed by the sheer, overwhelming impossibility of the situation. She forced herself to turn, her movements stiff and jerky, her eyes scanning the familiar space of the bakery. And there he was.

Julian Vance.

He stood just inside the entrance, his presence commanding the modest space. His dark hair was dusted with icy crystal. The snow that clung to his expensive wool coat seemed to shimmer under the warm bakery lights, as if even the winter itself bowed to his arrival. He was taller than she remembered, his shoulders broader, his face etched with a maturity that softened the boyish charm she'd once adored.

But his eyes, those impossibly blue eyes, were the same, direct, intelligent, and currently holding a flicker of something she couldn't quite decipher. Surprise? Regret? A carefully veiled assessment?

He was exactly as the whispers had described him. The local boy who had made good, the prodigy who had left their small town behind to conquer the culinary world. His restaurants were legendary, his name synonymous with innovation and exquisite taste. Julian Vance, the celebrated chef. And he was standing in her parents' bakery, a place that felt a universe away from the Michelin 5-star establishments he now presided over.

The air crackled. Decades of unspoken history surged between them, a tidal wave of shared memories threatening to drown the present. Every stolen kiss, every shared dream, every awkward goodbye. It all came rushing back with a dizzying intensity. Lani felt a blush creep up her neck, a telltale sign of the turmoil churning within her. She hadn't seen him since graduation, since the painful, messy implosion of their teenage romance, a casualty of diverging paths and youthful insecurities.

"Julian," her mother's voice was laced with a gentle surprise, a warmth that Lani hadn't heard directed at anyone outside the family in a long time.

"What a... surprise. We weren't expecting you."

"I know," Julian replied, his gaze finally settling on Lani. His expression softened infinitesimally, a subtle tightening around his eyes that spoke volumes. "I was in the area, visiting my Uncle. I thought I'd stop by, see how everyone was doing. And, of course, pay my respects to the legendary Shepard's Sweets."

His voice was smooth, practiced, a far cry from the earnest, slightly awkward tenor of the boy she'd known.

His gaze locked onto Lani, a slow burn that traced the curve of her cheekbone, the smudges of white dust clinging to her eyelashes. A phantom itch crawled over her, the rough weave of her apron suddenly a glaring testament to her current, flour-flecked reality. Her fingers twitched, yearning to brush away the tell-tale powder, to smooth the fabric into something less... domestic.

"Lani," he said, his voice a low rumble that seemed to resonate deep within her. It wasn't just a greeting; it was an acknowledgment, a recognition that spanned the years and the miles.

"Julian," she managed, her voice a thin, reedy sound that barely escaped her lips. It felt foreign, alien. She hadn't uttered his name in so long.

"You've got a bit of dust there," he said, his voice a low rumble that vibrated against the humming of the industrial mixer.

Lani's hand instinctively flew to her chest, then fell, the movement jerky, self-conscious. She could feel the sticky sweetness of the dough clinging to her forearms, the faint scent of yeast thick in the air, mingling with the metallic tang of the kitchen's stainless-steel surfaces.

Sunlight, thick with swirling motes, slanted through the grimy windowpanes, illuminating the frantic dance of her movements. Her apron, once a crisp shield, now bore the ghostly imprints of her work. A faint dusting on the bib, a heavier smear near the hem, each mark a whispered confession of the morning's labors.

She was Lani Shepard, back home, adrift. He was Julian Vance, soaring. The contrast was stark, almost painful.

Naomi, sensing the shift in the atmosphere, tugged at Lani's apron. "Mommy, who's the nice man?"

Lani's heart squeezed. Nice? Julian Vance had been her first love, the boy who had taught her the meaning of heartache.

"Naomi, this is Julian," she said, forcing a smile that felt brittle. "He... he used to know me when I was a little girl." A half-truth, a gross understatement.

Julian's lips curved into a subtle, knowing smile. "It's good to meet you, Naomi," he said, his voice taking on a softer, more playful tone as he addressed her. "Your grandmother makes the best cookies in town, doesn't she?"

Naomi beamed, her earlier curiosity replaced by shy delight. "Yes! And Mommy too!"

A beat of silence stretched, thick with unspoken history. Lani could feel Julian's gaze on her, a persistent, unsettling warmth. She wanted to look away, to retreat back into the familiar comfort of the dough, but something held her captive, a strange, undeniable magnetism. She remembered the intensity of his gaze in high school, the way it made her feel seen, understood, cherished. Now, it felt like an interrogation, a silent cataloging of the woman she had become.

Her parents, bless their pragmatic hearts, were already moving past the initial surprise, their ingrained hospitality kicking in.

"Julian, please, don't just stand there in the cold," Elenore said, wiping her hands on her own apron and gesturing towards a small table near the display cases. "Let me get you a cup of coffee. Thomas, why don't you show Julian the new espresso machine?"

Lani's father was a man of few words but full of great warmth, clapped Julian on the shoulder with a friendly grin. "Of course. Come on, son. You wouldn't believe the upgrades we've made."

As her father led Julian towards the back counter, Lani finally allowed herself to breathe, a shaky, gasping inhalation. Her heart was still pounding like a frantic bird trapped in her chest. She watched Julian's retreating back, the easy way he engaged with her father, the subtle confidence in his stride. He fit seamlessly into any environment, it seemed.

She returned to her dough, her movements still a little shaky. But the focus had shifted. The comforting rhythm of the bakery was now overlaid with the startling dissonance of Julian's presence.

He was a ghost from her past, materialized in the present, and Lani had no idea how to navigate this unexpected encounter. The scent of gingerbread, usually so reassuring, now seemed tinged with the bittersweet aroma of memory.

She quickly glanced at Naomi, who had returned to her cookie decorating with renewed fervor, her small hands still dusted with sugar. Lani felt a fierce pang of protectiveness. This was her daughter, her world, her responsibility. She couldn't let the ghosts of her past disrupt the fragile peace she was trying to build for them.

But Julian Vance was not just a ghost. He was a living, breathing reminder of a life she had outgrown, a love she had lost, and the vast chasm of experience that now separated them. He was a success story, a testament to ambition and talent.

She was... here. In her parents' bakery. Starting over.

The encounter had lasted mere minutes, but it had already irrevocably altered the atmosphere. The cheerful chatter of the bakery, the comforting scent of baking, the gentle snowfall outside, it all felt different now, imbued with a charged awareness of his presence.

Lani rolled out the cookie dough with renewed, almost desperate, energy. Each roll was a futile attempt to push away the memories, the feelings, the overwhelming sense of being seen by Julian Vance after all these years. He had been her first love, the boy who had carved his initials into the old oak tree behind the school, the boy who had held her hand as they planned a future that now seemed impossibly distant.

She remembered his passion, even then, for food. He'd spent hours in his grandmother's kitchen, meticulously recreating her recipes, experimenting with flavors, his eyes alight with fierce determination. Lani had been his first willing taste tester, his most fervent cheerleader. She had believed in him, in his dreams, with a fervor that had mirrored his own.

And now, here he was, a culinary titan, and she was... here. Back in the town she'd fled, back in the shadow of her family's legacy, her own ambitious career in ashes. The irony left a bitter, acrid taste on her tongue, far sharper than the sweet spice of the gingerbread.

"He's gotten so handsome," Elenore said softly, as if reading Lani's thoughts. She had a knack for that, her mother. A quiet observation that somehow managed to pinpoint the exact nerve Lani was trying to suppress.

Lani forced a shrug, her eyes still fixed on the swirling patterns in the dough.

"He was always handsome, Mom." That, at least, was a simple, undeniable truth.

"He always had that spark," Elenore continued, her voice tinged with nostalgia. "Remember when he used to enter those junior bakeoffs? Always winning, of course. He had a way with ingredients, even then. Said he could taste the stories they told."

Lani's breath hitched. She remembered.

She remembered the late nights spent poring over cookbooks with him, the shared excitement over a perfectly risen soufflé, the easy camaraderie that had blossomed into something so much more. She remembered the awkward, fumbling first kiss behind the bleachers after a football game, the scent of grass and his aftershave mingling in the cool autumn air.

"He's done remarkable things," Lani said, her voice carefully neutral. She couldn't afford to betray the rush of emotions that were threatening to overwhelm her.

Thomas returned, a wide smile on his face. "That Vance boy has certainly made a name for himself. Said he's back for Christmas, visiting his Uncle. Apparently, he's helping him with some renovations at his place." He slid a steaming mug of coffee across the counter to Elenore. "He remembered you liked it with just a splash of cream, Ellie."

Elenore's smile widened. "He always did have a good memory."

Lani felt a pang of something akin to jealousy. He remembered her mother's coffee preference, but what about her? Did he remember the way she liked her hair when it was humid? The silly song she used to hum when she was nervous? Or the way her heart had leaped every time he looked at her?

She stole a glance towards the counter where Julian was now engaged in a lively conversation with her father, gesturing with his hands, his voice animated. He seemed so... at ease. So confident. He had clearly moved on, forged a new life. Built an empire. And she was here, back in the past, her future uncertain.

The chime of the bell above the door sounded again, and this time, a gust of cold air swept into the bakery, carrying with it the scent of pine and woodsmoke. A group of bundled-up carolers, their faces rosy from the cold, entered, their voices raising in a cheerful rendition of "Jingle Bells."

The bakery, moments before filled with the quiet hum of preparation, now erupted in a cacophony of festive sound. Naomi clapped her hands in delight, her sugar-dusted fingers leaving streaks on Lani's apron. Elenore and Thomas greeted the carolers warmly, offering them samples of their freshly baked gingerbread.

And Julian Vance, the unexpected guest, the echo of a long-lost love, stood watching the scene unfold. A small, enigmatic smile played on his lips.

Lani felt a sudden, overwhelming urge to disappear, to melt into the background, to avoid his gaze. But as she turned back to her gingerbread dough, she knew it was too late. He had returned. A ghost from her past. And the quiet comfort of her present had been irrevocably shattered.

The scent of gingerbread was once a balm, was now carried the potent, undeniable aroma of love lost and a past revisited. Her carefully constructed composure felt as fragile as a spun-sugar ornament, and she braced herself for whatever storms this unexpected return might bring. The holidays, she realized with a sinking heart, had just become infinitely more complicated.

{ 4 }

Julian

The air, which moments before had hummed with polite, if surprised, greetings between her parents and Julian, was now marked with an entirely different energy. It was Lani's own internal echo, a tremor that had nothing to do with the festive carols and everything to do with the sheer, unadulterated shock of *him* being here. She'd instinctively turned back to her dough. The familiar anchor in a sea of unexpected emotion. But her hands felt clumsy, the practiced rhythm of cutting out cookies disrupted by the phantom sensation of Julian's gaze. She could feel it, even without looking, a palpable weight on her skin, a spotlight in the cozy, dimness of Shepard's Sweets.

She stole a quick glance, her eyes darting towards Julian, now a little closer to the counter, still engaged in conversation with her father.

The sight of him, framed by the warm glow of the bakery's lights, the faint dusting of snow still clinging to his dark, impeccably tailored coat, was like stepping into a photograph from another lifetime.

He was taller, yes, and the boyish angles of his face had sharpened into something more defined, more... experienced. There were faint lines around his eyes, the kind that spoke of laughter, perhaps, but also of long hours, intense focus, and the pressures of a life lived at a pace far removed from this quiet mountain town. Yet, beneath the veneer of sophistication, Lani saw it. The same steady intelligence in his gaze, the same subtle curve to his lips that she remembered so vividly. And in that fleeting, accidental glance, something shifted.

His eyes, those impossibly blue eyes that had once held her world, met hers across the bustling space. He pushed a piece of his dark hair back. For a heartbeat, the carolers' song faded, the clatter of baking pans receded, even Naomi's cheerful humming seemed to quiet.

It was as if time itself had snagged, a glitch in the continuum, and the years had dissolved into a fine mist. In his gaze, Lani saw not just the celebrated chef Julian Vance, but the Julian she had known. The boy who had scribbled love notes on flour sacks and whispered dreams into the quiet night. There was warmth there, deeper now, richer, seasoned with the years that had shaped them both. It was a look that acknowledged the impossible, the improbable reunion, and held a silent understanding of the shared history that bound them.

Julian caught her staring. A ghost of a smile touched his lips, a subtle crinkling at the corners of his eyes. It wasn't the easy, confident smile he offered her father, but something softer, more intimate. A private acknowledgment that resonated across the distance. And with that smile, Lani felt a warmth bloom in her chest, spreading outwards, painting a telltale flush across her cheeks.

She instinctively pulled her hands away from the dough, wiping them on her already flour-dusted apron, a sudden, overwhelming self-consciousness washing over her. She felt exposed, suddenly aware of her own disheveled state. The stark contrast between her current reality and the polished image of the man standing before her. He was the boy who had seen her at her most vulnerable, her most effervescent, and now, he was seeing her again, years later. A different woman, marked by experiences he couldn't possibly fathom.

This accidental encounter played out against the backdrop of twinkling fairy lights and the sweet, spicy aroma of gingerbread. It felt both utterly surreal and strangely, undeniably, meant to be.

It was as if the universe, in its own peculiar way, had orchestrated this moment, a punctuation mark in the quiet story of her return.

Cinnamon and molasses were thick in the air, which had always been a source of comfort, now seemed to carry unresolved feelings and of a past that refused to remain buried.

She remembered their whispered promises, the fierce, unwavering belief they'd had in each other, the naive certainty that their youthful love could conquer anything. And here he was, a testament to the very ambition and talent they had once shared. He was a shining example of the dreams they had dared to chase, albeit on different paths.

Julian's gaze lingered for a moment longer, a silent conversation passing between them that words could not have captured. It spoke of shared laughter in the dimly lit movie theater, of furtive kisses stolen under the vast expanse of a star-dusted sky, of the ache of goodbye when their paths had separated. It acknowledged the unspoken questions, the regrets, the lingering 'what ifs' that time had failed to erase.

Then, with a subtle nod, he turned back to her father, his professional composure seamlessly reasserting itself. The moment of suspended animation had passed, the years had snapped back into place, but the echo of that shared glance, the silent recognition, remained, a potent undercurrent beneath the surface of the festive chaos.

Lani, however, felt irrevocably changed.

The quiet hum of the bakery was no longer just the sound of her family's livelihood; it was the soundtrack to a reunion that had unearthed a buried part of her soul, a part she had long believed had faded into the mists of memory.

She returned to her cookies, but the dough felt different beneath her fingers. It was no longer just a task, a means to an end; it was a tangible connection to her family, to her roots, to the life she was trying to rebuild. And now, it was also the backdrop against which Julian Vance, the boy who had held her heart and then, inadvertently, broken it, had reappeared.

Naomi, oblivious to the seismic shift that had just occurred, tugged at Lani's apron. "Mommy, the man with the nice smile, is he going to buy cookies?" Her innocent question, a gentle splash of cold water on Lani's swirling emotions, pulled her back to the present.

Lani forced a smile, her heart still tapping a nervous rhythm against her ribs. "Maybe, sweet pea," she murmured, her voice softer than she intended.

She risked another glance at Julian, who was now laughing at something her father had said. He looked relaxed, comfortable, at home. It was a stark contrast to the turmoil churning within her. He had built a life, a career, a world that seemed so far removed from the simple existence of Evergreen Hollow. And she, Lani, had returned here, seeking solace and a fresh start.

The thought of him, of their shared past, had been a distant ache, a scar that had faded with time. But seeing him now, vibrant and successful, standing mere feet away, had reopened the wound, not with pain. But with a bewildering mix of longing and apprehension. She remembered the easy intimacy they had shared, the way he had known her thoughts before she'd even spoken to them. The way his touch had sent shivers down her spine. She remembered the fierce arguments, too, the passionate disagreements that had often ended in a tender truce, a renewed understanding.

Their love had been a whirlwind, a heady concoction of youthful idealism and undeniable chemistry.

Elenore, ever perceptive, placed a gentle hand on Lani's arm.

"He's grown into quite the gentleman, hasn't he?" she said softly, her gaze following Lani's toward Julian. There was a hint of pride in her voice, not just for Julian's success, but perhaps for the boy they had known, the boy who had once courted her daughter with such earnest devotion.

Lani nodded, unable to form a coherent sentence.

Gentleman. Yes, that was one word for him.

Polished, sophisticated, successful. But beneath the veneer, she hoped, still lay the boy who had loved stargazing and shared her passion for baking.

"He always had a certain presence," Lani managed, choosing her words carefully. "Even back then."

Thomas chuckled, clapping Julian on the back as if they were old friends. "More than a presence, Ellie. That boy was destined for bigger things. Always had that fire in his belly, that drive. Knew he'd end up in the culinary stratosphere."

He turned to Lani, his eyes twinkling. "You remember how much he loved helping his grandmother in the kitchen, Lani? Always experimenting, always tasting, always asking questions. Driven, that one."

Lani's breath caught. She remembered. How could she ever forget? The aroma of garlic and herbs wafting from his grandmother's small, cluttered kitchen, the clatter of pots and pans, the animated discussions about perfect pastry crusts and the art of caramelization. She remembered sitting on the worn linoleum floor, watching him, mesmerized, as he meticulously whisked and folded, his brow furrowed in concentration. He had seen food not just as sustenance, but as art, as expression, as a language. And she had been his eager audience, his quiet confidante, the one who understood his passion.

"He still has that fire," Lani said, her voice barely a whisper. It was a statement of fact, a quiet acknowledgment of his enduring talent. But it also felt like a confession, a reluctant admission that some parts of him, the parts that had once ignited her own spirit, were still very much alive.

Julian, sensing their eyes on him, turned. His gaze met Lani's again, and this time, the smile that spread across his face was more pronounced, more open. It was a smile that held no pretense, no artifice, just a genuine warmth that reached out and enveloped her.

"Lani," he said, his voice a low, pleasant rumble that seemed to reverberate through the quiet bakery. He spoke her name as if he were tasting it, savoring it.

Hearing him speak her name after all this time sent a jolt through her. It was a sound that belonged to a different era, a different Lani.

"Julian," she replied, her own voice a little unsteady. She managed a small, tentative smile, a mirror of his own, hoping it conveyed something of the complex emotions swirling within her.

Naomi, sensing the shift in the atmosphere, skipped over to stand beside Julian, her eyes wide with curiosity.

"Are you a famous chef?" she asked, her voice clear and bright.

Julian crouched down, his blue eyes crinkling as he met Naomi's gaze. "I cook, little one. And sometimes, people like what I cook. Is that famous?"

Naomi giggled. "Mommy says you used to know her when she was little."

Julian's smile widened, and he looked back at Lani, a knowing glint in his eyes. "I remember Lani when she had pigtails that flew when she ran, and a smile that could light up the whole town. I don't think she's changed one bit, really."

Lani's breath hitched. He remembered. He remembered the trivial details, the fleeting moments that had laid the foundation of their youthful romance. The pigtails, the smile – these were not things a casual acquaintance would recall. This was the memory of someone who had truly *seen* her. A blush, deeper and more insistent than before, crept up her neck.

"She's grown up a lot," Elenore interjected smoothly, deftly redirecting the conversation. "And Lani, she's done so well for herself, coming back here, helping us out."

Lani appreciated her mother's tact, her subtle attempt to steer them away from their shared past. But she also felt a pang of something she couldn't quite define. It wasn't resentment, not exactly, but a quiet acknowledgment of the life she had lost the career she had sacrificed. She was here, in her parents' bakery, starting over, while Julian was out there, living the dream they had once shared.

Julian stood up, his gaze returning to Lani. "It's good to see you back, Lani. Really good." His words were simple, but the sincerity in his voice was undeniable. It was more than just politeness; it was a genuine warmth, a recognition of her presence, her return.

And in that moment, surrounded by the comforting scent of gingerbread, the warmth of the bakery, and the joyful sound of carols, Lani felt a strange sense of peace settle over her. The years had melted away, not entirely, but enough to reveal the enduring connection that still existed between them.

He was here, a living, breathing reminder of a chapter closed but not forgotten. And she was here, ready to write the next one, perhaps with a familiar, yet entirely new, acquaintance by her side.

The air crackled with unspoken possibilities, and Lani knew, with a certainty that both thrilled and terrified her, that her life in this quiet mountain town had just become infinitely more interesting. The years had melted away in a shared glance, and the future, like the scent of gingerbread, was suddenly filled with a tantalizing sweetness and unexpected complexity.

Julian's presence was a gravitational pull Lani couldn't entirely escape. Even as she busied herself with the rhythm of the bakery, her senses remained acutely attuned to him. When he finally stepped forward, a subtle shift in the room's energy drew her attention. He moved with an effortless grace, a man comfortable in his own skin, yet there was an undeniable attentiveness in his approach, a quiet focus that seemed directed solely at her and her family.

"It's truly wonderful to be home, Thomas, Elenore," Julian began, his voice a rich baritone that carried a genuine warmth. He extended a hand to her father and a firm, confident grip was exchanged between them. "And to see Shepard's Sweets thriving like this. It's a testament to your hard work, and Lani's return, I'm sure, has only added to its magic."

Lani's heart gave a peculiar little leap at his words. He hadn't just acknowledged her parents; he'd acknowledged *her*. And he'd done it with a sincerity that belied the easy charm he was known for. She watched as he turned his attention back to her, a slow, disarming smile spreading across his lips. It wasn't the broad, practiced smile of a public figure, but something softer, more intimate, the kind that reached his eyes and made them sparkle.

"Lani," he said, and the way he pronounced her name was like a familiar melody, plucked from a forgotten playlist. "It's... it's so good to see you. Really good." He paused, his gaze holding hers for a beat longer than strictly necessary. "I heard you were back. I'm so glad you decided to return to where it all began."

The words hung in the air, heavy with unspoken history. *Where it all began.* It was a phrase loaded with memories, with shared laughter and stolen moments, with the heady rush of first love and the sharp sting of its abrupt end. Lani felt a blush creep up her neck, a betraying warmth that had nothing to do with the bakery's ovens.

"Thank you, Julian," she managed, her voice a little breathier than she'd intended. She gestured vaguely around the bustling shop. "It's good to be back. The bakery... it's always been home."

Her father's gaze flickered between her and Julian as he sensed the subtle undercurrent of their exchange. He interjected a hearty laugh.

"And she's been a godsend, Julian. Keeping us on our toes, introducing new ideas. Though I daresay some of your old favorites are still the best sellers!" He winked at Lani.

Julian's eyes, that impossibly blue expanse, flickered back to Lani. "I have no doubt," he said, his voice laced with amusement. "Some things, Lani, you just don't mess with. Like a perfect gingerbread cookie, or a sky full of stars. Or... well, you know." He let the sentence trail off, a playful challenge in his tone, a subtle invitation to acknowledge the shared understanding that simmered between them.

Lani's throat tightened. *Or... well, you know.* It was a perfect Julian-ism, a way of hinting at their past without explicitly stating it, a way of reminding her of all the things they had once held so dear. She quickly turned back to her cookies, her hands finding a familiar comfort as she placed them on the baking sheet. But even the tactile sensation of flour and sugar couldn't entirely ground her. She could still feel his gaze on her, a persistent, warm pressure.

He turned his attention back to her parents, engaging them in conversation about the intricacies of running a small business, the challenges and rewards. He spoke with easy familiarity, asking insightful questions that demonstrated a genuine interest, not just polite deference.

Lani half-listened, catching snippets of his stories. He'd traveled extensively, he mentioned, working in kitchens across Europe, honing his craft. He spoke of the relentless pace, the creative pressures, the exhilarating highs of a successful service. Yet, woven through the narrative of his impressive career, Lani detected a subtle thread of something else, a wistful undertone, a hint of something missing.

"It's a demanding life," he admitted, running a hand through his perfectly styled hair. "But incredibly rewarding. You get to create something tangible, something that brings people joy. It's a powerful thing, food." He paused, his gaze drifting back to Lani, who was now carefully arranging gingerbread men on a baking sheet. "It's a universal language, wouldn't you say, Lani?"

"Hmm?" She met his eyes, a silent acknowledgment passing between them. He remembered. He remembered their late-night conversations, fueled by sugar and dreams, where they'd dissected the emotional resonance of a perfectly baked pie, the comfort found in a warm loaf of bread. He remembered how they'd once believed that this passion, this shared love for creating, was the bedrock of their future.

"It is," she replied softly, her voice barely audible above the gentle hum of the bakery. "It's more than just sustenance. It's memory. It's emotion."

Julian nodded, a slow, thoughtful gesture. "Exactly. And you, Lani," he said, his voice dropping to a lower register, a confiding tone that drew her in, "you always had a gift for capturing that. For infusing your baking with something... special. I remember those lemon tarts you used to make. The scent alone could transport you."

Lani's breath hitched. Lemon tarts. She hadn't made them in years. Not since he left. They were his grandmother's recipe, a treasured heirloom, and Lani had been the only one he'd ever shared it with, the only one he'd trusted to bake them "just right." It was a small detail, a seemingly insignificant memory, but to Julian, to bring it up now, in this context, felt like a deliberate act. A deliberate reaching back into their shared past.

"They were your grandmother's recipe," she murmured, her gaze fixed on the intricate details of the gingerbread man's buttons. "A special lady."

"She was," Julian agreed, his voice softening. "And she saw that spark in you, Lani. She used to say you had a baker's heart." He smiled, a tender, almost wistful expression. "I think she was right."

The compliment, innocent on the surface, landed with the weight of years of unspoken longing. *A baker's heart.* It was what she had always strived to be, even when life had pulled her in a different direction. And Julian, of all people, remembered that. He remembered the core of who she was, the passion that had once burned so brightly between them.

Her mother, sensing Lani's slight withdrawal, stepped in smoothly. "Julian, you must tell us more about your latest venture. That new restaurant in the city, we've heard such rave reviews."

Julian readily launched into an animated description of his acclaimed establishment, the innovative menu, the challenges of sourcing sustainable ingredients, and the pressure of maintaining Michelin-star standards. He spoke with the eloquence and passion of someone deeply invested in his work. Lani listened, impressed by his drive, his dedication. He had achieved so much, built a life of substance and acclaim. It was everything they had dreamed of, and yet, he was here, in her parents' humble bakery, speaking of it with a certain detachment, as if recounting a story of someone else's life.

"It's... it's a lot," he concluded, a hint of weariness creeping into his voice. "Sometimes, you find yourself so caught up in the chase, in the next big thing, that you forget to savor the moment. To appreciate the simple things."

His gaze found Lani's again, and this time, there was no mistaking the undertone. He was drawing a parallel, an unspoken comparison between his whirlwind life and her seemingly quieter existence.

Lani felt a flicker of something akin to defensiveness, quickly followed by a wave of understanding. He wasn't judging; he was perhaps, in his own way, expressing a longing for something he'd lost, something he perhaps saw reflected in her return to a simpler life.

"The simple things have their own kind of magic," she offered, her voice gentle. "They're the foundations, aren't they? The things that ground you."

Julian leaned against the counter, his expression thoughtful. "They are. And sometimes, I wonder if I ever truly appreciated them when I had them in abundance." He looked around the bakery, his eyes softening. "This place... it's a reminder of that. Of where I came from. Of... certain people."

He allowed his gaze to rest on Lani for a moment longer, the unspoken implication clear.

The conversation continued, flowing seamlessly between the professional triumphs and the quiet reminiscences. Julian told them about his mentors who had shaped him and the culinary inspirations that had ignited his passion.

Lani found herself drawn into the conversation, offering her own observations, her own insights, drawing on the years she had spent in her parents' bakery, even when her career had taken her elsewhere. There was an unexpected ease to their banter, a comfortable rhythm that felt both familiar and new.

"You know," Julian said, a speculative gleam in his eyes, "I've been working on a new dessert. Something that requires a very specific, very delicate pastry. I've been struggling with the texture, trying to achieve that perfect balance of crispness and melt-in-your-mouth tenderness." He looked directly at Lani, a subtle challenge in his gaze. "I've tried everything, but it's still not quite there. It's like... like a missing ingredient, a certain touch that eludes me."

Lani felt a familiar flutter of anticipation, a spark of the old excitement. He was asking for her help, not just as a former acquaintance, but as a fellow baker. He was acknowledging her skill, her intuition.

"Sometimes," she began, her hands automatically moving as if to mimic the actions, "it's not about the ingredients themselves, but how they're treated. The temperature of the butter, the way you incorporate the flour, the patience you have in the chilling process. It's all about the handling, the gentle coaxing."

Julian listened intently, his eyes never leaving her face.

"Patience," he mused. "Yes, that's something that's often in short supply in my world. Always the next reservation, the next critic, the next review. The pressure to constantly come up with something new, to push the boundaries." He sighed, a sound that seemed to carry the weight of his demanding profession. "Perhaps I've forgotten the art of simply waiting, of letting the dough tell me when it's ready." He looked around the bakery, with a faint smile playing on his lips.

"This is a place of waiting, isn't it? Waiting for dough to rise, waiting for cookies to bake, waiting for customers to arrive. There's a quiet beauty in that anticipation."

The air between them seemed to thicken. He had pursued his dreams with a singular focus, leaving behind the small town, the quiet life, and Lani. She had returned, seeking solace and a sense of belonging, her own ambitions deferred. Now, here they were, standing in the heart of her family's legacy, a tangible symbol of the life they had once envisioned together.

"It is," Lani agreed softly. "And there's a certain satisfaction in that. In creating something beautiful, not out of a need for perfection, but a genuine love for the process. Out of patience."

His eyes softened and his smile became less of a charmer's tool and more of a genuine expression of connection. "I think you might be right, Lani," he said, his voice a low rumble. "I think perhaps I've been missing that 'certain touch' you mentioned.

He paused, the unspoken invitation hanging in the air. "Perhaps, if you ever have the time, you might be willing to share some of that wisdom? I'm sure my pastry chef would be eternally grateful, and... so would I."

Lani's heart gave a dizzying lurch. It was an offer, a request, a subtle overture that went beyond professional courtesy. It was Julian, the celebrated chef, asking for *her* help, for *her* touch. It was a chance to reconnect, not just as old friends, but as artists, as kindred spirits who had once shared a profound understanding. Wasn't it?

She met his gaze, a slow smile spreading across her face. The unfinished business of their youth, the abrupt separation, the roads not taken. It all swirled around them, a potent mix of memory and possibility. But in that moment, surrounded by the comforting aroma of gingerbread and the warm presence of her family, Lani felt a flicker of something new ignite. It wasn't just about revisiting the past; it was about discovering what new flavors could be created when two old souls decided to stir the pot once more.

"I think," Lani said, her voice steady and clear, "that I might just have some time to spare."

***

Naomi

Naomi perched on her usual stool by the window, the worn, smooth wood a familiar comfort beneath her. From this vantage point, she could survey the bustling heart of the bakery. Her large blue gaze, sharp and perceptive, flickered between her mother and the handsome man who had captured her mother's attention.

It wasn't just the man's undeniable charisma that drew Naomi's notice, though he possessed that in spades. It was the subtle shifts, the nuances anyone else would have missed.

She knew her Mommy better than anyone. They were a team. She saw the way Lani's cheeks bloomed with a soft, pink color whenever the man's impossibly blue eyes met hers. It was a blush that spoke of something more than mere politeness, a flicker of an old flame rekindled in the warm, sweet air of the bakery.

Mommy looked different today. She walked like she was lighter, like her feet didn't touch the ground all the way, and her voice sounded kind of like a song I hadn't heard before.

Grandma always says Mommy shines the brightest when she's really happy, and I think I was starting to see what she meant. When Mommy looked at the man named Julian, her eyes stayed on his, and it felt like they were sharing secrets without talking out loud. I scrunched up my forehead, not because I was worried, but because I wanted to know. Who was this man who made Mommy's smile look so sparkly, and how did he know her enough to make her act this way?

Julian—that's what he said his name was—didn't act loud or silly like some grown-ups do. He was calm, like he already knew how to fit everywhere without trying. When he talked to Grandma and Grandpa, he asked about the bakery and the old days, and even about Mommy coming back. He spoke slowly and carefully, like he wanted every word to mean something nice.

And when he wasn't talking, he really listened, leaning his head a little, like their words were the most important thing in the room. I could tell he didn't just think Mommy was baking bread. He looked at her like she was making magic with sugar and flour.

As if sensing Naomi's watchful gaze, his attention shifted. His smile widened, a genuine, disarming curve of his lips that reached his eyes, crinkling the corners. It was a smile that conveyed warmth and a touch of gentle amusement, the kind that made one feel instantly seen and welcomed.

He detached himself from the conversation with Lani's parents, his movements fluid and unhurried, and began to walk towards Naomi's perch by the window.

"And who is this discerning young lady?" he asked, his voice a low, melodious rumble that somehow managed to convey both kindness and a hint of playful curiosity.

He stopped a respectable distance away, his gaze meeting Naomi's directly. There was no condescension in his eyes, no dismissiveness of her youth. Instead, he seemed to regard her with a thoughtful interest, as if she held a unique and significant place in Lani's life.

Naomi was usually shy around strangers. But she found herself unexpectedly at ease. There was something about Julian's, a gentle honesty that enchanted her. It was like he didn't see a little kid, but a person, a fellow observer in the unfolding scene. Her heart gave a little thrum against her ribs. She pressed her hands against her belly, trying to stop the nervous rhythm. She offered him a small, tentative smile, her fingers unconsciously tracing the grain of the wooden stool.

"I'm Naomi," she said, her voice a soft murmur, barely audible above the clatter of trays and the whir of the mixer.

She shifted her weight, feeling suddenly self-conscious. She knew she was Lani's daughter, that her presence here was a given, but to be addressed so directly, so personally, by this stranger, was... different.

He made her feel important.

Julian's smile softened further. "Naomi," he repeated, the name rolling off his tongue with a gentle tone. "It's a pleasure to meet you. Your mother has told me so much about you."

Naomi's eyes widened slightly. Her mother? Lani didn't often speak of her. She was a private person; her emotions often tucked away like precious secrets. To think that Julian knew her well enough for Lani to speak of her... it was a revelation. A pleasant one, but a revelation, nonetheless.

"She has?" Naomi asked, a hint of wonder in her voice.

"Indeed," Julian confirmed, his gaze still holding hers with that same gentle curiosity. "I heard about your quiet strength, your good eye for detail. That you see things others miss."

He paused, his smile returning, a little more pronounced this time. "She's very proud of you, Naomi. Very proud indeed."

Warmth spread through Naomi, a soft bloom of pride that rivaled the blush on her mother's cheeks. To hear that from him, from someone who clearly held a special place in her mother's past, felt significant. It was an affirmation, a silent nod of approval that resonated deeply.

She felt a sudden urge to offer him something, a gesture of welcome, of acknowledgment. Her eyes scanned the display counter, her gaze landing on a plate of freshly baked shortbread cookies, their golden-brown surfaces sprinkled with coarse sugar. They were simple, but delicious, a testament to her mother's skill.

"Would you like a cookie?" Naomi asked, her voice a little steadier now, emboldened by his kind words. She reached out and carefully selected one of the smaller, perfectly formed cookies, its edges slightly crisp, its center still warm. She held it out to him, her small hand steady despite the tremor of nervousness that still lingered.

Julian's gaze dropped to the cookie, then back to Naomi's earnest face. He accepted the offering with a gracious nod, his large hand dwarfing her own as he gently took the treat.

"Thank you, Naomi," he said, his voice laced with a sincerity that made the gesture feel more significant than a mere cookie. He took a bite, his eyes closing for a brief moment as he savored the flavor.

"Mmm, that's exquisite. Your mommy's recipe?"

"Yes," Naomi confirmed, a small smile playing on her lips. "She makes them every Tuesday."

She watched him as he ate, her gaze cataloging every subtle expression, every minute movement. He was... different from the men her mother usually worked with. Different from the man who wasn't' her daddy anymore. There was more to him, a quiet that set him apart. He wasn't just a customer; he was someone who seemed to understand this place.

Julian finished the cookie, wiping his fingers delicately on a napkin. He looked around the bakery, his gaze lingering on the array of pastries, the neatly arranged loaves of bread, and the gentle hum of activity. It was as if he were taking in the entire scene, absorbing its essence. When his eyes returned to Naomi, they held a new layer of understanding, a quiet acknowledgment of her place within it all.

"Shepard's Sweets," he said, as if tasting the name. "It's more than just a bakery, isn't it? It's a cornerstone. A place where memories are baked into every recipe."

He looked back at her mother, who was now engaged in a conversation with Elenore, her laughter light and musical.

"And you, Naomi, you're a vital part of that, aren't you? You're not just the baker's granddaughter; you're a guardian of this wonderful place."

Naomi blinked, surprised by his perception. He saw her, not just as a child passing through, but as a part of the bakery's soul. He understood the quiet dedication, the unspoken pride that came with being a Shepard. She nodded, a silent affirmation.

"She loves it here," Naomi offered softly, her gaze following Julian's to her mother. "She... she missed it. While she was away."

The words tumbled out, a confession of sorts, an innocent revelation of her mother's inner feelings. It was rare for Naomi to speak so openly about her mother's emotions, but Julian's gentle nature encouraged it.

Julian's expression softened. A flicker of something crossed his face she didn't quite understand. Was it recognition, understanding, perhaps even a touch of regret? He met Naomi's gaze again, and this time, his eyes held a depth, a quiet empathy that resonated with her.

"I can see why," he said, his voice a low murmur, directed as much to himself as to her. "A place like this, with such heart, it's hard to stay away forever." He paused, a thoughtful expression on his face. "Your mother has a special gift, Naomi. A talent for bringing comfort and joy through her baking. It's a rare and beautiful thing."

He turned his attention back to Lani, a gentle smile playing on his lips. He didn't interrupt, but simply watched, his gaze filled with quiet appreciation.

Naomi watched him watching her mother, and a strange, new understanding began to dawn within her. Julian wasn't just an old friend; he was someone who saw Lani in a way that few others did.

And in his eyes, Naomi saw a reflection of connection.

It was as if, his being here in Lani's world, and by extension Naomi's, felt a little more complete, a little more understood. The air in the bakery, already warm with the scent of sugar and spice, seemed to thicken with an unspoken history, a shared understanding that transcended words.

Naomi, the silent observer, felt the knot in her tummy untie. A sense of peace settled over her. She knew, with certainty, that even at her young age, that this was a moment of significance, a turning point in the quiet narrative of her mother's life.

{ 5 }

Lani

The bell above the door chimed a soft farewell as Julian stepped out into the crisp afternoon air, his departure leaving behind a subtle ripple in the otherwise tranquil atmosphere of Shepard's Sweets.

Lani watched him go, a peculiar blend of sensations swirling within her. It had been years, no decades, since their paths had last crossed, and his sudden reappearance felt less like a chance encounter and more like a carefully orchestrated intrusion into the quiet sanctuary she had painstakingly built for herself. His parting words, a casual promise to "stop by" again, hung in the air, a loose thread threatening to unravel the neat tapestry of her present. She couldn't go there again

She turned back into the warmth of the bakery, the comforting aroma a stark contrast to the unsettling flutter in her chest.

Lani busied herself with wiping down the counter, her movements a shade more vigorous than usual, as if by sheer force of will she could scrub away the lingering presence of their meeting.

Julian.

The name itself was a whisper from a forgotten chapter, a melody that had once played a significant tune in the symphony of her youth. Now, it was a faint echo, a ghost of affection that had resurfaced with an unexpected potency.

She caught her reflection in the polished chrome of the espresso machine, her cheeks still faintly flushed. A tell-tale sign of the emotional tremor that had passed through her. It wasn't just a fleeting blush, she knew. It was a response to something deeper, something that lay buried beneath the layers of time and experience. She saw the lingering warmth in her own eyes, a warmth she hadn't consciously felt in a long time, a warmth that Julian's gaze had effortlessly rekindled. It was a surprising, almost disconcerting, surge of emotion, a reminder of a version of herself that had been dormant for so long.

Elenore was humming a cheerful tune as she meticulously arranged a display of lemon tarts, her back to Lani. Thomas was engrossed in a ledger, his brow furrowed in concentration. They had seemed, Lani thought, as oblivious to the undercurrents of her interaction with Julian as she herself had tried to be. They saw him as an old boyfriend of their daughter. A blast from the past. They couldn't possibly understand the tangled threads of memory that his presence had pulled tight. The years of unspoken words and broken dreams that his casual return had brought back to her heart that never mended.

Lani sighed, a soft, almost inaudible sound that was lost in the gentle whir of the industrial mixer.

Was it simply nostalgia that had colored her reaction? The natural tendency to revisit the past when a familiar face reappeared? Or was there something more to it? A genuine flicker of affection that had stubbornly refused to be extinguished by the passage of time? She dismissed the latter as preposterous.

Julian was a closed chapter in her life. A story that had reached its natural conclusion. To entertain any other notion would be to invite a disruption, a complication she simply didn't have the time or the emotional energy to navigate. Her life here at Evergreen Hollow was carefully balanced, and Julian's reappearance felt like an intrusion.

She glanced at Naomi, who had retreated to her usual spot by the window, her gaze now fixed on the street outside, her expression thoughtful. Lani wondered what her daughter had made of the encounter.

Naomi possessed quiet wisdom and uncanny perception for her age. She often saw more than she let on. Had she noticed the subtle shift in Lani's demeanor? The way her heart had inexplicably quickened at the sound of Julian's voice. Lani hoped not. She wanted to protect Naomi from the pain of her own past, to shield her from the messy, unpredictable nature of adult emotions.

"He sure has grown up. He seemed like a nice man, Lani," Elenore said, her voice bright and cheerful, as she placed the final tart with precision. "Polite. He certainly knows his way around a bakery, asking about the sourdough starter and all."

She turned, a gentle smile gracing her lips. "You haven't seen him in, what? Fifteen years?"

Lani's hand stilled on the counter. Fifteen years. The number felt both impossibly long and distressingly short.

"Something like that," she murmured, avoiding her mother's searching gaze.

"Julian Vance. Tall fellow, dark hair, always had a book tucked under his arm," Thomas murmured, looking up from his ledger. A aflicker of recognition in his eyes. "He was here all the time, back in the day. Before he moved away."

"That's the one," Lani confirmed, a ghost of a smile touching her lips. She remembered Julian's quiet demeanor, his intellectual curiosity, the way he'd always seemed to be observing the world around him with a thoughtful, discerning eye. He hadn't been like the boisterous, carefree boys of her youth. He was different, more introspective, and that had drawn her to him.

"He was a good lad," Thomas mused, turning back to his numbers. "Always polite. Shame he left the town."

A good lad. The words resonated with a bittersweet ache. He had been more than just a good lad to her.

He had been a confidante, a kindred spirit, a first love whose memory she had carefully filed away, deeming it too fragile, too painful, to revisit. His sudden appearance was a stark reminder of that buried emotion, a jolt that sent tremors through the foundations of her carefully constructed peace.

Lani took a deep breath, forcing herself to focus on the present, on the familiar tasks that grounded her. The sweet, cloying scent of frosting, the rhythmic thud of the dough hook, the comforting weight of her apron, these were the anchors that kept her steady. She couldn't afford to get lost in the memories of the past, not now. Not when her life had finally settled into a rhythm that was both satisfying and sustainable.

She began to prepare a batch of her signature gluten-free chocolate chip cookies. A small step towards making the bakery more inclusive for its customers. Her hands moved with an automatic grace that belied the turmoil within. The act of measuring sweet rice flour, creaming butter and sugar, and folding in the rich, dark chocolate was a ritual. A form of meditation. Each precise movement was a deliberate step away from the unsettling encounter with Julian, a reaffirmation of her commitment to the present. Yet, even as her hands worked, her mind kept drifting back to the wave in his dark brown hair, his impossibly blue eyes and the gentle curve of his smile. Surprising warmth bloomed in her chest.

Naomi, sensing her mother's distraction, pushed herself away from the window and walked over to the counter, her small hands reaching for a discarded piping bag.

"Mommy?" she asked softly, her voice laced with a hint of concern. "Are you okay?"

Lani forced a smile, her gaze meeting her daughter's. "Of course, sweetie. Just a little tired, that's all." She didn't want to lie to Naomi, but she also didn't want to burden her with the confusing complexities of her own feelings.

Naomi, however, seemed unconvinced. Her brow furrowed slightly, a mirror image of Lani's own habitual expression when something was amiss.

"You seemed different," she said, her gaze unwavering. "When he was here. Your cheeks were all rosy."

Lani's smile faltered. She knew Naomi saw everything. "It was just surprising, that's all. To see someone from so long ago." She tried to keep her tone light, dismissive. "It's not something that happens every day."

"He said he knew you from before," Naomi continued, her voice quiet but persistent. "He said you used to be friends."

Friends.

The word felt inadequate, a pale imitation of the depth of their past connection. "Yes," Lani admitted, her voice barely a whisper. "We were. A long time ago."

Naomi's gaze shifted, her eyes flicking to the door where Julian had stood moments before. "He looked at you like...like he remembered you. Really remembered you."

Lani's heart gave a painful lurch. Her daughter, with her innocent candor, had hit the nail precisely on the head. Julian *did* remember her. He remembered the girl she had been, the dreams they had shared, the future they had envisioned together. And in his eyes, Lani had seen not just a flicker of nostalgia, but a profound understanding, a quiet acknowledgment of the indelible mark they had left on each other's lives.

"He did," Lani said, her voice barely audible. She felt a strange mix of vulnerability and a reluctant sense of relief.

Naomi's awareness, rather than being a burden, felt like a strange sort of validation. Perhaps, she thought, it was time to acknowledge the past, not as a source of pain or regret, but as an integral part of who she was.

"We grew up together. He lived with his grandma a couple of years after his parents went to Brazil to become missionaries."

"Did you like him, like him, Mommy?" Naomi asked, her eyes wide and earnest. "Back then?"

Lani hesitated, her gaze drifting to the plate of cookies she had just finished preparing. The familiar comfort of their sweet scent filled the air, a stark contrast to the storm brewing within her.

"Yes, Naomi," she said, her voice soft but firm. "I did. I like him very much."

A small, knowing smile spread across Naomi's face. She didn't pry further, sensing that her mother had revealed all she was ready to share. Instead, she picked up a fallen chocolate chip from the counter and popped it into her mouth, her eyes still fixed on her mother.

Lani watched her daughter, a wave of affection washing over her. Naomi was her world, her anchor, her reason for being. And for Naomi's sake, she needed to ensure that her past, however complicated, didn't cast a shadow over her daughter's bright future. Yet, as she met Naomi's steady gaze, Lani couldn't shake the unsettling feeling that Julian's reappearance was more than just a fleeting coincidence. It felt like a deliberate turning of a page, an invitation to revisit a story she had long thought was finished.

She returned to her baking, the rhythmic creak of the mixer was a comforting counterpoint to the lingering questions in her mind. Julian's promise to "stop by" again echoed in her thoughts, a persistent, unsettling refrain. She told herself it was just a polite gesture, a social nicety. But a small, persistent part of her, a part that had been dormant for years, wondered if it was something more. A carefully planted seed of possibility, or a gentle nudge from fate, urging her to confront the ghosts of her past.

The encounter had been brief, a mere twenty minutes snatched from the fabric of an ordinary afternoon. Yet, it had been enough to stir a potent cocktail of emotions within Lani. Regret for the paths not taken, surprise at the return of buried feelings, and a startling flicker of an old affection that she had long believed was safely extinguished.

But Lani remembered.

Julian's presence in her life, after so many years of quiet solitude, felt like a sudden gust of wind, disturbing the carefully constructed peace she had sought.

She tried to dismiss it as mere nostalgia, a momentary weakness brought on by the unexpected reappearance of a familiar face from her youth. A ghost of her past, she told herself, conjuring a fleeting image of a younger Lani, her heart full of dreams and a future brimming with possibilities. But as she continued her work, the scent of warm cookies and melting chocolate filling the air, a small, undeniable part of her found herself wondering if this was truly just a coincidence, or if there was something more deliberate, something more meaningful, at play.

She imagined Julian walking away, his tall figure disappearing down the street, and she felt a strange pang of... what? Loss? Regret? It was hard to pinpoint. He had been a significant part of her life, a gentle presence who had seen her, truly seen her, in a way that few others had. His departure all those years ago had left a void. She learned to live with that quiet ache and moved on. And now, he was back, a living, breathing embodiment of a past she had tried so hard to outrun.

Lani watched her parents, their familiar routines a comforting balm to her unsettled spirit. They were so grounded, so present in the world of Shepard's Sweets. They saw Julian as a man who had once frequented their shop, a young man who had dated their daughter and moved on.

They didn't see the history he represented, the shared laughter, the whispered secrets, the first tentative steps towards a future that had ultimately never materialized. They didn't see the ghost of a love that still held a faint, persistent warmth within her.

She shook her head, trying to clear the lingering thoughts of Julian. This was not the time for reminiscing, for dwelling on 'what ifs'. Her focus needed to be on the present, on the bakery, on her family. She was Lani Shepard, a baker, a mother, a woman who had found her peace in the familiar rhythm of her days. She didn't need or want any more complications.

Yet, as she measured out the flour for her next batch of bread for the following day, she couldn't help but replay the brief exchange with Julian in her mind. His easy smile, the kindness in his eyes, and the way he had spoken to Naomi with such genuine warmth.

He had been so... present. So completely in the moment. It was a stark contrast to the way she often felt, constantly battling the echoes of her past.

And then there was the way he had looked at her. That lingering glance held a depth of understanding and silent acknowledgment of their shared history. It was a look that spoke volumes, a look that hinted at unspoken words, at memories that time had not managed to erase. It was a look that stirred something within her, something old and tender, a faint echo of affection that she had tried so hard to silence.

Was it possible that Julian had felt it too? This unexpected resurgence of feeling?

Or was she simply projecting her own turmoil onto his polite demeanor? Lani scoffed at herself. It was all in her head, a fanciful indulgence born of surprise and nostalgia. Julian was a man who had moved on, forged a new life for himself, miles and years away from the quiet streets of this town. His reappearance was a brief, unexpected detour, nothing more.

But the lingering warmth in her cheeks, the slight tremor in her hands, the persistent replaying of his words, they all suggested otherwise. The carefully constructed walls around her heart, built brick by painstaking brick over years of quiet resilience suddenly felt fragile. Seeing Julian was a threat to her heart.

She was a baker, skilled in transforming simple ingredients into comforting treats. But she was not equipped to handle the potent, unpredictable magic that Julian Vance seemed to possess, the magic of stirring embers that she had long believed had turned to ash. The echo, faint as it was, refused to be entirely silenced.

It whispered of forgotten moments, of roads not taken, and of a past that, however much she tried to confine it, refused to stay buried.

{ **6** }

Julian

The bell above the bakery door chimed softly as Julian stepped inside, and for a moment, his breath caught. **Lani.**

She stood behind the counter, a faint dusting of flour on her cheek, her laughter mingling with the hum of conversation and the sweet scent of sugar and cinnamon. Years had touched her gently, etching fine lines around her eyes, deepening her beauty in ways time could never diminish. Her dark brown hair was shorter but still thick and full. But her eyes were the same. That familiar light, bright and warm, struck something deep in him, something he hadn't felt in years.

She moved with a quiet grace, her gestures confident yet soft, like someone who had finally made peace with her place in the world. Watching her, Julian felt a sharp pang of regret, one he'd carried quietly for far too long. He should have asked her out all those years ago. The moment had been there, bright and waiting, and he had let it pass. He was too cautious, too afraid to risk what could have been.

Now, standing here, that missed chance felt heavier than ever.

He talked with her parents first, exchanging polite pleasantries while trying not to stare like a fool. They told him about the bakery and how it would become her bakery. They spoke about how she had come back after years away, how she would help rebuild the place. Every word carried a quiet pride, the kind that made his chest ache.

And when Julian spoke of her, he realized his tone had changed. Reverent. Careful. Like if he wasn't, the emotion might spill over.

Then there was Naomi, her daughter. Bright-eyed, curious, with that same open smile that had always been Lani's way of lighting up a room. She talked easily, her words tumbling out like a stream, and every time she grinned, he saw her mother. It was uncanny how much of Lani lived in her. It wasn't just a resemblance. It was a legacy.

And yet, standing there, Julian couldn't help but think he'd missed so much.

When Naomi ran off to help her grandmother,

He had leaned a hand on the counter and...couldn't get a word out that was anything close to being suave.

He pinched the bridge of his nose. "That's all I had?" he muttered under his breath. *I asked her to share her baking wisdom?* Not dinner. Not coffee. Baking.

He shook his head, half amused, half exasperated. "Smooth, Julian," he murmured. "Real smooth."

The truth was, the moment he saw her again, all that practiced confidence he'd built over the years evaporated.

The rhythm of her movements, the sound of her laugh, the way her hands worked the dough with that effortless precision, pulled him right back. And that ache in his chest, the one he'd buried under work and distance, came roaring back to life.

She looked the same, and yet not. Time had softened her edges, lent her a quiet kind of beauty that only comes from heartbreak and healing. But her eyes, those deep, familiar eyes, still held the same spark. The same girl who had stolen his heart before he even understood what love was.

Leaving Shepard's Sweets that day, years ago, had never been easy. It still wasn't. The chill of the autumn air outside did little to erase the warmth she'd left lingering in him. Her parting words had been polite, careful. But when he'd told her he would stop by again, she had smiled, a small, knowing smile that carried something fragile beneath it.

And as the door closed behind him, he couldn't help wondering if maybe she had felt it too. That flicker of what they used to be, still glowing quietly under the surface.

Coming back to this town had been impulsive, maybe even foolish. He'd told himself it was about business, about checking in on an old friend. But that was a lie he couldn't sell himself anymore.

As he stood on the sidewalk, the scent of fresh bread and sugar spilling into the cool evening air, he turned back. Through the bakery window, he saw her laugh at something Naomi said, her cheeks flushed from the oven's heat, her smile soft and unguarded.

And right then, it hit him. The simple truth was he'd spent years running from.

Lani wasn't just part of his past. She was everything he lost when he left. She was the missing piece of every plan that hadn't quite felt complete.

***

Julian lingered on the sidewalk long after the glow from Shepard's Sweets dimmed against the gathering dusk. Snow had begun to fall, soft and silent, dusting the brim of his coat. He shoved his hands into his pockets, staring through the bakery window one last time before turning away.

He didn't go back to the inn right away. His car seemed to move on its own, winding down the quiet streets of Evergreen Hollow until he found himself pulling into the gravel drive of a familiar farmhouse on the edge of town. The porch light was already on, casting a warm halo through the falling snow.

Uncle Jake was in his usual spot. An old armchair by the woodstove, a mug of coffee in one hand, and the newspaper spread out in front of him.

He looked up as Julian stepped inside, a slow grin tugging at the corners of his mouth.

"Well, I'll be," Jake said. "Didn't think I'd see you back here before Christmas."

Julian brushed the snow from his shoulders, a sheepish smile playing on his lips. "Yeah. Guess I surprised myself."

Jake's gaze sharpened, the way it always did when he sensed there was more to the story. "You went to see her, didn't you?"

Julian hesitated, then nodded. "Yeah. I saw Lani."

Jake leaned back in his chair, the faintest twinkle of amusement in his eyes. "And how'd that go?"

Julian exhaled, sinking into the chair opposite him. "She looks good, Uncle Jake. Better than I remember, somehow. Happier. More... herself." He rubbed the back of his neck, searching for words that didn't sound like the confession they were. "The bakery's picking up. Naomi's incredible. She's got Lani's spark, same eyes, same smile."

Jake gave a low hum of approval. "That girl's always had fire in her. Didn't let much stand in her way." He paused, studying his nephew. "And you?"

Julian let out a short humorous laugh. "Me? I stood there talking about baking techniques like an idiot. I wanted to ask her to dinner, but I froze. After all these years, I still can't seem to say the right thing when it comes to her."

Jake set his mug down and leaned forward. "Sounds like maybe the right thing ain't in the words, son."

Julian looked up, brow furrowed.

Jake shrugged. "Sometimes it's in showing up. You did that. After all this time, you came back. That says something."

Julian's throat tightened. He stared into the flicker of the fire, watching the flames dance around the logs.

"I never got over her, Jake. I told myself I had. I buried myself in work, in restaurants, in... everything. But seeing her again, it's like no time passed at all. She smiled, and suddenly every reason I'd ever had for leaving didn't make sense anymore."

Jake nodded slowly, the lines on his face softening. "That's how you know it's real. When time don't dull it."

Julian's voice dropped to a whisper. "She was it for me. Always has been." He shook his head, his tone thick with emotion. "I just didn't realize until now how much I wanted what she has. A life that means something. A place that feels like... like belonging."

Jake's eyes warmed with understanding. "You've been chasing a dream that looked good on paper, but maybe it wasn't yours anymore."

Julian nodded. "I've been thinking about that. About stepping back. Letting someone else run the restaurants. I've got good people in place. They don't need me to keep the wheels turning."

Jake raised a brow. "You thinking of staying here?"

Julian hesitated, then gave a slow, thoughtful nod. "Maybe. For a while. Maybe longer."

He gave a small smile. "I don't know what comes next, but when I was standing in that bakery, watching her laugh with her daughter... it felt right. Like I was standing where I was supposed to be."

Jake smiled knowingly. "You sound like your old man. He always said you'll know you're home when you stop looking for the next thing."

Julian's gaze drifted to the window, where the snow was falling harder now, blanketing the world in soft white.

"Yeah," he said quietly. "I think I finally understand what he meant."

The room fell silent for a moment, except for the crackle of the fire. Jake reached over and handed Julian his coffee mug.

"You've always been a hard worker, kid. Built yourself an empire out of food and determination. But maybe now it's time to build something else. Something that lasts."

Julian took the mug, the warmth seeping into his hands. "Something real."

Jake's smile deepened. "Something real," he agreed. "And if that something's got Lani Shepard written all over it, well, I'd say you're on the right track."

Julian chuckled softly, shaking his head. "You always make it sound simple."

Jake leaned back, eyes twinkling. "Love usually is. It's the people who make it complicated."

Julian looked into the fire once again, the flicker of light reflecting in his eyes. For the first time in a long time, he felt at peace. The kind of peace that came not from success or ambition, but from knowing where his heart was leading him.

"I think," he said quietly, almost to himself, "I'm done running."

Jake gave a satisfied nod. "Then it's about time you start staying."

{ 7 }

Lani

The predawn chill still clung to the air, a hushed promise of the day to come, as Lani pushed open the heavy oak door of the bakery. The familiar scent of flour, yeast, and a subtle sweetness, a comforting blanket woven from years of tradition, embraced her. It was a scent that had once represented childhood Saturday mornings, the comfort of her parents' presence, and now, the weight of responsibility.

Her fingers still bore the faint ache from the previous day's labor. She found the light switch, and the bakery bloomed into a soft, warm glow. The mixers, silent giants in the pre-dawn gloom, seemed to hum with anticipation as they awaited their daily dance with dough and batter.

Her mornings were practiced movements, a rhythm honed over years of observing her parents. Today, she embraced it with a new urgency. The large, industrial mixers, their stainless-steel bowls gleaming under the lights, were her primary instruments. Throughout her teenage years, she'd learned their quirks, the way each one responded to the different consistencies of dough. The yielding tenderness of brioche and the airy lightness of choux pastry. The low growl of the motor as it churned through flour and water was a familiar, grounding sound, a counterpoint to the persistent hum of thoughts she tried to keep at bay.

There was an art to managing the yeast, a living, breathing entity that dictated the pace of the bakery. Lani discovered a newfound respect for its temperamental nature. If it were too warm, it would ferment too quickly, resulting in a bitter, collapsed loaf. Too cold, and the dough would remain stubbornly inert, a testament to her impatience.

She had learned to gauge the room temperature by the subtle shifts in the air, to feel the elasticity of the dough between her fingers. Her hands, once accustomed to a gentler pace, the delicate precision of frosting cupcakes or arranging cookies on a tray, now grew strong and capable, accustomed to the substantial weight of flour sacks and the vigorous kneading of bread dough.

The delicate dance of pastry was another challenge entirely. Delicate tarts, their shells fragile as spun sugar, required a precise touch. Lani found herself captivated by the transfer of heat, the way a perfectly timed bake could transform simple ingredients into flaky, golden perfection. She learned to watch for the subtle signs, the slight puffing of puff pastry, the deep golden hue of a well-baked shortbread, the delicate blush on a fruit tart as the sugars caramelized.

Her mother, Elenore, was always, a constant, gentle presence offering quiet guidance. Her hands demonstrated techniques with an economy of motion that spoke of decades of mastery.

"Feel the butter, Lani," she'd murmur, her voice a soft melody. "It should be cold but yielding. Like a firm handshake, not a crushing grip."

Customer service in a town like this was less about transactions and more about relationships. Everyone knew everyone. And their reasons for visiting Shepard's Sweets were as varied as the pastries in the display case.

There were the hurried morning commuters grabbing a quick coffee and croissant. The mothers meeting for midmorning playdates with sticky-fingered children clamoring for cookies, the elderly couples seeking a familiar comfort in a slice of apple pie. Then there was the occasional tourist, wide-eyed at the array of delicious temptations. Lani learned to greet each face with a genuine smile, to remember their usual orders, and to engage in the gentle small talk that was the currency of a small town.

It was exhausting, at times, to maintain that cheerful façade, especially when her mind was a tangled knot of unanswered questions and resurfaced memories. Yet, the immediate, tangible act of satisfying a customer, of seeing the pleasure on their face as they took their first bite, provided a brief, potent antidote to her internal disquiet.

The physical demands of the bakery were relentless. Her muscles often ached by the end of the day, a deep, satisfying weariness that settled into her bones. But it was a welcome exhaustion and clean fatigue that left little room for overthinking. The constant motion, the focus required to manage multiple orders, to ensure everything was baked to perfection and ready on time, acted as a powerful balm to the emotional turmoil that Julian's reappearance had stirred.

She plunged her hands into mounds of flour, the soft powder clinging to her skin, and felt a sense of purpose, of tangible accomplishment, that was grounding. The scent of sugar caramelizing, the warmth radiating from the ovens, the rhythmic thud of dough being shaped creating a protective cocoon shield around her from the unsettling echoes of the past.

One particularly busy Tuesday, the kind where the bell above the door seemed to ring with a relentless urgency, Lani found herself wrestling with a particularly stubborn batch of croissant dough. Frustration began to prickle at her. She remembered her father, with his calm demeanor even when faced with a difficult bake. He would simply stop, take a deep breath, and reassess.

Taking his cue, Lani stepped away from the mixer, wiping her flour-dusted hands on her apron. She walked over to the window, her gaze falling on the familiar main street. A young couple strolled past, hand-in-hand, their laughter carried on the breeze. A group of teenagers, their faces illuminated by the glow of their phones, huddled on the corner.

It was the steady, unassuming pulse of the town, a rhythm she had known her entire life. Then, her eyes caught sight of the old oak tree in the town square, its branches reaching towards the sky like gnarled fingers. She remembered sitting beneath that tree with Julian, sharing a stolen ice cream cone on a sweltering summer afternoon, his quiet observations about the world around them a stark contrast to her own effervescent enthusiasm.

The memory, sharp and unexpected, jolted her. She remembered the thrill of that afternoon, the daring of their act, the shared secret that had bound them together.

Julian had leaned in, his breath warm against her ear, and whispered, "Forever, Lani. We'll be forever."

The word, once a sacred vow, now felt like a fragile echo. A beautiful promise broken by circumstances beyond their control

The rough bark of the oak tree scraped against her knuckles as she steadied herself. Julian stood beside her with a small, wickedly sharp penknife clutched in his hand. Sunlight dappled through the leaves overhead, painting shifting patterns on the ground around us.

"You sure about this, Julian?" she asked, her voice a little shaky. It was a big tree, old and full of secrets. He didn't look up from the trunk.

"Yeah. It'll be here forever, right? Like us." He paused, then added, "Well, maybe not forever forever. But a long time."

She watched him. His brow was furrowed in concentration, his jaw muscles tight. He had a smudge of dirt on his cheek, and his hair, usually a bit unruly, was plastered to his forehead with sweat. He was concentrating so hard, it was almost like he was performing surgery.

"It's a good spot," she offered, pointing to a section of smooth, unblemished bark.

"Nice and clear." Julian nodded, the corner of his mouth twitching upwards. He tested the edge of the knife against his thumb, a sound like a tiny whisper of steel. Then, with a decisive movement, he pressed the blade into the bark.

The *schriik* sound was surprisingly loud in the quiet afternoon. "L," he etched. The letters were a little wobbly, but clear enough. He wiped a bead of sweat from his forehead with the back of his hand.

"Now your turn." She took the knife. It felt surprisingly heavy. Her hands were clammy.

"What if I mess it up?"

"You won't," Julian said, his tone matter-of-fact. "Just do it like this." He mimed the motion with his finger. "Not too deep. You don't want to hurt it."

She took a breath and pressed the knife in. "A." The "A" was even wobblier than his "L." She traced the shape again, trying to make it neater, more deliberate. The bark yielded, offering satisfying resistance before giving way.

"Perfect," he declared, though she knew it wasn't. "Now for the last bit."

He took the knife back and carefully carved a heart. It was surprisingly well-formed, a little lopsided but recognizable.

He held it up, squinting. "There. L and A. Forever."

Lani leaned against the tree, the rough bark a comforting presence against her back. She felt a strange mix of pride and a prickle of something she couldn't quite name. It was a small act, carving initials, but it felt significant.

The sun continued to dapple through the leaves, and the air smelled of damp earth and pine needles.

Julian stood beside her, the penknife now tucked away, a satisfied look on his face. He turned to her, a grin spreading across his cheeks, revealing a gap where a tooth had recently been.

"Think anyone will see it in a hundred years?" he asked, his eyes bright.

"Maybe," Lani said, looking up at the vastness of the oak. "Maybe they will."

She shook her head, trying to dislodge the intrusive thought.

Focus, Lani, she chided herself.

The croissants. The butter was too soft. She needed to chill the dough and the butter again, to allow them to firm up. It was a simple fix, a matter of patience and temperature control.

She returned to her task, her movements more deliberate this time. She carefully rolled out the dough, placed the slab of butter precisely in the center, and folded it in, her movements slow and steady. This time, the dough responded. The layers began to form, thin and even, a promise of the flaky perfection to come.

The physical labor of the bakery was not just a distraction; it was a form of therapy. The repetitive motions of shaping dough, the precise measurements and the controlled heat of the ovens. They offered a sense of order and predictability that was a welcome contrast to the unpredictable nature of her own emotions. She found a quiet satisfaction in transforming simple ingredients. Flour, water, yeast, and salt transformed by heat and time into sustenance, into comfort, into something beautiful. Each perfectly risen loaf, each exquisitely decorated cake, was a small victory, a tangible testament to her growing competence, her resilience.

There were days, of course, when the exhaustion was bone-deep, when the early mornings and late nights felt like an insurmountable burden.

On those days, it was her parents support that sustained her. Elenore's quiet strength, her unshakeable faith in Lani's abilities, and Thomas's steady pragmatism, his unwavering support, were the foundations upon which she leaned. They saw her efforts, her dedication, and their unspoken approval was a powerful motivator. They had built this bakery, this legacy, and now, she was a vital part of its continued existence.

She learned to anticipate the ebb and flow of the day. The frantic rush of the morning, the relative lull of the mid-afternoon, the steady stream of after-school treat seekers, and the final push to prepare for the next day's opening. Each phase had its own demands, its own rhythm. She became adept at multitasking, at juggling orders, at anticipating needs before they were voiced. The scent of baking bread, the sweet perfume of fruit pies, the rich aroma of chocolate, these were the perfumes of her workday, a constant reminder of the life she had chosen, the life she was building.

Her hands, once prone to the slightest tremor when she thought of Julian, now moved with steady confidence. They were stained with berry juice from making blueberry jam filling and occasionally nicked by the sharp edges of baking tins. They were the hands of a baker, strong and capable, a baker who was not just surviving, but thriving, within the demanding, yet deeply rewarding, embrace of Shepard's Sweets.

The routine, the sheer physicality of her work, was a constant anchor, tethering her to the present, to the tangible reality of her life, leaving less space for the ghosts of the past to linger. Yet, even as she kneaded dough with practiced ease, the faintest whisper of a memory, a shared laugh with Julian, a lingering glance, could still surface, a fleeting shadow in the bright light of the bakery.

Each day she spent beside her parents drew her deeper into their world, a world shaped by careworn hands, warm ovens, and love that never seemed to fade. A world they had meticulously built, brick by brick, batch by batch, within the warm, flour-dusted confines of the bakery.

She saw them not just as bakers, but individuals who had poured their hearts and souls into this place. It was in the quiet moments, amidst the rhythmic sifting of flour or the careful weighing of sugar, that she began to truly understand the tapestry of their lives.

Her father moved through the bakery with quiet authority. He possessed a remarkable ability to coax perfection from even the most temperamental doughs.

Lani would watch, a silent observer, as he'd knead a challah dough, his strong, calloused hands working with a practiced grace that belied their robustness. He'd talk to the dough sometimes, low murmurs that seemed to encourage it, to coax out its best nature. It was a silent communication; a partnership built on years of intuition and respect.

He'd never lectured her, never pushed, but his gentle nods of approval, the slight crinkle at the corner of his eyes when she got a particular technique just right, were worth more than any elaborate praise. She'd learned from him the patience required for fermentation, the understanding that some things simply couldn't be rushed. He'd taught her to read the subtle signs of a loaf's readiness, not just by the clock, but by the way the crust yielded to a gentle tap, the hollow sound that indicated a perfect bake.

Elenore, on the other hand, was the heart of their operation, her warmth radiating as surely as the heat from the ovens. Her domain was the delicate artistry that adorned their creations. Lani found herself drawn to her mother's methodical approach to cake decorating, the steady hand that piped intricate rosettes and swirled elegant frosting patterns.

Elenore's conversations were often peppered with anecdotes from the bakery's past, stories of her own learning curve, of the triumphs and missteps that had shaped their family's journey. She spoke of the early days, when the bakery was just a fledgling dream, and how Thomas had been her unwavering rock, his steady presence a constant reassurance.

"Your father," her mother would say, her eyes twinkling as she meticulously placed a candied cherry atop a Black Forest gateau, "he always knew when I was about to give up. He'd just bring me a cup of tea, sit with me for a moment, and somehow, the problems seemed smaller."

She'd sigh, a contented sound, "We built this together, you know. Every crumb, every customer, every early morning. It wasn't just a business; it was our life. And now," she'd look at Lani, her gaze filled with an affection that was almost palpable, "it's yours too, in a way."

"No pressure, Mom," Lani replied.

These shared moments, these glimpses into her parents' lives, began to unravel layers of her own perception. She had always seen them as her parents, but now, as an adult she saw them as individuals, their strengths and vulnerabilities laid bare in the shared pursuit of their craft. She witnessed their unwavering dedication, the sheer force of will that propelled them through countless early mornings and late nights. It was a quiet dedication, devoid of fanfare, a testament to a love for their work that ran deeper than any fleeting trend or personal hardship.

During the quieter mid-afternoons when the lunch rush had ended and the afternoon tea crowd hadn't yet arrived, their conversations would often drift towards Lani's own life. The unspoken questions hung in the air, the gentle probing about her past, her present, and her uncertain future.

"Are you... happy, darling?" Elenore might ask, her voice soft, her hand reaching out to brush a stray strand of hair from Lani's forehead.

The question, though simple, carried the weight of years of maternal concern. Lani would offer a reassuring smile, a practiced deflection.

"Of course, Mom. It's... a lot, but I'm learning. And I'm here, aren't I?" She'd try to inject a lightness into her tone, to steer the conversation away from the choppy waters of her failed marriage.

But her parents, with their years of shared history and unspoken understanding, could see the subtle shifts in her demeanor and the fleeting shadows that crossed her eyes. They remembered the Lani who had left for college with such bright hopes, and the Lani who had returned, her spirit dimmed, after her divorce. They had seen the quiet resilience with which she had picked up the reins of the bakery. The determination that had replaced her youthful exuberance.

"We're proud of you, Lani," Thomas would say, his voice a low rumble that still held an authority that commanded attention. "You've stepped up. You're carrying on the tradition. That takes... strength." He wouldn't elaborate, wouldn't pry, but the unspoken message was clear: *We see you. We support you.*

There were moments, though, when the dam of polite conversation would crack, and a more vulnerable Lani would surface. One particularly quiet afternoon, while meticulously arranging a tray of éclairs, Lani found herself confessing to her mother.

"Sometimes, Mom," she began, her voice barely a whisper, "I wonder if I made the right choice. Coming back here, I mean. It feels like... like I'm hiding. Like I'm just going through the motions, trying to fill the space that... that Marc left." The name, spoken aloud for the first time in months, hung heavy in the air, a ghost in the fragrant atmosphere.

Elenore stopped her own task, her hands momentarily still. She looked at Lani, her expression one of deep empathy. "Oh, darling," she murmured, her voice laced with tenderness. "It's natural to question. It's natural to grieve. You went through something very difficult. And this bakery... it's a refuge, yes. But it's also your home. It's where you belong. And we're so glad you're here."

She then moved closer, her hands finding Lani's. "You don't have to hide, Lani. You're not just filling a space; you're creating your own. This is your legacy, too you know. And it's still unfolding." Her fingers gently squeezed Lani's. "Don't let the past define your future. Let it inform it, yes. Let it make you stronger, wiser. But don't let it chain you."

Thomas, from his usual station by the proofing racks, his back to them, cleared his throat. He didn't turn around, but his voice, steady and deep, carried a quiet reassurance.

"Your mother's right. Life throws us curveballs. The important thing is how we get back up. And you, Lani, you've always been a fighter." He finally turned, his gaze meeting hers, a silent testament to his unwavering belief in her.

"We're here for you. Whatever you need. We just want you to be... content."

The word "content," echoed in Lani's mind. It wasn't a grand ambition, not the soaring success she might have once craved, but it was a deep, fundamental desire. It was the quiet satisfaction of a perfectly baked loaf, the warmth of her parents' presence, the simple rhythm of a life lived with purpose. She realized that while observing their lives, their dedication to their craft and to each other, she was learning more than just the art of baking. She was learning about resilience, about the enduring power of family, and about the quiet strength that could be found in the most unexpected places, like the comforting, familiar embrace of a flour-dusted bakery. These were traits she wanted to pass to Naomi.

The bakery, in these moments, became more than just a workplace; it was a crucible for connection. The shared laughter over a dropped tray of cookies, the collaborative problem-solving of a tricky recipe, the quiet comfort of shared silence.

These were the ingredients that were forging their family bonds anew. There was still an unspoken current, a gentle undercurrent of concern for her happiness, a silent wish for her to find a lasting peace. But beneath that, there was an undeniable bedrock of love, a shared history, and a mutual respect that made even the most difficult conversations bearable, even comforting. Lani began to understand that her parents' love wasn't just in their words, but in the very air of the bakery, a constant, fragrant reminder of where she came from, and where she, perhaps, could finally find her footing.

The daily rhythm of Shepard's Sweets, the predictable shift of customers and tasks, had always been a comforting constant. But now, working alongside her parents, Lani saw that pace not just as a schedule, but as a life lived with intention. She'd watch her father as he guided a batch of brioche dough through its numerous folds. He had a way of explaining the 'why' behind a technique, not just the 'how,' imparting wisdom gleaned from decades of experience.

"You see, Lani," he'd say, his flour-dusted fingers demonstrating the gentle stretch and fold, "it's about developing the gluten structure without overworking the dough. Too much aggression, and it fights back. Too little, and it never reaches its full potential. It's a balance, much like many things in life." He'd then offer a rare, small smile. "Patience is a baker's best friend, and her harshest critic."

During the lull periods, conversations would naturally veer towards the more personal. Her parents, while never overtly intrusive, had an almost uncanny ability to sense when Lani was ready to speak, to share. They had witnessed the quiet devastation that had followed her divorce from Mark, the slow, painful process of rebuilding.

"He was a good man at the beginning, Marc I mean," Elenore once said, her voice tinged with a gentle melancholy, as she piped delicate sugar flowers onto a wedding cake. "I just... I never felt he truly understood the depth of your dreams, darling. He wanted you to be happy, I know he did, but perhaps in his own way, a way that wasn't fully aligned with yours."

She paused; her gaze meeting Lani's in the reflection of the glass display case. "It's hard when two paths diverge so dramatically. Sometimes, letting go is the bravest thing you can do."

Lani, wiping down the stainless-steel counter, found herself nodding, the familiar ache in her chest a dull throb.

"I thought I did, Mom. I thought we were on the same path. But then... it just felt like I was walking alone."

She sighed as the sound was lost in the gentle whir of the display case refrigerator. "I wish I'd seen it sooner. Wasted so much time trying to make it work."

Her father offered a simple, yet profound, observation from across the room. "Time spent learning is never wasted, Lani. Even if the lesson is a hard one. You're stronger for it. You know yourself better now." He'd then return to his task, the rhythmic thud of his hands on the dough, a silent affirmation of his words.

They had seen her navigate the challenges of her childhood and her teenage years, and now the complexities of adulthood. Their concern was not an attempt to control, but a genuine desire for her well-being. They wanted her to find not just success in the bakery, but happiness in her life, a sense of fulfillment that extended beyond the flour-dusted walls.

"We just want you to be happy, Lani," Elenore had said, her voice soft as she handed Lani a freshly baked croissant, still warm from the oven.

"Truly, deeply happy. And if that means finding new dreams, new paths, then we'll be right here, cheering you on. This bakery has always been a place of love and nourishment. It can be that for you, too. A place to heal, to grow, to discover what truly brings you joy."

This shared workspace, this venerable establishment that had been the backdrop to her entire life, was becoming something more. It was a sanctuary where the past could be acknowledged without being a burden, where the present was filled with meaningful work and the comforting presence of loved ones, and where the future, while uncertain, held the promise of growth and self-discovery.

The family dynamics within Shepard's Sweets were not always overtly expressed, but they were present with every shared glance, every quiet word of encouragement, every perfectly baked loaf. It was a testament to the enduring strength of family, a love that was as rich and comforting as the aromas that filled their beloved bakery.

The flour dust that settled on everything was a constant reminder of their shared labor, their shared history, and their shared future, a future that Lani was beginning to believe could be as sweet and satisfying as the pastries they created. She understood, more now than ever, that the legacy of Shepard's Sweets was not just about the recipes but about the enduring love and resilience baked into its very foundations, a love that was now enveloping her in its warm, comforting embrace.

The gentle rhythm of Shepard's Sweets had found a new, lighter atmosphere with Naomi's arrival. Even at her young age, she possessed an eagerness that was both endearing and surprisingly efficient. The early mornings, which once might have seemed daunting, were now met with a bright-eyed enthusiasm, her small figure bustling amidst the larger, more seasoned bakers. Lani found herself watching her daughter with quiet pleasure, a warmth spreading through her that rivaled the heat from the ovens.

Naomi, clutching a damp cloth, meticulously wiped down the gleaming stainless-steel counters, her pink tongue peeking out in concentration. Each smudge, each stray crumb, was met with a determined scrub until the glass shone. It was a small task, but performed with such dedication that it made Lani's heart swell.

"Almost done, boss," Naomi said, giving the surface one last rub.

"It looks great, sweet pea," she replied.

"Can I help arrange the cookies, Mom?" Naomi asked, her voice a melodic lilt, her eyes sparkling with anticipation. Lani smiled, nodding towards the cooling racks laden with an assortment of chocolate chip, oatmeal raisin, and delicate shortbread.

Naomi always approached the task with the precision of a seasoned artist, arranging the cookies on platters with an eye for symmetry and visual appeal. She'd create miniature landscapes of confectionery, ensuring no two cookies touched, each one presented as a jewel.

Her shyness, a characteristic that had once held her back, seemed to dissipate in the bakery's comforting embrace. When a customer approached the counter, Naomi's usual bashfulness would give way to a shy but genuine smile, a soft, "Hello, welcome to Shepard's Sweets," was offered with a quiet politeness that never failed to charm.

Her presence was a balm to Lani's often overwhelmed spirit. The demanding nature of the bakery, the constant pressure of deadlines and customer expectations, could weigh heavily on Lani's shoulders. But Naomi's cheerful chatter, her innocent questions about the different kinds of pastries, and her unadulterated joy in simple tasks served as a welcome distraction. It was a reminder of the lighter side of life, a world untouched by the trials and heartaches that had recently defined Lani's own existence.

"Mommy, look!" Naomi would exclaim, holding up a perfectly formed gingerbread man, its little button eyes made of chocolate chips. "I think he's smiling!"

Lani chuckled, the sound a genuine release of tension. "He certainly is, sweetie," she'd reply, her gaze lingering on her daughter's happy face.

This newfound engagement in the bakery was a revelation. Lani had worried that bringing Naomi into this environment, so tied to her own emotional turmoil, might be a mistake. But seeing Naomi embrace the routine, find joy in the small victories, and contribute in her own unique way, ease those anxieties.

It wasn't just the physical tasks Naomi excelled at. She possessed an innate understanding of the bakery as a whole. She'd sometimes hum softly to herself as she worked, a sweet, unassuming melody that blended seamlessly with the bakery's ambient sounds, the gentle whir of the mixers, the muffled clatter of trays, the low murmur of conversations.

One afternoon, a particularly discerning customer, a woman known for her exacting standards, arrived just as Lani was wrestling with a batch of croissants that refused to cooperate. The dough, it seemed, was stubbornly resisting Lani's efforts, threatening to become tough and unyielding. Lani felt a familiar knot of anxiety tighten in her stomach. This customer, Mrs. Thornton, was a regular, and her opinion carried weight. As Lani's frustration began to mount, Naomi, who had been diligently arranging a tray of fruit tarts, approached the counter.

"Good afternoon, Mrs. Thornton," Naomi said, her voice clear and steady, her shy smile in place. As her tiny body and big blue eyes looked up at Mrs. Thornton she gestured towards the tarts. "Would you like to try one of our fresh strawberry tarts today? Grandma just got them out of the oven." Her simple, honest enthusiasm seemed to disarm Mrs. Thornton, who had been tapping her fingers impatiently on the counter.

"Oh, aren't you a cutie! They do smell delightful, dear," Mrs. Gable replied, her tone softening. She picked up a tart and examined its glossy topping. "And you've arranged them so beautifully."

Naomi beamed, a quiet pride evident in her posture. Lani, witnessing this small interaction, felt a wave of relief wash over her. Naomi, with her innate grace, and genuine warmth and innocent smile, had navigated a potentially awkward moment without even trying. It was a talent Lani hadn't fully recognized in her daughter before. One that she would grow into as she got older.

Thomas and Elenore, too, seemed to appreciate Naomi's presence. Thomas would sometimes offer Naomi a brief, encouraging nod as she diligently polished the display cases. Elenore would often have a small, sweet task for Naomi, like dusting powdered sugar onto a fresh batch of madeleines or carefully placing delicate sugar flowers onto a cake.

"You have such a steady hand, darling," Elenore would praise, her eyes twinkling. "Just like your grandmother." These small affirmations, these moments of shared purpose, were weaving a new thread into the fabric of their family.

Of course, amidst the flour dust and the sweet aromas, the memory of Julian Vance continued to cast a long shadow. Lani found herself stealing glances at her phone, a nervous flutter in her stomach, half-hoping for, and half-dreading, a message from him.

The encounter at the bakery had been unexpected, a jarring reminder of a life she was trying to leave behind. His presence, his easy charm and the ghost of a shared past, had stirred a complex mix of emotions within her. Lingering affection, a deep-seated resentment, and a pervasive sense of unease.

She would be carefully piping frosting onto a cake, her concentration absolute, when a sudden image of Julian's wry smile would flash through her mind, making her hand falter. Or she'd be engaged in conversation with a customer, her focus sharp, only to have a stray thought about their last, contentious meeting intrude, causing her to lose her train of thought. It was a constant battle, this internal tug-of-war between the present realities of Shepard's Sweets and the persistent specter of her past entanglement with Julian.

When Lani found herself lost in thought, staring blankly at a row of muffins, Naomi would gently tug on her sleeve. "Mommy? Are these ready to be boxed up?" Her innocent query would snap Lani back to attention, grounding her in the tangible reality of their work.

On a particularly challenging afternoon, Lani received a curt email from Marc's legal team, a reminder of outstanding paperwork related to their dissolution. The impersonal, cold language sent a shiver down her spine, reigniting a familiar sense of dread and helplessness. She felt her carefully constructed composure begin to fray. Her hands trembled slightly as she tried to measure out flour, her usual precision wavering.

Naomi, sensing her mother's distress, though not fully understanding its source, approached her with a small, unopened bag of colorful sprinkles. "Mommy, can we decorate these cupcakes for Mrs. Henderson? She loves the rainbow ones." Her earnest plea, her innocent desire to bring a little brightness into their workday, was exactly what Lani needed.

Lani took a deep breath, forcing a smile. "Of course, sweetie. Let's make them the most beautiful rainbow cupcakes you've ever seen."

Together, they poured the vibrant sprinkles onto the freshly frosted cupcakes, a simple act that became a shared ritual, pushing the unwelcome thoughts to the periphery.

Naomi's cheerful commentary, her delight in the swirling colors, created a bubble of normalcy around them, a temporary sanctuary from the external pressures.

"Look, Mom, this one looks like a little unicorn!" Naomi giggled, holding up a cupcake adorned with an explosion of rainbow hues.

Lani laughed, a genuine, heartfelt sound. In that moment, the legal jargon and the lingering specter of Mark seemed distant, almost unreal. It was just her and her daughter, surrounded by the comforting scent of sugar and spice, creating something beautiful together.

She realized that her daughter's presence wasn't just a distraction; it was an active force for healing. Her unburdened spirit, her unwavering optimism, was a constant reminder of the good in the world, of the simple joys that could be found even in the midst of difficulty. It was a testament to the resilience of childhood, a resilience that Lani was also trying to cultivate within herself.

Elenore, observing the mother-daughter duo from her station at the pastry counter, offered a warm, knowing smile. She had seen Lani through darker days, through the painful aftermath of her divorce, and now she was witnessing a new chapter unfold. She saw the worry lines still etched around Lani's eyes, the occasional flicker of anxiety that crossed her face, but she also saw the growing strength, the renewed sense of purpose that her daughter was finding. Naomi's integration into the bakery was more than just a helping hand; it was a symbol of Lani's own journey towards peace and stability.

"She's a natural, isn't she?" Elenore commented to Thomas later that evening, as they cleaned down the ovens. "Naomi. She brings such lightness to the place. And Lani... she needs that. She needs to see that life can still be... sweet."

Thomas grunted in agreement, his movements slow and deliberate as he scraped the last remnants of dough from a large mixing bowl.

"Good for her. Good for Lani. Keeps her mind occupied. Stops her dwelling."

His pragmatism, though blunt, held a deep truth. Naomi's vibrant energy was a powerful force, capable of dispelling the lingering shadows that threatened to engulf Lani.

And it was true. As the days turned into weeks, Lani found herself more and more at ease within the familiar routines of Shepard's Sweets. The tasks, once a source of anxiety, now felt like a comforting rhythm. The early mornings, the bustling midday rush, the quiet afternoon lull. Each period had its own unique character, and Lani was learning to navigate them with growing confidence. Naomi's enthusiastic participation was integral to this newfound peace.

She'd help Lani set up the display cases each morning, carefully arranging pastries and cakes, her small hands surprisingly adept. "These eclairs look so shiny, Mommy!" she'd exclaim, her eyes wide with admiration.

Lani would smile, a genuine warmth spreading through her. "That's because we use the best ingredients, sweetie, and we take our time to make them perfect."

The afternoon would often find Naomi diligently wiping down tables, her movements quick and thorough. She'd greet customers with a friendly wave and a bright smile, her voice clear and confident, even as she offered a shy glance towards her mother for reassurance. The bakery, once a refuge from her past, was slowly transforming into a place of genuine growth and healing.

Lani would often catch herself observing Naomi, a sense of gratitude washing over her. This young girl, so full of life and optimism, was not only a help in the bakery but a beacon of hope in Lani's own life. Her daughter's presence was a constant, tangible reminder of what truly mattered – love, family, and the simple joy of creating something beautiful together. She could never regret her marriage to Marc when Naomi was the outcome.

Each smile Naomi shared, each perfectly arranged cookie platter, each compliment from a satisfied customer, chipped away at the hold he had once exerted.

The sweetness of the bakery, the genuine warmth of her family, and the simple, honest work was proving to be potent remedies, slowly but surely, for a wounded heart.

The flour dust settled gently on her daughter's hair, a subtle dusting of magic in the ordinary routine, and Lani knew with certainty that warmed her from the inside out.

They were going to be alright.

This place, this life, was becoming their own sweet haven, built on love, resilience, and the quiet strength of a mother and her daughter, side by side, amidst the comforting scent of baking.

The familiar hum of the small town was a symphony of routines and a predictable melody of lives lived in quiet unison. Yet, beneath the still surface, currents of curiosity and speculation churned, and Lani, despite her best efforts to remain unseen, found herself swept into their flow. Even as the memory of Julian Vance continued to surface, its power over her was slowly diminishing.

He hadn't called to work on his new pastry.

She wasn't surprised.

Her thoughts traveled back to that day her heart shattered.

***

The night was cool as they sat on Julian's grandparents' porch watching late summer twilight. Julian had been devastated by the death of his parents last week. They held onto each other like there would be no air left if they let go. The last of the sunlight filters through the trees, catching in Lani's hair like gold. A letter rests between them, unopened but heavy with promise and dread.

The tree frogs droned in the trees, a low, restless hum that filled the silence stretching between them. Julian's thumb brushed the edge of the envelope, the elegant script of the Culinary Institute gleaming faintly in the light.

"You're quiet," Lani said softly. "That's not like you."

He forced a laugh, but it sounded hollow. "Guess I don't know what to say."

"You got in, didn't you?"

Julian hesitated. Then he nodded. "Paris first. Then New York. It's... everything I ever wanted."

The words hung in the air like the smoke from her father's old wood stove—slow, thick, impossible to wave away.

Lani smiled, but it didn't reach her eyes. "That's wonderful, Jules. Really. You've worked so hard for this."

He looked at her then. The girl who'd known him before ambition had a name, before success became a dream that tasted like hunger.

"It is," he said quietly. "But it means leaving. For a long time."

Her hands stilled in her lap. "For how long?"

He shook his head. "I don't know. A few years, maybe more."

The porch creaked beneath them. Somewhere in the distance, an owl called, mournful and low.

"I thought..." she began, her voice trembling, "I thought we'd build something here. Together."

Julian's heart clenched. He wanted to say we still can, but the words caught like glass in his throat.

"If I stay," he said, barely above a whisper, "I'll spend my whole life wondering what could have been."

Lani turned to him, eyes shimmering in the fading light. "And if you go, you'll spend it wondering what you left behind."

He reached for her hand, but she pulled away—slowly, gently, as if afraid the act itself might shatter them.

"I can go with you," she offered hesitantly.

"You can't. I have to do this alone."

"But..." she began.

"No Lani. I don't want you to come with me," he replied with force.

She swallowed the thick lump that grew in the base of her throat, blinking back tears.

"Go, Julian," she said, her voice steady now. "Go and see the world. Just... don't expect it to love you the way I do."

She watched him as he looked down at the letter, the ink swimming in her vision, and realized for the first time that sometimes dreams came true only to break your heart.

Unfortunately, her quiet return to the place she had once fled hadn't gone unnoticed. It was as if the very air of Evergreen Hollow held a collective memory, and her presence was a catalyst that stirred it from its slumber. The news, it seemed, traveled faster than the scent of fresh bread from Shepard's Sweets, weaving through conversations at the bustling farmer's Market and the hushed aisles of the post office.

{ 8 }

Lani

Lani first noticed it at Mrs. Gable's flower stand. The air was thick with the sweet perfume of roses and the sharper scent of freshly dug earth. She was selecting a small bouquet of cheerful sunflowers, their faces turned towards the sky as if in perpetual confidence, when she overheard a hushed exchange between two women she vaguely recognized from years past. Their voices were lowered in an attempt at discretion. But they still carried clearly in the relative quiet of the morning.

"Did you hear? Lani's back. And... with *him* in town," one woman murmured, a subtle emphasis on the final word, laced with a hint of something that could have been pity, or perhaps something closer to scandal.

"Julian Vance? I can't believe it," the other replied, her voice tinged with a tone of disbelieving fascination. "After all this time, and all that happened... I thought she'd never set foot back here again. Especially not be seen with him."

Lani's hand froze, her fingers hovering over the vibrant yellow petals of a sunflower. A cold dread, as familiar as it was unwelcome, coiled in her stomach. She subtly shifted her weight, pretending to be interested in the delicate veins of a lily. She hoped her back was turned enough to render her invisible, as she listened to the roots of gossip grow.

"Well, they say he's been seen around town, picking her up," the first woman continued, her voice dropping even lower, a conspiratorial whisper.

"Saw them myself, just last week, leaving that little café by the river. Looked quite... cozy."

The implication hung in the air, heavy and suffocating. Cozy. The word conjured images Lani desperately tried to keep at bay. Where were they getting all this? She hadn't seen Julian since that day in the bakery.

A fleeting shared glance at the counter, a carefully constructed polite conversation, a strained formality that was anything but cozy. It was the weight of expectation. Like a phantom limb of a past she had tried to sever, they were seeing.

Her fingers fumbled with the leather of her wallet as she pulled out crisp bills and quickly paid for her sunflowers.

As she turned to leave, she caught a glimpse of the women's faces, their eyes meeting hers for a fleeting second, a mixture of recognition and something akin to pity in their gaze.

It was that look, more than their words, that pricked at her. It was the unspoken narrative they were already weaving, a story of predictable cycles and unavoidable fates.

Later that week, at the post office, the same unsettling current ran through hushed conversations. Lani was waiting in line to mail a package of delicate pastries to a customer in the next town over. She clutched the cardboard box as if it were a shield against judgment.

"Imagine that," a man behind her commented to his friend, his voice a low rumble.

"Lani Shepard and Julian Vance. Never thought I'd see the day. Remember how that whole thing ended? Messy."

"Aye," his friend agreed, a knowing sigh. "She was so young. And he was... well, he was Julian. Always knew how to charm the socks off everyone.

The first man shook his head. "Yeah, there was always something under the surface, wasn't there? Hey, I heard her husband left her too," he offered.

Lani's shoulders tensed. Under the surface. The words echoed the very doubts she wrestled with daily. They saw the familiar story, the prodigal daughter returning to the charismatic, perhaps dangerous, man who had once held a piece of her heart. Her failed marriage in the city.

They didn't see the painstaking effort she was making to build a new life within the comforting walls of Shepard's Sweets. They didn't see the quiet strength she was finding in the rhythm of baking, in the smiles of her customers, in the innocent chatter of her daughter, Naomi.

She felt a surge of frustration and a familiar prickle of anger. Why did her past, a chapter she had desperately sought to close, continue to haunt the present? Why did her return, her desire for a fresh start, invite such intense scrutiny?

It was as if the town held a collective memory of their passionate, tumultuous romance, and every interaction between her and Julian, no matter how innocent or professional, was interpreted through that lens.

"He always did have a way with the ladies," the first man continued, oblivious to Lani's growing discomfort. "And Lani... she was always so smitten. I suppose some things never change."

Lani gripped the package tighter, the cardboard digging into her fingers. Some things never change.The phrase was a cruel irony.

Everything had changed. She had changed.

Yet, to the people of Evergreen Hollow, she was still the young girl who had fallen head over heels for the charming, enigmatic Julian Vance. A story that had ended, as they so eloquently put it, messily.

Their whispers were like tiny, persistent insects, buzzing around her, their murmurs weaving a tapestry of assumptions. They spoke of her youthful infatuation, of the heartbroken girl who had vanished from town, and now, of her unexpected reappearance in the orbit of the very man who had likely caused her such pain. Each overheard conversation was a sharp reminder, a jolt that sent tremors through the fragile peace she was trying to cultivate.

At the bakery, the sweet, comforting aroma of vanilla and sugar was her sanctuary. But even there, the outside world intruded. A regular customer, Mrs. Peterson, a woman whose kindly face was etched with years of warm smiles, paused at the counter one afternoon, her eyes lingering on Lani with a look of gentle concern.

"It's good to see you back, Lani," she said, her voice soft. "Really good. It's been a long time. And... well, I hear you've been seeing Julian again." She hesitated, her gaze searching Lani's face. "I hope... I hope he's treating you right this time, dear. You deserve all the happiness in the world."

Lani forced a smile, her heart aching with a complex mix of gratitude for the concern and weariness from the constant rehashing of her past. "Thank you, Mrs. Peterson. We just... reconnecting. Professional matters, mostly." She kept her tone light, but she could see the flicker of doubt in Mrs. Peterson's eyes, the ingrained belief that this was more than just professional.

"Professional, of course," Mrs. Peterson murmured, though her tone lacked conviction. "It's just... that was quite a chapter, wasn't it? Between you two. Everyone remembers."

Everyone remembers.

The phrase was a heavy cloak, draped over her shoulders, a constant weight of shared history. It made the simple act of navigating her day feel like walking a tightrope, each step scrutinized, each move analyzed through the prism of her past relationship with Julian.

Even Thomas and Elenore, her parents and anchors in the bakery, sometimes caught the drift of the town's collective gossip. Eleanor, ever the pragmatist, would occasionally offer a knowing, almost apologetic, glance.

"They mean well, darling," she'd say, her voice gentle as she dusted a batch of madeleines with powdered sugar.

"Evergreen Hollow is a small town. People talk. Especially when there's a bit of... history involved."

Thomas, his gruff exterior hiding a deep well of affection, would simply grunt. "Let 'em talk. They're not paying your bills. They're not baking your bread. You've got your daughter, and you've got this place. That's what matters." His simple, unwavering support was a balm, a reminder that not everyone was caught up in the speculative currents.

But Lani couldn't always shield herself. The whispers, insidious and pervasive, chipped away at her resolve. They amplified her internal conflict, the constant battle between the desire to move forward and the undeniable pull of the past.

On the rare occasion she saw Julian, every time they exchanged professional courtesy, every time their paths crossed, she could feel the weight of those unspoken stories pressing down on her.

She would be kneading dough, her mind focused on the texture, on the feel of the flour yielding beneath her hands, when a fragment of overheard conversation would surface.

"Such a shame... he broke her heart, you know."

Or she'd be arranging a display of intricately decorated cupcakes, her artistic eye focused on color and symmetry, and the memory of a hushed argument, a whispered promise from years ago, would flash into her mind.

The scrutiny made her hyper-aware of her interactions with Julian. She found herself carefully moderating her tone, her body language, striving for an almost exaggerated neutrality. She wanted to avoid any perception of rekindling old flames, to maintain the professional distance that was so crucial for her own peace of mind.

Yet, in a town where their history was so well known, neutrality was a difficult and often impossible tightrope to walk.

The encounter at the art gallery, the one that had undeniably stirred the pot of the latest local gossip, was a prime example. It was meant to be a brief, cordial exchange, a professional courtesy.

But the moment she saw him, standing by a striking abstract painting, his familiar profile sharp against the gallery wall, a jolt went through her. Years melted away, and for a breathless instant, she was back in the whirlwind of their youthful romance.

She had approached him cautiously, offering a polite smile, her mind already rehearsing the carefully worded sentences she would use to discuss the possibility of working together.

But when he had turned, his eyes, those piercing blue eyes she remembered so vividly, met hers with an expression she couldn't quite decipher. A hint of surprise? A flicker of something that might have been regret? And that ever-present, disarming charm.

"Lani," he'd said, his voice a low, resonant sound that sent a shiver down her spine. "It's... good to see you."

The simple words, spoken in that familiar voice, were enough to set the town's rumor mill into overdrive.

She saw the sideways glances, the hushed whispers that followed them as they moved through the gallery discussing the talent of a particular artist with a forced casualness. She knew, with a sinking certainty, that this would be fuel for the fire, another chapter in the ongoing narrative of Lani Shepard and Julian Vance.

And so it was.

The whispers continued, a constant undercurrent in the fabric of Evergreen Hollow. They were not overtly malicious, not usually. Most were laced with a kind of nostalgic pity, a rehashing of a story they all thought they knew.

But for Lani, they were a persistent reminder of the weight of her past, a past that refused to stay buried. Each overheard word, each knowing glance, was a small erosion of the peace she so desperately sought. A subtle but constant pressure that amplified her internal struggle to build a new life, untethered from the shadows of what had been.

The aroma of baking bread, once a comforting balm, now sometimes carried with it the faint, melancholic scent of unspoken history, a reminder that in Evergreen Hollow some stories, no matter how much she wished it, were never truly forgotten.

She found herself longing for the anonymity of a larger city, a place where her past wouldn't follow her into every grocery store aisle and every post office visit.

But then she would see Naomi's bright, innocent face with her small hands dusted with flour, and she knew that this was where she needed to be. She just had to learn to navigate the whispers, to find a way to let them blow past, like the wind through the leaves, without taking root in her heart.

The air in town was usually laced with the gentle scent of woodsmoke and decaying leaves. Lately it had begun to carry a new aroma as December descended: the sweet, intoxicating perfume of gingerbread, cinnamon, and roasted nuts. Christmas was no longer a distant whisper; it was a thundering crescendo, and for Lani, it meant the beginning of the "Christmas Rush."

The familiar, comforting hum of the bakery transformed into a frenetic symphony of clanging pans, whirring mixers, and the rhythmic thud of dough being kneaded. Every surface, once artfully arranged with delicate pastries, was now a battlefield of flour, sugar, and meticulously piped icing.

Orders, which had previously arrived at a manageable trickle, now poured in like a winter flood.

Mrs. Gable, the flower shop owner, had placed an order for a dozen of Lani's signature gingerbread men, each one dressed in tiny edible holly leaves, for her festive window display.

The mayor's office had commissioned a towering, multi-tiered cake adorned with edible snowflakes and miniature chocolate-painted Santa's. It was to be a centerpiece for the town's annual holiday gala. And then there were the Yule logs. Lani's personal specialty, each one a masterpiece of chocolate roulade, ganache, and buttercream, meticulously decorated to resemble ancient, moss-covered logs.

The demand for these elaborate creations was staggering. The town, it seemed, had a collective sweet tooth for

Lani's talent. A talent she was only just beginning to fully reclaim.

Days blurred into a relentless cycle of early mornings and late nights. Lani found herself living by the clock of yeast proving and oven temperatures. She'd wake before dawn, the chill air a stark contrast to the warmth that would soon fill the bakery, and begin by preparing dough, coaxing it into submission with practiced hands. By mid-morning, the ovens would be roaring, a constant cascade of golden-brown cookies and perfectly baked cakes emerging from their fiery embrace.

The afternoons were a whirlwind of assembly and decoration. The delicate dance of piping frosting, the precise placement of marzipan figures, the careful dusting of edible glitter. Each task required an unwavering focus, a steady hand, and a mind that could hold multiple complex orders simultaneously.

Her initial anxiety and self-doubt that had been her constant companions since her return began to recede, not entirely vanquished, but certainly pushed to the edge by the sheer force of necessity. There was no room for doubt when confronted with a deadline for fifty custom sugar cookies, each one needing individual detailing.

There was no time for dwelling on Julian or the town's whispers when the intricate structure of a gingerbread house, complete with candied windowpanes and gumdrop chimneys, threatened to collapse.

Thomas, with his steady hand, was a man who could tackle any structural challenge and troubleshoot any oven malfunction, and he was invaluable. He'd arrive each morning with a thermos of strong coffee, his presence a silent reassurance.

Elenore, too, was a whirlwind of activity. Her organizational skills were honed over decades of managing the bakery, now in overdrive. She handled the phone, meticulously logging orders, confirming details, and politely managing the expectations of eager customers. She'd also taken on the bulk of the simpler baking tasks, freeing Lani to focus on the more complex, signature items.

"Ninety-six snowflake cookies for the Millers, fifty gingerbread men for Mrs. Gable, and that enormous Yule log for the town council needs to be delivered by noon tomorrow, Lani," Elenore called out, her voice a melodic counterpoint to the rhythmic whir of the mixer. "And Mr. Henderson just called again about his custom wedding cake consultation. He's getting impatient."

Lani nodded, her brow furrowed in concentration as she delicately placed a delicately spun sugar icicle onto a gingerbread mansion. "Tell him I can see him Friday morning, first thing. And remind me to start the marzipan fruits for the wedding cake on Thursday."

The pressure felt like a tangible force pressing down on her shoulders. There were moments, late at night, when exhaustion threatened to overwhelm her.

There were moments, late at night, when exhaustion threatened to overwhelm her.

Her hands would ache, her eyes would burn, and the scent of sugar would feel cloying rather than comforting.

She'd catch her reflection in the polished surface of the display case, a ghost of herself with flour streaked across her cheek and dark circles under her eyes. In those quiet, solitary moments, the old anxieties would try to resurface.

Can I really do this? Am I good enough? What if I fail?

But then she would look at the creations around her. The vibrant colors, the intricate details, the sheer volume of work accomplished. She'd think of Naomi, her bright-eyed daughter who would often appear in the bakery after school, her face alight with wonder at the edible wonderland surrounding her. Naomi's innocent admiration was a powerful antidote to any lingering doubt.

"Mommy, that gingerbread house is magical!" Naomi exclaimed, her voice full of awe. "It's like a fairytale castle!"

Lani smiled, a genuine smile that reached her eyes. "It *is* magical."

And she was creating that magic. She was the one conjuring these edible dreams into reality.

The sheer volume of work also forced Lani to embrace a level of improvisation and problem-solving she hadn't anticipated. When a crucial ingredient was unexpectedly out of stock, she'd find herself adapting recipes on the fly, substituting, creating new flavor combinations that often proved surprisingly successful.

A slight miscalculation in the oven temperature that threatened to brown the delicate meringue kisses too quickly led her to discover the perfect technique for achieving a lightly toasted, nutty flavor. She learned to trust her instincts, to rely on the years of ingrained knowledge that had been dormant for so long.

One afternoon, a particularly complex order arrived: a gingerbread replica of the town hall, complete with a working miniature clock tower. The customer was a local historian who wanted it as a surprise for the town's centennial celebration. It was a smaller event within the larger Christmas festivities.

The request was ambitious, bordering on audacious. Lani stared at the sketch, her mind racing through the structural challenges. The gingerbread itself would need to be extra sturdy, the mortar of royal icing had to be robust, and the tiny gears for the clock tower... that was the real puzzle.

For a moment, panic flickered. This was beyond anything she'd tackled since reopening. Then, her father's steady presence came to mind. He had an almost uncanny knack for engineering, even in the context of baking. She found him in the back, meticulously cleaning the industrial mixer.

"Dad," she began, her voice a little breathless. "I have a... challenge." She explained the request, her words tumbling out in a rush.

He listened patiently; his brow furrowed in concentration. He picked up the sketch, turning it over in his flour-dusted hands. A slow smile spread across his face.

"Well now, that's a proper undertaking, isn't it? Let's see... We'll need to reinforce the base, of course. And for the clock tower... I think I have an idea. Some strategically placed candy canes, perhaps to support the mechanism. And maybe a few cleverly placed fondant gears."

Together, they spent an entire afternoon sketching, calculating, and testing. Thomas's practical ingenuity, combined with Lani's artistic vision and baking expertise, created a formidable team.

They experimented with different consistencies of royal icing, built small structural prototypes. They discovered that by carefully embedding small, edible supports within the gingerbread walls, they could achieve the stability that was needed. Lani found such joy in the problem-solving, in the intellectual puzzle of making the impossible possible. It was a different kind of creativity, one that engaged a different part of her brain, but it was just as fulfilling.

The gingerbread town hall, when completed, was a marvel. Each tiny window was a clear, shimmering candy pane, the edible bricks meticulously laid, and the clock tower, with its fondant gears, actually ticked, even with a gentle, confectionery grace. The historian was beside himself with delight, his face beaming as he carefully transported it to the town hall. The praise he lavished on Lani, on the sheer artistry and engineering involved, filled her with quiet pride.

This challenge, more than any other, solidified a newfound confidence within her. She wasn't just a baker; she was a culinary architect, a creative problem-solver.

The Christmas rush, with its relentless demands and near-impossible requests, was not just a period of intense labor; it was a crucible that was forging her into something stronger, something more capable than she had ever dared to believe.

She was no longer just trying to survive; she was thriving, her hands moving with a skill and assurance that spoke of a deep, inherent talent finally unleashed. The whispers of the town and the shadows of her past all seemed to fade a little more with each perfectly decorated cookie, each perfectly risen Yule log, each successful, audacious creation. The magic of Christmas was transforming not just the town, but Lani herself.

{ 9 }

Lani

The crisp December air, carrying the faintest hint of woodsmoke from distant hearths, was a stark contrast to the bustling warmth of the Evergreen Hollow Farmer's Market.

Lani, wrapped in a thick wool scarf, found herself navigating the labyrinth of stalls, her basket already filled with chestnuts and a few Granny Smith apples. The "Christmas Rush" at the bakery had been relentless, and she'd promised herself a brief break. Her mind, usually a chaotic swirl of gingerbread construction and royal icing consistency, was surprisingly clear, though a lingering exhaustion still hummed beneath the surface.

She paused at a stall overflowing with handcrafted cheeses, the rich, earthy aromas, a welcome change from the cloying sweetness of her daily life. Her fingers brushed against a wedge of aged cheddar, when a familiar voice, warm and resonant, cut through the market's hum.

"You have excellent taste, I see."

Lani's heart gave an unexpected jolt.

Her head snapped around, a sharp inhale snagging in her throat.

Julian.

He stood a breath away. His lips curving into an unpracticed, honest curve. And those eyes, the rich cerulean loam after a spring downpour, pinning her. The market's business, the low hum of a hundred conversations and the chime of caroled melody. It all disappeared in a moment, leaving only the stark clarity of his presence.

Weeks had bled into one another since their last meeting, a brittle dance of averted gazes and the heavy weight of unspoken words. But now, his shoulders relaxed, not a hint of the old unease. He didn't flinch, didn't scan for an exit.

"Julian," she managed, her voice a fragile thread against the market's clamor. "It's... good to see you."

He took a half-step closer, the scent of woodsmoke and something faintly like spiced cider clinging to him.

"Lani," he replied, his voice a low rumble, like pebbles shifting in a stream. "I wasn't sure I'd see you here." He gestured vaguely at the overflowing crates of cheeses and the butcher's cart filled with glistening cuts of meat.

A ghost of a smile, tentative and uncertain, touched her lips. "The Christmas Market. Where else would I be on a Saturday?" The question hung, innocent on its surface, a barbed hook beneath.

He stepped closer, his gaze taking in her appearance, a hint of amusement dancing in his eyes. "And you, Lani. You look... well. Busy, I imagine, given the season." He gestured vaguely towards the town, a silent acknowledgment of the festive preparations she'd been so immersed in.

"You have no idea," she replied. A small, genuine smile finally breaking through.

The initial awkwardness that had threatened to descend was already dissipating, replaced by a strange sense of ease. It was as if the intervening weeks, the unspoken tensions, had simply melted away with the autumn frost.

"The bakery is in full Christmas swing. Gingerbread houses, Yule logs, enough sugar cookies to pave a small road."

He chuckled, a low, pleasant sound that resonated pleasantly in the brisk air. "I've seen the lights from your shop, the windows transformed. It looks... magical. Truly."

His admiration felt sincere, a balm to her weary spirit. "I've been meaning to stop by. To see... well, to see how you were doing."

The words hung in the air, a delicate offering.

"I'm doing well, Julian. Better than well, actually." She found herself speaking with a candor that surprised her. "The bakery is thriving. The orders are insane, but in a good way. It's good to be busy."

"That's wonderful to hear, Lani." His gaze softened, a warmth spreading through his eyes that made her feel seen, truly seen, for the first time in a long time. He wasn't looking at the baker struggling to reclaim her life; he was looking at *her*.

"I saw some of the... creations in your window the other day. That gingerbread town hall was incredible. A masterpiece of edible architecture."

Lani felt a flush of pride. "Oh, that was a challenge. A lot of engineering involved."

"I can imagine," he said, his eyes twinkling. "It looked like it. But then, you always had a knack for making the impossible seem... effortless."

The compliment, so simply delivered, resonated deeply. Effortless.

It was a word she hadn't associated with herself in years. The frantic pace of the bakery, the constant pressure, had been anything but effortless. Yet, looking at him, at his steady gaze, she felt a flicker of that lost confidence. Perhaps, in a way, it *was* becoming effortless again.

"Thank you, Julian. That means a lot." She gestured to the cheeses. "I was just picking up a few supplies. Trying to bribe myself with a treat for surviving another week."

He picked up a block of smoked gouda, rolling it thoughtfully in his hand. "A good choice," he said with an easy smile. "I've always had a soft spot for these kinds of cheeses. There's something comforting about them—a sense of simplicity and honest craftsmanship."

"Exactly!" Lani agreed, feeling a shared appreciation bloom between them. "It's a different kind of creation than what I do, but it feels just as real. Tangible."

"I understand," he said, his gaze holding hers. "There's satisfaction in building something, in bringing something beautiful and delicious into existence." He paused, a shadow passing over his face for a brief moment. "But you are creating something remarkable, Lani. Something that brings joy to people. That's a special kind of magic."

The conversation flowed with unexpected ease, a natural rhythm that felt both familiar and new. They spoke of the changing seasons, of the quiet beauty of Evergreen Hollow in winter. Of the anticipation building for the town's Christmas festivities.

Julian, it turned out, had been busy too, managing his restaurants throughout the holidays and preparing for the quiet slow season of the winter months.

"It's a different kind of rhythm," he explained, his voice calm and measured. "Slower, more contemplative. But no less demanding in its own way. It needs time. Patience."

"Patience," Lani echoed, a wry smile touching her lips. "That's a commodity in short supply at my place right now."

Julian laughed, a sound that seemed to chase away some of the lingering chill in the air. "I can only imagine. But I suspect you possess more patience than you give yourself credit for. Especially when it comes to your craft."

They lingered by the cheese stall, the conversation meandering through shared memories of Evergreen Hollow, of childhood summers and whispered secrets under starlit skies. There was a subtle shift in the atmosphere between them, a softening of the edges, a tentative rebuilding of bridges. The resentment and the hurt, that had defined their last meeting seemed to have receded. Replaced by a gentle curiosity, a recognition of the shared history that bound them.

"I remember," Julian began, his voice softer now, "that time you won the blue ribbon at the county fair for your apple pie. You were so proud. You practically glowed."

Lani blushed, a nostalgic warmth spreading through her. "Oh, that feels like a lifetime ago. I think I ate pie for a week straight just to prove it wasn't a fluke."

"It wasn't a fluke," he said, his gaze steady. "It was pure talent. You've always had that, Lani. A talent for bringing out the best in things. Whether it's fruit, or dough," he paused, "or people."

The last part of his statement hung in the air, a subtle implication that sent a tremor through her. Had he meant it literally? Or was it another one of his carefully veiled observations? She chose to interpret it in the context of her baking.

"I just try to use the best ingredients," she replied, her voice carefully neutral. "And treat them with respect."

"A valuable philosophy," he murmured, his eyes holding a depth of emotion she couldn't quite decipher. He glanced down at his watch, a flicker of regret crossing his face. "I should probably be going. I have a meeting to get to."

Lani felt a pang of disappointment, a surprising ache that she quickly suppressed. "Of course. Me too. I have dough to punch down."

They stood for a moment, an unspoken question lingering between them. Was this it? Another brief, fleeting encounter, swallowed by the demands of their separate lives?

Julian reached into his pocket. He pulled out a small, neatly folded card. "Lani," he said, his voice earnest. "I'd like to... I'd like to invite you to dinner. Sometime soon. When things aren't quite so chaotic for you. No pressure, of course, he added hurriedly. "I'd really like to catch up properly."

Lani took the card, her fingers brushing his. The simple act sent a jolt of warmth through her. The card was thick, embossed with the name of his restaurant chain.

"Julian," she began, her voice a little shaky.

"Just think about it," he said, his smile gentle. "No obligations. But I'd like that. A lot." He gave her a small nod, a final, lingering look, and began to walk away.

Lani stood there for a moment, the little card warm in her hand, his cologne still lingering in the air rich and familiar, like a memory she hadn't meant to stir. Around her, the scent of artisanal cheese and fresh bread wrapped the space in a comforting haze. But all she could really feel was the quiet thrum of her heartbeat.

It hadn't felt accidental, not really. Their paths crossing again carried a kind of gentle purpose, as if life itself had nudged them back into each other's orbit. There'd been something in his eyes—something steady, tender that spoke of old promises and unspoken things.

As she looked down at the card, a small smile tugged at her lips. Maybe it wasn't just a chance encounter. Maybe it was an opening gentle invitation from a past she'd never truly let go of.

A quiet hope, fragile and unexpected, began to unfurl within her, like a delicate pastry crust proving in the warmth of the oven.

His voice caused her jerk her head up. He came back.

"But for now, coffee?" Julian's voice was a low, warm rumble, cutting through the crisp market air and Lani's internal monologue. It wasn't a question posed with any expectation of refusal, but rather a gentle suggestion, a quiet confidence that she'd accept

"There's a little place, 'The Daily Grind,' just off the square. Their coffee is excellent, and it's usually quiet enough to actually hear yourself think. Especially this time of year."

Lani's gaze flickered from the card in his hand to his earnest, expectant eyes. A myriad of thoughts swirled within her.

Coffee. With Julian.

It felt... significant. Not in the way their last, painful meeting had been significant, filled with unspoken accusations and raw hurt. This felt different. It felt like a conscious choice, a deliberate step towards... what? Reconciliation? Curiosity? A simple, human desire to connect after a period of separation? Her mind, ever the strategist, began to calculate.

The market stand would be fine for an hour. Her mother could handle the booth. And truly, a break would be welcomed. The relentless sweetness of her days sometimes felt overwhelming, and Julian's world, so seemingly removed from the sticky sweetness of frosting, offered a different perspective.

"Coffee," she echoed, a small smile playing on her lips. "That sounds... lovely, Julian." The hesitation that had flickered within her was now replaced by a burgeoning sense of anticipation. 'The Daily Grind' is a good choice. I haven't been there in a while, but I remember it being wonderfully cozy."

He returned her smile, a genuine softening around his eyes. "Excellent. Then it's settled. Lead the way?"

They walked together, a comfortable silence falling between them, broken only by the crunch of their boots on the frosted earth and the distant, cheerful carols sung by a small choir near the town's ice-skating rink. The market was still vibrant with last-minute shoppers. It began to recede behind them as they turned onto a quieter side street, the charming storefronts of the small town offering a picturesque backdrop.

{ 10 }

Julian

The Daily Grind looked exactly as he remembered it, only better. Warm, welcoming, and unpretentious. The air carried the scent of freshly ground coffee, toasted nuts, and a hint of cinnamon. It smelled like comfort, like home—if home could be built on second chances.

Soft jazz drifted through the café, blending with the low hum of conversation. A few locals sat scattered at mismatched tables, reading or chatting quietly. His favorite corner booth by the window was open. Outside, snow dusted the street, turning Evergreen Hollow into something out of a memory he hadn't realized he missed.

"This looks perfect," he said, pulling out a chair for Lani before taking the seat across from her. He nodded toward the little chalkboard menu propped between them. "What can I get you? My treat, of course."

"Just a black coffee, please," she said, her voice soft and familiar. She looked around at the exposed brick walls and the colorful local art, smiling faintly. "And thank you, Julian."

He ordered for them, his tone easy, practiced. When he turned back, she was watching him with that same thoughtful gaze that used to undo him. He knew he'd changed; success had left its mark, but sitting here with her, he felt like the man he used to be. The one who cooked for joy, not acclaim.

When the coffee arrived, he leaned forward, resting his arms on the table.

"So," he said with a smile that came more easily than expected, "how have you been, Lani? Truly. Seeing you at the market was a surprise, but I've wanted to ask properly."

"I've been well," she said, wrapping her hands around her cup. "Busy. The bakery's doing better than I ever dreamed. This season feels different, stronger. We're even talking about expanding to catering next year."

He felt something ease in his chest at the pride in her voice. "That's incredible. You've always had the touch, Lani. I'm not surprised at all."

She smiled, gratitude softening her expression. "Thank you, Julian. It hasn't been easy, but it's worth it. Especially for Naomi."

Her tone gentled, and hearing her daughter's name brought a rush of tenderness he hadn't expected.

"How is she adjusting?" he asked quietly. "Kids grow so fast."

"She's wonderful," Lani said, her smile widening. "She'll be six next month. She's been helping at the bakery after school if you can believe it—turns out she has a real talent for keeping customers from losing their crap."

Julian chuckled. "Of course she does. She's her mother's daughter."

"Or it could be because she's five and adorable," Lani teased.

The warmth in her eyes nearly undid him. He looked down, swirling his coffee to steady himself. "You've rebuilt something beautiful, Lani.

Something lasting. I admire that more than you know."

She tilted her head, her gaze soft. "And you? You've built something too. Your restaurant's name is everywhere, magazines, and television. It must be incredible."

He hesitated before sighing. "It is... and it isn't. Success is exhilarating, yes, but it's also consuming. There's this endless hunger for more. More recognition, more perfection. It wears you down." He met her eyes. "The critics, the constant pressure, it's a lot to shoulder. And the higher you climb, the lonelier it gets."

Lani listened in that quiet, patient way she always had. "I can imagine. It sounds isolating."

"It is." He smiled faintly. "Sometimes, I miss the simplicity. In the early days, when I cooked because I loved it. When it was about making people happy, not headlines." He gestured around them. "This feels real. People sharing warmth, not chasing reviews."

He found himself talking more than he expected. About his grandmother's kitchen, the smell of butter and herbs, the joy of seeing someone's face light up at a first bite. Somewhere along the way, he had lost that joy, replaced it with ambition.

"Sometimes," he admitted softly, "I wonder if I've forgotten why I started. The perfection I chase has taken the place of the joy I once felt. But you found your way back to it."

She looked surprised, her eyes shimmering. "It wasn't easy," she said. "There were moments I almost gave up. Leaving the city, uprooting Naomi. But the bakery grounded me. It gave me a purpose again."

Julian watched her trace the rim of her cup, her fingers graceful and steady. He remembered those hands dusted with flour, the hum of her voice while she worked. The years hadn't dimmed her light. They'd deepened it.

"You've built something special, Lani," he said quietly. "Something real. You should be proud."

Her smile was soft and genuine. The kind that made the world around them fade away.

The café was filled, but Julian barely noticed. The world beyond that corner booth ceased to exist. It wasn't nostalgia pulling him back here. It was her. The warmth she carried. The peace he hadn't known he was missing.

As she spoke about her work and about Naomi, he felt something stir within him. Hope. Maybe some pieces of the past weren't meant to be left behind.

He listened, asking questions with genuine curiosity, grateful for the ease between them. This was what he missed, being seen, heard, and understood.

The afternoon light slanted through the window, painting their table gold.

"Do you remember Mrs. Gable's history class?" he asked suddenly, smiling. "The sheer terror we felt every time she called on us? Especially during the American Revolution unit. I swear, I still have nightmares about the Treaty of Paris."

Lani laughed, bright and unrestrained. "Oh, I remember! And the way you used to doodle elaborate battle scenes in the margins of your notebook instead of taking notes. I always wondered if you actually learned anything."

"I learned enough to pass," Julian said, eyes twinkling. "Mostly, I learned to anticipate her favorite questions. And to charm my way through the rest." He leaned forward, lowering his voice. "Remember that time I convinced her the Battle of Bunker Hill was actually fought on a Tuesday? I swear I almost got away with it."

"You were an absolute menace," Lani chuckled. "I think I even covered for you once, pretending I'd seen you taking notes when you were clearly sketching portraits of the Founding Fathers. My own grades probably suffered for your theatrics."

"Ah, but you were always the good student," Julian said softly. "The one with perfect attendance and color-coded binders. I admired that. Even then." He paused. "You were always so driven. Even with your art. I remember your sketches. You had a way of capturing people's attention with just a few lines. I always thought you'd have your own gallery someday."

Her eyes softened with nostalgia. "That was the dream, wasn't it? A little gallery, filled with light and color. A place where people could get lost in art, just like I used to." She looked down, smiling faintly. "Life has a way of rerouting even the most ambitious plans."

"Tell me about it," he said with a wry smile. "My plan was never to be... this." He gestured vaguely. "It was about food. About joy. About bringing people together. It sounds simple now, doesn't it?"

"It does," she said quietly. "And yet, so profound."

They shared stories of high school kitchens and burnt sauces, of laughter and smoke alarms. Her laughter filled the space like a melody he hadn't realized he missed.

He thought of the years between them, of what success had cost him. And when he finally reached across the table, letting his fingers brush hers, the gesture felt inevitable.

"Like this, Lani," he said softly. "Sitting here, talking. It feels familiar. Like coming home."

Her hand trembled slightly before she drew it back, not in rejection, but with a shy smile. "It's been a long time, Julian."

"Too long," he said, his voice low. "And I regret that. I regret letting life get so complicated that I lost touch with what mattered. People that mattered." He hesitated. "You look good, Lani. You've always had a light about you, but now there's strength too. A quiet confidence." He exhaled, the words slipping free. "I have missed you."

She blushed, the color warming her cheeks. "Thank you, Julian. You aren't so bad yourself."

He laughed softly. "It's been a journey. Exhilarating, but isolating too. My life—it's under a microscope. Every move, every word, judged."

"It's easy to get lost," she murmured.

"Yes," he said. "You lose sight of who you are. It becomes a cage, even when it's gilded." He met her eyes, open and vulnerable. "That's why this is so precious. This conversation. It feels like breathing again."

And it did. For the first time in years, Julian felt peace.

He realized then that this, her laughter, her warmth, this quiet connection was what he'd been chasing all along. Not fame. Not stars. Just this.

Sitting across from Lani, in a small-town café dusted with snow, Julian found what he hadn't even known he'd been searching for.

***

Lani spoke of the bakery with quiet conviction, her words carrying a warmth that seeped into the skin. She described how it had become her sanctuary. It was a space where she could channel her energy and passion into something tangible. Her art career, she admitted, was a dream left in another lifetime. But this, this was different.

"It's not glamorous," she said with a soft smile, "but it's real. And there's a deep satisfaction in creating something that brings comfort and happiness to people. Especially during the holidays. It feels meaningful."

Julian listened, his gaze never leaving her face. There was a sincerity in his attention, a rare stillness. He found himself captivated not just by her words but by the subtle inflections in her voice, the way conviction mixed with humility. It struck him how little authenticity he encountered in his world. People spoke to him about what he represented, not who he was. But Lani… she saw him, still, as the man beneath the accolades.

He asked questions gently, coaxing her to share more about her days, about Naomi, about how it felt to see people lined up outside her door on winter mornings. The conversation unfolded naturally, like a favorite song rediscovered after years of silence. Her laughter was softer now, touched by experience but no less radiant.

And somewhere between the sips of coffee and the fading afternoon light, Julian realized something had shifted. The years between them no longer felt like a divide, but like threads weaving them back together, familiar, inevitable.

Lani spoke with openness that stirred something deep in him. Her honesty invited his own. He found himself speaking of pressure, of expectation, of how even success could hollow you out when it became the only thing you chased.

He told her of the nights when the applause faded and the silence afterward felt heavier than the noise.

And she listened, really listened. Not with pity, but with understanding.

The air between them grew warmer, thick with memory and something else unspoken but alive. The coffee grew cold, the sun dipped low, and the murmur of the café faded into the distance, replaced by the rhythm of breath and quiet heartbeats.

Julian's gaze lingered on her. He studied her face with the discerning eye of someone seeing not the past, but the woman who had emerged from it. The faint lines near her eyes, the soft confidence in her posture, the calm strength radiating from her. All of it spoke of endurance. Of growth.

"You know, Lani," he began, his voice low and steady, "it's remarkable, seeing you like this." He gestured subtly, encompassing all of her. "There's a strength about you. I remember you always being so vibrant, so full of a kind of gentle fire. But this? This is different. It's forged. You walked through fire with your spirit intact, maybe even stronger."

Lani's smile faltered slightly, emotion flickering across her face. His words sank into her, and he saw it, the quiet pride, the vulnerability she rarely allowed to surface.

To see her like this. To witness the woman, she had become filled Julian with an ache that was part admiration, part longing.

He hesitated, the moment teetering on the edge of something deeper, then shifted slightly, his voice softening. "You know," he said, "speaking of significant events... my annual charity gala is coming up. It's a big night in the culinary world—chefs, patrons, artists. All gathering for a cause that means a great deal to me."

Lani looked intrigued, curiosity flickering in her eyes.

"This year, the proceeds will go toward a foundation that supports young artists," he continued. "It's personal for me. Most of us started with little more than a dream and the courage to chase it."

He paused, gauging her reaction. "It's a culmination of months of work. Yes, there's glamour and spectacle, but at its core, it's about creation, about giving back."

"That sounds wonderful," Lani said. "You're really giving back, Julian."

For a heartbeat, he said nothing. Then, quietly: "It occurred to me as we were talking... that you might find it interesting. To see that part of my world. To experience an evening that celebrates creativity, just as your bakery does in its own way." He leaned forward slightly. "I would be honored if you'd come. As my guest."

The invitation hung in the air like the faint echo of a bell.

Lani blinked, clearly taken aback. "Oh, Julian," she murmured, color rising to her cheeks. "That's... very generous. I don't know what to say."

He could almost hear her thoughts, the quiet tension between intrigue and hesitation. The world he was inviting her into the world of Michelin stars and flashbulbs was galaxies away from the warmth of her bakery.

"There's no pressure, of course," he said gently, reading the flicker of uncertainty in her eyes. "It was just a thought. A hope, really. I'd like to share a part of my world with you, that's all."

"I... I don't know what to say."

"Say you'll think about it," he replied, his tone easy but threaded with sincerity. "The gala is a celebration of passion and artistry. I think you'd see pieces of yourself there, the same dedication, the same heart. I'd love for you to witness that."

She looked down at her cup, her expression thoughtful. "We both know why you left, Julian."

He exhaled, his gaze steady. "We do. And maybe this isn't about the past. Maybe it's about showing you what that choice became. The kind of creation I built when I walked away."

Her eyes softened. "You make it sound almost poetic."

"Maybe it is," he said quietly. "Life doesn't always offer us equal balance, but sometimes it gives us the chance to bridge the space between what was and what could be."

She was silent for a long moment, her fingers tracing the rim of her mug. Then, almost shyly, she smiled.

"It sounds incredible, Julian. The food, the people, and the cause. It's just... I haven't been to anything like that in years. My life is pretty focused on Naomi and the bakery. I wouldn't even know what to wear."

Julian chuckled, the sound deep and easy. "Ah, the eternal dilemma. But that's half the fun. And if it helps, I know a very talented stylist who owes me a favor or two."

She laughed softly, the tension easing.

His voice gentled again. "You don't have to decide now. Just know the offer stands. I'd love for you to be there, Lani. Truly."

"It's a lot to take in," she admitted. "I'd need to think about it. About Naomi, about my schedule. But... I'm intrigued, Julian. Very intrigued."

The word lingered between them, rich with unspoken promises.

Julian smiled, warmth touching his features. "That's all I ask. Take your time. The gala's a week from Saturday. If you decide to come, it would mean a great deal to me."

He reached for his phone, jotting down the details and sliding it across the table. "Just in case," he said, a glimmer of playfulness in his eyes.

Lani glanced at the screen, then back at him. Her expression was softer now, her hesitation tempered by something else, possibility.

And Julian, watching her, felt a quiet certainty settle in his chest. The invitation had been more than an offer; it was an opening. A chance to reconnect two lives that had once moved in harmony, now finding their rhythm again.

The café had grown quieter, the last of the daylight fading to blue. Outside, the snow fell in lazy spirals. Inside, their mugs sat empty, the warmth of the moment stretching between them like the first stirring of something long dormant.

Julian didn't know what would come next. But as he watched Lani tuck a strand of hair behind her ear, her smile faint and thoughtful, he knew this, whatever happened, this day, this connection, would stay with him.

Like the lingering taste of something exquisite, unexpected, comforting, and profoundly real.

When they finally rose to leave, the late afternoon light had slipped into dusk. The café's windows glowed with soft amber, halos of warmth against the gathering cold outside. Lani buttoned her coat, her fingers brushing the edge of her scarf, and for a moment, Julian caught himself memorizing the small, ordinary grace of the gesture.

They stepped out together into the crisp evening. The snow had started again, fine, powdery flakes that swirled under the streetlights like slow-moving stars. The air held that clean, metallic scent that only came before nightfall in winter.

"Thank you for the coffee," Lani said, her voice quiet but sincere. "And for... the conversation. It was good to see you again, Julian."

He smiled, though something in him tightened at the finality of the words. "It was good to see you too, Lani. More than you know."

She hesitated, her breath clouding the air between them. For a heartbeat, he thought she might say something more, but instead, she offered a small smile, the kind that felt both warm and protective. Then she turned, her boots crunching softly against the thin layer of snow as she walked toward her car.

Julian watched her go, her silhouette framed by the glow of the café's window and the gentle cascade of snowflakes. Something in the sight so familiar, so achingly simple lodged itself in his chest.

He stood there a long moment after she walked away into the fading snowy distance. The street was quiet now. The town settled into its evening rhythm. He slipped his hands into his coat pockets and began to walk, his breath rising in slow, steady clouds.

The conversation replayed in his mind in fragments. The soft timbre of her voice, the flicker of her laughter, the way her eyes brightened when she talked about Naomi. The world he had built, Michelin stars, charity galas, televised perfection felt suddenly distant, abstract. A life filled with acclaim yet starved of this kind of connection.

The kind he'd just rediscovered, over lukewarm coffee in a small-town café. He passed the bakery on his way back to his car. The sign above the door, **Shepherd's Sweets,** was hand-painted, its edges dusted with snow. Through the frosted windows, he could just make out the soft glow of light inside. The smell of sugar and yeast lingered faintly in the air, wrapping around him like a memory.

He paused there, taking it in. The warmth, the simplicity, the life she had built. It wasn't glamorous. It wasn't loud. But it was real. And it was hers.

A flicker of movement caught his eye. Lani inside, moving around the counter, straightening things before closing up. She hadn't seen him. For a moment, he simply watched her, that familiar ache returning, quiet and insistent.

She belonged here, in this rhythm of creation and care. And he, he was a man who lived out of suitcases and schedules, a man whose life was a series of reservations and fleeting applause.

But for the first time in years, he didn't feel entirely comfortable in that narrative.

As he turned away, a cold gust swept down the street, sharp enough to make his eyes sting. He told himself it was the wind. But deep down, he knew better.

Walking back to his car, Julian couldn't shake the feeling that something had shifted. Not just between them, but inside him. Lani had reminded him of something he hadn't realized he'd lost: the quiet joy of creating for love's sake, not recognition. The simple act of showing up, day after day, and building something lasting.

He reached his car, hesitated with his hand on the door, and looked back one last time. The lights in the bakery had gone dim, the window now just a reflection of the soft falling snow.

Julian drew a slow breath, watching it cloud and fade in the cold air.

He didn't know if she'd come to the gala. Maybe she wouldn't. Maybe the worlds they occupied were still too different, too distant.

But for the first time in a long while, he felt the faint pulse of something steady, something hopeful.

Possibility.

As he drove away from Evergreen Hollow's quiet main street, the radio hummed low, a jazz standard he hadn't heard in years. The kind his grandmother used to play while stirring soup on Sunday afternoons. He smiled faintly, his fingers tightening on the wheel.

For the first time in years, the road ahead didn't feel like an escape. It felt like the beginning of something worth returning to.

{ 11 }

Lani

The memory unfurled like a shimmering tapestry, woven with threads of scent, sound, and a bittersweet ache.

Christmas. It wasn't just a season; it was a spectacle in the sprawling, elegant home of the Sterling family, a place where Lani, a shy girl from the more modest side of town, had often found herself on the outside watching in. They were legendary not just for their affluence but for their fabulous Christmas parties. These weren't mere gatherings; they were meticulously orchestrated events that held the entire town in thrall. Lani remembered them with a vividness that startled her, even now, years. And this was where Julian was holding the gala.

Lani was the girl who preferred shadows and would hover near the edges of the festivities, a quiet observer. When she and Marc attended parties, Lani would clutch a glass of sparkling cider, the bubbles a comforting fizz against her tongue and watch. She'd watch the effortless flow of conversation, the clinking of crystal glasses, the dazzling array of jewelry, and impeccably tailored suits.

It was a world of polished surfaces and refined manners, a world that felt impossibly distant from her own life back in Evergreen Hollow. She remembered the sheer scale of it all. Marc was always focused on becoming part of the inner circle.

Beneath the surface of all the dazzling festivity, there was always a thread of envy in Marc. All she wanted was a sense of effortless belonging.

The memory of the champagne glasses, the delicate *clink* as they touched, was particularly sharp. It represented a level of sophistication, a casual opulence so foreign to her own childhood, which was filled with warmth and love, but certainly not with crystal and orchestras. This life Marc strived for, held the scent of abundance, of a life lived large.

It was not the life Lani wanted for Naomi.

These memories were so potent and distinct they now cast a long shadow over Julian's invitation to his upcoming charity gala. The word "gala" itself conjured images that were eerily just like those parties. Elegance, exclusivity, a celebration of a world that Lani had left. No ran from.

The thought of attending, of being Julian's guest, sent a tremor of apprehension through her. It was a world so far removed from the comforting familiarity of her bakery, from the grounded reality of her new life with Naomi.

The contrast between those glittering evenings and her own life felt stark. Her days were a rhythm of early mornings, the comforting weight of flour in her hands, the sweet scent of proofing dough, the joyful chaos of Naomi's laughter.

Her evenings were filled with storybooks, the quiet hum of the dishwasher, and the simple, profound satisfaction of building a life on her own terms. It was a life of substance, of quiet achievement, but it was a world away from the grandeur of a gala at Sterling House.

Now, to be invited into *his* world, to step into the spotlight of his current success, felt like stepping into a dream that was both enticing and terrifying. The memory of those parties, so vivid and full of a distant, unattainable glamour, served as a stark reminder of the chasm between their lives, a chasm built over years of divergent paths.

Julian had forged his empire in the crucible of his ambition, while she had carefully, painstakingly, rebuilt her own life from the foundations of her past.

The invitation, as Julian had so eloquently put it, was an opportunity to "step outside her usual rhythm, to see a different landscape."

But that landscape felt like a place where she might easily get lost, a place where her own quiet strengths might be overshadowed by the sheer brilliance of the spectacle.

The ghost of those corporate parties past, with their intoxicating blend of merriment and opulence, seemed to whisper a cautionary tale, a reminder of the dazzling allure of a world that was not her own.

It was a memory that amplified her hesitation, making the prospect of the gala a much more complex proposition than simply attending a social event. It was a step back into a world she had long since left behind.

The scent of evergreen and the echo of champagne glasses were no longer just nostalgic memories; they were specters that hovered at the edge of her current reality, prompting a profound question: was she ready to face the ghost of high-class Christmas business parties past, and step into the glittering future Julian was offering?

***

The aroma of freshly baked bread, a comforting balm that usually soothed Lani's anxieties, did little to quell the knot of apprehension coiling in her stomach. She'd been wrestling with Julian's invitation all afternoon, the embossed card a constant, reminder of a world so far removed from her own.

It was a world of polished surfaces and hushed tones, a world where she felt perpetually out of step, like a waltz dancer attempting the intricate steps of a tango. She'd finally decided to talk about it with Naomi, her spirited, precocious daughter, hoping the child's unvarnished perspective might offer some clarity.

"Mommy?" Naomi's voice, bright and inquisitive, cut through Lani's internal monologue. The almost six-year-old was perched on a stool at the kitchen island, meticulously arranging a collection of brightly colored pebbles into what she declared was a "fairy village." Her tongue poked out from the corner of her mouth in concentration, a familiar gesture that always made Lani's heart swell.

Lani took a deep breath, the scent of vanilla and sugar a welcome distraction. "Yes, sweetie?"

Naomi's eyes, the same startling blue as Lani's, flickered up from her project. "You look, thinking-y. Like when you're trying to figure out how many sprinkles go on a cupcake."

Lani managed a small smile. "Something like that. Remember Mr. Vance? The chef who invited Mommy to his special dinner?"

Naomi's face lit up, her concentration dissolving into pure, unadulterated excitement. "Julian! Yes! He was so nice! And he said my cookies were pretty!" Her voice rose with each word, her small hands gesturing wildly, nearly dislodging her pebble masterpiece. "He invited you to a party! A big, fancy party!"

Lani's breath hitched. She hadn't quite articulated it like that, not out loud. The invitation had felt like a delicate, fragile thing, something she was afraid to handle too roughly, lest it crumble into dust. "He did, yes," Lani confirmed, her voice a little softer than she'd intended. "It's called a gala."

"A gala!" Naomi echoed, her eyes widening as if the word itself held a magical, untold promise. "What's a gala, Mommy?"

"It's... it's a very special party," Lani explained, searching for words that would convey the essence without overwhelming her daughter. "A bit like a very fancy dress-up party, but for grown-ups."

Naomi's brow furrowed, not in confusion, but in deep contemplation. "So, like a ball?" she ventured, her imagination clearly working overtime.

Lani chuckled. "A little bit like that, I suppose. There will be lots of people, and it will be very elegant." She hesitated, the internal debate replaying itself. "And Julian is hosting it."

This was the part Lani had been dreading, the part that felt most exposed. She was an observer by nature, a creature of comfortable routines and familiar landscapes. The idea of stepping into Julian Vance's dazzling orbit of attending an event that conjured echoes of her life with Marc filled her with a deep-seated unease. She was Lani, the baker, the mom who smelled faintly of flour and sugar. What business did she have at a gala?

But Naomi's reaction was immediate and effervescent. "Julian! He's going to be there? Oh, Mom! You have to go!"

Naomi scrambled off the stool, her pebble village momentarily forgotten, and rushed around the island to Lani, her hands reaching out to pull her mother closer. "It would be so fun! You could wear that pretty dress you have in your closet! The long, flowy one!"

Lani's heart softened at the sheer, unadulterated joy radiating from her daughter. Naomi saw the world through a lens of pure possibility, a prism of delightful anticipation. Where Lani saw potential for awkwardness and social missteps, Naomi saw an adventure.

"I don't know, sweetie," Lani began, the familiar refrain of her own self-doubt starting to surface. "It's a very grown-up event. And I'm not sure I have the right things to wear, or..."

"Nonsense!" Naomi declared, her voice ringing with authority that sounded suspiciously like her grandmother. She patted Lani's arm with a small, determined hand. "You always look pretty, Mom. And we can find something! Maybe Grandma can help! She knows all about fancy clothes!"

Naomi's eyes sparkled with a new idea. "And maybe you'll see that chef on TV! The one who makes the funny hats!"

Lani couldn't help but laugh. Naomi's references were always so delightfully specific. "I don't think there will be any funny hats, darling," she explained gently, "but there might be very important people. And Julian is a very important chef."

"Exactly!" Naomi beamed, nodding her head while filling the space with undeniable energy. "So, you have to go! It's a chance to see something new! You always say we should try new things, Mommy. And this is a new thing for *you*!"

Her daughter's words, spoken with such innocent conviction, struck a chord deep within Lani.

She squeezed Lani's hand. "You always tell me to be brave, and this is a chance for you to be brave too!"

Naomi's unhesitating belief in her, in Lani's ability to navigate this unfamiliar terrain, was a powerful antidote to Lani's own ingrained hesitations. Naomi saw her mother not as the shy baker, but as a woman capable of grace and sophistication, a woman who deserved to experience the magic of a gala. It was a perspective Lani hadn't fully allowed herself to consider.

Lani looked down at her daughter's expectant face. Naomi's innocent enthusiasm was a beacon, illuminating a path that Lani had been too afraid to tread. The idea of a gala, which had previously conjured images of daunting formality and potential embarrassment began to shift, subtly reshaped by Naomi's infectious delight. It was no longer just about Julian or her opulent past; it was about a shared experience, a chance to create a new, glittering memory for her.

"You really think I should go?" Lani asked, her voice laced with a dawning sense of possibility.

Naomi nodded vigorously, her blue eyes shining. "Yes! It'll be an adventure! And we can practice our fancy manners!" She curtsied dramatically, her sparkly dress rustling. "Good evening, esteemed guests! May I offer you a delightful crumb?" She giggled, stumbling over the words.

Lani smiled, a genuine, unforced smile that reached her eyes. Naomi's pure joy was contagious. It was a reminder that sometimes, the most significant steps outside one's comfort zone were taken not for oneself, but for the sheer delight of sharing something special with a loved one.

The gala now felt a little less daunting, a little more accessible, thanks to the unwavering optimism of her bright, bubbly daughter.

Perhaps, just perhaps, she *could* do this. Perhaps she could trade her familiar apron for an elegant gown, her well-worn baking tins for a crystal flute, and step, however tentatively, into a world of glittering possibility without losing sight of herself.

The thought, once terrifying, was now tinged with a hopeful shimmer, thanks to Naomi's unshakeable belief. She saw the invitation not as a test of her social standing, but as an opportunity to bring a spark of magic into her everyday life. It was the innocent, unvarnished enthusiasm of a child that was slowly, surely, chipping away at the walls of her apprehension, allowing a sliver of Julian Vance's glittering world to seep into her own, familiar reality.

The following morning, Lani found a small, heavy envelope nestled amongst the usual bills and junk mail. It was different, immediately distinguished by the exquisite quality of the paper – a creamy, thick stock that felt substantial in her hand, embossed with a subtle, elegant crest. Her breath caught as she recognized Julian Vance's familiar, confident script, elegantly gracing the front. This was no mere formality; it was a personal missive.

Inside, a card, equally luxurious, held his words, penned with an ink that seemed to shimmer with sincerity. It wasn't the stark, printed invitation for the general guest list. This was personal, intimate.

"Dearest Lani," it began, and the simple address, so unexpectedly warm, sent a tremor through her.

He wrote of the upcoming charity gala, reiterating the cause with a passion that Lani recognized from his days in her father's kitchen. It was a genuine desire to give back. But he quickly moved beyond the official details.

He confessed that while he was thrilled to be hosting, a significant part of his anticipation stemmed from the prospect of seeing her there.

He'd addressed her apprehension directly, albeit with a gentle touch. "I know such events can sometimes feel a little... overwhelming," he wrote, his words a silent acknowledgment of her nature.

"But I truly want you to feel comfortable. Please consider this less of a grand obligation and more of an informal gathering of friends and supporters. The focus is entirely on the evening's beneficiaries, and of course," he added with a flourish that Lani could almost hear, "on enjoying some delightful culinary discoveries. I'm particularly eager for you to sample my latest creations. I've been working on a few innovations I believe you might appreciate, drawing inspiration, as always, from the unexpected."

The implication, subtle yet profound, was that her presence wasn't merely an addition to his guest list; it was something he genuinely desired, something he believed would enrich the occasion. He assured her that the atmosphere would be relaxed, encouraging conversation and camaraderie rather than stiff formality.

He painted a picture of an evening where smiles were more prevalent than stern glances, where genuine connection trumped superficial posturing. He underscored the philanthropic nature of the event, framing it not as a display of wealth or status, but as a collective effort for a worthy cause.

This was Julian's gift to her: reassurance, validation, and a pathway to participate without feeling entirely out of her depth.

Lani's breath caught in her chest as she read the final line.

"Your company would mean a great deal to me, Lani. Please do consider accepting. It would be a genuine pleasure to reconnect, however briefly, in a setting that I hope you will find both enjoyable and meaningful." He signed off not with a formal "Sincerely," but with a warm, "Warmly, Julian."

Lani reread the note several times, the elegant script and carefully chosen words weaving a spell around her. The paper itself felt like an embrace, the embossed crest a subtle mark of distinction that somehow, in this context, felt more personal than ostentatious.

It wasn't a demand; it was a gentle, persistent invitation, delivered with such consideration that it began to chip away at her ingrained reticence. He hadn't just sent an invitation; he had sent a bridge carefully constructed to span the distance between their vastly different worlds. He had recognized her hesitation and responded not with more pressure, but with thoughtful persuasion, making her feel not just remembered, but *valued*.

He saw her, Lani the baker, the single mother, and invited her into his world with a grace that made her feel capable of accepting. The emphasis on the charity, the relaxed atmosphere, and the promise of new culinary experiences.

It all resonated with her desire for substance and authenticity.

He understood that the glitz and glamour weren't what would draw her in; it was the genuine connection, the shared purpose, and the quiet acknowledgment of her unique perspective. This wasn't the Julian of her hazy memories, the dazzling prodigy; this was a man who had grown, who understood nuance, and who, in his own inimitable way, was reaching out to her with a sincerity that was hard to resist.

The note had been accompanied by another, more official invitation card, detailing the date, time, and venue of the gala. This one was printed, undeniably formal, but Julian had clearly instructed the stationer to match the paper and typeface to his personal note, creating a cohesive presentation.

It listed the event as a "Gala for the Future Foundation," a reputable organization dedicated to providing educational resources for underprivileged youth. Julian Vance was listed as the Patron and Host. The sheer elegance of the card, the crisp lettering, the subtle sheen of the paper, all spoke of a world Lani rarely encountered. Yet, compared to his handwritten words, the formality felt less intimidating, more like a beautiful frame for the genuine sentiment within.

She traced the embossed crest again, a stylized intertwining of a chef's toque and a subtle laurel wreath, a symbol of his culinary mastery and his recognized achievements. It was a testament to how far he had come and how much his life had evolved since their paths last crossed

And here he was, extending a hand, inviting her to witness it, to be a part of it, even if only for a single evening. The invitation wasn't just a request to attend; it was an offering of his time, his respect, and his genuine desire for her companionship.

He knew with certainty that Lani had to admire that simply asking her to attend wouldn't be enough. He needed to allay her fears, to reassure her that she would be welcomed, not judged, and that her presence would be a gift, not an imposition.

Lani walked over to the window, the heavy envelope still in her hand. The afternoon sun cast long shadows across her small kitchen, illuminating the dust motes dancing in the air. It was a world of quiet routines, of predictable rhythms. The gala, with its implied opulence and social intricacies, felt like a jarring counterpoint to her everyday life. Yet, Julian's words... they had a way of softening the edges of her apprehension. He spoke of "culinary discoveries" and "informal gatherings." He had even acknowledged that such events could be overwhelming. A direct nod to her own unspoken reservations.

It was this empathy, this understanding, that resonated most deeply. He wasn't just inviting her to a party; he was inviting her to share an experience, to witness his passion for his work, and to reconnect with him on a level that transcended their past.

She thought of Naomi, her daughter's bright eyes, her unadulterated excitement at the mere mention of a "fancy party." Julian had sent this, she realized, with Naomi in mind too, perhaps subconsciously. His note hinted at a desire to foster a connection not just between him and Lani, but between him and the daughter she cherished. He knew, from their brief encounter, how much Naomi adored him and his creations.

By framing the invitation with such warmth and reassurance, he was, in essence, creating an opportunity for Lani to offer her daughter a glimpse into a world of wonder, a memory to treasure. This wasn't just about Lani stepping out of her comfort zone; it was about expanding Naomi's horizons, too, albeit in a carefully managed way.

The idea of "innovations" he was eager for her to sample sparked a flicker of her old curiosity, the professional interest that had always been a part of her. Julian had always been a culinary visionary, pushing boundaries and experimenting with flavors. To taste his latest creations, to engage with him on a professional level, even in a social setting, held a certain allure. It was a chance to see the artist at work, to understand the evolution of his craft. He had cleverly woven together the threads of his personal and professional lives, creating an invitation that appealed to both the woman and the chef in her.

He was persistent. Maybe it was the unwavering assurance in his tone or the quiet confidence that she would find a way to navigate the event that began to sway her.

He made it clear that her presence was not a demand but a privilege he wished to extend, and that he believed she was capable of embracing it. The handwritten note felt like a tangible anchor, a direct line to the man himself, bypassing the impersonal nature of a formal invitation. It was a gesture that spoke volumes about his respect for her, his understanding of her character, and his sincere hope for her participation. He was, in essence, offering her a seat at his table, not just as a guest, but as someone whose perspective he valued.

The invitation, a tactile whisper of cream-colored cardstock and Julian's elegant script, lay on Lani's worn oak kitchen table, a stark contrast to the chipped Formica and the lingering scent of yeast.

For three days, it had been the silent epicenter of her world, drawing her gaze, her thoughts, her anxieties. The mountain air, usually so crisp and clear, seemed to hold a nervous tension, mirroring the tempest brewing within her. Each gust of wind rattling the windows sounded like a whisper of doubt, each snowfall a blanket of uncertainty.

Her days unfolded in their usual, comforting rhythm: the early morning bake, the school run, the precious hours spent at the bakery, her hands shaping dough, her mind wrestling with the gilded invitation. She'd reread Julian's words countless times, dissecting each phrase, searching for hidden meanings, for reassurance.

"Less of a grand obligation and more of an informal gathering of friends and supporters," he'd written. But the words "gala" and "Patron and Host" on the official card pulsed with undeniable glamour, a world away from her quiet existence. The glitter was undeniable, a siren song of an opulent past she'd long since traded for a more grounded reality.

The internal debate was fierce, a relentless tug-of-war. On one side, there was Julian, the dazzling prodigy, the man who had once occupied a significant, if hazy, corner of her heart. A part of her yearned for the echo of that connection, for the intellectual sparring, the shared passion for culinary artistry that had once defined their relationship. There was also the undeniable allure of networking possibilities—the chance to mingle with influential people and perhaps even glean insights that could benefit her own burgeoning business.

Julian had spoken of "culinary discoveries," of "innovations," and the chef in her, the artist who lived beneath the baker's apron, felt a prickle of professional curiosity, a longing to see what he had created, to understand his evolved vision.

But the other side of the scale was weighed with a more potent, more visceral fear. The fear of being an imposter, a fish out of water. She pictured herself in her simple, practical attire, surrounded by women draped in silks and jewels, their conversations flitting between haute couture and exclusive vacation spots. Would her hands, roughened by flour and kneading, feel out of place? The thought of the scrutiny, the unspoken judgments, sent a shiver down her spine, a familiar echo of insecurity her ex-husband instilled in her.

She had built a life here, a strong, stable foundation for herself and Naomi, brick by careful brick. This glittering world felt like a whirlwind, capable of uprooting everything she had painstakingly constructed.

She found herself pacing her small living room, the plush rug underfoot a stark contrast to the worn linoleum of her kitchen. Outside, the snow continued its silent descent, blanketing the world in a pristine white. It was a landscape she knew intimately, a comfort zone that offered no respite from her internal turmoil.

She brewed endless cups of tea, each one growing colder as her thoughts spun in circles. The image of Naomi's eager face, her excitement about Julian's pastries, was a constant, gentle pull. She wanted to give her daughter this experience, this taste of magic, but at what cost to her own peace of mind?

On the fourth day, as the first hint of dawn painted the snow-laden peaks with soft hues of rose and gold, Lani finally turned to her parents. Elenore, with her kind eyes and practical wisdom, and Thomas, a man of quiet strength and unwavering support, were her anchors.

She found them in the sun-drenched kitchen, the aroma of coffee and woodsmoke a comforting embrace. She laid out the invitation, Julian's note, and then, haltingly, poured out her heart, articulating the anxieties that had been churning within her. She told them about the dazzling world Julian lived in, the stark contrast to her own life, the fear of judgment, the feeling of being utterly out of her depth.

Elenore listened intently, her hands resting on Lani's, her gaze steady and reassuring. When Lani finished, her mother squeezed her hands gently.

"Oh, my darling," she said, her voice a soft melody. "That sounds like quite the dilemma. But let me tell you something. You are not the girl you were fifteen years ago. You have built a life, run a successful business, and are raising a remarkable daughter. You possess strength and grace that are entirely your own."

Thomas, who had been stirring his coffee, looked up, a thoughtful expression on his face. "Julian invited you because he values you, Lani. Not for the dress you wear or the company you keep. He knows who you are. He knows your talent, your integrity. Don't let all that richy rich stuff make you doubt your own worth. You have a fire within you, child, a quiet flame that burns brightly."

Her father's words, a direct echo of the respect he had always shown her, resonated deeply. He had always believed in her, even when she'd doubted herself.

Her mother's gentle reminder of her own growth, her inherent strength, was like a balm to her frayed nerves.

"It's not about the glamour, Lani," Elenore continued, her eyes twinkling. "It's about the opportunity. To see Julian, to see what he's achieved, and yes, to experience something different. And for Naomi! Imagine her delight. You can be a gracious guest, my dear. You don't have to be someone you're not. Just be Lani. The talented baker, the loving mother. That is more than enough."

Lani's eyes darted back and forth between her parents. They didn't dismiss her fears, but they offered a different perspective —one that highlighted her resilience and inherent value.

Thomas nodded, adding, "And think of it this way. If you feel out of place, well, then you know for sure that it's not where you belong. But if you go, with your head held high, you might surprise yourself. You might find that those dazzling chandeliers cast a warm light, not a harsh glare. You've always had an eye for detail, for quality. Judge the event by its substance, not just its sparkle. And if it's all a bit much, you can always find a quiet corner with a good glass of wine and observe. You're a good observer, Lani."

Their words were not a command, but a gentle nudge, an offering of support that eased the weight of her decision. They reminded her of the foundation she had built, the strength she possessed, the inherent dignity that transcended any social setting. They saw not the hesitant woman afraid of being judged, but the capable, resilient individual who had overcome so much.

She left her parents with a renewed sense of purpose, the snow-covered landscape no longer a symbol of her isolation, but of a quiet strength, a steadfast beauty. The internal debate hadn't vanished entirely, but the scales had tipped.

The fear was still present, a low hum beneath the surface, but it was now tempered by a budding sense of courage, a desire to honor the trust her parents had placed in her, and the quiet, persistent invitation that Julian had extended.

The pull of the past had always lingered like a familiar melody, soft, haunting, and impossible to forget. But now, it wasn't just nostalgia that tugged at her. It was a possibility. The chance to reconnect, to see what time had changed… and what it hadn't.

The thought of Julian, of stepping for one night into his glittering world, no longer felt intimidating. It felt like an invitation, not to lose herself, but to remember who she had become. She wasn't that uncertain girl anymore. She was Lani. Steady, grounded, shaped by heartache and healing in equal measure. She could walk into any room, even his, and still be wholly herself.

The idea stirred something warm inside her. A spark of anticipation that felt dangerously close to hope. The snow fell thick and lazy against her windshield as she wound down the mountain road, the world around her bathed in soft white. The headlights caught the glimmer of ice on the trees, and for the first time in a long while, she smiled to herself.

It wasn't just about the gala, or even about Julian. It was about saying yes to life, to change. To the quiet flutter in her heart, she thought she'd long since silenced. Somewhere between the mountains and the valley below, the fear that had held her back began to loosen its grip.

But she had to think about Naomi. Lani knew her daughter was not prepared for another letdown from a man she trusted. And she seemed to be clinging to the idea of Julian being around more often. If she decided to attend, it would be without Naomi. He would have to prove himself before becoming a part of her daughter's life.

By the time she reached town, the hesitation had melted away like morning frost. What lay ahead was unknown, yes but it also shimmered with promise.

And as she drove through the falling snow, she realized that maybe this wasn't just another chapter. Maybe this was the beginning of something she hadn't dared to dream of in years.

Julian

Julian had been staring at the phone for the better part of an hour, the screen dark and silent, his thoughts circling back to Lani with frustrating persistence. He told himself he was being foolish, that she'd moved on, that her quiet mountain life didn't have room for the noise of his world. But even as he tried to convince himself, his heart refused to listen.

He'd always admired her courage, that quiet determination that came so naturally to her. When he'd extended the invitation, he wasn't sure what he was hoping for. Maybe a chance to bridge the years between them, or maybe just to see her step into his orbit again. Not as someone from his past, but as someone who still mattered.

The phone rang then, sharp and unexpected in the quiet of his apartment. He reached for it without thinking, the sound startling him more than it should have. His breath caught when he saw her name on the screen.

"Lani."

Her voice was soft, hesitant but it carried that familiar steadiness that had once grounded him through every storm. The sound of it, after all this time, hit him square in the chest.

"I... I've been thinking a lot about your invitation," she said. A pause followed, the kind of pause that made the air feel electric. "I've decided to accept."

For a moment, Julian forgot how to breathe. Then the words spilled out, unguarded and full of warmth.

"Lani! That's... that's wonderful! I'm so glad. Truly." He couldn't help the smile that broke across his face, the one that came from somewhere deeper than mere relief. "I was hoping you would," he admitted, his tone softening. "It means a great deal to me."

He could almost picture her then, standing by the window of her cozy mountain home, her hair falling loose around her shoulders, that same mix of uncertainty and quiet strength in her eyes.

Her next words came carefully, each one chosen like a stone placed on solid ground.

"It's not quite what you might think." Lani's words came carefully. "I'm not looking for a grand romantic gesture, Julian. I see this as an experience. A chance to see a different world, to challenge myself, and perhaps, to find a part of myself I've misplaced."

Julian laughed softly, the sound genuine, touched with memory. "And that's precisely why I hoped you'd say yes," he said. "I wouldn't want it to be anything less than what you need it to be, Lani. And believe me, I've always admired that grounded strength in you. That quiet resolve."

He hesitated, the truth sitting heavy but honest in his chest. "It's one of the things I never forgot."

There was silence then, not empty, but full.

The kind of silence that carried meaning, memory, and the faint hum of something being rekindled.

Julian leaned back against the counter, a faint smile tugging at his lips. He could feel the warmth of her presence through the phone line, could almost smell the faint sweetness of her bakery, could almost see her looking out at the snow.

"Thank you," he said finally, his voice quieter now, almost reverent. "For saying yes. It'll be good to see you and Naomi again, Lani. Not as the chef or the celebrity, but just... me."

"I've decided to come. But I won't be bringing Naomi. She isn't ready for all of this," Lani replied.

"I understand," Julian replied, trying to hide his disappointment.

"I hope you do. I will see you then."

When the call ended, he didn't move for a long while. He just stood there, staring out the window at the city lights stretching endlessly beyond the glass. The noise, the shimmer, the unrelenting pace. It all felt so distant compared to the soft steadiness he'd just heard in her voice.

For the first time in months, maybe years, Julian felt something he hadn't allowed himself to feel. Hope.

Lani was a mother first. He understood why she chose to leave Naomi at home. He truly did. She was stepping, however cautiously, into his world. But deep down, he knew the truth. It was *he* who was stepping back into hers.

And that thought alone made the glittering city outside his window seem just a little warmer.

{ 13 }

Lani

The worn cardboard boxes, stacked precariously in the attic, offered a familiar landscape of forgotten treasures and dusty memories.

Lani knelt before them, the afternoon sun filtering through the grimy windowpane, illuminating dancing motes of dust. Each box was a Pandora's Box of sorts, holding remnants of a life lived before the mountains became her sanctuary.

She'd hoped, with desperate optimism, that somewhere in these containers was a flicker of what she needed.

A dress.

Not just any dress, but one that could somehow bridge the distance between the Lani who kneaded dough and the Lani who Julian, a man of refined taste and exquisite social circles, had invited to his gala.

She lifted the lid of the first box. A cascade of faded cotton blouses, a few sensible skirts, and a rather unfortunate floral print sundress that hadn't seen the light of day since a regrettable summer picnic a decade ago lay untouched.

No. This wouldn't do.

The next box held more of the same: practical sweaters, well-worn jeans, and a surprisingly large collection of aprons. Her baker's uniform. Her comfort. Her shield. But for this occasion, a shield wouldn't be enough. She needed armor, or perhaps something more akin to a spotlight.

The hours blurred into a monotonous dig into her past. She found a sensible tweed suit her mother had insisted on for a long-forgotten job interview, a few cocktail dresses from her early twenties that now felt wrong, too young, too eager. They were remnants of a woman who had been trying too hard, a woman who was desperately seeking validation. This Lani, the one who had made peace with her solitude and found joy in the simple rhythm of her days, felt a quiet disdain for that younger self.

Frustration began to prickle at the edges of her resolve. It wasn't just about finding a dress; it was about finding *herself* within the confines of such an event. Could she possibly embrace the sophistication that such an occasion demanded without sacrificing the authenticity she had so painstakingly built? The thought was daunting, a looming shadow cast over the excitement Julian's invitation had sparked.

With a sigh that felt heavier than the accumulated dust of years, Lani closed the last box.

Nothing. Absolutely nothing.

She needed a change of scenery, a wider selection, and a more professional eye. She needed to venture out of her carefully constructed cocoon.

The drive to the city was a journey in itself, a slow shedding of the mountain's quietude. As the sprawling metropolis came into view, a familiar hum of nervous energy began to thrum beneath her skin. This was Julian's world, a world of shimmering lights and hushed tones, a stark contrast to the earthy scent of pine and the rustle of leaves. She parked the car and took a deep, fortifying breath, reminding herself of the conversation with Julian, his genuine desire to have her there, not as an imposter she once felt like, but as herself.

She found herself drawn to a boutique nestled on a tree-lined street, its windows displaying an array of gowns that seemed to whisper tales of elegance and allure.

The air inside filled Lani's senses. It was a sophisticated fragrance. The hushed reverence with which the sales assistants moved added to the sense of occasion. This was not her usual shopping experience, which typically involved a brisk trip to a department store for sturdy footwear or a practical long-sleeve tee.

The racks brimmed with a dazzling spectrum of colors and textures. Silks shimmered like liquid moonlight, velvets were as deep and rich as midnight, and intricate beadwork sparkled like captured starlight.

Lani ran a hesitant hand over a cascade of sapphire blue, then a daring crimson. They were beautiful, undeniably, but still felt like costumes, like she was trying on someone else's skin.

She was about to turn away, a familiar sense of inadequacy creeping in, when a gown, hanging slightly apart from the others, caught her eye. It was a deep, lustrous emerald green, the fabric a heavy, luxurious silk that seemed to absorb and reflect the light simultaneously.

It wasn't ostentatious, not overtly flashy, but there was a quiet power to its understated elegance. The cut was simple, a graceful A-line that skimmed the body, with a modest V-neckline and delicate cap sleeves. It spoke of timeless sophistication, a style that felt grounded, yet undeniably glamorous.

"May I help you, madam?" the sales assistant asked, her tone polite

Lani turned to find a woman with kind eyes and an impeccable sense of style standing beside her.

"This dress," Lani said, a little breathless, "it's... it's beautiful."

The sales assistant smiled warmly. "Ah, the emerald silk. A truly special piece. It has a way of... bringing out the best in whoever wears it."

A flutter of curiosity, a nascent hope, began to stir within Lani. "Could I try it on?"

"Of course," the assistant replied, her smile widening. "Follow me."

The fitting room was a sanctuary of plush velvet and soft lighting. Lani shed her clothes and slipped the emerald gown over her head.

The silk felt cool and smooth against her skin, a stark contrast to the rougher textures she usually wore. It draped perfectly, falling with a graceful weight that felt both substantial and liberating.

She stood in front of the full-length mirror, and for a long moment, she simply stared. The woman staring back was and yet wasn't, Lani.

The divorced, practical baker, with her flour-dusted apron and perpetually rosy cheeks, had receded, replaced by someone else.

The emerald silk seemed to deepen the hazel of her eyes, to lend a subtle sheen to her usually untamed brunette hair, which now fell in soft waves around her shoulders. The modest cut of the dress accentuated her natural grace, and the subtle shimmer of the fabric gave her an almost other-worldly glow.

This wasn't just the dress. This was about the way it made her *feel*. It gave her quiet confidence, a sense of poise she hadn't experienced in years. The nervousness that had accompanied her to the city began to dissipate, replaced by a tremor of something long dormant. A rediscovered sense of self.

She saw a hint of the woman Julian had once fallen in love with, not the polished socialite he might have expected, but a woman of quiet strength and undeniable allure, a woman who could stand with grace in any room.

The woman in the mirror was elegant, yes, but more importantly, she was still *her*.

The Lani who had nurtured a garden, the Lani who found solace in the quiet hum of her oven, the Lani who had, against all odds, rebuilt a fulfilling life for her daughter and herself.

The dress hadn't transformed her into someone else; it had, rather, revealed a facet of herself she had almost forgotten existed. Beneath the layers of practicality and routine, there still resided a woman who could captivate, who could command attention, not with grand pronouncements, but with a quiet, inherent grace.

She turned slowly, observing the fabric's sway and how it caught the light. The emerald silk clung to her like a second skin, a promise of an evening where she would not just attend but truly *be*. It was a subtle transformation. This wasn't about becoming someone she wasn't but about embracing a part of herself that had been dormant for too long.

She imagined herself at Julian's gala, not as a shy observer, but as a woman who belonged, a woman who could hold her own. The thought brought a genuine smile to her lips, a smile that radiated from within, a smile that truly belonged to the woman in the emerald dress.

"It's perfect," she whispered.

"It looks beautiful on you," the sales assistant admired.

It wasn't just a dress; it was a key, unlocking a door she hadn't realized had been closed. She was stepping outside her comfort zone and embracing the unknown.

She felt a surge of gratitude for the sales assistant, for the gown, and for the quiet courage that had led her here. This was more than just an outfit; it was a statement of intent, a declaration that Lani, the baker from the mountains, was ready to step into a different light.

The reflection in the mirror was no longer a stranger; it was a familiar, yet newly discovered, friend. She saw not just a dress, but the quiet confidence it inspired, the subtle shift in her posture, the spark in her eyes.

This was Lani, ready to face whatever lay beyond the familiar peaks of her mountain home.

The sales assistant offered a knowing smile. "It's as if it were made for you," she murmured, her voice soft with appreciation.

And in that moment, looking at her reflection, Lani felt that it truly was. décolletage beautifully, hinting at the femininity she often carefully kept tucked away. Her shoulders, usually squared with the effort of lifting heavy sacks of flour, seemed softer, more relaxed.

She gave a twirl. A small, almost involuntary movement, and the emerald silk swirled around her, a whisper of movement that was surprisingly graceful. The fabric, with its subtle sheen, seemed to capture the ambient light, making her skin glow with a healthy luminescence. It was a perfect reflection of the woman Lani was discovering within herself, strong, resilient, and possessing a beauty that ran far deeper than mere appearance.

"I'll take it," Lani announced.

She thought of Julian, of his discerning eye, his appreciation for artistry. Would he see *this* Lani? The thought sent a fresh wave of butterflies through her stomach, but this time, they were not entirely of apprehension.

They were mingled with a thrill of anticipation, a sense of excitement for the evening ahead.

This dress was more than just a garment; it was a bridge, connecting the Lani of the mountains to the woman who was about to enter Julian's glittering world. It was a tangible representation of her courage, her willingness to embrace change, and her quiet determination to show up as her most authentic, yet perhaps, most radiant self.

The sales assistant approached, holding out a delicate silver necklace. "A little something to complement the gown," she suggested.

It was a simple pendant, a single, teardrop-shaped emerald that mirrored the dress's rich hue. Lani fastened it around her neck, the cool metal a pleasant weight against her skin. It was the perfect finishing touch, a subtle accent that enhanced rather than overpowered the gown.

Looking in the mirror one last time, Lani smiled.

The quiet tremor she felt wasn't fear; it was the stirring of a long-dormant spirit, a subtle awakening of a part of herself that had been waiting for the right moment to emerge. The decision to accept Julian's invitation had been the first step, but this emerald dress and the reflection it held was the embodiment of that step.

She was ready. She was, at this moment, more than ready. She was luminous.

14

Julian

Julian couldn't take his eyes off her.

"Lani," he said, his voice a low, steady baritone that still carried the weight of memory. He saw the faint shiver that ran through her. "You came."

The words were simple, but the meaning between them ran deep; recognition, relief, and something that felt like triumph.

"Julian." Her voice caught slightly, warm and a little breathless. "It's... quite a sight." She gestured toward the glittering ballroom, her hand sweeping over the gleam of crystal and candlelight. "You've really outdone yourself."

His smile curved easily, though it reached deeper than charm. "It's an occasion," he said, his gaze holding hers. "And I wanted it to be worthy of the company."

The air between them shifted. The compliment lingered, quiet and deliberate.

"You look... stunning, Lani."

For a heartbeat, she seemed unsure what to do with the words, and then the faintest color rose to her cheeks. Around them, the room moved in soft motion, the hum of conversation, the clink of crystal, the mellow strains of a string quartet, but it all seemed distant, muffled.

She spoke about home, about the mountain. Of still mornings and snowfall whispering through pines. Of her bakery, and the rhythm of creation that had become her peace. Her words came with an effortless grace, small fragments of a life built on meaning rather than spectacle.

Julian listened. He didn't interrupt, didn't fill the spaces with commentary or charm. He simply absorbed her voice, the warmth of it, the way it smoothed over the noise of the world. Each detail she shared felt like a brushstroke against the edges of his own carefully curated existence.

When she paused, he let the silence stretch before speaking, his voice low, thoughtful.

"It sounds... perfect, Lani. A life built on something real. You've found your own kind of artistry."

Her eyes lifted to his, surprised, touched. "It's my own kind of masterpiece, I suppose. Small, but meaningful."

He leaned in, a quiet conviction threading his tone. "All art is meaningful. Scale doesn't define worth. It's the heart behind it, the devotion. That's where the beauty lives."

He glanced briefly around the room, the glimmering ice sculptures, the silver platters, the meticulously plated dishes, and then back at her.

"This," he said softly, "is my canvas. But your bakery, Lani... that's yours. And they're both art."

He reached out, his hand brushing her arm. It was brief, almost tentative, but the contact sent a pulse through him.

Her skin was warm beneath his fingertips, familiar in a way that felt both startling and inevitable.

"Julian," she whispered, her voice trembling just enough to betray her heart, "I didn't come here expecting..."

He smiled gently, finishing for her. "To see me like this? Or to see yourself reflected in it?"

Her gaze fell to the orchids on the table. "Perhaps a little of both," she said quietly.

He let out a slow breath. "You'r being here, it means more than you know." His voice dropped, steady and unguarded. "You were the inspiration behind so much of what I've built, even when you weren't there. The drive to make something lasting, something beautiful... it started with us. With you."

For a long moment, neither of them spoke. The space between them pulsed with something unspoken and familiar, delicate as glass.

Julian had seen hundreds of people step into rooms like this, elegant, poised, carefully composed, but when Lani arrived, the world had simply gone still.

The emerald gown caught the chandelier light and shimmered softly, the color deepening where it brushed her skin. He could hardly look away.

"Thank you," she said, a hint of nervous laughter in her voice. "The dress... it was an adventure to find."

An adventure. Of course it was. Julian smiled faintly. Everything with Lani had always been an act of quiet bravery.

"Well," he said, his gaze lingering, "it was an adventure worth taking. That color... it's extraordinary on you. It brings out the fire in your hair, and..." His voice softened, reverent. "It's just so unmistakably you."

Her blush deepened, and something in his chest tightened.

"It felt like the right choice," she said.

"It is," Julian replied. "It's you. Just... illuminated."

He reached for her hand without thinking, his fingers hesitating in the air for half a second before brushing hers. The contact was simple, innocent even but it grounded him, sent a warmth spreading through his chest that no crowd or spotlight could ever rival. Her skin was soft, her pulse steady beneath his thumb as he let it drift lightly across her knuckles.

"Come," he said gently, reluctant to let go. "Let me show you what I've been working on. I think you'll appreciate the artistry."

She hesitated only a moment before placing her hand in his. Her touch was small but sure, grounding him in a way the world's applause never had. As he helped her to her feet, the emerald silk of her gown caught the light and for a moment, Julian forgot the room.

His breath caught in his chest. All he saw was her, luminous, steady, achingly real.

And as she smiled up at him, something in his chest shifted. A quiet, certain understanding.

He led her through the throng of glittering gowns and tuxedos, the sounds of polite conversation fading as they stepped into a quieter alcove where light danced on frozen glass. Here, the air was cooler, touched by the crisp scent of ice and citrus.

"This one," he said, gesturing toward a sculpture of a swan poised mid-flight, its wings carved with delicate precision, "was inspired by a storm that hit the mountains last spring. The wind was fierce, untamed, but there was beauty in it too. The way it shaped the snow, the way it reminded me that creation and chaos are often the same thing.

He paused, his eyes still on the frozen sculpture but his thoughts elsewhere, on her.

"I thought of you when I made it," he admitted softly. "The strength of something graceful. The way you always seemed to find beauty in the mess of things."

Lani turned to him, surprise flickering in her gaze, and he saw it then. The same spark he'd carried with him all these years, quietly waiting for this moment.

For her. He was still in love with her.

And maybe, just maybe, this time, he wouldn't let her slip away.

15

Lani

His eyes, a startling shade of cerulean, swept across the room, pausing, then locking with hers. A slow smile, one that crinkled the corners of those expressive eyes, spread across his face. It was a smile that held a wealth of unspoken acknowledgment, a silent greeting that cut through the hum of the crowd. Lani's heart, which had been beating a steady rhythm of nervous appreciation, began to quicken its pace. The emerald silk felt suddenly more alive, the cool fabric a counterpoint to the sudden warmth blooming in her chest.

She straightened her shoulders, a small, involuntary gesture of readiness, of acknowledgment. Lani watched his hands as he spoke, the elegant gestures that accompanied his words. He talked about the viscosity of the ice, the precise temperature needed to achieve certain textures, and the way light would refract through different densities. It was a language she understood, a language of creation, of coaxing beauty from raw materials. He explained the challenge of working against time, of how fragile his creations were, how quickly they could melt away, no matter how much care he poured into them. There was a passion in his voice, a fire that mirrored the passion she felt for her own craft.

"It's magnificent, Julian," she said, genuinely impressed. "The detail, it's breathtaking."

She traced the curve of the swan's neck with her gaze, imagining the hours of painstaking work and the focused concentration required to bring such a vision to life.

"It's a fleeting beauty," he mused, his gaze distant for a moment, as if lost in the memory of the creative process. "Like so many things, it exists for a moment, then it is gone. But the memory, the impact, that can linger." He turned his gaze back to her, a thoughtful expression on his face. "Much like... certain connections."

The subtle allusion didn't escape her. A prickle of awareness, a delicate tension, settled between them. She didn't respond directly, choosing instead to focus on the intricate details of another sculpture. The swirling vortex of ice seemed to capture the dynamism of a whirlpool.

"And the food," Julian continued, shifting gears smoothly, his attention now turning to the culinary aspect of the evening. "Tonight, it's a celebration of contrasts. The robustness of aged cheddar against the delicate sweetness of honey-glazed pears. The earthiness of wild mushrooms paired with the bright zest of preserved lemon. I've been experimenting with textures, Lani."

Lani nibbled on a wafer-thin tuile. The crispness shatters on her tongue, leaving behind the softness of a slow-braised lamb, and a surprising pop of pomegranate seeds.

"You really are a genius. This is delicious," she stated.

Julian smiled. A full, true smile of the boy she used to know. Used to love.

"There's more!" He led her through a series of tasting stations, each one a miniature masterpiece.

He introduced her to a chef, a young woman with a quiet intensity in her eyes. She explained the intricacies of a delicate consommé, its clarity a testament to hours of careful simmering and straining.

Julian watched Lani's reaction as she sampled a small bite of seared scallop, its sweetness perfectly balanced by a whisper of chili heat.

"The balance," he said, his voice low, "that's always the challenge, isn't it? To achieve that perfect equilibrium where no single element overwhelms, but each plays its part in the symphony."

Lani nodded, her mouth full of the exquisite flavor. "It's a dance," she agreed. "A very intricate dance." She remembered the days spent perfecting her own sourdough, the endless adjustments to hydration, fermentation times, oven temperatures. The pursuit of that elusive perfection, the moment when all the elements transformed into something extraordinary.

"Exactly," Julian affirmed, a spark of shared understanding in his eyes. "And tonight, I wanted to showcase the dance between art and sustenance. The beauty of form, the pleasure of taste. They are not mutually exclusive, are they?"

"They shouldn't be," Lani replied, her gaze meeting his. "But sometimes, in the pursuit of one, the other can be... neglected."

"A mistake I've tried to avoid," he said, his voice holding a subtle challenge.

He gestured towards a display of miniature pastries, each one a tiny work of art.

"The construction of a perfect tart, for instance. The crispness of the pastry, the smooth richness of the filling, the precise arrangement of fruit. It requires as much precision, as much artistic sensibility, as any sculpture or painting."

He picked up a tiny chocolate mousse tart, its surface adorned with a single, glistening raspberry. "Taste," he instructed. He offered it to her.

Lani accepted it, the delicate pastry cooled against her fingertips. She took a bite, the dark chocolate melting on her tongue, followed by the subtle tartness of the raspberry.

"It's divine," she breathed, closing her eyes for a moment to savor the sensation.

"And yet," Julian continued, his voice a low murmur beside her, "it's also a product of careful calculation. Understanding the Maillard reaction, the emulsification of chocolate, and the correct ratio of sugar to butter. It's science, Lani. But it's also art."

He was making a point, she realized, a deliberate one. He was drawing parallels, constructing a bridge between their respective disciplines, and between their past and their present. He was showing her that the passion and dedication she knew so well, the very essence of what had drawn them together, was still alive and thriving within him, manifested in this grand, opulent arena.

"You've always had a gift for seeing the artistry in things, Julian," she said softly, her voice barely above a whisper. "Even in the simplest of ingredients."

He leaned closer, his gaze intense. "And you, Lani," he said, his voice dropping even lower, "you always had a gift for bringing out the best in everything you touched. The way you could transform simple flour and water into something magical. The way you truly care for your customers. That's a kind of artistry, a profound one."

The unspoken words hung heavy in the air between them. The memory of their shared past, of quiet evenings spent discussing dreams and aspirations, of the raw, unadulterated passion that had fueled their younger days, seemed to shimmer around them. He was not just showcasing his current success; he was reminding her of what they had once shared, of the creative fire that had burned between them.

He steered her gently towards a quieter seating area, away from the main flow of guests. Two plush armchairs were arranged to overlook a breathtaking display of cascading orchids, their delicate petals a vibrant contrast to the surrounding opulence.

"Please," he said, gesturing for her to sit. "Tell me more about your life, your plans. I've seen the occasional photograph you post online, but it's not the same as hearing it from you."

Lani hesitated for a moment, then sank into the soft embrace of the armchair. The emerald silk settled around her, a comforting weight. She felt a sense of ease, a familiarity in his presence that was both comforting and disquieting.

"It's. Well, it's a different world, Julian," she began, choosing her words carefully. "Quieter. More grounded. I spend my days with my hands in the dough. Right now, I am trying to boost the bakery's sales and bring my parents' books up to the 21st century. I've found a rhythm there, a peace that I didn't know I was missing."

"I've missed it," he admitted. "Funny how you can live somewhere for years and not see it for what it is, until you walk away from it."

Lani's eyes widen in surprise. He was so quick to leave all those years ago.

Julian shrugged. "Surprised?" He asked.

"A little," she admitted.

He reached out, his hand resting lightly on her forearm, his fingers gently curling around the fabric of her sleeve in a reassuring touch. The contact sent a jolt through her, a familiar spark that ignited a cascade of memories.

"Julian," she began, her voice catching slightly. "I... I didn't come here expecting..."

"To see me like this?" he finished for her, his eyes twinkling. "Or to see yourself reflected in it?"

His question hung in the air, sharp and insightful. Lani looked away, her gaze falling upon the intricate patterns of the orchids. She had come to step out of her comfortable solitude for a night.

"Perhaps a little of both," she confessed, her voice barely a whisper.

Julian waited intently for her to continue, his gaze never wavering from her face.

"I came back to start a new life for me and Naomi. I wasn't looking for anything more."

Julian's smile softened. He squeezed her arm gently before releasing her.

"Lani," he said, his voice laced with a sincerity that resonated deeply. "Relax. Your presence here tonight is a gift. You were the inspiration for so much of what I've created, even when we were apart. But for right now, let's just get to know each other again."

Warmth spread through Lani at his words. It was a validation, a recognition of what they once had together."

He stood up, extending his hand to her, palm open and steady.

"Come," he said, his gaze steady and warm. "Let me introduce you to some of the people I admire. And then, perhaps, we can try some of these 'contrasts' I've been so eagerly anticipating."

Lani took his hand, the familiar warmth of his touch grounding her. As he pulled her to her feet, she met his gaze, a silent acknowledgment passing between them.

The journey from her corporate job in the city, her failed marriage, her quiet mountain bakery to this glittering ballroom felt less like a leap and more like a natural progression. Stepping into a new stage in life. Julian's cherished creative spark is now fully her own.

The night was just beginning, and Lani, in her emerald silk, felt ready to paint her own vibrant strokes upon Julian's magnificent palette.

The initial wave of acquaintances Lani had navigated in Julian's grand ballroom had been a gentle ebb and flow, a series of polite smiles and murmured pleasantries.

But as the evening progressed, the currents began to pull her towards more familiar people. The faces from her past emerge from the glittering throng like constellations appearing in the twilight sky. Each encounter was a subtle test, a gentle unfolding of the person she had become versus the Lani they remembered.

The first to catch her eye was Sarah Jenkins, her former high school classmate, whom Lani hadn't seen since graduation day. Sarah was now a polished woman with a sleek auburn bob and a dress that whispered of expensive tailoring. She approached Lani with a disarming blend of surprise and calculated charm. Her eyes, sharp and discerning, swept over Lani's emerald gown, lingering for a moment before meeting Lani's gaze.

"Lani? Is that really you?" Sarah's voice was a little higher than Lani remembered, laced with an almost theatrical astonishment. "Good heavens, you've transformed! I barely recognized you."

She tilted her head, a faint smile playing on her lips. "That emerald green is simply divine on you. Absolutely stunning. Though I must admit, I wouldn't have pegged you for a Julian Vance kind of event."

Lani felt a familiar tightening in her chest, a phantom echo of the shy, uncertain girl who had always felt out of place in Sarah's polished orbit. But the years had woven a different fabric for Lani. The emerald silk of her gown felt like armor, and Julian's steady and encouraging presence, even at a distance, was a silent anchor.

"Sarah, it's good to see you," Lani replied, her voice steady and clear. She offered a small, genuine smile. "And yes, it's me. Life has a way of leading us down unexpected paths, doesn't it?" She gestured vaguely around the opulent room. "Julian and I, well we reconnected recently. He's quite the host, isn't he?"

Sarah's eyebrows rose infinitesimally. "Oh, I'm aware," she said, her tone shifting, becoming more conspiratorial. "Everyone is talking about Julian's incredible resurgence. And *you*, Lani, appearing by his side. Well, it's quite the story. What have you been up to all these years? Last I heard, you were taking over your parents' bakery. Quite the rustic endeavor, I imagine."

The word "rustic" was delivered with a subtle, almost imperceptible air of condescension. Lani felt a prickle of annoyance, but she suppressed it. This was not the Lani who would shrink from such observations.

"It is my parents' bakery, yes," Lani confirmed, her smile widening slightly. "And it's a life I've rebuilt with great care and joy. It's not 'rustic,' Sarah, it's grounded. And I've been thriving there, creating something beautiful and real with my own hands. It's a different kind of skill, perhaps, but deeply fulfilling."

She met Sarah's gaze directly. "And as for Julian and me, our paths were always meant to cross again. Some connections, you see, are simply too strong to break."

The subtle confidence in Lani's voice seemed to catch Sarah off guard. Her carefully constructed façade flickered for a moment, genuine surprise, perhaps even a touch of envy.

"Well, isn't that fascinating," Sarah murmured, her gaze drifting back to Lani's gown. "You certainly know how to make an entrance, Lani. Truly."

Before Sarah could delve further into her probing questions, Lani saw a familiar face weaving through the crowd.

It was David Chen, a fellow student from her early days, before her life had taken a sharp turn towards the mountains. David, who had always possessed an earnest, almost boyish charm, now sported a distinguished beard and a suit that fit him with precision. He spotted Lani, and his face lit up with genuine warmth, immediately putting her at ease.

"Lani? No way!" David exclaimed, navigating the space between a towering ice sculpture and a cluster of animated guests to reach her. He extended a hand, his smile wide and unreserved. "It's been ages! You look incredible. That dress is... wow."

Lani laughed, a genuine, unforced sound. "David! It's so good to see you too. You haven't changed a bit, except for the beard, which suits you."

"And you've changed spectacularly," David returned, his gaze earnest. "Seriously, Lani, you're glowing. I always knew you had it in you, but this... this is a whole new level.

And here, of all places! I heard Julian was throwing an event, but I never imagined I'd see you here. What's the story?"

Lani felt a familiar pang of nostalgia, warmth spreading through her at David's easygoing nature. He had always been one of the few who saw her passion for art and food, her dedication to the craft. He didn't judge or show reservation.

"It's a long story, David," she admitted, her gaze flicking towards Julian, who was engaged in conversation nearby, but still subtly aware of her.

"But the short version is that you know Julian and I have a history. And tonight, he invited me to celebrate with him."

David nodded, his eyes twinkling with understanding. "I remember you two. You were inseparable for a while. He always said you had the most intuitive palate he'd ever encountered. And seeing you tonight, I believe it more than ever. I hear this whole event is a testament to his vision. And you're right here, looking like you're about to step onto a runway yourself."

"Julian's artistry is undeniable," Lani agreed, feeling a sense of pride in them both. "He's created something truly magnificent. But my own path has taken a different direction. I'm running the bakery now, up in the mountains."

David's eyes widened. "Shepard's Sweets? That's fantastic! I've always loved your dedication. I can picture you there, surrounded by the smell of fresh cookies. It's perfect for you." He leaned in slightly, his voice lowering.

"Julian always talked about how much he missed that connection, that pure passion for creation that you both shared. It seems like you've both found ways to keep that fire alive, just in different arenas."

His words were a balm, a confirmation of the journey she had taken. He didn't see her as someone who had abandoned her dreams, but as someone who had found a new, equally valid expression of her creative spirit.

"That's a lovely way to put it, David," Lani said, genuinely touched. "It feels that way, too. Different mediums, perhaps, but the same heart behind it."

Just then, a woman with a familiar, kindly face approached. It was Mrs. Gable, her neighbor from her childhood home, a woman whose lemon bars were legendary and whose garden was a riot of vibrant color. Mrs. Gable, her silver hair neatly coiffed and her dress a soft lavender, beamed at Lani.

"Lani, dear child! Is that truly you?" Mrs. Gable's voice was warm and melodious, carrying the comforting cadence of home. "My goodness, you've grown into such a beautiful woman! And that dress... it's breathtaking, darling. You look like a Hollywood starlet."

Lani's heart swelled with affection. Mrs. Gable was a constant, a warm beacon in her memories of their small town.

"Mrs. Gable! It's wonderful to see you!" Lani exclaimed, embracing her warmly. "You look wonderful as well. That lavender is so elegant on you."

"Oh, this old thing," Mrs. Gable demurred, patting her dress. "But you, my dear, you are simply radiant. I heard you were back in town for Julian's event, but I never imagined you'd be well, quite like this. So poised, so sophisticated. I remember you as such a quiet, thoughtful girl. Always with your nose in a book or helping your parents in the kitchen."

Lani chuckled. "I was that girl, Mrs. Gable. And in many ways, I still am. Just with a bit more experience under my belt." She gestured towards Julian, who had momentarily glanced over and offered a brief, knowing nod. "Julian and I have been reconnecting. He's putting on quite the spectacle tonight."

Mrs. Gable's eyes twinkled. "Julian Vance. Of course. He was always such a bright spark, wasn't he? Talented, ambitious, I always knew he'd go far. And you two. I remember you always had a special connection. Like two peas in a pod, you were. Always discussing something, your heads bent together." She paused, her gaze thoughtful. "So, are you thinking of going back to the big city, Lani?"

"Not quite," Lani clarified gently. "I've built a life for myself here in Evergreen Hollow, running the bakery. It's quiet, but it's fulfilling. I needed to get my hands back in the dough. Create new cake flavors again. So, I did."

"The bakery!" Mrs. Gable's face lit up. "Oh, I love a good loaf of bread! Your parents make the best. Bless your heart, that's always been your gift, hasn't it? I'm so pleased to hear you've found happiness. And to see you here, with Julian. It warms my old heart." She squeezed Lani's hand. "You always did have a knack for finding the truly good things, Lani. And Julian was always one of them, wasn't he?"

The question, so simply put, held a world of unspoken history. Lani met Mrs. Gable's warm, knowing gaze.

"He was," Lani admitted softly, a gentle smile gracing her lips. "And it seems some good things are worth revisiting."

*****

As the evening continued, Lani encountered more faces from her past, a cousin she'd rarely seen, former schoolteachers, even a childhood friend who had married and moved away years ago.

Each interaction was a brushstroke on the portrait of her present. Some were genuinely delighted to see her; their surprise laced with sincere affection. Others offered compliments that felt a little too pointed, their curiosity barely veiled. There were subtle questions about her relationship with Julian, about her return to Evergreen Hollow, and about her sudden reappearance in his opulent world.

But with each exchange, Lani felt a subtle shift within herself. The anxieties that had once plagued her, the fear of not belonging, of being judged, of being out of her depth seemed to recede.

Julian's presence was a steady, reassuring current in the swirling tide of the ballroom. He moved through the throngs of guests with an effortless grace that spoke of a lifetime navigating such circles. Yet his gaze consistently sought Lani out. It wasn't a possessive stare, nor was it one of public display for the sake of appearances. Instead, it was a subtle tether, a silent assurance that she was precisely where he wanted her to be.

He would occasionally pause in his conversations, his eyes meeting hers across the glittering expanse. A flicker of a smile, a slight inclination of his head gestures so small they might have been missed by anyone else.

But Lani felt them like a warm current flowing between them. Each acknowledgment was a quiet confirmation, a silent declaration that she was his focus, his esteemed guest.

As the evening wore on, Julian began to introduce Lani to some of the key figures he was hosting. His voice, when he spoke her name, held a distinct note of pride.

"Arthur," he'd say, turning to a distinguished gentleman with a shock of silver hair, "allow me to introduce Lani Shepard. Lani, this is Arthur Sterling, a cornerstone of the Sterling Foundation."

The introduction was delivered with a warmth that transcended mere professional courtesy. His hand would briefly, possessively, rest on the small of her back, guiding her slightly closer, as if to emphasize their shared space. It was a subtle claim, a quiet assertion of her presence beside him.

Arthur Sterling, a man whose handshake was firm and whose eyes held the keen intelligence of someone who had brokered countless deals, offered Lani a warm smile. "A pleasure, Ms. Shepard. Mr. Vance has spoken of your unique talents. It's an honor to finally meet you."

The emphasis on "unique talents" was delivered with a knowing glint, a subtle acknowledgment that Julian had, indeed, spoken of her, and not in a superficial manner.

Lani, feeling a surge of confidence that Julian's presence seemed to amplify, met his gaze.

"Thank you, Mr. Sterling. It's a pleasure to meet you as well. Julian has been a most gracious host."

The slight emphasis on "gracious host" was her own subtle acknowledgment of his attentiveness.

Julian's smile widened. A genuine expression that Lani was beginning to cherish. He placed a hand on her arm, his touch light yet firm, a silent signal of shared understanding.

"Lani's insights have been invaluable to me, Arthur," he stated, his gaze never leaving Lani's. "She possesses a grounding perspective that is often missing in my own world."

The words, casual as they were, resonated deeply with Lani. He wasn't just acknowledging her presence; he was validating her and her experiences, her very essence, in front of his influential peers.

The sentiment wasn't lost on Arthur Sterling. He nodded thoughtfully, his expression one of genuine interest.

"A grounding perspective? That is indeed a rare and valuable commodity. Especially in circles like these. One can easily lose sight of what truly matters when caught in the whirlwind of ambition." He turned his attention back to Lani, his eyes holding a newfound respect. "I can see why Julian values your company, Ms. Shepard."

As Julian continued to navigate the room, introducing Lani to a succession of important individuals from a renowned art curator to a prominent philanthropist and even a leading figure in technological innovation.

Each introduction was a carefully crafted affirmation. He didn't simply point her out; he presented her. He shared small anecdotes, sometimes about her work, sometimes about her character, weaving a narrative that painted her not as a mere plus-one, but as an integral part of his world.

To the art curator, Ms. Genevieve Dubois, Julian spoke of Lani's discerning eye for beauty, her innate understanding of form and balance, and her ability to find artistry in the unexpected.

"Lani has a remarkable ability to see the soul of things, Genevieve," he'd said, his hand resting lightly on Lani's shoulder. "It's a talent I've long admired."

Genevieve, a woman whose sharp eyes missed nothing, gave Lani a knowing look.

"The soul of things," she mused, her voice a low purr. "A rare gift indeed. Mr. Vance, you have impeccable taste not only in art, but in people as well."

The philanthropic leader, Mr. Davidson, was told about Lani's quiet dedication to her community, her commitment to nurturing growth, both in her bakery and in her personal endeavors.

Julian spoke of her tireless work ethic and the profound satisfaction she derived from creating something tangible and beautiful. Mr. Davidson, a man known for his pragmatism, was visibly impressed.

"A woman who builds with her hands and her heart," he commented, extending a hand to Lani. "Such dedication is the bedrock of any true progress, Ms. Shepard. You are an inspiration."

"Indeed, she is," Julian agreed, giving Lani a secret smile.

With each encounter, Lani felt less like an interloper and more like a valued companion. Julian's subtle gestures were orchestrating a symphony of acceptance. A gentle squeeze of her arm as a particularly probing question was posed by an inquisitive guest, a reassuring smile when she paused, searching for the right words, a shared glance that communicated volumes of unspoken encouragement.

These were not the grand romantic gestures of a public proposal, but the intricate, understated courtship of a man who understood the power of quiet affirmation.

Julian shot her a sidelong glance as the guest he had just introduced her to drone on.

"Remind me to never take culinary advice from a man who thinks champagne pairs with chili."

Lani bit back a laugh, and their eyes met. A spark of shared humor that said more than words.

He never monopolized her time, understanding that she needed space to breathe and observe. But he also ensured she was never adrift. He would subtly steer conversations towards topics he knew she could contribute to, drawing her out without making her feel spotlighted.

There was a moment, as they stood by a magnificent floral arrangement that seemed to spill from a crystal urn, when Julian turned to her, his expression thoughtful.

"Are you comfortable, Lani?" he asked, his voice a low rumble that cut through the ambient noise. "This is a lot, I know. But I wanted you to see this. To be part of it."

Lani met his gaze, her heart softening. "I'm more than comfortable, Julian. I'm fascinated. And grateful. Thank you for including me."

He reached out, his fingers brushing lightly against her cheek, a touch so fleeting it might have been a figment of her imagination.

"You belong here, Lani," he said, his eyes holding hers. "As much as anyone."

It was a declaration, veiled in a simple statement of fact. He was telling her, in his own quiet way, that she was not just a guest, but an equal, a partner in his present, and perhaps, his future.

Lani felt her breath catch at his words, the sincerity in them wrapping around her like warmth on a cold night. For a heartbeat, she couldn't look away from him or from the earnestness in his eyes, from the quiet strength behind his touch.

She managed a soft smile, her voice steady but laced with emotion.

"I'm not sure I belong here, Julian," she said gently. "But standing here with you... it feels like I could."

Julian's expression softened, the corners of his mouth curving into that faint, knowing smile that always seemed to undo her. His hand lingered just long enough for her to feel the steady warmth of it before he drew it back, the connection between them humming in the space left behind.

"You were never missing, Lani," he said quietly. "Maybe just waiting to be found again."

The words hung between them, delicate and intimate, like the last notes of a familiar melody. Around them, the gala moved on with laughter, clinking glasses and the soft swell of music. But it all felt distant, blurred by the gravity of that moment.

Lani swallowed, her pulse fluttering.

"You always did know what to say," she murmured, a hint of a smile tugging at her lips. "Even when I didn't want to hear it."

Julian chuckled softly, the sound rich and low.

"I don't know about that," he replied. "I just know what I mean — and I mean this. You're part of my story, Lani. You always have been."

Her eyes shimmered, reflecting the golden light from the chandeliers above. Something inside her shifted. The quiet acknowledgment of how deeply she had missed this: the easy honesty between them, the way he looked at her as if she were the only one in the room.

She drew in a breath, steadying herself.

"Then maybe," she said softly, "it's time we stopped pretending our stories don't overlap."

Julian's gaze deepened, a quiet promise glimmering there.

"I'd like that," he said. "More than you know."

An important delegation had arrived. He turned to Lani. "Stay here for a moment," he instructed, his voice soft.

"I'll be back as soon as I can. Don't let anyone corner you into talking about bread unless you want to."

A playful glint danced in his eyes. "Though," he added, a hint of a smile playing on his lips, "I suspect you can hold your own in any conversation."

{ 16 }

Lani

He was gone for only a few minutes, but during that time, Lani felt a subtle shift in the atmosphere around her. Guests who had previously offered polite but distant smiles now approached with a more direct, curious interest. They had seen her with Julian, had heard his introductions, had witnessed the quiet way he attended to her. They understood, on some unspoken level, that she was more than just a pretty face on his arm.

A distinguished-looking woman, Mrs. Albright, who Lani recognized from a brief introduction earlier, approached her with a warm smile. "Ms. Shepard," she began, her voice carrying a gentle authority. "Julian is a remarkable man, isn't he? And it's refreshing to see him with someone who clearly brings him such joy."

The observation, delivered with a genuine smile, was a testament to Julian's own outward display of affection. He wasn't hiding his regard for Lani; he was subtly showcasing it.

Lani felt a blush creep up her neck, but she met Mrs. Albright's gaze with a steady smile. "He is," Lani agreed softly. "And I'm very fortunate to be here tonight."

Mrs. Albright nodded. "He mentioned you run a bakery. It's in town, is it? I've always admired that kind of dedication. To create something with your own hands, from the ground up." Her eyes scanned Lani's elegant gown, then returned to her face. "You look... radiant."

The compliment, like so many others, felt more substantial tonight. It wasn't just about her dress or her appearance. It was about the entire package, the woman Julian was presenting to the world, the woman he clearly admired.

"Thank you, Mrs. Albright. It's actually my parents' bakery. It's been in the family for three generations. I've worked hard to bring it up to date. And it brings me a great deal of happiness."

Julian returned, a subtle smile gracing his lips as he overheard the tail end of their conversation. He offered Mrs. Albright a polite nod of acknowledgment and then turned his full attention to Lani.

"I hope you weren't being subjected to too much interrogation, Lani?" he inquired, a touch of concern in his voice.

Lani shook her head, a genuine smile blooming on her face. "Not at all, Julian. Mrs. Albright was just being kind." She met his gaze, her own eyes conveying a depth of gratitude. "And I'm very happy to be by your side."

His thumb brushed lightly against her hand, a silent acknowledgment of her words. "The feeling is entirely mutual," he murmured, his voice barely audible above the noise.

It was a simple statement, but in the context of the evening, of his introductions, of his attentiveness, it was a profound declaration.

Julian Vance was laying his heart, in his own understated way, at Lani's feet. The ballroom, with its glittering chandeliers and influential guests, had become the grand stage for his quiet, yet undeniable, pursuit.

The polite chatter and the clinking of glasses had settled into a comfortable hum, a testament to the success of Julian's soirée. Lani had navigated the labyrinth of introductions with surprising ease, Julian's steady presence acting as her anchor.

Each conversation, each shared glance, had woven a tapestry of connection between them, stronger and more intricate than she could have ever imagined.

She found herself watching him, observing the effortless way he commanded attention, the genuine warmth he extended to each guest, and a quiet pride bloomed within her. He was a force, a presence that both commanded respect and invited admiration, and to be by his side, to be *seen* by him, felt like a privilege.

As the evening began to subtly shift gears, a new melody unfurled from the orchestra, a slow, languid waltz that seemed to exhale romance into the very air.

The music swelled behind them, a slow and melodic rhythm and without another word, he extended his hand.

She turned, her breath catching as Julian stood before her, his eyes, those deep, thoughtful pools, holding hers with an intensity that made her pulse quicken.

He offered her a smile, a gentle curve of his lips that held a world of unspoken understanding. In his hand, he held a single, perfect white rose, its petals unfurling like a silent vow.

"Lani," he began, his voice a low, resonant timbre that seemed to vibrate through her very being. "Would you do me the honor of this dance?"

The invitation was simple, yet it carried the weight of a thousand unspoken sentiments.

Lani's heart gave a joyful leap. She hadn't danced since... well, since they were younger, before life had pulled them in separate directions. The memory of those stolen moments, of clumsy steps and breathless laughter, flickered through her mind.

"Julian," she replied, her voice a little softer than she intended, a tremor of anticipation running through it. She accepted the rose, her fingers brushing against his, a jolt of awareness shooting up her arm.

"I would be honored."

He extended his hand, his palm open, a silent offering of strength and support. Lani placed her own hand in his, the warmth of his skin a familiar, comforting sensation. As their fingers intertwined, a silent acknowledgment passed between them. It was more than just a greeting; it was a reunion of souls, a tangible connection that transcended the years and miles that had separated them.

The music seemed to slow as Julian led her toward the center of the dance floor. His movements were graceful. The crowd around them blurred into a soft haze of color and motion, shimmering gowns, muted laughter and the glint of crystal under golden light. But for Lani, there was only the steady rhythm of Julian's heartbeat as his hand found the small of her back.

His touch was confident and gentle. A wordless reassurance that she was safe here, that this moment belonged to them alone.

"It's been a while since we've done this," she said softly, a smile ghosting across her lips.

"You still move like you remember how," he murmured, his breath brushing against her temple.

She laughed, the sound low and genuine. "I think that's because you're doing all the work."

"Hardly," he said, smiling down at her. "You make it look effortless."

They swayed together, the rhythm carrying them through the space like an echo of something long lost but never forgotten. Lani could feel the tension of the evening, the uncertainty, the careful boundaries, melting away with each turn. The scent of his cologne mixed with the faint sweetness of orchids nearby, stirring up memories she'd thought time had buried.

When she finally looked up at him, his gaze was steady, unguarded.

"You look happy," he said quietly. "Really happy. I didn't realize how much I missed seeing that."

Her heart fluttered. "I didn't realize how much I missed being seen," she admitted.

Julian's fingers tightened slightly against hers, his expression softening with something like reverence.

"I see you, Lani," he said simply. "Not the dress, not the moment — *you*. The same woman who once made the best peach pie in the county and still managed to beat me at every card game."

She laughed again, her head falling briefly against his shoulder. "You let me win half the time."

"Not once," he said, smiling. "I just liked watching you celebrate."

They moved in quiet harmony as the song shifted into something slower, more intimate. The world outside that moment ceased to exist. Every worry she'd carried about fitting in, about reopening old wounds. It all dissolved in the warmth of his closeness.

And when the music finally began to fade, neither of them stepped back.

"You make it hard to leave," Lani whispered, almost to herself.

Julian's thumb traced a slow circle against her hand, his voice low and certain.

"Then don't," he said. "Not yet. Stay a little longer. Just be here with me."

Lani lifted her gaze, meeting the deep sincerity in his eyes. The air between them hummed, tender, fragile, full of all the words they hadn't yet dared to speak.

And as the orchestra began the next song, she found herself smiling. Not with hesitation this time, but with quiet, full-hearted acceptance.

"All right," she whispered. "A little longer."

Julian's answering smile was soft, but it reached his eyes. And as he drew her close once more, guiding her into the next dance, it felt less like a beginning and more like a homecoming. Two souls finding their way back to the same rhythm after far too long apart.

He drew her closer, his arm encircling her waist, his touch firm yet tender. Lani placed her hand on his shoulder, the fabric of his impeccably tailored jacket, a familiar texture beneath her fingertips.

As they began to move, a sense of effortless synchronicity flowed between them. Their bodies remembered the rhythm. The dance was slow and unhurried, allowing a carefree stillness to settle around them.

In Julian's arms, Lani felt a sense of peace wash over her. The anxieties and uncertainties of the evening, the weight of her unexpected return into his orbit, all seemed to dissipate like mist under the morning sun.

Here, in this suspended moment, surrounded by the soft glow of the chandeliers and the hushed reverence of the music, she felt utterly and completely present. It was a feeling she hadn't realized she'd been missing, a sense of belonging that resonated deep within her core. She could dance in his arms all night.

Julian's blue gaze remained fixed on hers, and in those depths, she saw not the famous chef but the boy she had once known.

There was a vulnerability there, a tenderness that softened the edges of his sophisticated demeanor. He didn't speak, and neither did she, but a silent conversation unfolded between them. It was a language of shared glances, of subtle shifts in posture, of the almost imperceptible tightening of his embrace.

His thumb traced slow, soothing circles on her back, a gesture so intimate it sent shivers down her spine. Lani found herself leaning into him, her head resting lightly against his chest, the steady beat of his heart a comforting rhythm against her ear.

The music swelled mirrored the emotions swirling within her. It was a bittersweet melody, a reflection of their shared history. The joy of their youthful infatuation, the ache of their separation, and the unexpected tenderness of their reunion. Each note seemed to evoke a memory, a phantom echo of laughter, a whisper of shared dreams.

She remembered dancing like this in the moonlit gardens of her childhood home, his arms around her, the world a blur of youthful innocence and boundless possibility. Back then, their worries were few, their futures unwritten. Now, the years had etched their lines onto their faces and had brought them both challenges and triumphs. Yet, as they swayed together, those differences seemed to melt away, leaving only the pure, unadulterated connection that had always existed between them.

Julian's hand moved from her waist to gently cup her jaw, tilting her head so their eyes met again. His gaze was intense, filled with a depth of emotion that made her breath hitch.

"You look beautiful, Lani," he murmured, his voice a low rumble that vibrated against her cheek. "Even more beautiful than I remembered."

The compliment, so simple, so sincere, struck her with a force she hadn't anticipated. She felt a blush creep up her neck, a testament to the lingering shyness that still resided within her, despite the confidence Julian had so carefully nurtured.

"Thank you, Julian," she whispered, her voice thick with unshed tears. "You... you haven't changed either. Not the important parts, anyway."

He smiled, a genuine, heartfelt expression that reached his eyes. "Some things," he said, his gaze softening, "are worth preserving. Worth returning to."

The unspoken words hung heavily in the air between them: *us.* He was acknowledging the enduring pull, the undeniable thread that had connected them for so long. It wasn't just nostalgia; it was a recognition of a foundational bond, a truth that had persisted through time and distance.

As they continued to dance, Lani felt an intense sense of gratitude wash over her. Gratitude for Julian's persistent belief in her, for his unwavering support, and for this unexpected moment of grace. He brought her into his world, introduced her to his esteemed colleagues, had made her feel not just accepted, but valued.

And now, he was sharing this intimate dance, a silent affirmation of the deep affection that had clearly grown between them.

The music began to slow, the final notes weaving a tender, lingering farewell. Julian's embrace tightened almost imperceptibly as they completed their final turn, bringing them to a gentle halt. He held her for a moment longer, not releasing her immediately, as if wanting to prolong the intimacy of the shared space.

Lani could feel the warmth of his chest against hers, the steady rhythm of his breathing.

When he finally released her, his hands lingering on her waist for a beat longer than necessary, Lani felt a sense of pleasant disorientation. The world around them slowly reasserted itself. The gentle hum of conversation returned. But the quiet world they had escaped to on the dance floor lingered.

He still held the white rose he had offered her, its petals now slightly brushed from their embrace. He raised it to her; his eyes filled with tender amusement.

"This," he said, his voice low and intimate, "is just a small token. A reminder."

Lani accepted the rose, its coolness a stark contrast to the warmth that still radiated from her skin. She brought it to her nose and inhaled its delicate fragrance. "A reminder of what?" she asked softly, her gaze meeting his.

A hint of a smile played on his lips. "Of potential," he said, his eyes twinkling. "Of music. Of moments like these." He paused, his expression growing more serious.

"And perhaps," he added, his voice barely a whisper, "of new beginnings."

The word hung in the air, a promise and a question all at once.

New Beginnings.

The words vibrated deeply within Lani, echoing the sense of possibility that had been stirring within her since her arrival. She looked at Julian, at the man who had so deftly arranged this evening, who had shown her such unwavering kindness and respect. She saw not just the powerful businessman, but the sensitive, thoughtful man who had once stolen her heart.

"New Beginnings," she echoed, a soft smile gracing her lips.

As she held the rose, its petals a pristine white against the backdrop of the glittering ballroom, Lani knew, with the certainty that settled deep within her soul, that this was not an ending, but a beautiful new chapter.

As the final notes of the song melted into the hum of conversation, Julian felt Lani's hand still resting in his, her warmth grounding him more than the applause rippling through the ballroom ever could. For a long moment, neither of them moved. It was as if the rest of the room, the lights, the people, the glittering spectacle, had receded to the edge of their awareness.

He leaned down slightly, his voice brushing against her ear. "Come with me," he murmured. "It's too warm in here."

Lani nodded, her pulse skipping. His hand slid from her waist to her fingers, guiding her through the maze of silk gowns and tuxedos, through a pair of glass doors that opened to a quiet terrace bathed in the soft glow of string lights.

Outside on the balcony, the night was still and cool, carrying the faint scent of pine and distant snow. The evening lights shimmered below like fallen stars, but all Julian saw was her and the way the soft breeze teased a few strands of her hair loose, the way her cheeks were flushed from dancing.

"It's beautiful," she whispered, folding her arms lightly against the chill.

Julian slipped off his jacket without a word and draped it over her shoulders.

"You always did love the cold," he said, his tone touched with quiet affection. "I remember you used to stand outside the bakery in December just to watch the snow fall."

She laughed softly, the sound mingling with the night air. "I still do. Old habits, I guess."

"Some habits are worth keeping," he said, his eyes lingering on her face.

The silence that followed wasn't awkward. It was charged, full of unspoken memories and everything they hadn't yet dared to admit.

Julian noticed the sprig of mistletoe hanging just above them, its green leaves and white berries catching the soft glow of the terrace lights. A slow, knowing smile touched his lips.

He stepped closer, the faint scent of vanilla and sugar clinging to her like something familiar and utterly irresistible.

"Lani," he said quietly, tilting his chin upward. "Look."

Lani followed his gaze. When she saw it, her eyes widened just slightly, the soft light catching the luminous depths of her gaze.

"Lani..." he began, his voice a low murmur. "I don't want to make this complicated. I just..."

She looked up, her eyes luminous in the soft light. "It's already complicated, Julian," she said gently. "It always has been."

He smiled faintly. "Maybe. But right now, it doesn't feel that way."

Her breath caught as he reached up, his fingertips brushing the edge of her jaw. The touch was hesitant at first, reverent, as though he were memorizing her all over again. She tilted her head slightly, and that small motion, that unspoken invitation, was all he needed.

Julian closed the distance between them, his lips finding hers with a tenderness that was both new and achingly familiar. The kiss was slow, deliberate. A careful rediscovery rather than a claim.

Her hands lifted to his chest, fingers curling into the fabric of his shirt as if to steady herself against the rush of emotion.

When they finally drew apart, their foreheads rested together, breaths mingling in the cool night air.

"That," Julian whispered, a faint smile curving his lips, "was long overdue."

Lani's answering laugh trembled with emotion. "You always did have terrible timing," she teased softly.

"Maybe," he said, brushing a stray brunette curl from her cheek, "but I'm hoping this time... I got it right."

She looked at him for a long moment, really looked, and then, with quiet certainty that surprised even her, she nodded.

"I think you did."

They stood there, wrapped in silence and the warmth of shared history, as snow began to fall. It was soft, unexpected, and perfect. The world beyond the terrace faded until there were only the two of them, and the promise of something real taking shape between them once more.

The dance under the starlight, though indoors, had been a celestial event. She felt breathless, not from the exertion of the dance, but from the sheer, overwhelming depth of emotion that Julian's presence. His words, spoken and unspoken, had awakened something within her.

With his kiss, it felt like a homecoming, like finding a missing piece, of a future that suddenly seemed luminous with promise.

{ 17 }

Lani

The morning after the gala dawned with a gentle, persistent light, coaxing Lani from the lingering tendrils of sleep. The first rays of dawn, shy and hesitant, crept through the familiar lace curtains of her childhood bedroom. Lani blinked, the softness of the light a stark contrast to the dazzling opulence of the previous night.

Her thoughts lingered on Julian, the music, and the hushed intimacy of their dance. The emerald gown draped over her vanity chair was a silent testimony to the magic that had unfolded. It felt like a vivid, intoxicating dream, but the subtle ache in her feet and the lingering scent of the white rose on her nightstand confirmed its reality.

She swung her legs out of bed, her feet sinking into the plush, faded rug. The room was exactly as she'd left it, a time capsule of her youth. The worn teddy bear on the shelf, the framed photographs of her parents, the stack of well-loved books. They were all comforting anchors to a life that now seemed a world away.

But last night, last night had been different. Last night, Julian had been there, not as a world-famous chef, but as the boy who had once made her heart flutter with a single glance. His eyes, in the soft glow of the ballroom, held a depth of emotion that thrilled and unnerved her. The way he had looked at her, the way he had held her, it had stirred a potent cocktail of exhilaration and apprehension within her.

After Julian left her, she moved to the city. When her art career didn't even get off the ground, she found a job in an office and focused on graphs and numbers. It kept her fed and a roof over her head. When Marc strolled into her life, she knew she could never love anyone as much as she loved Julian. But she took the chance.

Look where that got her. She moved on, but there was always something missing. Marc was a good man at the beginning. He just loved her more than she loved him and it turned bitter. Without Naomi, her life would have been worthless.

She walked over to the window and pulled back the curtain to reveal the quiet street below. It was a picture of serene normalcy. It was so unlike the glittering spectacle of the previous evening.

Lani traced the pattern on the windowpane, her mind replaying fragments of the night. Julian's hand, warm and firm, as it had cupped her jaw.

His murmured compliment, "You look beautiful, Lani. Even more beautiful than I remembered." The sincerity in his voice had been disarming, stirring a blush that she hadn't felt in years. And then there was his offer of the rose, his words, "And perhaps of beginnings."

The implication had hung in the air, a delicate thread of possibility spun between them. She felt a warmth that came not from the air, but from a sudden hope for a future she had never imagined.

She remembered the sheer ease with which she had fallen back into his orbit. It was as if their years apart had been mere seconds, a brief interlude before they had naturally gravitated back towards each other.

He had introduced her to his colleagues, not as an afterthought, but with a clear pride, a subtle possessiveness that had made her heart swell. He had seen her, truly seen her, not just the baker from the small town, but the woman she had become.

And in his eyes, she had seen a flicker of the boy who had once confessed his deepest secrets under the stars, a boy who had believed in her dreams with an unwavering faith.

The weight of it all settled upon her as she turned from the window.

The gala had been a whirlwind, a dazzling display of Julian's world. But it was the quiet moments, the stolen glances, the almost imperceptible squeeze of his hand that had truly resonated. He had managed to weave a spell, a subtle enchantment that had left her feeling both cherished and utterly bewildered.

The life she had so carefully constructed, so proudly maintained, felt suddenly incomplete. The bakery's routine-the familiar rhythm of her days-now seemed to pale in comparison to the vibrant, intoxicating possibility that Julian represented.

She walked to the emerald gown, her fingers brushing its cool, smooth fabric. Last night, in its embrace, she had felt like a different, more sophisticated woman. But in the morning light, the familiar Lani reasserted herself-the baker who knew the scent of a perfectly baked cupcake-though even she felt subtly changed by the encounter.

The apprehension she felt wasn't a fear of Julian, but a fear of what he had awakened within her. A yearning for something more, something she hadn't realized she'd lost, or perhaps had never truly found.

The memory of his touch, the way his arm had encircled her waist, sent a cascade of shivers through her. She could almost still feel his hands on her. It had been a gesture of possession, yes, but also of protection, of a deep, unspoken tenderness. He had held her as if she were made of spun glass.

And she, in turn, had leaned into him, finding a solace, a sense of belonging, that had surprised her with its intensity. The world outside their dance had faded into a soft, indistinct hum, leaving only the two of them, suspended in a moment that felt both ancient and brand new.

Julian's words, "Some things are worth preserving. Worth returning to," echoed in her mind. He had said them with such quiet conviction, his gaze unwavering.

It was a declaration, a silent acknowledgment of the enduring bond between them. It wasn't just about nostalgia for their shared youth; it was a recognition of a fundamental truth that had persisted through the years, reinforced with every shared glance, every stolen moment at the gala.

Lani felt a tremor of excitement, a nascent hope that perhaps, just perhaps, this was more than a fleeting encounter.

She remembered the weight of his gaze as he'd handed her the rose. "A reminder," he'd said, his voice a low, resonant murmur that had sent a thrill through her. His eyes had twinkled with a knowing amusement, "of beginnings." The word had settled in her heart like a promise, a soft whisper of a future she hadn't dared to dream of.

The sheer audacity of it, the possibility of a new beginning with Julian, made her breath catch in her throat.

But then, reality began to assert itself and she heard Naomi bound up the stairs.

"Mommy!" Naomi called out as she pounced on the bed.

"Morning, Sweet Pea. Did you have fun last night with Grandma and Grandpa?"

"Oh yes, Mommy," she exclaimed. Grandpa let me stay up late and Grandma let me have hot chocolate with whipped cream before bed." She quickly covered her mouth. "Opps ,that was a secret," she whispered.

"A secret, huh?" Lani couldn't really blame her parents. After being apart for so long, they deserved some time to spoil Naomi..

"Did you dance like Cinderella last night?" Her eyes were bright and well aware of Lani's exhaustion.

"I did. I had a wonderful time," she replied. "But now it's time to get you to school and me to the bakery."

Christmas break was coming quickly and Lani had a lot of work she needed to get ahead of before Naomi would be in the bakery full-time.

Naomi ran out of the room to get dressed. Lani turned to her nightstand and picked up the white rose, its petals cool and soft against her fingertips. It was a fragile thing, yet it held the promise of something substantial, something enduring.

Julian had a way of making promises feel real, of imbuing even the most casual of gestures with profound meaning. She had always known he was destined for great things, that he would shape the world around him. But she had never imagined that she would be a part of that shaping, a recipient of his attention, a contender for his affections.

Lani closed her eyes, trying to recapture the feeling of being in his arms. The quiet strength of his hold, the steady beat of his heart against her ear, the sense of absolute safety and belonging. It was a feeling she hadn't realized she'd been craving, a void she hadn't known existed until Julian had filled it. He had a way of making her feel seen, valued, and cherished, in a way that went beyond anything she had ever experienced.

Lani closed her eyes, trying to recapture the feeling of being in his arms: the quiet strength of his hold, the beat of his heart, the sense of safety and belonging. She hadn't realized she'd been craving such a feeling until Julian filled that void. He had a way of making her feel seen, valued, and cherished beyond anything she had known.

Julian's presence in her life had stirred the embers of a past love, and now, they were beginning to glow with a renewed intensity.

The scent of the rose, delicate and sweet, filled the air. It was a reminder of their shared history, of the stolen glances and whispered confessions of their youth, but more importantly, it was a reminder of the present, of the undeniable connection that still existed between them.

She had gone to the gala wanting to support Julian. She left with something more profound--a heart full of hope and trepidation.

She walked towards her wardrobe, her gaze falling on her everyday clothes. The comfortable jeans, the soft sweaters, the practical aprons. They were the uniform of her life, a life she had accepted.

But now, a new possibility loomed, a possibility that involved emerald gowns and stolen dances. The thought sent a shiver of excitement through her, quickly followed by a wave of apprehension. Could she really be the woman who attracted Julian's attention, who inspired such a profound reaction in him?

She remembered the way he had looked at her when he'd said, "You haven't changed either, not the important parts, anyway." It had been a statement of recognition, an acknowledgment of the core of who she was, a core that he had always seen, even when she had doubted herself. That thought gave her strength. He saw something in her, something that had endured the passage of time, something that had perhaps even deepened.

Lani sighed, a soft sound that barely disturbed the quiet of the room.

The mundane reality of the bakery beckoned, the familiar routine a comforting, yet now somewhat stifling, presence. But the encounter with Julian had irrevocably altered her perspective. She couldn't unsee the intensity in his eyes, couldn't unfeel the electric current that had passed between them. He had reminded her of a part of herself she had long since buried, a part that yearned for passion, for connection, for a love that could transcend the ordinary.

She was no longer just Lani the baker or Lani the mother; she was Lani, a woman on the cusp of something new, something that had been waiting for her in the quiet corners of her heart, and in the intense gaze of a man from her past.

The path ahead was uncertain, shrouded in the morning mist, but for the first time in a long time, Lani felt a spark of anticipation, a deep-seated hope that the future, like Julian's smile, held a radiant promise.

{ **18** }

Lani

The remnants of their shared meal sat between them, a testament to the hours that had slipped away with an unnerving, yet welcome, ease. The diner, once a bustling hub of midday activity, had quieted, leaving them in a pocket of hushed intimacy. Julian swirled the remaining coffee in his mug, his gaze fixed on Lani, a thoughtful intensity in his blue eyes.

"You mentioned your divorce, that it was difficult," he began, his voice a low murmur, carefully devoid of judgment. "I can only imagine the weight that carries. Particularly after so many years of marriage. It's not an easy thing to disentangle one's life from another's."

Lani nodded, her fingers tracing the rim of her own mug.

The warmth of the ceramic was a small comfort against the sudden chill that traced its way down her spine.

"Difficult is an understatement, Julian," she confessed, her voice barely above a whisper. "It felt like the end of everything I'd ever known. My entire identity had been so intertwined with being a wife, with building a life *with* someone. When that dissolved, it felt like I was left with...

nothing. Just an empty space where a future was supposed to be."

She managed a wry smile, though it didn't quite reach her eyes. "And then, of course, there's the nagging question of 'what now?' I'm... I'm not entirely sure how to even begin to figure that out. The bakery is my passion, my solace, but it doesn't... it doesn't fill every void. The sheer uncertainty of it all can be paralyzing, to be honest."

Julian reached across the table, his hand covering hers for a brief, grounding moment. The touch was gentle, a silent acknowledgement of her vulnerability.

"I understand," he said softly. "The feeling of being adrift. Of having the roadmap you'd been following simply vanish. It can be terrifying. My own path has been different, of course. Less about building a shared life with one person, and more about navigating the often-treacherous currents of the corporate world."

He withdrew his hand, his gaze drifting back to his coffee. "The pressures are intense. Constant demands, relentless competition. And there's a pervasive sense of superficiality, at times. So many people, so many interactions, that feel devoid of genuine feelings. It can be incredibly isolating, even when you're surrounded by people."

Lani met his gaze, a sudden wave of empathy washing over her. He wasn't the powerful businessman, but a man wrestling with his own demons, with the existential weight of his success.

"It sounds like you've been carrying a heavy burden too," she said, her voice laced with genuine concern. "The expectations, the constant need to prove yourself. It must be exhausting."

"It is," he admitted with a sigh.

He paused, a shadow crossing his features. "I've often felt like I'm performing, rather than living. Playing a role that's expected of me, rather than truly being myself. It's a lonely existence, Lani. And it makes one wonder, after a while, what the point of it all is. What are you building towards when the foundations feel so unstable?"

The years had undeniably left their Marc, etching lines of experience and perhaps a touch of sorrow onto both their souls.

"It all makes it so difficult to trust. To believe that people see the real you, rather than the persona, the success."

"Julian," she began.

He quickly continued. "That's one of the things I admired about you, even all those years ago. You were always so authentic, so grounded, so... real. Even then." He offered a small, almost wistful smile. "I suppose that's why seeing you again. It was such a jolt. A reminder of a time when things felt simpler, perhaps more genuine."

The pain of their separation, the abruptness with which their youthful romance had been severed, still held a faint echo in the quiet of the diner.

"I often wondered what happened to you," Lani confessed, her voice softer now, more intimate. "After everything. It was a painful time. I

She looked down at her hands, the memory still sharp, still capable of drawing a faint ache from her heart.

"I tried to build a life, a good life, for myself. And I think, in many ways, I have. I wouldn't give up Naomi for the world. And the bakery has become my sanctuary. It's where I can feel a sense of purpose. But there are still moments."

"What kind of moments?" He asked.

"Moments when I feel the weight of what was lost."

Julian's gaze was steady, his eyes holding hers with a profound understanding.

"I carry my own share of regrets, Lani," he admitted, his voice low. "I made choices that I've had to live with. That we had to live with."

Lani blinked back the tears that were quickly welling up.

"And the way we parted," he sighed. "It was a wound that took a long time to heal. I was young, perhaps too proud, too consumed by my own ambitions. I didn't handle it with the grace it deserved. And I've regretted that, more than you know."

He paused, his thumb gently stroking the back of her hand, which rested on the table between them. "Seeing you last night, being with you Lani. It was like everything was set back into place. Perhaps some things, some connections, aren't meant to be entirely severed."

"The ghosts of the past, they're always there, aren't they?" She broke eye contact and stared at the chip in the corner of the table.

He leaned forward, grabbing her attention, his voice dropping to an even more intimate register.

"I don't know what the future holds, Lani. And I don't want to rush anything. I know you have Naomi to consider. But the conversation we're having now, this feeling of ease, of being able to talk about, and the present, with such honesty. This is rare. And it's something I don't want to dismiss lightly."

Her slight smile sent a flicker of hope to his heart.

"Our past doesn't have to dictate our present. Or our future. We can acknowledge them, learn from them, and then choose to move forward. To build something new," he said.

Lani felt a tremor of emotion run through her. Julian's words resonated deeply, touching upon the very fears and uncertainties that had been swirling within her. His acknowledgement of their shared past, of the pain that had marked their separation, was not a source of renewed hurt, but rather a gentle validation. It was as if he, too, had been carrying the weight of their history, and in acknowledging it, he was offering a pathway towards its release.

"That's... that's a beautiful way to put it," she said, her voice thick with emotion. "The ghosts... they can be so powerful. So overwhelming. It's easy to let them define you, to let them hold you back. I've certainly struggled with that. With the fear of making the same mistakes, of getting hurt again." She took a deep breath, the scent of coffee and pastries a comforting anchor in the swirling currents of her thoughts. "My divorce... it was a profound loss. And the process of rebuilding... it's been slow, arduous. There are days when I feel like I'm finally on solid ground, and then

there are days when the earth feels like it's crumbling beneath me."

She met his gaze, a newfound courage blossoming
within her. "But you're right, Julian. We can't let the past
dictate everything. And the connection I felt last night...
the conversation we're having now... it feels different. It
feels like an opportunity. A chance to... to explore. To see if
there's a way to weave the threads of our past into a new
tapestry, one that's not defined by what was lost, but by
what might still be found." She managed a small, genuine
smile. "It's a frightening prospect, but also... a deeply hopeful one."

Julian returned her smile, his eyes crinkling at the corners. "Hope," he echoed softly. "Yes. That's exactly it. A
cautious, hopeful search. It's not about erasing what came
before, Lani. It's about understanding how it has shaped us
and then deciding how we want to move forward. You've
built a beautiful life for yourself, Lani. A life filled with passion, with purpose, with tangible creation. And I... I'm still
searching for that sense of solid ground. That genuine connection that cuts through the noise."

He gestured around the diner, a subtle movement that
encompassed their shared space.

"This feels like a real step," Julian said softly. "Like we're
finally moving away from all the noise, the expectations,
the pretending and just... being here. Talking. Remembering. Seeing what's still between us."

He paused, his eyes searching hers. "I don't want to pre-
tend that our past doesn't exist, Lani. It does. It's a part of

who we are. It shaped us. But I also don't want it to stand in the way of what could come next. Maybe we can take what we had, the good parts, and build something new from it. Something honest. Something that lasts."

"This is a step, isn't it? A deliberate step away from the glamour and the expectations. A moment to simply... be. To talk. To remember.

The air between them seemed to hum with new energy, quiet anticipation. The conversation had shifted from re-counting past hurts to tentatively sketching out possibil-ities. It was a delicate dance, the careful navigation of shared history and present desires. The ghosts of their sep-aration, while acknowledged, no longer held the dominant presence they once had. Instead, a new narrative was be-ginning to unfurl, whispered in hushed tones over lukewarm coffee. A story of tentative hope and the quiet courage to embrace the unknown.

"It's... it's a lot to consider," Lani admitted, her voice laced with a mixture of trepidation and excitement. "The idea of being part of each other's lives again. It's a concept I haven't dared to entertain, even in my wildest dreams. Af-ter the divorce, I felt so fragile. So afraid of any kind of vulnerability. And yet..." She looked at Julian, a newfound clarity dawning in her eyes. "And yet, sitting here with you, talking like this... it doesn't feel fragile. It feels... strong. It feels like a possibility, not a threat."

Julian's expression softened, a genuine warmth radiating from him. "That's what I'm hoping for, Lani. That this feels like a possibility. Not a demand, not an obligation, but a gentle unfolding. You have a strength that I've always admired, a resilience that's evident in everything you do. And I... I've spent so long building walls, protecting myself from the world. Perhaps it's time to let some of those walls down. To see what lies beyond them. To see if, perhaps, there's a space for something real. Something... lasting."

He reached out again, this time his hand resting fully on hers, his thumb stroking slow, comforting circles. "Your bakery... it's a testament to your dedication, to your ability to create something beautiful and enduring from the simplest ingredients. I see that same potential, in us, Lani. In what we might build, if we're brave enough to try."

The weight of his words settled over her, not as a burden, but as a promise. The memory of their youthful love, once a painful reminder of what had been lost, now felt like a seed, dormant for years, finally beginning to stir beneath the surface.

The gala had been a dazzling spectacle, a grand reintroduction. But this quiet conversation, this intimate exploration of their shared past and uncertain future, felt like the true genesis. The journey ahead was undoubtedly filled with complications and lingering shadows of past disappointments, but for the first time in a long time, Lani felt a profound sense of hope. A hope that was not naive, not blind to the challenges, but a quiet, steady flame, kindled by the rekindled spark of a connection that refused to be extinguished. The whispers of 'what if' and 'maybe' that had danced on the edges of her consciousness were now taking center stage, not as anxieties, but as invitations. And she found herself, with a startling sense of conviction, ready to accept.

The afternoon sun cast long shadows as they left the diner, the conversation still flowing, the connection between them deepening with every shared word, every knowing glance. Julian's thoughtful breakfast had been more than just a meal; it had been an affirmation, a quiet declaration of interest, and a gentle step forward on a path that Lani was beginning to realize she wanted to explore.

*****

The clatter of dishes and the murmur of conversations had faded into a comfortable hum by the time Lani and Julian finally rose from their booth. The late afternoon sun cast long shadows across the diner's checkered floor, a golden light that seemed to bless the tentative peace they had found. As they stepped out into the crisp air, the familiar silhouette of Naomi's bright yellow backpack was a welcome sight, perched on the steps outside the bakery. Her daughter was meticulously rearranging a display of sugared violets, her brow furrowed in concentration.

"Mommy! You're back!" Naomi's face lit up, her earlier pout dissolving like sugar in warm tea. She scampered down the steps, her questions tumbling out in a rush. "Did you have fun? Did you talk to... um... the man from the bakery?" She pointed a small, flour-dusted finger in the general direction Julian had been standing. "The one with the really pretty blue eyes? He dropped off those yummy little cookies, remember?"

Lani's heart gave a small, unbidden leap. Julian. Even the mention of his name sent a ripple of warmth through her. She knelt to meet Naomi's enthusiastic gaze, her smile genuine. "Yes, sweetie, that was Julian. And we did talk."

She chose her words carefully, seeking a balance between honesty and the gentle unfolding that Julian had spoken of. "He's... he was a very special friend of mine from a long, long time ago. And we're getting to know each other again, now that we've found each other again."

Naomi's eyes widened, a spark of curiosity igniting within them. "A long time ago? Like, when you were a kid?" she asked, her voice laced with the wide-eyed wonder of a child who had just discovered a secret passage. "You said you used to play together?"

Lani chuckled, the sound light and easy. "Something like that," she conceded, avoiding the more complicated truth of stolen kisses behind the old oak tree and handwritten love letters tucked into shared textbooks. "

We were young, and friends. And then we lost touch for many years. And now... well, now we're reconnecting."

She watched Naomi's reaction, bracing herself for a barrage of questions about Julian and his personal life. At this age, Naomi had no filter. But her focus was blessedly and wonderfully simple.

"So, he's a baker too?" Naomi asked, her gaze drifting back to the elaborate gingerbread house displayed in the bakery window. Julian had commissioned a miniature mas terpiece for the Christmas season years ago. It still stood, a testament to his appreciation for the craft, even if it wasn't his own creation.

"Because those cookies he brought, they were *so* good. The little swirls he made on top, they looked like tiny waves. Did you see the gingerbread house! It had so many windows! Did he build that one?"

Lani felt a wave of relief wash over her. Naomi's innocent focus on Julian's culinary connection provided a safe harbor for Lani to discuss with him, to share details without feeling exposed or vulnerable. It was a familiar landscape, built on flour, sugar, and the shared language of baking.

Lani laughed, "He's not a baker in the same way I am, sweetie," Lani explained, "he has a very important job that involves a lot of numbers and planning. But he loves good food and beautiful creations. He's very artistic, you know? He is very creative."

She gestured towards the gingerbread house, its intricate details still holding their charm. "He ordered that gingerbread house, Naomi. He gave me the design idea, and we worked together to bring it to life.

"He has a good imagination when it comes to those kinds of things, huh Mommy?"

"Yes, he does, sweet pea, he was telling me about some of the things he used to bake when he was younger, and how much he enjoyed it. He said he used to make elaborate gingerbread villages. Can you imagine? Whole villages made of gingerbread!"

Naomi's eyes sparkled. "Gingerbread villages? Wow! Like a whole town? Did they have little gingerbread people?" she breathed, her imagination already running wild. "Did they have gingerbread cars?"

Lani laughed. "I'm sure they had all sorts of things! He told me about how he used to spend hours on them, making them look just right. That's part of what makes him so good at his job."

She glanced at Julian, who had been standing off to the side and listening patiently. A faint smile played on his lips. His presence, so close and yet so unobtrusive, felt like a comforting anchor. "He said he even made a gingerbread replica of a famous landmark once. I forget which one, but it was apparently very impressive."

"Which landmark?" Naomi pressed, hopping from one foot to the other with eagerness. "Was it a castle?"

"He didn't say, but I suspect it was something grand," Lani replied, feeling a lightness she hadn't experienced in years.

Discussing Julian through the lens of his past baking adventures and Naomi's innocent questions felt natural and easy. It was as if the shared love of creation had bridged the years and the unspoken complications. It felt like they created a simple, understandable connection.

"He has a real passion for it, even though his work is different now. He still uses his skills to make something beautiful from scratch. He was telling me how much he liked the way the icing was piped to look like snow, and the little sugar pearls he insisted on having around the windows."

Julian stepped forward, his voice a warm baritone that blended seamlessly with their conversation. "It was quite the project, wasn't it, Lani? I remember giving you that sketch, and you immediately understood my vision. You were able to turn an idea into something tangible, something delicious and beautiful. It is truly remarkable.

He looked at Naomi, his blue eyes crinkling at the corners. "Your mother makes the most wonderful cakes, Naomi. And her cookies are almost as good as the ones I used to make when I was a boy."

Naomi giggled, a sound of pure delight. "Almost?" she echoed, a playful challenge in her tone. "Are you saying you make better cookies than my mom?"

Julian chuckled, a deep, resonant sound. "When I was young, maybe. But your mother has had many more years of practice, and she's incredibly talented. I'm sure she's surpassed my childhood efforts by a long shot. I do, however, remember being rather proud of my gingerbread castles. They had quite elaborate turrets, if I recall correctly."

"Castles?" Naomi's eyes widened further. "Wow! Did you have moats?"

"Indeed," Julian confirmed with a twinkle in his eye. "And drawbridges that actually worked, or at least, they worked for a little while before the royal gingerbread knights decided to test their structural integrity."

Naomi looked confused for a moment then seemed to shrug it away.

Lani watched the exchange, a soft smile gracing her lips. It was surreal, and yet wonderfully grounding, to see

Julian interact with Naomi. There was such an easy camaraderie blooming between them. Naomi's uncomplicated curiosity had provided the perfect entry point, a way for Lani to acknowledge Julian's presence in her life without going into a deeper discussion about their rekindled romance.

"He has a very good memory for detail," Lani said, her voice light, as she addressed Naomi. "He remembers things from a long time ago. He remembers the gingerbread villages he used to make, and he remembers how much he liked the way I decorated that house for him. It's nice when people remember those things, isn't it? It makes you feel like you've made an impression."

"It does," Julian agreed, his gaze meeting Lani's.

There was a depth in his eyes, a shared understanding that passed between them, unspoken but profound. "And you, Lani, have always made a profound impression. On everyone you meet, I imagine. But especially on those of us who were lucky enough to know you when we were younger." He turned his attention back to Naomi.

"Your mother has a special gift, Naomi. She can create beauty and joy with her hands. It's something I've always admired."

Naomi beamed, clearly pleased with the praise for her mother, and perhaps a little flattered by Julian's attention. "She makes the best cupcakes too!" She declared, her loyalty to her mother's baking evident. "With the swirly icing!"

"Ah, yes, the swirly icing," Julian mused, a fond smile gracing his lips. "A signature design, wouldn't you say? He turned to Lani, his expression softening. "It's wonderful to see you so happy, Lani. The bakery is a reflection of that happiness, I think. It's so welcoming."

Lani felt a blush creep up her neck. His words, so sincere and gentle, had a way of disarming her, of easing the lingering anxieties she had carried for so long.

"Thank you, Julian," she murmured, meeting his gaze. "It's... it's my passion. It's what I love to do. And it's been a journey, coming back here, this life."

"A journey that's clearly been filled with creativity and dedication," he replied, his voice a warm rumble. "And seeing you now, Lani." He paused, a subtle shift in his tone. "You mentioned earlier how difficult your divorce was. To find your footing again and to create something new. You've done that beautifully." He raised a hand to touch her. But dropped it quickly as his eyes flickered toward Naomi.

Naomi, having seemingly absorbed all the relevant information about Julian's culinary history, now shifted her attention to a loose thread on her backpack.

"Can we get ice cream after this, Mom?" she asked, her voice laced with the hopeful optimism of a child who knew that dessert was often the reward for a day's good behavior.

Lani smiled, a genuine, unforced smile that reached her eyes. "Of course, sweetie," she said, relief washing over her once more.

The conversation had been perfectly navigated. Julian had been introduced, his connection to her past acknowledged, his character subtly highlighted through shared interests and Naomi's innocent questions. It had been an easy conversation that could easily have been filled with the weight of years and unspoken emotions.

"Ice cream sounds like a wonderful idea," Julian chimed in, his tone warm and agreeable. "Perhaps a strawberry swirl for Naomi, and for Lani a classic vanilla, or maybe something a little more adventurous?" He looked at Lani, a playful question in his eyes.

Lani's heart fluttered. The simple act of choosing ice cream, of sharing a sweet treat, felt laden with unspoken possibilities. It was a step, a small one perhaps, but a step nonetheless, towards weaving their past and present into a new, uncharted future.

"Vanilla sounds perfect, Julian," she said, her voice soft, a hint of a smile playing on her lips. "Sometimes, the classics are the best."

As they walked towards the ice cream parlor, the setting sun painting the sky in hues of orange and pink, Lani felt a sense of peace settle over her.

Naomi chattered excitedly about her choice of toppings, her innocent questions about Julian having paved the way for a more comfortable interaction. Lani realized, with a quiet sense of gratitude that sometimes, the most profound conversations, the ones that truly begin to mend old wounds and build new bridges, are the ones that are initiated with the simplest of questions. And spoken by the most innocent of hearts.

The gingerbread villages and swirly icing had become the unexpected, yet perfect, foundation for their own unfolding story.

{ **19** }

Julian

The remnants of their breakfast told a quiet story. Two coffee cups, nearly empty; a scatter of crumbs on mismatched plates; sunlight filtering through the diner's fogged window, softening everything it touched.

To Julian, it felt strangely intimate, as if the years that had stretched between them were nothing more than a pause in conversation rather than a chasm carved by time.

He watched her absently trace the rim of her mug, her fingertips delicate and deliberate, as they used to be when she shaped dough or brushed egg wash on a pastry. Lani had always had a kind of quiet grace, a steadiness that grounded him. Sitting across from her now, that steadiness felt like a balm, familiar and yet new in ways that made his heart ache.

"Think about it, Lani," he said, leaning forward slightly, the words tumbling out before he could temper the enthusiasm behind them. "Your grandmother's recipes, they're the soul of the bakery, the reason people keep coming back. But there's room to grow, to explore. Imagine taking those beloved classics and giving them a subtle, modern twist. Not changing them just elevating them."

He picked up his fork, gesturing unconsciously as ideas poured out of him. "Your lemon drizzle cake, for instance. What if, for spring, we added a touch of elderflower? Or lavender for a summer special? Think of the floral notes, soft, fragrant, unexpected. It's about keeping the heart of the recipe but giving it... a new breath of life."

Lani's eyes lifted from her cup, curiosity sparking in their depths. Julian felt a flicker of something stir in his chest. The same thing that had always drawn him to her. She didn't just listen; she absorbed. When she gave you her attention, it was total.

He pressed on, the rhythm of his thoughts syncing with the low hum of the breakfast shop.

"And seasonality, that's where the real magic is. People crave connection now, to place, to time, to the moment. Imagine a 'Harvest Moon' tart in autumn. Spiced apples and pears from a local orchard, maybe a drizzle of maple syrup infused with smoked paprika for depth. Or a winter special. Dark chocolate ganache with a whisper of chili and orange zest. Comfort, but with an edge. Something that makes them remember."

As he spoke, he watched her expression shift. Interest softening into wonder. He could almost see her imagination at work, tasting, adjusting, shaping the vision in her mind. It filled him with a quiet thrill. This...this exchange of ideas, of passion, it felt like coming home.

"Hmmm," was all she said.

Julian leaned back slightly, smiling. "It's not just about flavor either," he said. "It's the experience. We could create moments. Seasonal tastings. Collaborations with local artisans, cheese makers, and coffee roasters. Imagine a croissant with fig and gorgonzola compote. Or rosemary scones with artisanal honey. You could make the bakery a destination, not just a stop, but an experience."

The excitement in her eyes made his pulse quicken. For a moment, it was easy to forget the years he'd spent chasing success, the sterile perfection of hotel kitchens and Michelin stars. None of it compared to watching Lani's face light up with inspiration.

"But it's not *my* bakery. Not yet. It belongs to my parents," Lani explained.

He reached across the table, almost without thinking, and placed his hand over hers. Her skin was warm, familiar. "You've already begun rebuilding something incredible," he said softly. "But tradition and innovation, they don't have to fight each other. They can exist side by side. Surely your parents will see that. You honor your grandmother's legacy every day, Lani. Maybe now, it's time to let your own legacy take root right beside it."

Her gaze met his, wide and searching. He could feel her hesitation. That quiet fear of reaching too far, of losing something precious in the process. It was a fear he understood all too well.

"You're right," she said after a long pause, her voice barely above a whisper. "I've been so focused on preserving what works, on not disappointing anyone, that I stopped asking what *else* was possible."

He smiled, pride swelling quietly in his chest. "Then maybe it's time to ask again."

He withdrew his hand slowly, though the warmth of her skin lingered. He didn't want to push. What he wanted, more than anything, was to see her believe in her own brilliance again.

"I could help," he said finally. "Not taking over the kitchen that's your domain. But with planning, strategy, growth. You've built something with heart, Lani. I could help you build it into something lasting. Something that reaches beyond the mountains."

Her breath caught slightly, surprise and something softer, hope, maybe flickering across her face. "You'd do that? You'd help me?"

Julian nodded, his voice steady. "If you'll let me. I believe in what you're trying to build. And I believe in *you*."

For a heartbeat, silence hung between them. The kind of silence that hums, alive with unspoken things. He could feel the weight of their

"I've always loved how you see the world," he said, his voice softening. "How you find beauty in the simple things. You take flour and sugar and turn them into something that feels like love. I lost sight of that kind of meaning for a while. Maybe... maybe helping you build this dream is my way of finding it again."

Her smile, small and tremulous, undid him.

"Then maybe we can build it together," she said quietly.

The words struck him like a slow sunrise, warm and full of promise. He felt something uncoiled in his chest, something he hadn't allowed himself to feel in years: hope.

"I will talk to my parents. See what they think about all of this," she declared.

Julian leaned back, watching her as she asked what he envisioned for spring, her tone light, her eyes bright. He answered eagerly, describing berries and lavender, marzipan and macaron pastels. But beneath the words, a quieter truth pulsed through him.

This wasn't just about business. Or food. Or even legacy.

It was about *her*.

About rediscovering the woman who had once been his anchor and realizing, with a quiet ache, that she still was.

The late morning light had shifted by the time they stepped outside. The air was crisp, edged with that faint sweetness that came just before snow. A promise of renewal whispered through the mountain breeze. Julian held the door open for Lani, and she brushed past him with a soft smile, the faint scent of flour and citrus following her like a memory.

They fell into step naturally, as if no years had passed between them, as if this was just another morning walk home from school, or one of those quiet strolls they used to take down the main street after his late shifts at the diner, when the world felt small and perfectly theirs.

The town was slowly waking up around them. Storefronts flickered to life, someone laughed across the street, and the church bell chimed the half-hour. Lani tucked a stray strand of hair behind her ear, her fingers brushing her cheek, and for a moment Julian's hand twitched with the instinct to reach out, to tuck it away for her like he used to. He didn't. Not yet.

"You really haven't changed this place much," he said finally, his voice light. "Shepard's still has that same red awning, and the bookshop still smells like dust and coffee."

Lani chuckled softly. "That's the charm of this town; it refuses to keep up with the times. You can't get a decent Wi-Fi signal, but everyone knows your birthday."

He smiled, glancing sideways at her. "I missed that. I missed *this*." He paused, searching for the right words. "You don't realize you were home the whole time until you leave it."

Lani looked up at him, her eyes soft, her expression un-readable. "You always did make things sound poetic," she said quietly.

"Maybe," he murmured. "Or maybe I just spent too long convincing myself that the city could replace what I had here." He hesitated, his throat tightening around the truth.

"What I had with you."

They walked a few steps in silence. The only sound was the crunch of gravel beneath their feet and the faint whistle of wind against the eaves.

When they reached the bakery, Lani stopped at the door. The painted sign *Shepards Sweets* swung gently in the breeze, its letters worn at the edges, but still proud. She turned toward him, her expression a blend of warmth and uncertainty.

"Julian," she began, her voice soft but steady. "I'm glad you came back. Not just for the bakery ideas or the business talk, but…" She paused, glancing down, her fingers fumbling with the strap of her purse. "For this. For being here."

Julian swallowed hard. He hadn't realized until that moment just how much he'd needed to hear those words. "You have no idea what that means to me," he said. "Being here, with you. It feels like the first real thing I've done in years."

Something flickered in her eyes, surprise, tenderness, maybe even longing. She reached for the door, then stopped. "Would you like to come in? I've got a new batch of brioche cooling."

He smiled, that familiar, easy warmth spreading through his chest. "You're tempting me, Lani."

"Good," she teased lightly, though her voice trembled just enough to betray the emotion beneath.

Inside, the bakery was quiet and sunlit, the air filled with the sweet scent of butter and sugar. The counters gleamed, and a faint trail of flour dusted the wood floor like snow. Julian felt a strange mix of nostalgia and awe. This was *her* world, the life she and her family had built with their own hands.

Lani crossed to the counter, cut two small pieces of brioche, and placed them on a plate. "It's not quite your fancy city fare," she said with a smile.

He stepped closer, close enough to see the gold flecks of light in her hair. "It's better," he said softly. "Because it's yours."

She looked up at him then, really looked and something in the air shifted. The hum of the bakery seemed to fade, replaced by the steady rhythm of his heartbeat. He reached out, brushing a bit of flour from her cheek. Her breath caught.

"Julian," she whispered.

He hesitated only a moment. Long enough to see the way her lips parted, the way her gaze lingered on his. And then he closed the distance between them.

The kiss was soft, tentative, a rediscovery. This wasn't a kiss to release sexual tension. It was something deeper, slower, threaded with memory and quiet awe. Her hand came to rest against his chest, his heart beating wild beneath her touch. For a moment, the years dissolved. The pain, the distance, all of it until there was only this: the taste of home, the sweetness of second chances.

When they finally drew apart, Lani's eyes shimmered with uncertainty, but unafraid. Her breath came a little unevenly as she whispered,

"Julian... you can't just kiss me like that."

Julian's smile was quiet, the kind that reached his eyes before his lips. His thumb traced the curve of her cheek, a touch both steady and reverent.

"Maybe I can," he murmured, his voice low and sure, "because this time... it's where we were always meant to be."

Outside, the bell above the bakery door chimed softly as a breeze slipped through the mountain air. A gentle reminder that even after the longest winters, spring always found its way back.

The world seemed to still after the kiss.

The faint hum of the refrigerator, the creak of the old bakery floorboards, even the low whistle of wind against the windowpanes. All of it faded into a soft, distant hush.

Julian stood close enough to feel the warmth of her breath against his skin, to see the faint tremor in her fingers as she brushed a strand of hair behind her ear.

He wanted to speak, to fill the silence with something that could make sense of the moment. But the words, like the years between them, felt too heavy, too full.

Lani was the first to step back, her hand resting lightly on the counter as if she needed something solid to hold onto.

"Julian…" she began, her voice barely above a whisper. "I don't know what that was."

He swallowed hard. "It was real," he said quietly. "That's all I know."

She looked down, tracing a small circle on the counter with her fingertip. "It's been a long time. People change."

Julian let out a slow breath, his voice rough with honesty. "I've changed, yes. But not in the way you think. The city, my career, it all gave me what I thought I wanted. But somewhere along the way, I lost the part of me that mattered most." He hesitated, meeting her gaze. "The part that felt like *home*."

Lani's eyes flickered, a mix of tenderness and fear passing through them. "You can't just come back here after all these years and say things like that," she murmured. "You left, Julian. You built a whole life somewhere else."

"I did," he admitted. "But it never felt whole."

Julian hadn't planned what to say. He'd rehearsed a thousand versions of this moment on lonely hotel balconies, in empty kitchens after midnight service, in dreams that always ended with her walking away again. But now, standing before her, the words trembled at the edge of his tongue like something fragile and alive.

"You look like you've been carrying something," Lani said gently, her voice the same melody he remembered, steady, warm, threaded with concern. "You've had that look before."

Julian exhaled, long and uneven. "There's something I never told you," he began. His hands flexed uselessly at his sides, fingers curling as if trying to hold on to something that had slipped through them long ago.

"About why I really left."

Lani tilted her head slightly, her brow furrowing. "I know why you left. You got the offer. You followed your dream."

He shook his head slowly. "That was part of it. But it wasn't the whole truth."

The mountain wind stirred around them, carrying the faint scent of pine and fresh bread. Julian's voice dropped, raw and unsteady. "My parents... they died that same week, Lani. The night before, I was supposed to tell you about the letter."

Her breath caught. "What?"

He nodded, the words breaking free at last, years of silence splintering like glass.

"Car accident. The roads were slick, and a storm rolled in. They were back from their mission trip. They were coming to see me after visiting my aunt in Silver Creek." He paused, swallowing hard. "I was supposed to be with them to visit my aunt. I'd told them I'd stay to see you instead."

The world seemed to still around them. Even the wind quieted. Lani's hand came to her mouth, her eyes shining with unshed tears.

"Oh, Julian..."

"I couldn't face you after that," he said hoarsely. "I couldn't stand the thought of you looking at me and seeing what I'd lost, or worse, what I'd survived. I felt guilty I was with you and not in that car."

He tugged on his dark curls and continued. "I left because it was the only way I knew how to breathe again. I told myself I was leaving for my career, but the truth is..." He looked down, his voice trembling. "I was running. From grief. From guilt. From the life we were supposed to have."

He lifted his gaze to hers then, and the years between them seemed to collapse, all the distance, all the silence, all the longing. "Every success I've had, every award, every gleaming kitchen, none of it meant anything, Lani. Not without you. Because I didn't just lose them that night. I lost *us.*"

Her tears fell freely now, though her expression held no anger, only heartbreak, tempered by understanding.

"You should've told me," she whispered. "You didn't have to go through that alone."

He took a slow step closer. "I didn't know how to stay. Everything here reminded me of what I'd lost... and everything I'd ruined." His voice broke. "You were the one bright thing left, and I was terrified I'd destroy that too."

Lani's breath came out in a shaky exhale. "All these years, I thought you'd chosen ambition over love."

Julian's eyes glistened. "No," he said quietly. "I chose survival. But I've learned something, Lani. Survival without love isn't living. It's just... existing."

For a long moment, she said nothing. The air between them shimmered with everything unspoken, the pain, the what-ifs, the tenderness that had never really died. Then, she stepped forward, closing the last of the distance, and lifted her hand to his face. Her touch was soft, trembling,

"You've carried this alone for too long," she murmured.

His breath hitched as he turned into her palm. "I don't want to carry it anymore," he whispered. "Not if I can carry it with you."

Their eyes met in the kind of gaze that reaches across years, across heartbreak, and finds something still alive, still possible. And in that fragile, golden light, Lani rose onto her toes and kissed him.

It wasn't the desperate kiss of youth. It was tender, searching, reverent. A kiss that spoke of loss and forgiveness, of two souls finding their way home. His hands found her waist, drawing her closer, and for the first time in years, Julian felt still. Whole.

When they finally broke apart, her forehead rested against him.

"You came back," she whispered.

Julian's voice was rough with emotion. "I never really left."

The mountain wind sighed through the trees, carrying the faintest scent of cinnamon and pine. The world felt smaller then, quieter as if everything, finally, had come full circle.

He moved closer again, careful not to touch her, though every instinct in him screamed to close the distance.

"I know I hurt you. And I've carried that with me every day since. But being here again, seeing you, hearing you talk about the bakery, about your life, it reminded me that not everything beautiful has to be fleeting. That maybe some things... some *people*... are worth coming home for."

For a moment, she didn't respond. The clock on the wall ticked softly, marking time in the quiet between them. Finally, she drew in a breath.

"Coming home isn't the same as staying, Julian," she said, her tone gentle but cautious. "And I can't go through losing you again."

He nodded, understanding more than she realized. "I'm not asking you to trust me overnight," he said softly. "But I came back for more than nostalgia. I came back because I finally realized what I've been missing wasn't opportunity or acclaim. It was *belonging*. It was you."

Lani looked at him for a long moment, the conflict in her eyes deep and raw. Then, almost imperceptibly, her expression softened.

"You always did have a way with words," she murmured, though her lips curved in the faintest, wistful smile.

He smiled back, that old spark flickering to life. "Maybe," he said quietly, "but this time, I mean every one of them."

Her gaze dropped to the tray of cooling brioche between them. "You should probably take one for the road," she said, her voice steadier now, though he could hear the emotion threading through it.

Julian chuckled softly, reaching for a piece. "You're still taking care of me, aren't you?"

"Someone has to," she said lightly, though her eyes betrayed her heart.

As he turned to leave, she called after him. "Julian?"

He paused at the door. "Yeah?"

She hesitated, then said, almost shyly, "Don't make this another goodbye."

His chest tightened, emotion clawing its way to the surface. He stepped closer, his gaze steady.

"I won't," he said. "Not this time."

And when he stepped out into the bright mountain morning, the scent of fresh bread and coffee still clinging to him, Julian felt something shift inside, something equal parts hope and ache.

He wasn't sure what the future held. But for the first time in years, it didn't feel like running. It felt like coming home.

***

The evening had settled softly over Evergreen Hollow, a hush blanketing the mountain town in that familiar, comforting way. The streetlights glowed amber through the faint mist, and the air carried the scent of pine and distant woodsmoke. Julian's car engine had long since cooled, but still he sat behind the wheel, staring across the street at **Shepards Sweets.**

He hadn't meant to come back. Not tonight. Not so soon. But some invisible thread had tugged him here, the same one that had drawn him to her door that morning, to her laughter over coffee, to the kisses that still burned on his lips.

Through the wide front window, the bakery looked like something out of a dream. The soft, golden light poured from within, washing the street in warmth. And there she was, **Lani**, framed in that glow like a portrait he'd never stopped carrying in his heart.

She moved with quiet grace, her auburn hair pulled loosely back, the sleeves of her cardigan rolled to her elbows as she worked. The world outside might have been wrapped in night, but inside that little bakery, everything felt alive. She dusted flour across a countertop, leaned over a tray of pastries, and smiled, just a faint, private smile, the kind she probably didn't even realize she wore.

Julian leaned forward, resting his forearms on the steering wheel. That smile hit him like a rush of memory. Summer nights by the lake, her laughter echoing through the dark, the taste of cinnamon sugar on her lips when they'd kissed under the bleachers after the homecoming dance.

He hadn't realized how much he'd missed the **sound** of her being. The quiet hum when she was content. The soft sigh she made when she was lost in thought.

He'd chased applause, built restaurants that gleamed with Michelin stars and marble countertops, but none of them ever felt like this...this fragile, human warmth glowing in a mountain bakery window.

For a long moment, he just watched her. It wasn't voyeurism, it was reverence. A reminder that some beauty didn't need to be owned or claimed; it just needed to be witnessed.

Then, almost without thinking, he got out of the car. The air was sharp and cold, biting at his skin as he crossed the street. He paused outside the bakery door, his breath fogging the glass, his heart drumming hard in his chest.

Inside, Lani looked up. Their eyes met through the glass. She froze for a moment, then smiled, hesitant at first, then warmer, that familiar crinkle touching the corners of her eyes. She gestured toward the door, and he stepped inside, the bell chiming softly above him.

"You came back," she said quietly, wiping her hands on her apron.

He gave a small, almost sheepish laugh. "I was driving by," he lied, though they both knew better.

"Uh-huh," she said, that teasing note in her voice. "Just happened to be driving by the bakery after closing, did you?"

Julian spread his hands. "What can I say? The coffee here is unbeatable."

She raised an eyebrow, clearly unconvinced. "The coffee? Or the company?"

"Both," he said simply.

Something softened in her face, and for a moment, the air between them shifted. That delicate mix of nostalgia and something new, something fragile but undeniable.

Lani moved to the counter and poured two mugs from still warm pot. "If you're here for coffee," she said, sliding one toward him, "you might as well earn it. You can help me box up the scones."

Julian smiled, setting down his coat and rolling up his sleeves. "You always did know how to put me to work."

"Old habits die hard," she said, and there was a warmth in her tone that went deeper than humor.

As they worked side by side, the silence between them felt easy, companionable. The years seemed to fall away. Every so often, their hands brushed, and each touch carried that quiet electricity that neither of them dared acknowledge aloud.

Finally, Julian glanced over at her. "You know," he said softly, "I think this is what I've been missing."

Lani looked up from the pastry box, brow furrowed. "What do you mean?"

"This," he said, gesturing around them. "The quiet. The work. The... feeling." He hesitated, then added, "You."

She froze, her breath catching. "Julian..."

He stepped closer, his voice barely above a whisper. "I'm not asking for anything. Not tonight. I just needed you to know that being here, with you, feels more right than anything I've done in years."

Her eyes shimmered, though her smile remained steady. "You always did know how to make words sound like promises," she said gently.

Julian's lips curved into a faint smile. "Maybe this time," he murmured, "they are."

And as they stood there beneath the soft glow of the bakery lights, surrounded by sugar, flour, and the scent of something warm and familiar, the world outside seemed to hold its breath.

For the first time in a long time, Julian didn't feel like a man chasing success.

He felt like a man finding his way back.

{ 20 }

Lani

The first hint that the world outside had changed was the profound, almost oppressive silence. Lani stirred from a deep, dreamless sleep, the kind that only comes after a day filled with a heady mix of professional inspiration and unexpected long-lost emotions. She lay for a moment, listening, trying to place the absence of sound. No distant traffic hum, no early morning birdsong, not even the usual whisper of wind through the eaves. The silence so complete, it felt as though the air itself had been muted.

A prickle of unease, quickly followed by a wave of curiosity, drew her from the warmth of the comforter. She padded barefoot across the cool wooden floor and down the stairs, her gaze fixed on the window.

The dawn was pearly grey, and through the panes, the world was a study in white. Snow. Not just a dusting, but a deep, unbroken blanket that had transformed the familiar street into an ethereal landscape.

Her breath hitched as she pressed her forehead against the cold glass. Fat, heavy flakes continued to drift down from a sky that had lost all definition, merging seamlessly with the snow-covered rooftops and the skeletal branches of the oak tree in the small square.

The streetlights, usually sharp beacons, now glowed diffused and softened by the falling snow. She stepped onto the porch. She looked down the street.

The bakery sign, usually bold and inviting, was now a muted silhouette against the pristine canvas. It was breathtaking. And utterly still.

She imagined Julian, who had been planning to head back to the city this morning, would be equally surprised. Their conversation last night had left her on a euphoric high, a whirlwind of potential and renewed feelings.

They had talked for hours, their initial tentative discussions about the bakery evolving into something deeper, more personal. He had stayed late, and she had found herself reluctant to let him go, the comfortable camaraderie that had always existed between them now tinged with an undeniable, electric current.

She turned from the window, a soft smile playing on her lips. The snow had effectively cancelled Julian's departure.

They were trapped.

The thought, instead of being an inconvenience, sparked a flutter of excitement in her chest. The blizzard had brought the world to a halt, but for them, it felt like an invitation. An invitation to what? To continue exploring the possibilities they had discovered. To confront the undeniable attraction that had been simmering between them for weeks.

The air held the lingering scent of yesterday's baked goods her father had brought home, a comforting blend of yeast, sugar, and vanilla. She made her way to the kitchen. The familiar routine of brewing coffee grounded her, a comforting ritual paired with the extraordinary stillness outside. As the rich aroma began to fill the air, she heard it—a soft thud from the back door.

Julian

Of course. Who else would make the morning thump like a knock on memory's door?

The old oak groaned in protest as her hand twisted the cold brass knob. A gust of wind, sharp with the scent of pine needles and frost, pushed the door inward.

There he was, framed by the swirling white. Snowflakes, like scattered diamond dust, clung to the raven darkness of his hair, melting into tiny rivulets on the broad expanse of his coat's shoulders. His gaze, the deep, cerulean blue snagged hers.

A breath hitched in her throat as she saw the sudden wideness of his pupils, then the slow unfurling of a smile that crinkled the corners of his eyes, a silent acknowledgment passing between them.

"Looks like you braved the blizzard," Lani said, voice husky, words blending warmth and disbelief as they echoed through the hall's hush.

He chuckled, the sound a warm counterpoint to the wind's howl. "Just a little stroll. I didn't want to miss seeing you like this." His eyes, a deep, oceanic blue that seemed to catch and hold the light, flickered toward the softly lit room behind her, a silent question hanging in the air.

"Didn't you have to check on your restaurants?" She raised a brow in question.

"Looks like the weather had other plans for my departure," he said, his voice a low rumble that seemed to resonate in the quiet space. He brushed a snowflake from his sleeve, his gaze sweeping over the snow-laden street.

"I haven't seen it snow this hard, this fast in a very long time. It's like the world decided to hit pause."

"It's magnificent," Lani breathed, stepping aside to let him in. "I feel like I woke up in someone else's world. A very quiet world."

Julian stepped into the house, bringing with him the crisp, cold air of the blizzard. He shook the snow from his coat, the movement creating a small flurry of white.

"Quiet is an understatement. I already checked out of the hotel. My car is buried. I'm not going anywhere today." He looked at her then, his eyes holding a question, an unspoken invitation.

"Unless... you'd have me?"

The warmth that bloomed in Lani's chest was more potent than the coffee brewing, more invigorating than the sight of the transformed town.

"Of course, I would," she said, her voice a little softer than she intended. "There's plenty of room. And coffee's just about ready."

As she poured two steaming mugs, the silence of the kitchen became a shared space, a sanctuary against the swirling storm outside. They sat at the small, sturdy tables near the bay window. The white world was a mesmerizing backdrop to their conversation. The snow continued its relentless descent, blanketing everything in a soft, ethereal hush. The world beyond the glass was frozen, immobilized, but within the cozy confines of the room, a different kind of warmth was beginning to thaw.

"I was up late," Julian admitted, stirring his coffee, the spoon clinking softly against the ceramic. "Thinking about what we talked about yesterday. The ideas, Lani, they're brilliant. Truly. You have a gift for that bakery, a real legacy."

Lani's heart did a little flutter. Julian's gaze pinned her in place, and she felt suddenly naked—in the best way. "It's my family's legacy," she said, soft as sugar sifted over freshly baked loaves. "I just try to do it justice."

"And you do," he affirmed, his eyes holding hers. "But you're also building on it. Your own vision. Those seasonal twists, the collaborations, it's incredibly exciting."

He took a sip of his coffee, his gaze drifting out to the window. "This snow... it's forcing a pause, isn't it? For everyone. For us. It's like the universe is saying, 'Slow down. Look around. Reassess.'"

He turned back to her, a thoughtful expression on his face. "Sometimes, these unexpected interruptions are the most important moments. They force us to confront things we might otherwise keep pushing aside."

Lani knew exactly what he meant. The conversation last night had been a revelation, an unexpected outpouring of shared dreams and unspoken feelings. They talked about everything and nothing. Her passion for baking, his work, their past, and the tantalizing, terrifying possibility of a future. He had spoken with such clarity about his belief in her, in the bakery, in her potential, that it had felt like a validation of years of hard work and solitary dedication.

"I've been so focused on the day-to-day," she admitted, tracing the rim of her mug. "Making sure Naomi has what she needs, the bakery thrives, the books are in order, the customers are happy. The bigger picture, the strategic growth... it's always felt a little overwhelming. That mountain looks so high some mornings, I forget where I left my boots."

"But you don't have to climb it alone," Julian said, his voice gentle. "That's what I was trying to say last night. I see the potential, Lani. And I have the tools and experience to help you build the strategy. It's not about changing your vision but about helping you realize it. Making it tangible."

"It's just... it's been a while," Lani said, her gaze drifting to the intricate patterns of frost blooming on the windowpane. "Since I've allowed myself to... to really dream about something like that. About building something bigger. And about... well, about letting someone else in."

Julian reached across the small table, his fingers brushing hers. It was a fleeting touch, but it sent a jolt through her, a familiar warmth that was both comforting and exhilarating.

"I understand," he said softly. "But Lani, you've already let me in. With your passion, with your talent, with the warmth of this place. And yesterday... you let me see a little more of your heart."

"I never expected... this," Lani murmured, gesturing vaguely at the snow-covered world. "I thought you'd be gone this morning."

"Me neither," Julian admitted, his thumb gently stroking the back of her hand. "But I'm not disappointed. Not at all. This... this feels like an opportunity. A chance to really talk, without the rush of everyday life. And maybe," he paused, his gaze holding hers, "a chance to see where this connection between us might lead."

His words hung in the air, heavy with unspoken emotion. The physical tension that had been building between them, a subtle undercurrent for weeks, now felt like a palpable force, amplified by the isolation and the quiet intimacy of the kitchen.

He withdrew his hand, but the warmth lingered on her skin. The silence of the snowfall seemed to deepen, to press in on them, creating a bubble of shared intimacy.

"Julian!" Elenore called out in surprise. "This is an early visit."

Julian turned toward the sound of Elenore's voice, the soft rhythm between him and Lani breaking like a sigh. The warmth of her hand still lingered on his palm. The echo of their unspoken words suspended in the hush of the kitchen.

"Early visit, perhaps," Julian said, flashing Elenore a sheepish grin, "but I promise it's a productive one."

Elenore arched a flour-dusted brow, smirking. "Productive, hm? As long as 'productive' doesn't mean you two get flour all over my clean counters, I suppose I'll allow it."

Julian chuckled, lifting both hands in mock surrender. "No promises," he said lightly.

Before Lani could reply, the sound of boots crunching against the old pine floor cut through the soft hum of the ovens. The back door swung open, bringing with it a rush of cold air and the faint scent of pine and snow.

"Morning, looks like we are snowed in," Thomas greeted, stepping into the kitchen with a grin that warmed the space instantly. His hair was wind-tousled, his flannel collar dusted with snowflakes.

"Didn't expect to find *you* here so early, Julian."

Julian extended a hand in greeting, genuine affection lighting his face. "Thomas," he said. "Good to see you. I was going to head to the airport, but couldn't seem to find my car. Or the road."

Thomas grunted. "You'll have to stay here until it clears."

"Thank you," Julian responded.

Lani turned, her expression brightening. "Dad! You're just in time. We were talking about the bakery."

"We were tossing around a few ideas, nothing set in stone yet, but exciting things," Julian added.

Thomas shook his head, glancing between them with mild curiosity. "Exciting things, huh? That usually means trouble in this kitchen."

Elenore, still hovering by the pantry door, laughed. "You're not wrong about that."

Julian grinned, undeterred. "Hear me out," he said, motioning toward the counter where parchment paper was spread out, covered in hastily drawn notes and sketches.

"Your family built this bakery on tradition and heart. It's the soul of this town. You and Elenore have done an incredible job keeping that alive. But now..." He glanced at Lani, his tone softening. "Now it's time for the next chapter. Time for Lani to shape the legacy she'll inherit."

Lani's cheeks flushed, her eyes flicking toward her parents.

"I'd never want to change what you've both built," she said earnestly. "You've worked so hard keeping the bakery the way grandma did."

Elenore wiped her hands on her apron, her expression gentle. "Oh, sweetheart," she said with a fond smile, "we've only been keeping it warm for you. It's always been yours. And one day it will be Naomi's. We just wanted it to still be standing when you were ready to take it on."

Thomas nodded, his voice steady and kind. "Your name's on the deed, Lani. Has been for the last couple of months. We're getting too old to be here all the time. We were just waiting till you decide the time's right."

Julian watched Lani's face soften, pride and emotion warring in her expression. He could see the moment it sank in. The realization that *this* was hers to shape, to nurture, to make new.

"We want to honor what's already here," Julian continued, sensing her hesitation. "Keep the heart intact. Just... add a few brushstrokes. A tasting nook, maybe, by that front window. Somewhere people can sit, slow down, and savor what Lani creates. Seasonal events, small, intimate, centered around her recipes and the stories behind them."

Thomas leaned against the counter, his arms folding comfortably. "A café corner, huh? Not a bad idea. Folks do like to linger, and with the view from that window, they'll never want to leave."

Lani smiled, the spark of excitement lighting her features.

"Exactly. I've always dreamed of that space being more than a quick stop for coffee and pastries. I want it to feel like a gathering place again. Like it did when Grandma ran it."

Julian nodded. "We could celebrate each season, elder-flower and lemon in spring, spiced maple in fall. Partner with local farms, maybe even the orchard up the road. Keep everything rooted right here in the valley."

Thomas's grin widened. "That's the spirit. You're talking about keeping it local. Keeping it *ours*. I like that."

Julian smiled back. "Growth without losing the roots."

He turned to the parchment again, sketching lightly. "And over here, a rotating centerpiece pastry. Something seasonal, something with a story.

We could call it *Shepard's*. Keep the tradition but state the change."

Lani's eyes lit up. "I love that. It feels personal."

Thomas chuckled softly. "Sounds like you two have been busy. Should I be worried this place is about to get too fancy for me?"

Julian laughed. "Not a chance. This place has heart. We're just giving it a little polish. Think of it as adding a few new colors to an old painting."

Thomas nodded, his tone teasing but approving. "Well, if it keeps the coffee strong and my cinnamon loaf on the menu, you've got my blessing."

Lani laughed, warmth filling her chest. "You'll always have that, Dad. That's a Shepards Sweets promise."

Elenore reappeared, carrying a tray of warm croissants. "Blessings or not, I think it's time you all eat before making any more grand plans." She set the tray down with a satisfied thud. "Dreams are hungry work."

Their laughter filled the kitchen, mingling with the scent of butter and sugar and the soft hum of the ovens. Outside, snow fell in slow, silvery flakes. The world hushed, as if holding its breath.

Julian broke a croissant in half and offered one piece to Lani, his voice low. "To new beginnings," he said.

Her eyes met his, bright with emotion. "And to keeping the heart of what matters."

Thomas raised his mug of coffee, smiling. "I'll drink to that."

The kitchen door creaked open with a gust of chilly air and the unmistakable patter of small boots against the tile.

"Mommy! It's snowing!" Naomi's voice rang out, high and bright as a bell. She burst into the room, her pink mittens clutched in one hand, her hat slightly askew, dark curls peeking out in every direction. A clear sign she had been in the backyard.

Her cheeks glowed crimson from the cold, and her eyes sparkled with wonder. "The whole world's white! It looks like sugar!"

Lani laughed, bending down just in time to catch her daughter as she flung herself forward. "It does look like sugar, doesn't it?" she said, brushing a few stray flakes from Naomi's hair. "But not the kind we eat, sweetheart."

Julian, standing by the counter, couldn't help smiling. Naomi was all energy and light, the very image of her mother. The same expressive eyes, the same unfiltered joy.

"You brought the snow in with you," he teased gently, reaching for a dish towel to wipe up the little puddle forming around her boots.

Naomi grinned up at him, unabashed. "Hi, Mr. Julian!" she chirped, her small voice lilting with familiarity. "Guess what? No school today. And Grandma made croissants! The kind with chocolate inside!" She lifted her mittened hands toward the counter where a tray of golden pastries still steamed beside the coffeepot.

"Can I have one? Pleeease?" The ends of her chocolate colored hair were covered in melting snow.

Elenore chuckled from near the stove, wiping her hands on her apron. "You don't have to ask twice, my darling girl. They're still warm. Come take off your wet things and sit, and I'll get you one with a bit of cocoa to chase away the chill."

Naomi climbed up onto her favorite chair. The one Thomas had painted a cheerful yellow just for her and swung her legs while Elenore placed a plate before her. The croissant was almost too big for her small hands, but she tore into it with pure delight, chocolate smudging her fingertips and chin.

"Grandma," Naomi mumbled around a mouthful, "you make the best ones. Mommy's are good too, but yours are extra-fluffy."

Lani feigned offense, hand over her heart. "Extra-fluffy? I see how it is. Grandma gets the glory."

Naomi giggled as the crumbs scattered. "You make the cookies, Mommy. The ones with the sprinkles! You're the cookie queen."

Julian laughed softly at that, the sound low and warm. He leaned closer to Lani and murmured, "I think that's a title worth keeping."

Lani glanced at him, her lips curving into a soft, knowing smile. "I think so too."

Across the table, Naomi hummed happily to herself, swinging her feet and watching the snow swirl beyond the window. "Can we make a snowman after this?" she asked between bites. "A big one! With a hat and a carrot nose and maybe a cookie mouth!"

Thomas chuckled from his spot by the coffee pot. "A cookie mouth, huh? That's a first. We'll have to talk to the cookie queen about that."

Naomi clapped her chocolate-smudged hands together in delight. "Yay! Mommy cookies for the snowman!"

The room filled with laughter, soft, genuine, the kind that wrapped around the heart and made even the coldest morning feel warm. Outside, the snow kept falling in slow, steady flakes, blanketing the little mountain town in shimmering white.

Inside, between the smell of butter and cocoa and the sound of a little girl's laughter, everything felt exactly as it should be.

{ 21 }

Julian

The snow kept falling, slow, steady, unhurried. From where Julian sat, it looked as if the world outside had been erased and redrawn in shades of white.

The street beyond the bakery window had vanished, muffled under the storm's quiet insistence. Inside, the warmth of the kitchen wrapped around them, all soft light and the faint scent of sugar and coffee. It felt almost suspended. Like time itself had taken a deep breath and decided to wait.

He glanced across the table at Lani. The curve of her profile, the way her hair caught the glow of the pendant light. It stirred something in him that had lain dormant for too long. She didn't realize how magnetic she was when she was listening, when her attention was wholly fixed on something. He could still remember the way she used to listen to him when they were kids, the same focus, the same quiet intensity.

She looked up suddenly, catching his gaze. "What were you thinking about when you were talking about the bakery earlier?" she asked softly.

He smiled faintly, leaning back in his chair. "Lots of things."

"You talked about it with such conviction. Like it was your own dream too," she questioned.

"It is, in a way," he said after a pause. "I've spent years in meetings surrounded by spreadsheets and predictions of restaurant success. It's a different kind of creation, efficient, measurable, but sterile. All precision, no heart." He looked down at the faint dusting of flour on the counter and brushed a thumb across it.

"Your bakery isn't like that, Lani. It's not just a business. It's," he stopped, searching for the right word. "It's alive. It gives people something real. Comfort, joy, a little piece of belonging. You've built something that connects people, something I've been missing."

Her eyes softened. She didn't interrupt, and that, more than anything, made him want to keep talking.

"When I watched you yesterday," he continued, "your hands in the dough, your eyes lighting up as you talked about your grandmother's recipes, I realized how rare that is. To love something so completely. And it made me want to be part of it. Not as some consultant with a checklist, but as someone who believes in what this place could become."

He exhaled slowly, the next words quiet but certain. "And maybe as someone who believes in you."

A silence settled. The kind that didn't need filling. The snow pressed softly against the window. A whispering backdrop to the rhythm of his heartbeat.

He stood and walked toward the wide front window. Outside, Main Street was gone, swallowed in a white haze. Only the faint glow of the lamppost across the street pierced through the snow, a single, steady light.

"Imagine it," he said quietly. "Shepard's not just a local favorite, but a place people seek out. Seasonal menus, warm evenings filled with laughter and light, maybe even a small corner where people can sit and watch the snow fall, just like this."

Behind him, he could hear the soft shift of her chair as she joined him. Their reflections stood side by side in the glass, faint, blurred, but together.

"I've always thought of this place as home," she murmured, her voice almost lost to the hum of the heater. "But sometimes home can feel... lonely."

He turned to her, his voice gentler now. "And I've spent so long chasing success that I forgot what it means to build something with soul. This storm," he gestured to the window, "maybe it's a reminder. That we don't have to keep moving so fast. That maybe there's something worth slowing down for."

For a long moment, neither of them spoke. The world beyond the glass was nothing but white and quiet. Inside, though, there was warmth. Like a pulse of connection that neither could quite name.

Julian let out a breath he hadn't realized he'd been holding. "We could make something extraordinary, you and me. You bring the heart, the flavor, the history... I bring the structure, the vision. Together, we could build something that lasts. Something that feels like us."

When Lani looked up at him, there was a spark in her eyes, soft, cautious, but real. "That sounds like the start of something," she said.

"It does," Julian agreed, his lips curving into a slow smile. He didn't reach for her. Not yet. But the distance between them felt smaller somehow, the air charged with promise.

Outside, the snow kept falling. But inside, it felt like something had begun to thaw, quietly and tenderly between them. A second chance wrapped in warmth and sugar and the gentle hush of winter.

The morning had settled in with an ethereal hush, the world outside painted in shades of white and silence. Lani stood by the window, a mug of coffee warming her hands, the lingering scent of yeast and sugar a comforting counterpoint to the stillness.

Julian, his dark hair still flecked with melting snow, was a sight that made Lani's pulse stumble. The storm had trapped him here.

His car was buried somewhere beneath the heavy drift. Instead of frustration, there was a spark in his eyes. He looked almost *alive* in the way city people rarely did anymore, his cheeks flushed from the cold, his breath still carrying the bite of winter.

Being snowbound might have felt suffocating to some, but to Lani, it felt strangely intimate. A quiet reprieve. A pause in the rhythm of her life. One she hadn't realized she needed.

And Julian, standing there with that half-smile and the quiet confidence in his voice, made the bakery feel smaller, warmer... charged.

"So," Julian said, his tone rich, velvet-soft, as he stepped into the main baking area. He brushed a stray flake from his sleeve, his eyes catching hers. "Looks like I'm officially on snow-day duty. Anything a stranded city boy can do to keep this place running?"

Lani's lips curved. "Well," she began, her voice light, teasing, "we're a bit short-staffed today. My parents are here, but it's mostly just us." She nodded toward the counter, dusted in flour. "And the dough."

"The dough?" he echoed, stepping closer.

"It requires a bit of persuasion."

Julian's mouth tilted in a knowing smile. "Persuasion," he repeated, tasting the word. "I'm fairly skilled at that. You'll have to show me your technique."

He came to stand beside her, close enough that she caught the faint scent of him, cedar, citrus, and the crispness of snow. The air shifted; even the hum of the ovens seemed louder, the space between them charged.

"It's all in the touch," she said, sliding the bowl toward him. "You have to coax it, not force it."

His gaze drifted to her hands, strong, sure, dusted in flour, then back to her face.

"Show me," he murmured.

She placed her hands over his, guiding his palms into the cool dough. Their fingers overlapped, skin to skin, her warmth against his. The movement was steady, almost intimate.

"Push, fold, turn," she whispered.

The dough gave beneath their joined touch, sticky at first, then smooth. The sound of it, soft and rhythmic, filled the quiet.

Julian's breath brushed her ear. "It's... slower than I expected."

"You can't rush it," she replied, fighting the heat rising in her neck. "You have to feel it yield."

He looked down at her, his eyes dark with focus and something else. "Like this?" His voice was low, his hands moving in sync with hers.

She nodded, though her breath caught when his thumb brushed the inside of her wrist, maybe by accident, maybe not, lingering just long enough to make her shiver.

"So, it's a dance," he murmured. "Push and pull. Resistance and surrender."

Her pulse quickened. "Something like that."

For a while, they worked in silence. His movements grew more confident, his forearms flexing as he pressed the dough forward. Lani found herself watching the way the flour clung to his skin, the curve of his shoulders, the rhythm of his breath.

"You're getting the hang of it," she said softly.

Julian grinned, a spark in his eyes. "Good teacher. Though I think I'm starting to like this lesson for reasons beyond the bread."

Her laugh came out quiet, breathless. "You always did have a way with words."

"And you always underestimated how much I was listening."

The air thickened again, a silent pulse between them. She turned back to the counter, trying to focus, but his nearness made it impossible.

When the dough was finally set aside to rise, Julian reached for a towel and brushed a bit of flour from her cheek. His touch was light, almost reverent.

"You missed a spot," he said quietly.

Her heart skipped. "Thanks."

He didn't move away. "You've got a little more..." His fingers traced her jaw, brushing another speck of flour, lingering just a fraction too long.

"There. Perfect." His voice had gone low, roughened by something unspoken.

The storm outside beat gently against the glass, echoing the rhythm of her pulse.

He still didn't move.

Her breath caught as Julian's thumb lingered just beneath her chin, the lightest touch, enough to tilt her face toward his. Neither of them spoke.

The air hummed with the scent of flour and warmth and something far more dangerous.

Julian's eyes searched hers, asking for permission, for forgiveness, for a chance to rewrite what had been lost. Whatever he found there made his jaw tighten, his breath hitch.

"Lani..." he whispered. Her name left his lips like a secret he'd kept too long.

She didn't answer, not with words. Just a soft tilt forward, a surrender.

His lips met hers, hesitant at first, then sure.

This kiss wasn't cautious or tentative. It carried memory and ache, the kind of knowing that comes only from losing something and finding it again.

Julian's lips moved against hers with quiet hunger, as if the space between them had been waiting for this moment all along. His hand slid to the back of her neck, fingers threading into her hair, the slow drag of his thumb at her pulse drawing a shiver from her.

Lani leaned into him, tasting the faint trace of coffee on his lips, the warmth of his breath mingling with hers. The world beyond the bakery, the storm, the snow, the low hum of the ovens, blurred into nothing. There was only him, solid, familiar, heartbreakingly close.

He deepened the kiss, slow and deliberate, as if savoring something fragile and long-awaited. His other hand found her waist, steadying her against the counter. Flour dusted his sleeve, smudging against her skin when his fingers brushed her side.

It was grounding. Intimate. Two people rediscovering what they'd thought was gone.

When they finally broke apart, their foreheads rested together, breaths tangled. The silence between them thrummed with energy, the kind that made her skin hum.

Julian's voice came low, roughened with desire and something gentler beneath it. "Third time's supposed to be the charm, isn't it?"

Lani smiled against his lips, her pulse still racing. "Then maybe we shouldn't stop at three."

He laughed softly, warm, dangerous, full of promise, before kissing her again, slower this time, as if to prove her right.

His thumb brushed her bottom lip once more before he stepped back, giving her space, though the air between them still vibrated with what had just happened.

"Tea?" she offered, needing to breathe.

Julian smiled. "Only if you're having one too."

They moved around each other easily, familiar yet newly aware. The air smelled of yeast and cinnamon, but beneath it lingered something sharper: tension, curiosity, want.

As they worked side by side again, conversation came in gentle teasing and quiet laughter, the kind that softened the edges of something powerful. When Julian broke a warm roll in half and offered it to her, his fingers brushed against hers again, deliberate this time.

"See?" he said, his voice low, intimate. "Magic."

Lani took a bite, the heat of the bread spreading through her. The flavor was rich and tangy, but it was Julian's eyes on her lips that made her breath hitch.

Outside, the world was swallowed by snow. Inside, it was all warmth and scent and the soft thrum of inevitability, the kind of slow burn that began with laughter and ended with lips that couldn't quite stay apart.

The day slipped into twilight. The storm pressed harder against the windows, wild and unrelenting. The house glowed, alive with heat, with light, with something neither of them dared to name.

{ **22** }

Lani

Inside the cozy confines of Lani's parents' living room, a different kind of warmth was unfurling. The roaring hearth, a comforting heartbeat in the heart of the house, cast dancing shadows on the walls, painting the room in hues of amber and gold.

Lani and Julian, their earlier camaraderie now deepened by the hours spent together, found themselves drawn to its primal allure. The lingering scent of yeast and sugar from the bakery had given way to the subtle, earthy aroma of burning oak, a scent that spoke of refuge and timelessness.

Lani curled up on the plush rug before the fire. She pulled the thick, hand-knitted blanket around her shoulders, cradling a mug of steaming hot cocoa. The rich, dark liquid warmed her from the inside out, its sweetness a gentle counterpoint to the quiet introspection that had settled over her.

Julian sat beside her with a similar mug in his hands fixed, his gaze on the hypnotic dance of the flames.

The easy banter of the afternoon had softened, replaced by a more profound stillness, a comfortable silence punctuated by the crackle and hiss of the logs.

"It's incredible how isolating this weather can feel, even when you're surrounded by people," Julian murmured, his voice low, almost a confession. He stirred his hot chocolate, the spoon clinking softly against the ceramic.

"You can see the world outside, but it's like looking through a thick pane of glass. Everything feels distant."

Lani nodded, her eyes mirroring the introspection in his. "I know what you mean. It forces you to look inward, doesn't it? To face whatever's lurking in the quiet."

She traced the rim of her mug, the warmth seeping into her fingertips. The firelight caught a subtle tremor in her hand. She felt a flicker of the vulnerability she rarely allowed herself to show. The storm outside was relentless in its power and untamed nature.

It was like a mirror to the tempest that had raged within her for so long after her divorce. It had been a period of upheaval, of shattered assumptions, and a profound sense of being adrift.

"And sometimes," Julian continued, his voice laced with a weariness that surprised her, "the quiet can be the loudest place of all. Especially when you're used to a certain kind of... noise." He offered a faint, self-deprecating smile. "The constant activity, the demands, the expectations. When that stops, and it's just you... it can be deafening."

Lani looked at him, truly looked at him, beyond the charming facade and the easy grace. She saw the shadow of loneliness in his eyes, a stark contrast to the public persona she imagined he wore. His world, so outwardly glittering, seemed to hold a profound solitude.

"You're talking about your work, aren't you?" she ventured softly. "The fame, I suppose. The constant attention."

Julian sighed, a sound that seemed to carry the weight of a thousand performances.

"It's a strange kind of paradox, isn't it? To be constantly surrounded by people, to be recognized everywhere you go, and yet to feel utterly alone. You build walls, you create a persona, and eventually, you forget who's behind them. Or worse, you start to believe the persona is the real you, and the person underneath... well, they get lost."

He paused, his gaze drifting to the fire again. "It's hard to let people in, when you're not even sure what you're letting them in to. And the fear... the fear of being truly seen, of being rejected for who you are, not who they think you are. It's paralyzing."

His words resonated deep within Lani. She understood that fear, that gnawing anxiety of exposure. Her own experience had taught her the harsh lesson that vulnerability could be weaponized, that the tender places within could be exploited.

The divorce had been a brutal shedding of a life she'd carefully constructed, and in the wreckage, she'd found herself hesitant to rebuild, afraid of investing her heart in something that might crumble again.

"I know that fear," she confessed, her voice barely a whisper. "When you've been hurt, really hurt, the instinct is to retreat. To build walls. I spent so long making myself small, trying to disappear, so I wouldn't be a target any-more."

She looked down at her hands, the flour dust from ear-lier still faintly visible on her skin. "I was afraid of my own passion, even. Afraid that if I poured everything I had into something, like this bakery, and it didn't succeed, or worse, if it did and it somehow wasn't 'enough'... it would prove something I didn't want to believe about myself."

Julian turned to her then, his expression gentle, under-standing. "But it is enough, Lani. You see it every day the way people react to your creations, the comfort and joy you bring them. That's not small. That's huge."

He reached out, his hand hovering for a moment before resting lightly on her knee. The touch was electric, a silent confirmation of the growing connection between them. "And you're not a target. You're a creator. You bring beauty and sustenance into the world. That's a powerful thing."

His words, so earnest and genuine, chipped away at the defensive walls she'd painstakingly erected. It was easier to believe him than to continue arguing with her own insecu-rities. The warmth of his hand on her knee was a gentle in-vitation, a silent assurance that she was seen and accepted in this moment.

"It's hard to shake off the old narratives, though," she admitted, her voice thick with emotion. "The ones that tell you you're not good enough, or that you'll always end up alone. My ex... he had a way of making me feel that way. Like my dreams were frivolous, my efforts were misguided."

The memory still stung, a dull ache beneath the surface. "It took me a long time to realize that his opinion wasn't the absolute truth."

Julian's thumb stroked her knee in a slow, comforting rhythm. "People can project their own insecurities, even their own limitations, onto others. And if we're not careful, we start to internalize them. I've had plenty of people trying to define me, to box me in. 'The golden boy,' they call me. Or 'the heartthrob.' But when the staff goes home and the food critics' reviews die down, I'm just... me. And 'me' is a lot more complicated than they'd ever imagine."

He looked away for a moment, his gaze distant, as if lost in a memory. "There were times, early on, when I felt like I was drowning in it all. The constant scrutiny, the pressure to be perfect. I craved anonymity, a quiet corner where I could just... be. But it felt impossible."

The fire crackled, sending a shower of sparks upwards, illuminating their faces. In that brief, incandescent glow, Lani saw a flicker of the pressure Julian must have endured, the weight of a world's expectations.

"It must be lonely," she said, the word feeling wholly inadequate.

"It can be," he agreed. "The worst is when you crave genuine connection, but you don't know how to find it. How do you tell the difference between someone who's interested in you and someone who's interested in your public image? Eventually, you learn to keep people at arm's length, just to protect yourself from the inevitable disappointment."

He met her gaze, a vulnerability in his eyes that mirrored her own. "I haven't had a real, honest conversation like this in, well I can't even remember how long."

Lani felt a stirring within her, a sense of profound connection that transcended the circumstances. Here, in the heart of a snowbound town, with the world outside a white, wild expanse, they were stripped bare of their usual defenses. The blizzard had created a cocoon, a sanctuary where they could finally breathe, and speak, their truths.

"It's the storm," she whispered, a small smile playing on her lips. "It's forcing us to slow down, to be present. To let the outside chaos create a pocket of inner peace."

Julian returned her smile, a warmth spreading through his eyes. "Perhaps it is. Or perhaps... it's just the fire." He gestured towards the hearth, the flames licking at the logs, their heat radiating outwards. "There's something primal about fire, isn't there? It draws people together. It strips away the pretense. It invites honesty."

He leaned closer, and Lani's breath hitched. The scent of woodsmoke and something uniquely Julian, his subtle cologne filled her senses. The dancing firelight cast a warm glow on his features, softening the lines of his face, making him seem more approachable, more real than she'd ever seen him.

"It's like this," he said, his voice dropping lower, more intimate. "When you're kneading dough, you're forcing it, coaxing it, shaping it. It resists, but eventually yields, becoming something stronger, more resilient.

Our emotions, our fears, they can be like that too. If we try to suppress them, to push them away, they just build up. But if we can face them, acknowledge them, even acknowledge the pain, they can transform. They can become a source of strength, not weakness."

Lani felt a wave of understanding wash over her. He wasn't just talking about dough; he was talking about the human condition, about the art of healing and growth.

"So, the storm outside," she mused, her voice gaining a new confidence, "it's not just a force of nature. It's a catalyst. It's showing us what we're made of, by pushing us to our limits."

"Exactly," Julian agreed, his gaze unwavering. "And in the face of that, it's easier to be honest. Because what else is there? When you're truly vulnerable, what's the point of pretense?" He paused, a flicker of uncertainty crossing his face, then he continued, his voice barely above a whisper. "I used to think that being strong meant never showing weakness. That being successful meant always being in control. But I'm learning that true strength lies in acknowledging those moments of vulnerability. In allowing ourselves to be seen, even when it's terrifying."

The weight of his confession settled in the air between them, heavy and precious. Lani felt a sense of privilege, of being allowed into the guarded spaces of his heart. She, who had spent so long guarding her own, found herself opening up in ways she hadn't thought possible.

"The divorce... it felt like a failure, at first," she admitted, the words tumbling out before she could stop them. "Like I'd made all the wrong choices, invested my heart in the wrong place. It took me a long time to understand that sometimes, even the most carefully constructed plans can fall apart. And that doesn't make you a failure. It just makes you human."

Julian reached out and gently cupped her cheek, his thumb stroking the soft skin. "You are not a failure, Lani. You are resilient. You are beautiful. And you have an incredible gift." His gaze held hers, warm and steady. "And you're not alone. Not anymore."

In the heart of the roaring fireplace, with the blizzard swirling outside, a new kind of warmth was blooming. It was the warmth of shared vulnerability, of unspoken understanding, of a connection forged in the crucible of honesty.

The snow kept falling outside, tapping gently against the windows. Inside, the world felt smaller and warmer. Lani and Julian sat near the fire, the glow painting soft light across their faces. The room was quiet except for the occasional pop from the logs and the steady rhythm of the storm beyond the glass.

They talked for hours, though it didn't feel like it. The conversation moved easily, with laughter here and long pauses there. The kind of flow that happens when two people forget to guard themselves. They talked about everything and nothing: about what they'd dreamed of when they were younger, about the turns their lives had taken, about the quiet, stubborn feeling that they both wanted something more than just getting by.

At some point, Lani realized how close they were sitting, their knees almost touching, the warmth of the fire blurring the edges between comfort and something deeper. There wasn't any grand declaration, no dramatic moment, just the soft understanding that maybe, after all this time, they'd found their way back to a space where things made sense.

The snow outside showed no sign of stopping, but neither of them minded. The storm had given them this, stillness, a place to breathe, a chance to remember how it felt to really be real with someone.

Their quiet conversation flowed through the living room. But a different energy pulsed from the heart of the house, a smaller, more vibrant force fueled by the sheer magic of a snow day.

Naomi, oblivious to the profound confessions and budding emotions unfolding around her, had discovered her own wonderland just beyond the kitchen door.

The world had been transformed into a vast, white playground, and she was ready to explore every glittering inch.

With a squeal of delight that cut through the quiet hum of the blizzard, Naomi had flung open the back door, her face alight with anticipation. The air, frigid and sharp, was a welcome contrast to the cozy warmth of the house.

"It's play time!" Naomi announced, bursting through the door with snow dripping from her boots and hat, leaving a glittering trail on the floor.

"Mommy, Julian! Why are you sitting in here?" Her little face was flushed pink from the cold, her brow creased in confusion.

Lani couldn't help but smile at her daughter's energy, the kind of boundless joy that filled a room just by existing.

"Aren't you cold, sweetheart? Would you like some hot cocoa?" she asked, trying perhaps in vain to steer Naomi's attention away from the snow-covered yard that had clearly captured her heart.

"Yes, but later," Naomi insisted, her eyes bright with determination. "Come build a snowman with me!" She rocked impatiently from foot to foot, knowing she wasn't supposed to go any farther inside with her wet boots.

Julian laughed, the sound rich and unguarded.

Before either of them could say another word, Naomi darted back outside, a streak of pink and motion. Lani followed her with her gaze, heart full and aching all at once.

Through the window, she watched her daughter plunge her mittened hands into the fresh, powdery drifts that had gathered on the doorstep. Naomi's small form was alive with movement and joy, her laughter carrying through the glass.

The snow was perfect, soft, light, and endlessly moldable, and Naomi wasted no time turning it into her playground. Her bright pink snowsuit stood out like a spark against the silvery expanse, her every movement pure energy.

First came the snow angels. Naomi had always adored them, the way they left behind something delicate and beautiful in the snow's untouched surface. Lani watched her daughter lie back, spread her arms and legs wide, and move with gleeful abandon, the motion rhythmic and full of life. Snow clung to her lashes, dusted her rosy cheeks, and tangled in the curls escaping her hat, but she didn't care. She was lost in the joy of the moment, creating fleeting little masterpieces destined to vanish beneath the next flurry.

Lani felt a familiar warmth stir in her chest, the simple, aching beauty of childhood wonder.

Outside, Naomi sprang up again, brushing snow from her sleeves, already plotting her next creation. Her voice rang out, full of excitement. The snow angels, it seemed, were only the beginning.

Soon, her giggles turned into gleeful shrieks as she began packing snow into balls with determined little hands, ready for the next grand adventure, a snowball fight.

Lani exchanged a glance with Julian, a quiet smile passing between them, the kind that needed no words. Outside, their world was white and wild and full of laughter, and for a moment, everything felt exactly as it should.

***

Lani's father, bless his heart, had been lured outside by Naomi's infectious enthusiasm. He'd emerged, bundled in a thick wool coat, a playful glint in his eyes that mirrored his granddaughter's. Their initial skirmishes were tentative, playful tosses that barely reached their intended targets. But soon, the intensity escalated.

Round, perfectly formed snowballs flew through the air, landing with satisfying thuds and exclamations of mock outrage. Naomi, surprisingly agile for her age, would duck and weave, her laughter echoing through the quiet street. Her grandfather, a seasoned snowball warrior, would act surprised at her accuracy, his own throws aimed with a gentle precision that ensured no one got hurt, only playfully splattered.

It was in the middle of one particularly spirited volley that Naomi's gaze drifted towards the back door. There, silhouetted against the warm glow of the doorframe, stood Julian.

He'd been drawn out by the sounds of their merriment. A slow smile spread across his face as he watched the playful combat unfold, the sheer delight radiating from Naomi infectious. He stepped out, the cold air biting at his exposed skin, but he didn't seem to notice.

"Looks like a serious battle is going on here," Julian called out, his voice warm, carrying easily over the wind.

Naomi, mid-throw, spun around, her eyes widening with delight. "Julian! You came to play!"

Lani, who had ventured to the doorway, watched with a quiet ache in her chest. Seeing Julian here, in this element, was a revelation. He shed the polished, almost detached air he often carried and embraced the playful spirit of the day with an easy grace. He didn't just stand there; he plunged in.

Julian picked up a snowball, his movements fluid and natural. He didn't hesitate, didn't overthink it. He formed a perfect sphere and, with a grin, lobbed it towards Lani's father. The shot was accurate, hitting him squarely on the chest.

"Hey!" Thomas exclaimed, feigning indignation, but his eyes twinkled. "You're on her team now, are you?"

"Always," Julian declared, his gaze briefly meeting Lani's, a shared amusement passing between them.

What followed was a riot of snowy chaos. Julian, with his larger frame and athletic prowess, was a formidable opponent, yet he never once overwhelmed Naomi.

He'd shield her from her grandfather's playful attacks, create diversions, and expertly dodge her own well-aimed snowballs, all while laughing with genuine abandon.

Lani watched, her heart swelling with a tenderness she hadn't anticipated. The way Julian interacted with Naomi was more than just polite engagement; it was a genuine warmth, an inherent understanding of childhood joy. He didn't just humor her; he *played* with her. He got down on her level, his laughter mingling with hers, his eyes alight with a mirth that was utterly captivating.

He'd lift her onto his shoulders for a better vantage point, her small hands gripping his hair. She giggled a cascade of pure happiness. He'd help her build a mini snow fort, his larger hands working in tandem with her smaller ones, their collaboration a silent testament to a shared purpose.

He'd even endure a direct hit from a slightly too-hard snowball from Naomi, only to react with exaggerated surprise and a mock dramatic stumble, eliciting a fresh wave of giggles from his snow-day companion.

For Lani, watching Julian with Naomi was like seeing a different side of him, a more authentic, unguarded self. His willingness to embrace this childish pursuit, to shed his public persona and simply be present, spoke volumes. It wasn't just about entertaining her daughter; it was about embracing the spirit of the moment, about finding joy in the simple act of play.

She saw the ease with which he navigated Naomi's boundless energy, the patience he displayed, the genuine delight he took in her every exclamation. He didn't seem to be performing; he seemed to be *enjoying* it. This was not a calculated move to impress her or win her over; this was him, unadorned, reveling in the simple, uncomplicated pleasure of a snow day with a child.

This uninhibited playfulness dissolved a subtle reservation that had begun to form in Lani's mind. She'd been so cautious, so guarded about letting anyone new into Naomi's life, and by extension, her own. The scars of her past were still too tender, the fear of another heartbreak too potent. But seeing Julian's genuine affection for her daughter and the natural way he interacted with her, chipped away at those defenses. It wasn't just about his charm or his intellect; it was about his heart. And in that moment, his heart seemed remarkably open and kind.

He didn't just tolerate Naomi; he seemed to revel in her presence. Lani watched him kneel down to listen to her elaborate explanations about the proper way to construct a snowball. His full attention on her, as if she were the most important person in the world. He'd offer gentle encouragement when she struggled to pack snow tightly, his voice soft and reassuring. He was present, truly present, in a way that few people managed to be.

When Naomi, flushed with exertion and exhilaration, finally declared a truce, collapsing into a giggling heap in a snowdrift, Julian sat down beside her.

Lani had to chuckle at his dishevel as his own breath came in slightly ragged puffs.

He pulled Naomi close, laying a protective arm around her small shoulders, and Lani watched as he brushed stray snowflakes from her hair. It was a gesture so tender, so natural, it made Lani's own heart ache with a newfound warmth.

"You're a formidable snowball opponent, Naomi," Julian said, his voice laced with amusement. "I might have to strategize for our next encounter."

Naomi beamed, her eyes shining. "I'm really good at snowballs, Julian!"

"That you are," he agreed, his gaze lingering on her for a moment before turning to Lani, who stood a few feet away, a silent observer to this intimate scene. His smile widened, a genuine, unforced smile that reached his eyes. "She's quite the force of nature, isn't she?"

Lani felt a blush creep up her neck. "She certainly is. She gets her enthusiasm from... well, she gets it from somewhere." She smiled back, a soft, private smile that acknowledged the unspoken connection forming between them.

The sight of Julian playing in the snow with her daughter, so completely at ease, so full of genuine affection, was a powerful image. It was a picture of him she hadn't imagined, a side of him that resonated deeply with her own maternal instincts.

It was one thing to be charmed by his wit and his vulnerability in the quiet of the living room, but it was another entirely to witness him embrace the messy, joyous, uninhibited spirit of childhood.

As the light began to fade and the snow continued its relentless descent, Naomi, tired but happy, was coaxed back inside by her grandfather.

Julian lingered for a moment longer, the playful energy of the snowball fight slowly receding. It was replaced by the same quiet contemplation that had settled between him and Lani earlier. He turned to Lani, his expression softened by the fading light and the lingering glow of shared play.

"She's an incredible child, Lani," he said, his voice a little huskier now. "Full of life."

Lani's gaze met his, and she felt a flutter in her chest. "She has her moments," she admitted, a small smile playing on her lips. "She gets it from her mother."

Julian chuckled, a low, warm sound. "I have a feeling there's a lot of you in her, and that's a very good thing. She has your warmth, your spark." He paused, his eyes searching hers. "And seeing you two together, it's truly beautiful."

The sincerity in his voice and the genuine admiration in his gaze were disarming. Lani had spent so long protecting herself and shielding her heart from potential pain. But watching Julian with Naomi, seeing the effortless way he'd stepped into their lives and embraced them both was melting away her reservations. He wasn't just a visitor; he was a potential presence, a gentle force weaving himself into the fabric of their lives.

The world was blanketed in a pristine white silence. The blizzard outside had brought the world to a halt, but for Lani, it had also paused her internal struggle, allowing her to see the possibility of a future brighter than she had dared to imagine. And in Julian's eyes she saw a promise of that warmth, a reflection of a heart that was not only capable of deep introspection but also of pure, unadulterated joy.

"It's been a long time since I've seen Naomi this happy, this... free," Lani confessed, her voice barely above a whisper. The storm had done more than just bring snow; it had brought a thawing in her own internal landscape.

"She's been through a lot, and sometimes... sometimes I worry I haven't given her enough of that lightness."

Julian pushed off the counter, taking a tentative step towards her. The air between them crackled with an unspoken electricity, a recognition of shared vulnerability. He stopped just a breath away, close enough for her to feel the warmth radiating from him, close enough to see the intricate flecks of gold in his deep blue eyes.

He raised a hand, his fingers hovering for a moment before gently, almost reverently, touching her cheek.

His touch was feather-light, a tender caress that sent a shiver through her. Her skin felt impossibly sensitive beneath his fingertips, attuned to every subtle shift in his presence. She tilted her head slightly, seeking the warmth of his hand, a silent invitation. His thumb brushed against her cheekbone, a simple gesture that conveyed a world of understanding, of shared experience.

Julian's words caught Lani off guard, settling deep in her chest before she could even respond.

"You've given her everything, Lani," he said quietly, his voice roughened by something raw and real. "You've given her your strength, your resilience. And today... you've given her joy. And me as well."

The sincerity in his tone undid her. For a moment, she couldn't speak. She could only meet his gaze, blue and steady, full of emotion she wasn't sure how to hold. Something unspoken passed between them then, a recognition of everything that had led to this point.

The confessions by the fire, the laughter outside in the snow, the quiet rhythm they'd found in the kitchen all seemed to converge here, in this breathless stillness between them.

Lani could see the empathy in his eyes, the way he seemed to read the flicker of doubt that always lingered at the edges of her heart. He didn't look away from it. Instead, he met it head-on, his presence steady and grounding.

She knew he had noticed the way she'd watched him with Naomi and how easily he'd folded himself into their small, imperfect world. Watching him like that, laughing and light, had stirred something inside her that she hadn't felt in years: safety, connection, the quiet ache of belonging.

"I haven't felt this connected in a very long time," Julian said, his voice low and unguarded. "Not since, well, it doesn't matter. What matters is this. This moment. This quiet after the storm."

Lani's breath caught. There was something so simple and honest in the way he said it that left her disarmed. The air around them seemed to hum, soft, charged, fragile.

She looked into his face, really looked. Gone was the man from magazine covers, the one whose life seemed untouchable. Standing before her was Julian. The man she had once known, now tempered by loss and time was searching for something real.

Her pulse thrummed in her ears as he stepped closer. His eyes held hers, asking and offering all at once. Naomi's laughter faded through the house; the muffled hush of snow still fell outside. Everything seemed to blur until there was only this: warmth, breath, and the space between them growing smaller.

When his lips met hers, it was tentative at first. It was a soft, questioning brush that made her heart stutter. But then it deepened, slow and sure, a pull she couldn't resist. The kiss carried the weight of everything they hadn't said, and the fragile, impossible hope of something beginning again.

His lips were warm, a stark contrast to the lingering chill of the snowstorm outside. They tasted of the subtle sweetness of the pastries they'd shared earlier, and something uniquely him, a hint of mint, a trace of the day's fresh air.

It wasn't a demanding kiss, but one filled with a profound tenderness, a hesitant rediscovery. It was a kiss that spoke of shared loneliness finding solace, of guarded hearts tentatively opening, of a quiet hope blossoming amidst the remnants of a storm.

Lani's hands, as if guided by an instinct she hadn't realized she possessed, rose to cup his face. His skin was warm beneath her touch, his jaw firm and familiar. His hands trembled slightly as they moved from her cheek to her waist, drawing her closer, deepening the connection.

This kiss was a revelation of unspoken desires, of shared vulnerability. It was a promise of something more, a symbol of rekindled feelings sealed by the enchantment of the snowstorm and the comforting aroma of the bakery.

In that moment, the world outside ceased to exist. The lingering snow, the quiet of the bakery, the sleeping child upstairs. It all faded into a soft blur. There was only Julian, his lips on hers, his arms holding her close, and the overwhelming sense of finding something precious and unexpected in the heart of a storm.

The kiss sent her soaring, a breathtaking reaffirmation that even after the deepest winters, spring, and the promise of warmth, could always find a way to bloom. It was a kiss that spoke not of a grand declaration, but of a quiet, profound understanding, a mutual acknowledgment that the connection forged between them was not fleeting, but something that held the potential for enduring warmth and a shared future.

For a heartbeat, everything stopped. The world, the snow, even the fire's crackle and all that remained was the taste of cinnamon and a kiss that felt like a fresh start.

$$\{\ 23\ \}$$

Julian

The world outside the town had transformed overnight. What had been a roaring, merciless storm only hours before was now a vision of pure stillness. It was the kind of beauty that demanded quiet reverence. Snow blanketed every surface, softening edges, reflecting the pale morning light like scattered diamonds. The town, usually brisk and busy, seemed to be holding its breath, caught between slumber and renewal.

Julian lay awake earlier, watching the soft morning light spill across the room. The fire had long since gone out, leaving only the faint scent of smoke and something sweeter. Lani's perfume was clinging to the quilt beside him. He could still feel the weight of the night before in his body, in the quiet ache of muscles that remembered her touch.

He hadn't meant for it to happen. Not at first. They'd been talking by the fire, laughter mingling with the sound of the wind outside. It had been easy, familiar, like slipping into a memory he'd almost forgotten. But then the space between them had shifted.

She'd looked up at him, with eyes soft and full of something unspoken, and he'd known there was no turning back.

He remembered the way her hand had felt in his, small, warm, trembling just a little. The taste of her lips, the way she'd said his name like it was both a question and an answer. The heat of her skin, the softness of her breath against his neck. The storm had raged outside, but inside there had been only warmth, the slow rhythm of their hearts finding each other again after years apart.

In the hush of morning, everything felt different. Calmer. Certain. Lani had slept beside him, her hair spilling across the pillow, her face relaxed in a peace he hadn't seen before. He reached out, fingers trembling as he traced a finger lightly along her shoulder, barely daring to touch her for fear of breaking the quiet spell that lingered between them.

Last night had changed them. It had taken away years of distance and careful restraint, leaving only truth. No performance, no pretense, just two people who had finally stopped running from what had always been there.

Julian closed his eyes and exhaled slowly, letting the echo of her warmth settle in his chest. What had happened between them wasn't planned, but it was real. Deeply, undeniably real. The intimacy, the laughter, the way her breath had caught against his skin...and last night. And for the first time in a long while, he felt something he hadn't dared to hope for—home.

Their past feelings weren't fleeting anymore. They weren't just whispers carried away by the storm. They were real now, tangible, and they lingered in the air between them like the faint scent of sugar and spice that always clung to the walls.

Julian stood and walked to the window, watching as the sunlight spilled across the snow. Behind him, the faint crackle of the old radiator and the comforting scent of cinnamon hung in the air. Reminders that the world was still waking up, even after everything that had happened the night before. He glanced toward the back of the kitchen, where Lani moved to, refilling the kettle. Her hair was slightly tousled; her cheeks still flushed from sleep. The sight made his chest tighten.

The morning light stretched softly across the worn wooden surface of the kitchen table. Lani moved quietly towards him, her hair loose, her expression calm but thoughtful. He could still feel the warmth of her touch, still hear the quiet rhythm of her heartbeat from the night before. Everything about her felt like something he'd been waiting for and now that he'd found it, the idea of leaving felt heavier than he'd ever imagined.

As she reached him, she leaned over and placed a gentle kiss on his lips.

Reality was creeping back in, steady and certain. His restaurants, his team, his responsibilities waited for him miles away, part of a world that for the first time, suddenly felt distant and strangely hollow.

He glanced toward her, the soft light catching on her profile. "I should tell you," he said quietly, his voice rougher than he meant it to be. "I need to head back soon. There are things I have to take care of."

After filling her mug with coffee, she turned to look at him, her eyes steady, though he could see the flicker of understanding there. No surprise, just a quiet acceptance.

He leaned back, rubbing a hand over his jaw. "It's not that I want to leave," he said voice thick with regret. "I don't. I just... need to make things right before I can decide what comes next."

The words hung there, heavy but honest. He watched her nod slowly, the faintest smile curving her lips.

Her calmness only deepened the ache in his chest.

He released a sigh. "It's beautiful," he said softly, gesturing toward the window. His voice still felt rough from sleep. "Like the whole world got a fresh start."

Lani joined him, wrapping her hands around her mug. Her eyes followed the light dancing on the snow.

"It does," she said quietly. "It feels different this morning. Like anything's... possible."

Julian turned slightly, studying her profile. He gently traced the soft curve of her jaw memorizing every detail as a faint smile played on her lips. He longed to freeze her in this instant: serene, radiant, achingly real.

"Maybe it is," he murmured. "Maybe the storm was exactly what we needed."

She smiled faintly, though there was a question in her eyes. "And now what? The roads will open soon. People will start coming in for coffee and bread. Life picks up again."

Julian nodded, slowly. "Yeah," he said, his words wrapped in longing. "Life always picks up again." He hesitated, thumb sliding along her sleeve, fighting to hold onto the moment. "But that doesn't mean we lose this. What happened here was real...more real than anything."

Her eyes met his, and in them he saw everything he'd been afraid to hope for, affection, uncertainty, and longing.

"Last night..." she began, her voice soft, "it felt like the world stopped for a while."

He smiled, just barely. "Maybe it did."

For a moment, neither of them spoke. The room felt suspended in time. The quiet hum of the oven, the glow of the morning light, the scent of sugar and spice wrapping around them like a secret. Julian reached up and brushed a strand of hair from her face. His hand lingered, cupping her cheek, his thumb grazing her skin in a slow, familiar rhythm.

"I meant what I said," he murmured. "I don't want to leave this behind, Lani. I want to see where it leads."

Her breath caught, and she nodded once, small and certain. "So do I," she whispered.

Outside, a snowplow rumbled down the street, breaking the silence. The world was stirring again but inside, wrapped in the soft light of morning, Julian felt something rare and steady take root. It wasn't just the quiet after the storm. It was the beginning of something he hadn't known he'd been waiting for.

He reached for her hand, their fingers intertwining with the gentle assurance of two people who had finally found a rhythm that made sense. The snow outside gleamed brighter as the sun rose higher, and for the first time in a long while, Julian felt... content.

That's when he heard the soft creak of the back stairs. Light footsteps. A sleepy yawn.

"Mommy?"

Lani turned, her hand instinctively slipping from his, though the warmth lingered between them. Naomi appeared in the doorway, wrapped in a too-big sweater, her curls sticking out in every direction. She rubbed her eyes with one small fist and blinked toward the light spilling through the front window.

"Hey, sweet pea," Lani said softly. "Did we wake you?"

Naomi shook her head, her voice still thick with sleep. "No... the snowplow did." Her gaze shifted toward the window, and her eyes widened. "Whoa! It's so shiny! Did it all fall last night?"

Julian couldn't help but smile. "Every last flake," he said, crouching down so he was eye level with her. "Looks like someone painted the whole town white while we were asleep."

Naomi grinned, clutching her stuffed rabbit. "It looks like sugar! Like the frosting you put on cookies, Mommy!"

Lani laughed. "You always think about sweets first thing in the morning," she teased gently.

"Because they're the best thing!" Naomi said matter-of-factly, then turned to Julian. "Do you like sweets too?"

Julian's eyes twinkled. "I do. Especially when your mom makes them."

Naomi's grin widened. "Me too! Grandma says Mom's croissants are magic."

"Well, Grandma's right," he replied. "I've had a lot of croissants in my life, and none of them come close."

Lani shook her head, but the blush that crept into her cheeks betrayed her smile. "You're both terrible liars," she said, but her voice was warm, teasing.

Naomi giggled, then pressed her nose to the window, fogging up the glass. "Can we make a snowman later? Please?"

"After breakfast," Lani said. "But first, I think we need something warm. Croissants sound good?"

Naomi's cheer erupted like sunshine. "Yes, please!"

Julian stood, watching as Lani led her daughter toward the kitchen stool.

The sound of laughter and the gentle clatter of dishes filled the kitchen. Ordinary sounds, yet to him, they felt almost sacred.

He lingered by the window a moment longer, looking out at the bright, glistening morning. The world outside had been remade overnight, so had he.

When he finally turned to join them, Lani was kneeling beside Naomi, helping her reach a plate from the lower shelf. Their heads bent close together, curls mingling, laughter spilling softly between them.

And just like that, Julian felt the shape of his world shift. This woman had stolen his breath, but it was her little girl who had wrapped herself around his heart without even trying. This was the warmth of family, the easy cadence of love in motion, this was what he hadn't known he was searching for.

And as the morning light poured across the flour-dusted floor, he realized with quiet certainty that the storm hadn't trapped him here. It had delivered him home.

***

The sun had climbed higher, flooding the snow-washed world outside with a soft golden light. Through the bakery windows, everything looked impossibly still, like the storm had been nothing more than a wild dream. The scent of cinnamon and coffee lingered in the air, mixing with the quiet hum of the ovens.

Julian stood near the counter, still half-lost in the haze of the morning after. The night had changed something between them. There was no awkwardness, no need to fill the silence, just that fragile, steady peace that comes when two people finally stop pretending.

The doorbell jingled.

He blinked, half expecting the world to still be asleep. But there, framed by the soft light and the smell of snow, stood Mrs. Hammonds. Her cheeks were flushed, her arms full with a thermos in one hand and a plate of cookies in the other.

"Lani, dear!" she exclaimed, bustling in with a rush of cold air and motherly concern. "We were worried sick! When the snow stopped, no one knew if the roads were clear. Are you and little Naomi alright?"

Lani's eyes flicked to him for just a heartbeat.

He saw it. The tiny ripple in her calm, the silent acknowledgment that their little bubble had burst. He watched her straighten, heard the quiet strength in her voice when she replied, "We're perfectly fine, Mrs. Hammonds. Naomi is excited for more snow."

Julian found himself smiling. "It was quite the storm," he said, stepping forward to take some of the weight from Mrs. Hammond's hands. "But Lani here handled it like a pro. I think I was more of a liability than a help."

Mrs. Hammond's gaze turned toward him then, sharp and curious. There was that flicker of recognition. It was the look he'd seen a thousand times before, but somehow it felt different here. Less like a spotlight, more like a surprise.

"Well," she said slowly, her lips curving into a knowing grin, "this *is* a pleasant surprise. We don't often get celebrities snowed in with our bakers."

Lani's breath hitched, and Julian felt her tension from across the room. He wanted to take her hand right then, to remind her that the world couldn't touch what they'd found here. Instead, he offered Mrs. Hammonds an easy smile.

"Just a very lucky traveler, ma'am," he said lightly. "Our town has a way of drawing people back home."

Mrs. Hammond's eyes twinkled as she set the cookies down. "Oh, I'm sure it does," she replied, her tone warm but threaded with mischief. "Well, I'll leave you two to... settle back in. The plows have been through, and everyone's coming out of hiding. Roads are open, though I imagine some of us wouldn't have minded staying snowed in a little longer."

Julian caught the glint in her eye as she reached for the door.

"Don't be strangers, now," she added, pausing just long enough to glance at him again. "Especially *you*, Mr. Big-Restaurant Owner. But I suppose you've got other places to be soon, hmm?"

The bell jingled again, and she was gone, leaving behind the faint smell of coffee and curiosity.

For a moment, neither of them spoke. The world beyond the glass was beginning to stir. The sound of scrape of shovels, the distant growl of an engine, but in the bakery, it was still and warm.

"She knows," Lani said finally, a flush creeping up her neck. "Mrs. Hammonds. She knows something's going on."

Julian laughed softly, taking one of the cookies and breaking it in half. "Let her know," he said, offering her a piece. "Let the whole town know, if they want. Would that really change how you feel?"

Her eyes softened as she took the cookie, her fingers brushing his. "It might make things harder," she said quietly. "People talk. And I have Naomi to think about."

He nodded, hearing the truth beneath her words. The instinct to protect her daughter made her a steady, grounded woman.

"I know," he said, his voice low. "But we don't have to rush anything. We just have to be honest about what's here."

She looked up at him then, and he saw it again. A flicker of hope beneath her careful composure. "What we found here," she said, her voice barely above a whisper, "it's worth protecting. Even if the world's watching."

Julian's chest tightened, an ache of something fierce and real. He reached for her hands, his thumb tracing lazy circles across her knuckles.

"Then we'll protect it," he said simply. "Together."

The shared secret was no longer just theirs; everyone would know soon enough. The storm had passed, but its legacy remained. The roads were clear, the town was waking up, and it was back to the real world. But as Lani looked into Julian's eyes, she knew that they were ready to face it, together.

{ 24 }

Lani

The intimacy, the shared vulnerability, the tender kisses...and last night. These were no longer just whispers of the night, but solid truths that now demanded navigation.

Julian's presence had been a comforting anchor throughout the blizzard, but now held a different weight.

The news of his impending departure had settled over them like the softest snowfall, muffling the immediate joy of the morning but not erasing the warmth it promised. His obligations, a world away from the quiet rhythm of Lani's life, had called him a reminder of the delicate balance they now had to strike. He had to leave, but the way he did it, the words he spoke, the look in his eyes, suggested a departure that was more a preamble than a conclusion.

"I have to go," he said, his voice a low rumble that seemed to vibrate with an unspoken regret.

He stood by the door, his hand still resting on the polished wood, as if a physical barrier between them. The morning light caught the fine lines around his eyes, the very lines that Lani had traced with her fingertips last night. He looked... different in the daylight, more grounded, yet the same magnetic pull, the same intensity, remained.

Lani nodded, her throat tight. She watched him, cataloging every detail. The way his dark hair was slightly disheveled, the faint shadow of stubble on his jaw, and the quiet strength in his posture.

"I understand," she managed to say, though the words felt inadequate, hollow. Understanding didn't diminish the pang of sadness that tightened her chest. It felt as though a part of the newfound peace she had found had to be packed away with his luggage.

Julian met her gaze, his blue eyes earnest and unwavering. "This isn't goodbye, Lani. Not even close."

He stepped forward, closing the small distance that separated them. His hand lifted, his thumb gently caressing her cheekbone, his touch sending a familiar warmth through her. "This is just... a pause. A moment before the next chapter begins."

He leaned in then, his lips finding hers in a kiss that was both a promise and a farewell. It was different from the breathless urgency of their first kiss, this one imbued with a deep, quiet knowing. It was a kiss that spoke of shared secrets, of a connection forged in the heart of a storm, and of a future that was still uncertain but undeniably present.

When he finally pulled away, his forehead rested against hers, his breath mingling with hers.

"I'm going to see Naomi," he murmured, his voice husky. "Before I head out. I want to say goodbye properly. And then... I'll be back."

The conviction in his voice was a balm to Lani's anxieties. It wasn't just words; it was a promise etched in sincerity. "I need her to know this is for a short time, Lani. And I need you to understand I have to leave, as much as you're willing to. We found something special here, something I don't want to lose. Something I need to explore."

Lani could feel the tremor of emotion in his voice, the raw vulnerability that he had shown her throughout the night. It was this genuine openness that had chipped away at her defenses, that had allowed her to hope again.

"I... I'll miss you," she admitted, the words escaping before she could censor them. "And I'll miss this. This quiet. Us."

A gentle smile touched Julian's lips. "And I'll miss you. Terribly." He took a step back, his hands falling to his sides, the tangible connection broken. He looked around the cozy bakery, the scent of cinnamon and yeast still clinging to the air. "This place... it's become more than just a refuge from the storm. It's become a part of my story now." He gestured towards the staircase, a soft smile playing on his lips. "Naomi has such a fierce spirit. I can see why you're so proud."

He walked towards the stairs, and Lani followed, a silent escort. The morning sun, now brighter, streamed through the windows, casting long shadows across the floor. Naomi fell back asleep, a peaceful figure tucked under her blankets, her breathing soft and even. Julian stood by her bedside for a long moment, his gaze filled with a tenderness that Lani hadn't seen before. He didn't touch her, but his presence seemed to radiate a silent warmth, a paternal love that was both beautiful and surprising.

"She's amazing, Lani," he whispered, turning back to her, his eyes shining. "You've done a remarkable job. She's so resilient. And kind. I can see so much of you in her." He paused, then added, his voice a little softer, "And maybe in time she'll pick up some of my good habits, perhaps?" He offered a wry smile, a flicker of hope in his gaze.

Lani felt a blush creep up her neck. The idea of Naomi being a part of their shared future, of their lives intertwining, was still a fragile concept, one she was just beginning to embrace. "She deserves all the best," Lani said, her voice thick with emotion. "And so do you, Julian."

He reached out, his hand brushing hers as he turned to leave. "And we'll find that best, won't we?" he asked, his voice laced with an optimistic conviction. "Together."

He gave Naomi's door a final, lingering look before descending the stairs, Lani close behind.

The snowplows had already begun their work, carving paths through the deep drifts, the rumble of their engines a herald of the town's return to normalcy. Julian paused, his gaze sweeping over the transformed landscape, then settling back on Lani.

"I'll call you," he promised, his voice firm. "As soon as I can and explain everything to Naomi. And I'll be back. Sooner than you think."

He hesitated, then reached out, his hand cupping her face once more. His touch was a benediction, a tangible reminder of the connection that now bound them.

"Don't let the world outside make you forget what we found here, Lani. Don't let fear win." He leaned in and kissed her again, a quick, intense kiss that left her breathless.

Then, with a final, lingering look that spoke volumes, he turned and walked out into the bright, sun-drenched snow.

Lani watched him go, her hand instinctively rising to her lips, still tingling from his kiss. He climbed into his sleek, dark car, a stark contrast to the rustic charm of her town, and with a final wave, he drove away, leaving behind a trail of tire tracks in the pristine snow.

The silence that descended upon the bakery was profound, an echoing void where Julian's presence had been. The scent of his cologne, a subtle blend of sandalwood and something distinctly masculine, still lingered in the air. Lani stood on the threshold, the biting cold a stark reminder that the enchanted bubble of the blizzard had burst. The world was back, the roads were clear, and Julian Vance, the chef and restaurateur, was returning to his world.

But as she watched the diminishing silhouette of his car disappear down the freshly cleared road, Lani realized that something had fundamentally shifted within her.

The fear, the ingrained caution, was still present, a persistent whisper in the back of her mind. But it was no longer the loudest voice. It was being drowned out by the sweet memory of Julian's kiss and the certainty of his promise. He had left, but he had left behind more than just an absence.

He had left behind the lingering promise of a future that they would build.

Her parents arrived at the bakery as the morning progressed, their faces etched with a mixture of relief and concern. They found Lani in her element, a whirlwind of flour dust and frosting, her concentration absolute.

Elenore watched her daughter with a knowing gaze. A soft smile played on her lips. She'd seen this before, this fierce dedication that Lani poured into her baking, but there was something different this time. A spark, a self-possession that hadn't been as pronounced.

"You're working at lightning speed, Lani," Elenore observed, her voice warm with admiration as she carefully arranged a tray of precisely decorated sugar cookies. "It's like you've been supercharged."

Lani paused, a delicate sugar snowflake poised in her hand. She met her mother's eyes, a genuine smile gracing her lips. "Just trying to catch up after the snow. And well, Christmas is almost here."

Her father, Thomas, a man of few words but keen observation, nodded in agreement, his gaze lingering on the intricate details of Lani's work.

"You've always been good, Lani," he said, his voice a low rumble that carried the weight of years of quiet pride. "But you seem... more than good today. You seem very sure of yourself." He gestured with a flour-dusted hand towards the array of cookies. "These are remarkable. More detailed than usual."

Lani felt a blush creep up her neck. She knew her parents had noticed Julian's presence, the quiet intensity of his stay. They had seen the shift in her, the subtle but undeniable change in her demeanor. While they might attribute it in part to Julian's influence, to the rekindled connection they had glimpsed, Lani knew it was also something deeper, something that had been awakened within her.

"Maybe I just needed a good storm to shake things up a bit," she quipped, a playful glint in her eye. She dusted the snowflake with a touch more glitter, its tiny facets catching the light. "It's good to be back in the thick of it. Feels right."

Elenore placed a gentle hand on Lani's arm. "It's good to see you like this, sweetheart. You seem happy. And I know Julian's visit meant a lot to you." There was no probing, no judgment, just a simple acknowledgment of the connection they had witnessed. "He seems like he has grown into a good man, Lani. Kind."

Lani's heart gave a soft lurch at the mention of Julian. The image of his earnest blue eyes, the gentle touch of his hand, flashed in her mind.

"He was," she confirmed, her voice soft. "He is." She looked around the bustling bakery, the familiar scent of baking, the comforting weight of her apron. "And this is my world. And I'm good at it."

It was a simple statement, yet it held a profound truth. The demanding, often relentless, rhythm of Shepard's Sweets was not just a job; it was a testament to her resilience, her skill, her enduring passion.

The Christmas rush, with its early mornings and late nights, became demanding. Lani handled it all with a new-found confidence. She seamlessly juggled orders for elaborately decorated cakes, meticulously crafted pastries, and mountains of holiday cookies.

The pressure of deadlines, the occasional demanding customer, and the sheer volume of work all served to anchor her. The business helped to keep her mind focused on the present and on the task at hand.

She found herself anticipating her customers' needs. She suggested pastry-and-coffee pairings and offered recommendations with an assuredness that surprised even herself.

The quiet conversations with her parents at the end of each long day were filled with a lighter tone. They spoke of sales figures, of inventory, of the challenges of the season, but beneath it all was a current of unspoken pride. They saw their daughter not just as the baker who would inherit their legacy, but as a woman stepping fully into her own power, both in her craft and in her life.

One afternoon, as she was piping intricate holly leaves onto a festive Yule log, Elenore brought her a cup of steaming tea.

"You know," Elenore said, settling onto a stool beside Lani, her gaze sweeping over the organized chaos of the decorating station, "I remember when you were just a little thing, always trying to 'help' me bake. You'd get more flour on yourself than in the bowl." She chuckled softly. "You've always had this in you, Lani. This knack."

Lani smiled, the memory bringing warmth to her cheeks. "I think I learned from the best."

"But you've taken it further," Elenore continued, her voice laced with a deep maternal pride. "You've found your own style, your own voice. And it's beautiful. This confidence you have now, it's not just about the baking, is it?" Elenore's eyes held a gentle, knowing inquiry.

Lani met her mother's gaze, a small, genuine smile touching her lips. She didn't need to elaborate. The unspoken understanding passed between them. The storm had indeed shaken things up, and while Julian's departure had left a void, it was a void that was already being filled with something new.

It was the quiet hum of her own rediscovered strength, the reassuring rhythm of the bakery, and the nascent hope that pulsed within her. The sweet scent of Christmas baking filled the air. She was back, and she was more present, more capable, and more undeniably herself than ever before.

The world outside was bustling with the holiday spirit. Inside the bakery, her hands moved with practiced ease, shaping dough, swirling frosting, creating edible masterpieces, each creation a silent affirmation of her own enduring resilience. The familiar weight of the rolling pin in her hands felt like a comforting extension of her own being, a tool that had been with her through countless seasons and would continue to be a constant in the ebb and flow of her life.

The scent of cinnamon and sugar was more than just the aroma of her livelihood; it was the fragrance of her own strength, a constant reminder of what she was building and what she was capable of.

She was not just keeping the bakery alive; she was breathing new life into it and infusing it with her own renewed spirit. In doing so she was rebuilding her life, her craft, and the unfolding promise of her future. The demanding pace of the Christmas rush, far from being overwhelming, was a welcome challenge, a vigorous exercise for both her body and her spirit.

Her parents' observations, though subtle, were deeply felt. They saw not just the improved efficiency but the subtle shift in her bearing, the quiet confidence that emanated from her, a self-assurance born not just from Julian's attention but from her own capabilities and new ideas, now amplified and recognized.

She found deep satisfaction in the predictable chaos of the holiday season, the rhythmic clang of mixing bowls, the hiss of the ovens and cheerful chatter of customers. These were the sounds of her life, the soundtrack to her resilience.

The memory of Julian was a tender warmth, a cherished secret that fueled her resolve, but it did not define her. Her identity was rooted in the flour dust on her apron, the calluses on her hands, the artistry in her creations. Lani found herself not just surviving but truly thriving. Her beloved bakery was just as ready for whatever the coming season and the future might bring.

***

Naomi's bright, excited chatter filled the warm kitchen, a stark contrast to the quiet hum of the bakery ovens. She was perched on a stool, her small hands still dusted with a faint shimmer of edible glitter, gesturing wildly as she recounted the previous day's adventures. Lani, meticulously piping delicate, snowy white icing onto a batch of sugar cookies, listened with a soft smile playing on her lips.

"And then, Mommy, Julian said he'd never had a *real* snowball fight before!" Naomi's eyes sparkled, her voice high and full of infectious glee. "He was so surprised when I hit him right in the middle of his jacket! He just laughed, this big, rumbling laugh, and then he threw a snowball back that was *huge*! It landed right beside me, but it was so soft, like a fluffy cloud. He's really good at it, you know. Much better than me, I think, but I made him laugh!" She giggled, a pure, unadulterated sound that warmed Lani's heart.

Lani paused her piping, tilting her head to better catch Naomi's enthusiastic description. The image of Julian, the man who had arrived like a tempest and settled like a gentle snow, engaging in a playful snowball fight with her daughter, felt like a scene from a heartwarming holiday movie. It was so perfectly... *them.*

Naomi's immediate and unreserved affection for Julian had been a balm to Lani's own tentative feelings. It was one thing for her to feel a connection, a flutter of hope, but to see it reflected in Naomi's innocent joy. Well, that was something else entirely. It solidified her belief that Julian wasn't just a visitor in her life; he was potentially something more.

"He sounds like he had a lot of fun, sweetie," Lani said, her voice soft.

She imagined Julian, his usually composed demeanor softening with laughter, the playful glint in his eyes as he engaged in the simple, unadulterated joy of a snowball fight. It was a side of him Lani was only beginning to discover, and it was utterly captivating.

"Oh, he did!" Naomi insisted, bouncing slightly on her stool. "And then, guess what? We decorated the gingerbread house together! The big one I made for the window display? He helped me put on all the little candy canes and the gumdrop pathway. He said he'd never decorated a gingerbread house this pretty before either but he knew just where to put the icing to make it stick. He helped me build a little chimney, and he put a tiny gumdrop on top like a little hat! It looks so amazing now, Mommy. Everyone will love it."

Lani's heart swelled with a tender affection for both of them. Naomi's excitement was so genuine, so pure. And the fact that Julian had so readily embraced the childish delight of decorating a gingerbread house, that he had participated with such enthusiasm, spoke volumes about his character. It wasn't just about indulging Naomi; it was about finding joy in the simple, collaborative moments.

And Naomi, she had been talking about Julian for weeks.

Seeing Julian connect with Naomi so easily, so naturally, was profoundly reassuring. It dissolved any lingering doubts she might have had, any anxieties about introducing him into their lives. Naomi's simple, unvarnished happiness in his company was the most potent validation Lani could have asked for.

"That sounds wonderful, sweet pea," Lani said, turning back to her cookies, her hands moving with a newfound lightness. "I'm sure it's the most beautiful gingerbread house in town. You and Julian make a great decorating team." The words felt easy, natural. They weren't forced, nor were they an exaggeration. They were simply the truth, a reflection of the warmth that had settled in her chest.

Naomi beamed, her small chest puffing out with pride. "He's really nice, Mommy. Really, really nice. He tells funny stories, and he smells nice too, like... like warm wood and sunshine." She wrinkled her nose in thought.

"And he helped me find my blue mitten when it fell off in the snow. It was hidden under a big snow pile, and he dug it out for me. He's strong."

Lani smiled, the image of Julian, strong and kind, digging through snow for a lost mitten, solidifying her positive impression. He was patient, considerate and clearly good with children. These were qualities Lani had always valued, qualities she secretly hoped for in a partner. The thought that she might have found them in Julian, and that Naomi so clearly saw and appreciated them too, was a powerful comfort. The storm had brought them together, and now, in its aftermath, a quiet season of warmth and connection was beginning to bloom.

"He sounds like a very good friend, Naomi," Lani said, her voice a little softer than before. She carefully placed another perfectly formed sugar cookie onto the cooling rack. "I'm so glad you enjoyed your time with him."

The word 'friend' felt almost too small, too insignificant for the burgeoning feelings that had been stirring within her since Julian's arrival. But for Naomi, for now, it was the perfect word. A bridge between their shared experience and the promise of more.

"I wish he lived here," Naomi declared, her voice tinged with a slight wistfulness. "Then we could have snowball fights every day! And he could help me bake cookies all the time. He ate so many of the ones we made. He said they were the best he'd ever tasted." She looked up at Lani, her brow furrowed in thought. "When is he coming back? Will he come back soon?"

Lani's heart gave a little leap at the question. It was a direct echo of her own quiet longing and old fears briefly surfaced.

"I don't know exactly when, sweet pea," she admitted, choosing her words carefully. "But I hope he'll visit again soon. I think he liked it here, don't you?" She watched Naomi's face, searching for any flicker of doubt, any hint of confusion. But there was none. Only bright, eager anticipation.

"Oh, yes!" Naomi exclaimed, her face lighting up. "He said he liked the snow, and he liked the pretty lights, and he liked our house. And he liked *us*," she added, her voice dropping slightly, as if sharing a precious secret. "He said he liked *us*."

Lani's breath hitched. That he had said that, that he had expressed such a sentiment, even to a child, felt like a profound gift.

It was a validation not just of his growing affection for her, but of his genuine appreciation for their world, their home, their shared moments. For Lani, it was a subtle but significant step, a quiet acknowledgment of the bond that was forming.

"And I liked him, Mommy," Naomi continued, her voice earnest. "He makes me feel... happy. Like when you finish a really big puzzle, and all the pieces fit."

Lani knelt beside Naomi's stool, her hand gently resting on the child's small shoulder. Naomi's simple analogy struck a chord deep within her. Julian made her feel that way too. Like disparate pieces of her life, once scattered and seemingly unconnected, were finally beginning to fall into place. He brought a sense of order, a quiet strength, and a surprising warmth that had been missing for too long.

And to know that Naomi felt it too, that their shared experience had brought her such simple, profound joy, was more comforting than Lani could express.

"That's a wonderful feeling, isn't it?" Lani said, her voice thick with emotion. She squeezed Naomi's shoulder gently. "And I think he felt it too, Naomi. I think he felt happy with us."

She met Naomi's bright, inquisitive gaze, a soft smile gracing her lips. The idea of Julian visiting again, of him being a regular part of their lives, no longer felt like a fragile wish, but like a tangible possibility. A sweet, warm prospect that she embraced with open arms.

"So, he'll definitely come back?" Naomi pressed, her hope palpable.

Lani nodded, a genuine sense of optimism blooming within her. "I have a good feeling about it, sweet pea. A very good feeling."

She looked around the bakery, the familiar scent of cinnamon and sugar, the comforting sight of her baking tools laid out, suddenly felt even more welcoming and full of promise.

"He's a good man, Naomi," Lani said, her voice firm, filled with a quiet certainty. "A very good man."

And as she turned back to her cookies, her movements steady and purposeful, she knew that Naomi's innocent pronouncements had solidified something within her.

Julian was not an interruption; he was an invitation. An invitation to a future that felt brighter, warmer, and infinitely sweeter than she had dared to imagine. The memory of his laughter during their brief, unexpected snow globe encounter, the warmth of his hand that had briefly touched hers, the quiet strength in his eyes. These were no longer just fleeting moments.

They were the foundation stones of something real, something beautiful, something she was ready to build upon. And in Naomi's simple, unadulterated acceptance,

Lani found the courage to embrace that burgeoning hope, to believe that this unexpected arrival might indeed be the beginning of a cherished new chapter.

She imagined his return. The anticipation was a sweet ache in her chest. And in that quiet moment, surrounded by the comforting aroma of her craft and the innocent joy of her daughter. Lani allowed herself to believe in the possibility of shared snowball fights, of collaborative gingerbread house constructions, of a future where his warm smile and kind presence were a regular, cherished part of their lives. The sweetness of her baking now seemed to mirror the sweetness of the burgeoning hope that bloomed within her, a testament to the unexpected gifts that sometimes arrive in the aftermath of a storm.

Flour clung to Lani's apron, a pale dusting against the faded cotton. Sunlight, still hesitant, painted pale stripes across the worn wooden table where Naomi's spoon scraped rhythmically against the bottom of her cereal bowl.

"When's Julian coming back, Mommy?" Naomi's voice, a high, sweet chime, echoed in the quiet kitchen.

A smear of jam, the color of crushed berries, bloomed on her cheek. Lani's hand stilled mid-knead, the dough giving a soft sigh under her touch. She smoothed a stray curl from Naomi's forehead.

"Soon, little one. Very soon." Her gaze drifted past the steaming mugs, past the window framing the dew-kissed rose bushes that clawed at the glass, towards the silent, waiting road.

The scent of woodsmoke, sharp and comforting, hung heavy in the air, a constant companion to the silence Julian's absence had carved into their home.

It had been two weeks since Julian's departure. Two weeks that had settled back into the predictable rhythm of early mornings and flour-dusted afternoons.

Naomi, of course, had been full of questions about him, her small voice a constant, gentle reminder of the warmth he had brought into their lives. But Lani, while reassuring her daughter with hopeful responses about his potential return.

There was a softness that had replaced the brittle edges of her long-held caution. The fear that had once been a constant companion, a quiet sentinel guarding her heart, had receded, leaving behind a more permeable space.

It wasn't that the fear was entirely gone; perhaps it never would be. But it no longer dictated her every step, no longer cast a shadow over every potential joy.

Instead, a fragile, yet persistent, optimism had taken root, pushing through the compacted earth of her reservations. It was a subtle shift, like the slow, almost imperceptible turning of the earth towards the sun, but it was profound. The world, which had often felt like a minefield of potential hurt, now held the promise of gentle discoveries.

The bakery also seemed to have undergone a transformation in her perception. For so long, it had been her sanctuary, a fortress built of flour and frosting where she could control every variable. It had also her self-imposed isolation.

But now, she saw it differently. It was no longer just a shield but a place of quiet strength from which to engage with the world. Her craft was no longer just a means of survival; it was her pride. The bakery had once sheltered her; now it felt like a launchpad.

She looked at her parents with new clarity, their steady support and quiet presence filling her with renewed gratitude.

They had weathered their own storms, navigated their own heartaches, and yet they had always provided a stable, loving harbor. She saw the wisdom in their gentle counsel, the strength in their quiet endurance. Their love, a constant, unadorned gift, was a reminder that connection, even in its most enduring and unassuming forms, was a powerful force.

And Naomi. Her daughter was the bright, beating heart of her world. A constant source of wonder. Lani had always loved her fiercely, but now, with this newfound openness, she saw Naomi's innocent joy, her unbridled enthusiasm, as a reflection of a deeper truth. Naomi's ability to embrace Julian so easily, to welcome him into their lives with such open arms, was a mirror to Lani's own budding hope. It was a reminder that vulnerability, when met with genuine warmth, could lead to the most beautiful of connections.

Naomi's laughter, the way her eyes lit up when she talked about Julian, was a powerful affirmation that love was not to be feared, but to be savored.

The quiet hum of the ovens, the rhythmic whisking of batter, the gentle clinking of ceramic mugs, they were the soundtrack to a life that, while still grounded in the familiar, now held a wider horizon.

She found herself lingering over the details and plans to revamp the bakery. Julian's absence, while noted, was no longer a gaping void.

Instead, it was a quiet space that allowed these newly appreciated aspects of her life to breathe and expand. His presence had disrupted the predictable stillness and in the ensuing quiet. Lani had begun to hear the subtle changes of her own life, desires she had long suppressed.

He had shown her a glimpse of a different possibility, a warmth that extended beyond the familiar confines of her carefully curated existence. And that glimpse, however brief, had been enough to stir something dormant within her, to awaken a longing for more, a willingness to explore the terrain beyond her own well-trodden path.

She remembered the way Julian had looked at her. Not with pity or judgment, but with quiet curiosity, a genuine interest that made her feel cherished. That look had chipped away at the layers of self-protection she'd so carefully maintained. It suggested he saw not a broken woman, but someone with depth, with a story, with a future not solely defined by her past.

The realization had been slow but steady: maybe the narrative she'd told herself about her own limits wasn't the full truth.

The fear of vulnerability was like an old coat, familiar, worn, but no longer fitting. She had worn it for so long she'd almost forgotten what it felt like to be without it. Yet Julian's gentle persistence, his quiet kindness, had begun to loosen the seams. He never demanded, never pushed, but his open-hearted presence created a space where she could finally breathe. And when she did, the air felt startlingly liberating.

Her openness didn't arrive with fanfare; it came like a slow thaw. The frozen parts of her heart began to soften. She found herself humming as she worked, smiling at customers with a warmth that surprised her.

Julian's stories lingered with her.

They weren't tales of adventure, but of quiet moments and shared meals. Through him, she was reminded that simplicity had its own kind of richness. The contentment she'd once dismissed as naïve now felt profound, even aspirational.

Her relationship with her parents had also begun to shift. Their talks once stayed safely on the surface, weather, work, and the bakery. Now, she found herself sharing more of her thoughts, her gratitude, her growing sense of peace. They listened with gentle understanding, and in their quiet affirmations, she felt something deepen between them. It was no longer just a family obligation. It was a connection, simple and real.

Naomi's future, once a mountain to be conquered, now felt like a garden to be tended. Lani was still protective, still determined to give her daughter every opportunity, but the anxiety that once shadowed those thoughts had eased. She trusted her ability to guide Naomi, to nurture her growth. Her daughter's resilience and joy filled Lani with quiet confidence.

Whatever the future held, she knew they would face it together, rooted in love, strength, and a new openness to whatever blessings might come.

"Mommy!"

The small, bright voice broke through the quiet rhythm of Lani's thoughts. She looked up just as Naomi came bounding through the bakery door, pink cheeks flushed from the cold, a scattering of snowflakes melting in her dark curls.

Lani smiled, brushing the flour from her hands as Naomi ran to her. The little girl's mittens were mismatched again -yellow and pink - and her grin was wide enough to light the room.

"Look what I made at school!" Naomi announced, pulling a crumpled paper from her coat pocket. It was a drawing. Stick figures stood beneath a big, uneven sun. Three figures. Herself, Naomi, and one more, taller, with hair the color of midnight.

"That's you, Mommy," Naomi said proudly, pointing at the middle figure. "And that's me. And that's Julian. He makes you smile."

Lani's breath caught for a moment. The drawing was simple and childlike, but something about it. Maybe it was the way the sun shone over them, the way their hands were joined, it felt achingly real. She knelt beside her, smoothing the paper with gentle fingers.

"He does make me smile," she said softly. "You do too."

Naomi giggled, leaning into her mother's arms. Her small body was warm, smelling faintly of cocoa and the outdoors. Lani held her close, pressing a kiss to her hair.

Outside, the snow lay on the ground. The scent of freshly baked bread filled the air, mingling with laughter, with hope, with something new taking root.

Lani set the drawing on the counter, letting it dry beside the rising dough. She caught her reflection in the glass. Dark circles showed under her eyes. She was tired but content.

"Come on," she said, taking Naomi's hand. "Let's make something sweet for dinner."

Naomi's face lit up. "Can we make the kind Julian likes?"

Lani laughed, the sound soft and certain. "Yes, sweetheart. I think he'd like that."

And as they turned back to the flour-dusted counter, the warmth of the oven wrapped around them. The world outside could wait. For now, there was only this-her daughter's laughter, the soft promise of the rising dough, and the steady heartbeat of a life finally beginning to bloom again.

{ 25 }

Julian

Snow fell in lazy spirals through late-afternoon light, softening the edges of the street, blurring the world into something hushed and almost dreamlike. Julian slowed as he reached the corner, his headlights glinting off the bakery window. The sight stopped him cold.

There she was.

He stepped closer, drawn to the light, to her. And as if she'd felt it—the pull—she looked up.

Their eyes met through the glass.

For a breath, neither of them moved. The years seemed to fold in on themselves, collapsing the distance that had lived between them for too long. Her expression flickered: surprise first, then something like disbelief, and finally, that soft, unmistakable warmth that had once undone him completely. It hit him hard, right in the chest, the quiet knowing that he'd missed her far more than he'd ever let himself admit.

When she smiled, just faintly, the cold didn't seem to bite anymore.

He pushed open the door, the bell chiming above him. Warmth enveloped him instantly. The scent of butter and sugar, the low hum of the ovens, and beneath it all, something that was purely her.

"I told you I'd be back," he called as he pushed open the door, his voice carrying easily in the crisp winter air. "And I didn't come empty-handed."

Her mouth curved into that familiar half-smile, part amusement, part invitation. "Something tells me it's not another novelty mug."

He laughed, the sound echoing lightly in the small shop. "No mugs this time." He set a box on the counter between them, the heat from the ovens wrapping around him like a welcome. "A challenge," he said, flipping open the flaps. Belgian butter. The real thing."

Her lips curved into that familiar, half-amused smile, and the sound of his name, unspoken but alive in her eyes, was somehow louder than anything she could have said.

"Something tells me it's not another novelty mug," she teased, though her voice was softer now, colored with something that sounded like relief.

Julian laughed, the sound rumbling low in his chest. "No mugs this time." He set the box on the counter, the heat of the bakery wrapping around him as if the space itself had been waiting. "A challenge," he said, lifting the flaps to reveal his find. "Belgian butter. The real thing."

Her breath caught, her composure slipping into wonder. "You didn't."

"Oh, I did," he said, grinning. It wasn't about the butter—it never had been. It was about that look she gave him now, like he'd brought her something rare, something only he would know to bring. "And I propose we use it for a proper test. The art of the croissant."

It was meant as a lighthearted jab, but the air between them shifted again. Softer. Closer.

"You want to make croissants here? With me?"

He nodded, his voice gentling. "It's a dance, really. Science and instinct. I've got the theory... and you've got the touch."

Her blush deepened, but her eyes held his. The tension between them was almost tangible now, delicate but undeniable.

"Alright then," she said, brushing a stray lock of hair from her face, a small smile tugging at her lips. "Let's see if your theory can keep up with my instincts."

He chuckled, but it came out quieter than he expected—less amusement, more reverence. "Deal."

Their fingers brushed as she reached for the butter, a fleeting touch that felt anything but accidental. The ovens hummed, the snow whispered against the windows, and in the charged stillness, something in him steadied, then came undone.

Before he could think, she moved around the counter and into his arms.

It wasn't tentative. It wasn't hesitant. It was certain, the way two people fit when words had already said enough. Julian closed his eyes and breathed her in, his hand finding the small of her back, the warmth of her body seeping into his. The faint sweetness of her hair, the rise and fall of her breath, the quiet tremor when she exhaled against his chest—it was all achingly real.

"I'm glad you're back," she murmured, her voice soft against his shirt.

He exhaled, the tension of weeks dissolving in a single breath. "Me too," he said quietly. "More than you know."

When she stepped back, her eyes held something lighter, freer. Julian felt it too. It was the quiet certainty of belonging. He hadn't realized until that moment how much he'd missed this: her laughter, her calm, the way the world seemed to slow when they were together.

Standing there in the glow of the bakery, her smile reflected in the polished glass, he knew better.

And at that moment, surrounded by sugar and warmth and the faint scent of bread, Julian knew he hadn't just returned to a town or a memory.

***

The oven timer chimed, a bright, clear note cutting through the bakery's symphony. Julian opened the door, and a wave of pure, unadulterated heaven washed over them. The croissants. They were magnificent. A deep, burnished gold, their surfaces glistening as if kissed by the sun. They had puffed up dramatically, the crescent shapes defined and elegant, each curve holding the promise of flaky, buttery layers within.

The scent of butter and caramelized sugar still hung in the air like a soft memory, but it was Naomi's laughter that gave the space its real warmth.

It filled the corners that had once felt sterile, seeped into the quiet places of his mind that he hadn't realized had gone hollow over the years.

Watching her and her little hands waving animatedly as she compared croissants to "buttery clouds" and "happy food," Julian felt something inside him ease, a quiet, unspoken ache he hadn't wanted to name.

He'd come to this town chasing a craft, chasing the kind of perfection that only existed in lamination charts and baking temperatures. But here, kneeling beside a five-year-old with a smear of butter on her cheek and her mother smiling softly in the background, Julian realized he'd stumbled into something far rarer. This wasn't just the perfection of pastry. This was the perfection of belonging.

Naomi was radiant, perched on a stool far too big for her, swinging her legs with the effortless confidence of someone who knew she was adored.

"Julian," she said through a mouthful of croissant, "you should open a bakery with Mommy. You could call it... um..." She paused, brow furrowed in thought. "*Butter Clouds!*"

Lani laughed, a bright, melodic sound that wrapped around him. "Butter Clouds, huh? That's actually kind of cute."

Julian grinned, unable to resist her infectious joy. "I'll admit," he said, resting his elbows on the counter, "it's got a nice ring to it. Has a certain... honesty."

Naomi nodded vigorously, utterly convinced. "And I could be the taster. Forever."

"Forever?" Julian teased, raising an eyebrow. "That's a long time to eat croissants."

Naomi giggled. "That's okay. I'm brave."

Her answer drew another ripple of laughter from Lani, the kind that softened the edges of the world. Julian found himself studying her in the golden afternoon light streaming through the window: the gentle curve of her smile, the quiet pride in her eyes as she watched her daughter, the faint dusting of flour that glimmered like snow in her hair.

She looked... at peace. And that, he realized, was the truest triumph of all.

He hadn't meant for this to happen. The easy camaraderie, the shared laughter, the slow intertwining of their rhythms. But it had, as naturally as dough rising in a warm room. He'd shown her how to coax butter into layers; she'd shown him how to let joy in again.

Naomi leaned against the counter, content now, her small hand resting trustingly on his. The weight of it was so light, yet so certain. It struck him deeper than he expected. He glanced at Lani, and their eyes met. There was something wordless there: gratitude, understanding, and a question neither of them needed to voice just yet.

Outside, the snow had begun to fall again. Soft flakes drifted past the window, catching the light like the fine dusting of flour that lingered in the air. The world beyond the glass seemed hushed, holding its breath.

Inside, the warmth of the oven still glowed, the scent of their labor of love wrapping them in quiet contentment.

Julian carefully lifted one of the croissants from the sheet with a spatula. It was impossibly light, its delicate shell crackling softly as he moved it.

He held it out to Lani. "Go on," he encouraged, his gaze warm. "The first one is always special."

Hesitantly, Lani took it. She brought it to her lips, and with a gentle bite, the outer layers surrendered with a satisfying crispness.

Julian took a bite.

The interior was an explosion of pure, buttery bliss. Layers upon layers, impossibly thin and tender, melted on her tongue, creating a delicate, airy honeycomb structure. It was sublime. A wave of pure delight washed over him, followed by an overwhelming sense of accomplishment.

"Oh, Julian," she managed to say, her voice muffled by the pastry. "It's... It's incredible." Tears pricked at the corners of her eyes.

The hours they spent meticulously folding, chilling, and shaping the dough, the moments of frustration and the sparks of insight, had all led to this. This golden, flaky masterpiece.

Julian reached over to gently dust a crumb from Naomi's chin, and she looked up at him with the kind of unguarded trust only a child could give.

"You make good croissants," she declared solemnly. "And you make Mommy smile."

That simple statement, so honest, so devastatingly true, settled in his chest like an ember. He felt Lani's gaze on him again, and when he looked at her, she was smiling that same hesitant, hopeful smile she'd worn the first time he'd seen her soften.

He smiled back. "Guess that makes this my best batch yet," he said quietly.

Naomi giggled, crumbs still on her fingers. Lani's laughter joined hers. And in that moment surrounded by warmth, sweetness, and the faint sound of snow brushing against the window. Julian felt something unfold inside him. Something simple.

Something steady.

The storm had passed. What lingered now was light and fragile, tender, but real.

And for the first time in a long time, Julian didn't just taste success.

He tasted home.

{ 26 }

Lani

The lingering scent of perfectly caramelized butter and toasted flour was no longer just the aroma of success; it was the perfume of possibility. Lani watched Naomi, her small frame still buzzing with the residual joy of her croissant critique, and then her gaze shifted to Julian.

His smile, a quiet, contented curve of his lips, was a familiar and comforting presence, seamlessly woven into the fabric of their lives. The triumph of the croissant, the tangible, flaky, buttery picture of their shared effort, had opened a new opening in Lani's world. One she'd previously only dared to imagine in fleeting, hopeful moments.

"He's a super good baker, you know!" Naomi had declared her pronouncement a sweet, innocent endorsement that had resonated deeper than any professional review could.

It was more than just praise for Julian's technical skill; it was a testament to the genuine affection she felt for him.

As Naomi's enthusiastic descriptions of the "buttery cloud" croissants filled the air, Lani and Julian found themselves in that quiet, post-victory lull, a space ripe for introspection and, perhaps, for the planting of new seeds.

"You know," Julian began, his voice a low rumble that drew Lani's attention from where she was tidying a stray dusting of flour, "seeing Naomi so happy with the croissants... it's incredibly rewarding. It makes me think about what else we could create, together."

He gestured vaguely, his eyes holding a spark of professional ambition, the same spark that had driven him to meticulously hone the lamination of those very croissants.

"Your understanding of flavor profiles, your intuition with ingredients... and my, well, my slightly obsessive attention to technique." He gave a self-deprecating smile, but Lani knew there was more than just modesty in his words.

Lani paused, a half-wiped counter beckoning. "I know what you mean," she admitted, her voice soft.

The bakery, once a traditional family endeavor, was weighed down by her own aspirations and the quiet hum of her own efforts. Now it felt different. Julian's presence had injected energy, a sense of shared purpose that was both exhilarating and deeply grounding.

"It's like... when you have a really good idea, but you need someone else to help you bring it to life, to add a piece you didn't even know was missing."

"Exactly," Julian confirmed, stepping closer.

The easy familiarity between them now felt like a well-worn path, comfortable and sure-footed. He reached out, his fingers brushing hers as he gestured towards the cooling racks, still bearing faint imprints of their recent triumph.

"This isn't just about making a perfect croissant, Lani. This is about potential. We have a knack for this, both of us. Separately, we're good. But together..." He let the implication hang in the air, heavy with unspoken promise.

Lani's heart gave a little flutter. She had always been fiercely independent, her bakery a sanctuary built on her own sweat and tears. The idea of relying on someone else, of sharing the creative and financial risks, had been a formidable hurdle. But Julian... Julian was different. He didn't diminish her vision; he amplified it. He understood the artistry, the passion, and he brought a complementary set of skills that were, frankly, indispensable.

"I've been thinking about that too," she confessed, her gaze meeting his. The warmth that bloomed in her chest was a stark contrast to the cool pragmatism that often governed her business decisions. "I've been so focused on just helping my parents keep this place afloat, on making it *my* own. But you've... you've shown me that it can be more. That we can be more."

"More of what?" Julian prompted gently, his thumb now tracing a slow circle on the back of her hand. The simple touch sent a jolt of warmth through her.

"More... collaborative," Lani said, the word tasting new and exciting on her tongue. "More ambitious. I've had so many ideas for new products, for different kinds of pastries, even for catering small events. But I always felt overwhelmed, like I didn't have enough hands, or enough. Or even expertise in certain areas." She looked at him, a hopeful question in her eyes.

"Your precision, your understanding of patisserie techniques, marketing, building a new business, it's incredible, Julian. And with my creativity, my love for unique flavor combinations," she paused.

Julian's smile widened. "We could create something truly special, Lani. Imagine a line of signature pastries. Not just croissants, but éclairs with unexpected fillings, tarts that blend classic techniques with modern twists, perhaps even artisanal breads that tell a story with every slice."

His mind was clearly racing, a familiar cascade of ideas spilling forth. "We could explore wholesale opportunities, supplying to local cafes that are looking for something unique, something with a story behind it. Or even develop a small, curated menu for special orders, for parties and celebrations."

"Catering..." Lani mused, the word resonating with a long-held dream. She pictured elegant dessert tables, artfully arranged pastries that spoke of quality and care. "That's something I've always wanted to do. But the thought of managing larger orders, of ensuring consistency and quality on a bigger scale... it felt daunting."

"And that's where I come in," Julian said, his voice firm but gentle. "I can handle the production side, the precision that ensures every single item meets our standard. You can be the creative director, the visionary. We can divide and conquer, Lani. You can focus on developing new recipes, on the artistry and inspiration, and I can focus on the execution, on making sure we can deliver on that vision, consistently and beautifully."

The vision they were sketching out wasn't just about expanding the bakery; it was about building a shared future. For so long, Lani had navigated the choppy waters of single parenthood and entrepreneurship alone. Her parents agreed to the initial plans and have already begun transferring ownership to her solely.

The prospect of a partner, not just in business but in life, had been a distant, almost unattainable star. But Julian's quiet strength, his unwavering support, and now, his tangible contribution to their shared success had made that star feel like it was descending, closer and closer, until it was within reach.

"And Naomi," Lani added, her voice softening as she thought of her daughter, who was now meticulously arranging the fallen croissant shards into a miniature, edible sculpture on the counter. "She loves being here. She loves watching us bake. This isn't just my dream anymore, Julian. It's going to be hers too. I can feel it."

Julian's expression shifted, the professional gleam in his eyes softening into something far more personal and profound. He knelt beside Naomi, his voice a warm invitation.

"Naomi, you know how much fun it is to bake with your mom and me, right?"

Naomi nodded enthusiastically, her mouth already full of a pastry shard. "It's the bestest! Can we bake a cake tomorrow?"

Julian chuckled. "Maybe not a whole cake just yet, but perhaps some special cookies? And your Mommy and I were just talking about how much we both love baking with you. We were wondering if you'd like it if we did it... more often. Like, a lot more often." He looked at Lani, a clear question in his gaze.

Lani felt a wave of emotion wash over her. Naomi's innocent question and Julian's gentle inclusion of himself in the equation were a beautiful, unspoken affirmation.

"Julian wants to be a bigger part of our lives, sweetie," Lani said, her voice thick with feeling. "He's been helping us make the most amazing things in the bakery, and he wants to keep helping. He wants to be here, with us, making delicious treats and having fun."

Naomi looked from Lani to Julian, her brow furrowed in thought. Then, her face broke into a wide, radiant smile. "You mean... like a family?" she asked, her voice filled with hopeful wonder.

The word hung in the air, potent and life-altering. Lani's breath caught in her throat. She looked at Julian, and in his eyes she saw a mirror of her own burgeoning hope, tender apprehension, and profound willingness to explore this beautiful, unexpected possibility.

He gave a slow, deliberate nod. "Something like that, Naomi," he said, his voice laced with deep, resonant sincerity. "If that's something you and your mom would like."

Lani found herself nodding too, a silent agreement that transcended words. The idea of a blended family, once a distant concept, now felt warm, tangible, and incredibly real. It was built on shared passions, on mutual respect, and on the undeniable joy of a child who, with her characteristic openness, had given them both her blessing.

"Yes, Julian," Lani said, her voice steady and clear, meeting his gaze. "I think... I think that's exactly what we'd like."

The bakery, which had always felt like Lani's personal sanctuary, was slowly but surely transforming into something more. It was becoming a space of shared creation, of shared dreams, and Lani dared to hope, the foundation of a shared life.

The discussion that followed wasn't just about business plans and product lines. They were about timelines, about shared responsibilities, and about the quiet, steady commitment to building something lasting. Julian spoke of wanting to invest his skills and his time, not just as an employee or a partner, but as a permanent fixture in their lives.

"I want to be part of it all," he admitted. "Naomi's school plays, lazy Sunday mornings... I want to be someone she can depend on. Someone who's there."

Lani listened, her heart swelling with a tender, exhilarating emotion.

"I don't just want to help you open a new business and walk away. I want to bake with you, Lani," he said, his hand finding hers across the worn oak table in her small apartment kitchen, a space that was slowly starting to feel like 'theirs' as much as 'hers'. "I want to build a life with you. And with Naomi. This bakery is a perfect place to start. It's already filled with so much heart, so much love. I want to add to that. I want to be a part of that future."

The fear of vulnerability and the ingrained habit of self-reliance began to recede replaced by a sense of trust and optimism. She had spent years protecting herself, building walls around her heart to shield it from potential pain. But Julian's patience and genuine affection, and his willingness to embrace both her and Naomi with such open heartedness had, brick by brick, dismantled those defenses.

"I... I want that too, Julian," she admitted, the words a soft whisper, yet carrying the weight of a profound declaration. "I want a future with you. I'm ready to explore what that looks like. Not just as business partners, but as... as something more. A family."

The future they were now consciously planning felt tangible. It was no longer a concept born of chance encounters and shared glances over flour-dusted counters. It was a deliberate construction, built on the solid foundation of their mutual respect, their shared love for creating delicious things, and their undeniable connection.

They talked about financial planning, about Julian buying into the business, about how they could combine their resources and talents to create something truly remarkable. The possibilities seemed boundless.

"We could expand the space," Julian suggested one evening, sketching ideas on a napkin while they shared a quiet dinner. "Knock down that wall to the old storage room. Create a dedicated pastry kitchen. And maybe a small seating area, for those who want to enjoy their croissants fresh from the oven, with a good cup of coffee."

Lani's eyes lit up. She had always loved the cozy intimacy of her small bakery, but the idea of a more defined space, one that could accommodate more customers and perhaps even small workshops, was incredibly appealing.

"And we could offer baking classes!" she exclaimed, her own ideas bubbling to the surface. "For adults, and maybe even for kids, like Naomi. Imagine teaching them the basics, passing on the joy of baking."

"Exactly," Julian agreed, his gaze meeting hers, a shared excitement passing between them. "It wouldn't just be about selling pastries anymore. It would be about sharing our craft, about building a community around what we love. And it would be a testament to your family, to us."

The word *us* resonated deeply. It was no longer just her family bakery, or *Lani and Naomi's bakery*. It was *their* bakery, *their* future. The anxieties that had once gnawed at Lani, the fear of financial ruin, the loneliness of single parenthood, uncertainty of her romantic future. All of it was slowly being replaced by steady confidence. Julian's presence was a constant source of reassurance, his belief in her, in *them*, a powerful catalyst for change.

"I never thought I'd be in this position," Lani confessed one quiet afternoon as they carefully arranged a tray of fruit tarts for a new catering client. Sunlight streamed through the window, glinting off the glossy berries and casting a warm glow across the counter. "I was so afraid of opening myself up again, of the risk in letting someone in. Not just professionally, but personally."

She hesitated, watching Julian pipe a perfect swirl of cream with that steady focus she had come to find grounding. "But you make it feel safe," she continued softly. "You make it feel not just possible, but... wonderful."

Julian looked up then, meeting her eyes. His smile was quiet but certain, the kind that began in his chest and worked its way outward.

"Lani," he said, setting the piping bag down, "you make me feel like I've finally found where I belong. This bakery, your passion, Naomi's laughter, it's everything I've been looking for. I want to be a part of this. I want to build it with you."

Outside, beat soft and silent against the window pane. Lani nibbled softly on her bottom lip.

"I didn't know how to start over," he admitted. "So I built walls instead. Kitchens. Menus. I kept chasing something I couldn't taste anymore. But being here..." He looked around, shaking his head slightly, as if in disbelief. "I remember what it felt like to *feel*. To create because it mattered, not because someone would write about it."

Lani's throat tightened. "You always created because it mattered, Julian. Even when you didn't know why."

A silence settled between them. Years of loss and longing threaded through it, softening into something fragile and new.

Julian's gaze found hers again. "I used to dream about this place," he said quietly. "About walking through that door and seeing you behind the counter. About saying all the things, I never got to say."

Lani swallowed hard. "And now that you're here?"

He took a slow step forward, then another, until he was close enough to feel the warmth radiating from her and the ovens behind her. "Now I don't want to wake up."

Her breath caught. His hand rose, tentative at first, then steady, brushing a strand of hair from her cheek. His thumb lingered there, tracing the faint curve of her jaw, and the world seemed to narrow to that single point of contact with the quiet hum of the ovens, the soft ticking of the clock, their hearts moving in time.

"Lani," he whispered, her name barely a breath. "I don't know if I deserve another chance. But I'd give anything just to be part of your world again. Even a small part."

Her eyes glistened. "You don't have to earn it, Julian," she said softly. "You just have to stay."

That was all it took. The words, simple and true, cut straight through the years of distance.

Julian leaned forward, his lips finding hers with quiet reverence, as though he were afraid she might vanish if he moved too quickly. The kiss was slow, tender, and full of memories. The echo of their youth, the ache of their separation, and the fragile, hopeful promise of something new.

Lani melted into him, her hands rising to rest against his chest. The steady beat of his heart thrummed beneath her fingertips. When they parted, their foreheads remained pressed together, breaths mingling in the soft glow of the bakery.

Julian smiled faintly, his voice husky. "You know, I've cooked in Michelin-starred kitchens and served meals to presidents... but nothing has ever felt as right as standing here with you."

Lani let out a soft, teary laugh. "You always did have a way with words."

"And you always did have a way of making me believe them," he murmured.

She looked up at him, her expression open, unguarded. "Then believe this, your home, Julian. For as long as you want to be."

He kissed her again, slower this time, the warmth of the ovens wrapping around them like a blessing.

He reached for her hand, his thumb brushing across her knuckles with gentle certainty. "The future we're talking about, the one with more baking, more laughter, more family, it's not just an idea anymore. It's what I want. With you. And Lani..."

He paused, the words rough but true. "I love you."

The words seemed to hang in the air between them, simple but immense. Lani's breath caught, her fingers trembling slightly in his grasp. For a moment, she could only look at him. The man who had walked into her life with patience instead of pressure, kindness instead of pretense.

Her eyes softened and she let out a shaky laugh that was half sob, half relief. "Julian," she whispered, her voice thick with emotion, "I love you too."

He drew her closer, and she went willingly, their hands still dusted with flour, the faint scent of sugar and butter wrapping around them like a benediction. When his arms circled her, she felt the tension that had lived in her shoulders for years melt away as their lips touched.

They stood there for a long moment, the world narrowing to the warmth of their embrace, the steady beat of his heart against hers.

When they finally pulled apart, Lani smiled through the shimmer in her eyes. "You realize this means you're officially part of the bakery now," she teased, her voice lighter. "Long hours, early mornings, and very little glory."

Julian laughed, brushing a stray lock of hair from her face. "As long as I get to do it with you," he murmured, "I'll take every bit of it."

She leaned in again, her forehead resting against his. "Then it's settled," she said softly. "You, me, Naomi... and a whole lot of butter."

Julian smiled, his thumb tracing small circles on her hand. "That sounds like the perfect recipe."

The scent of the tarts filled the air, sweet and warm, as they stood together in the quiet bakery.

Lani's smile lingered, but there was curiosity in her eyes now, something hopeful.

"What happens next?" she asked softly. "For you, for us?"

Julian exhaled; the answer was already clear in his mind. "I've been thinking about that," he admitted. "About what it means to really *be* here. Not halfway between places, not running back and forth to the city. I've already spoken with my partners."

His thumb traced a slow, absent circle over her hand. "I'm going to appoint someone else to manage the restaurants. Someone I trust. They can handle the day-to-day, hell, they've earned it."

He looked around the bakery then, the light catching on the rows of glass jars and polished trays. "My place is here now. With you. I want to take everything I know, operations, marketing, finance, and help make this place thrive. Not just survive but *grow*. You've built something beautiful, Lani. I just want to help make sure it lasts."

Lani's throat tightened. "You'd really do that?" she asked, her voice barely above a whisper.

"I already have," he said simply, and the quiet conviction in his tone sent warmth blooming through her chest. "I've spent years building other people's dreams. This," he gestured gently to the bakery, to her, "this is the first time I want to build *ours*."

Her eyes shimmered as she smiled, wide and unguarded. "Then it's settled," she murmured. "You, me, Naomi... and a lot of early mornings."

Julian chuckled, brushing a stray lock of hair from her cheek. "I know, and a lot of butter," he added.

She laughed, leaning into his touch. "The perfect combination."

He kissed her again, softly, reverently, sealing a promise. And when they finally parted, the future didn't feel uncertain anymore. He stepped away, transitioning into the businessman he was.

"I've been doing some research," he said, pulling out a sleek tablet. "There are grants available for small businesses looking to expand, especially those with a focus on artisanal production. And I've been looking into different POS systems and inventory management software. Things that will streamline our operations and free up more of your time for recipe development and creative direction."

Lani was impressed not just by his competence but also by his genuine desire to invest in *their* future. It wasn't just about him joining her bakery; it was about him building it with her, from the ground up.

"You've really thought this through," she said, with a sense of awe washing over her. "It feels so real. Like we're not just dreaming anymore."

"We're not," Julian confirmed, his gaze steady and reassuring. "We're building. And we're going to build something incredible, Lani. Something that will last." He paused, then added with a hopeful smile, "And maybe, just maybe, we'll make some of the best pastries the world has ever tasted along the way."

The conversation flowed effortlessly, a seamless blend of professional ambition and personal affection. They discussed the possibility of hiring additional staff in the future to manage the increased workload. Even the idea of eventually opening a second location in a neighboring town in the future.

Each idea, each suggestion, was met with thoughtful consideration and an enthusiastic collaboration that felt entirely natural. The fear that had once held Lani captive was now a distant memory, replaced by a vibrant sense of excitement and possibility. The future was once a hazy landscape of uncertainty. Now coming into sharp focus, a canvas upon which they would paint their shared dreams, one delicious pastry at a time.

{ 27 }

Lani

The air in her parents' small, cozy home crackled with a festive energy that was as familiar as it was invigorating.

Christmas Eve.

The words themselves felt like a warm embrace, a promise of twinkling lights, comforting aromas, and the gentle hum of cherished traditions.

Lani surveyed the scene with a contented sigh, her heart swelling with a sense of belonging that had been slowly, beautifully rebuilding itself since she'd returned to her childhood town. Her parents' faces were etched with the quiet joy of the season. Naomi's eyes were wide with anticipation, darting between her mother and her grandparents. A tiny whirlwind of excitement, her small hands eager to contribute to the unfolding magic.

The magnificent Fraser fir tickled Lani's nose with the crisp scent of forest air. The tree stood proudly in the corner with its branches already adorned with a colorful medley of ornaments. Each bauble, each delicate glass figure, was a tiny vessel holding a memory, a moment frozen in time.

Lani found herself drawn to a set of hand-painted wooden stars, a gift from her grandmother years ago. She remembered tracing the swirling patterns with her finger as her small voice attempted to mimic the carols her parents sang. Now, as she carefully hung them amongst the glowing fairy lights. The familiar shapes seemed to glow with an inner warmth, a silent testament to the enduring love that permeated their family.

Her father's large hands were surprisingly nimble as she carefully draped a shimmering garland around the boughs with a contented hum vibrating in his chest.

Her mother's silver hair caught the light and was untangling a strand of twinkling lights. Her brow furrowed in concentration while a slight smile playing on her lips. It was a scene of beautiful, chaotic domesticity, and Lani wouldn't have traded it for anything.

"Naomi, darling, can you hand me those red stars, please?" her mother asked, her voice gentle.

Naomi, who had been meticulously arranging pinecones at the base of the tree, scampered over with her small arms filled with the shiny spheres.

As she carefully placed them on a low branch, Lani watched them, a pang of nostalgia mixed with present-day joy. It was during these moments, bathed in the glow of the tree and the warmth of her family, that Lani felt most herself, most grounded. The uncertain, exhilarating developments with Julian felt like a separate and vibrant thread woven into the tapestry of her life.

The scent of baking was, of course, an essential part of their Christmas Eve. This year, the honor of Santa's favorite treat fell to a batch of classic shortbread cookies. Their buttery aroma filling the kitchen with a comforting sweetness.

Lani, her parents, and Naomi were all gathered around the counter earlier in the day in a flurry of flour and rolling pins. Lani and her mother worked side by side, their movements synchronized, a silent understanding passing between them. Elenore, a woman of quiet grace, had always been her rock, her first culinary mentor. Lani remembered countless hours spent in this very kitchen, her small hands sticky with dough, her mother patiently guiding her through the mysteries of baking.

"These need to be perfectly crisp, for Santa's reindeer too," her mother instructed, her eyes twinkling. "He'll need a good, hearty snack after his long journey."

Naomi, armed with a small star-shaped cookie cutter, was diligently pressing shapes into the dough, her tongue poking out in concentration. Her creations, while perhaps not as perfectly uniform as her grandmother's, were made with an abundance of love, and that, Lani knew, was the most important ingredient. Lani found herself watching Naomi with a tenderness that threatened to overwhelm her. Seeing her daughter so happy, so engrossed in the simple joy of creating something special, was a profound gift.

"Remember when you used to make these, Lani?" her father chimed in, his voice warm. "You'd always sneak a piece before they were even baked. Said the raw dough tasted like pure happiness."

Lani laughed, a soft, melodic sound. "I still think it does," she admitted, a hint of her childhood mischief returning. "But these ones are strictly for Santa."

She carefully placed a row of perfectly formed shortbread stars onto a baking sheet. Each one was a tangible link to Christmases past and the promise of many more to come.

The conversation flowed as easily as the dough, a gentle current of shared memories and quiet observations. Her parents spoke of their own childhood Christmases, of the simple pleasures that had meant the most.

Lani listened, absorbing their wisdom, feeling the foundations of her own life solidified with each spoken word. The anxieties that had once felt so overwhelming, the uncertainties about her future with Julian, seemed to disappear into the background, replaced by a deep sense of peace.

This was where she belonged, here, surrounded by the people who had loved her unconditionally, who had shaped her into the woman she was today.

As the afternoon wore on, the kitchen transitioned into a culinary hub for the evening's feast. Lani's father, a man who relished the role of family chef, began to prepare the centerpiece: a succulent roast turkey, its skin already glistening with herbs and butter. The aroma of roasting poultry soon mingled with the sweet scent of shortbread, creating an intoxicating symphony of festive flavors.

Lani helped him with the side dishes. She chopped vegetables with a practiced hand, her mind a calm, happy space. She peeled potatoes and arranged a medley of roasted root vegetables. Their colors were a cheerful contrast against the rustic wooden cutting board.

Meanwhile, Elenore was in charge of the dessert. This year, it was a traditional Christmas pudding, rich with dried fruits and spices, its preparation a ritualistic dance of stirring and simmering. Lani watched her mother stir the pudding, a tradition passed down through generations. It had been a symbol of continuity and enduring love.

"You know," her mother said, her voice soft, "this recipe has been in our family for over a hundred years. It's seen Christmases of joy, Christmases of hardship, but it's always been there."

Lani felt a profound connection to that sentiment. Her own life had recently seen its share of challenges, of uncertainties. But like the Christmas pudding, she, too, was finding her way back to a sense of constant, enduring love. The bakery, her relationship with Julian, and her reconnection with her parents. These were the ingredients that were slowly, steadily, altering her life into something beautiful and strong.

As dusk began to settle, a warm golden glow set over the snow-dusted landscape outside. Naomi, anticipation grew as her face flushed with excitement.

"Santa would be arriving soon, and the shortbread cookies needed to be put on the hearth. They need to be perfect," Naomi exclaimed

Lani helped her daughter arrange the cookies on a festive plate, alongside a glass of milk, a sweet offering to the magical man in red. The simple act was so familiar, so ingrained in her childhood memories that Lani was filled with a profound sense of contentment. It was these small, seemingly insignificant moments that truly defined Christmas, acts of love and tradition that bound families together.

The doorbell chimed. The cheerful sound cut through the gentle hum of the house. Lani's heart gave a familiar, hopeful leap.

Julian. He was here.

She glanced at her parents, who offered her warm, encouraging smiles. Naomi, however, was already at the door. Her anticipation overruled any sense of shyness. Lani followed, her steps light, a smile gracing her lips. The evening was unfolding precisely as she had hoped, filled with the warmth of family, the comfort of tradition, and the promise of shared joy.

The uncertainties of the future were still there, a quiet murmur beneath the surface, but for tonight, in this warm, festive atmosphere, they felt manageable, even exciting. She was ready for whatever this Christmas Eve and the future would bring.

Julian stood on the doorstep, a festive sprig of holly tucked into his coat, his eyes crinkling at the corners as he saw Lani. He carried a small, beautifully wrapped gift.

"Merry Christmas Eve," he said, his voice a low, warm rumble that always sent a pleasant shiver down Lani's spine.

Naomi launched herself into his arms. "Julian! You're here!" she exclaimed, her voice muffled against his chest.

He chuckled, hugging her tightly.

"Of course, I'm here, little one," he said, his gaze meeting Lani's over Naomi's head.

In that shared look, Lani saw a reflection of the deep, burgeoning affection that had taken root between them.

"Welcome, Julian," Lani said, her voice soft but clear, stepping forward and taking his hand. "Come in, come in. We're just about to sit down for dinner."

Her parents greeted Julian with genuine warmth, their acceptance of him as a part of their lives evident in their easy smiles and welcoming gestures. Her father clapped him on the shoulder, a hearty, friendly gesture.

"Glad you could make it, Julian. We've got plenty of roast turkey to go around."

Her mother offered him a glass of mulled wine, its cinnamon-scented steam curling invitingly in the cool evening air.

"We were just talking about how much you'd enjoy Lani's mother's Christmas pudding," he said, her eyes twinkling. "It's a family secret, you know, but I think she might be willing to share it with you... eventually."

Julian accepted the wine with a grateful smile, his eyes lingering on Lani for a moment longer. "It's an honor to be here," he said, his sincerity evident. "Thank you for inviting me."

As they gathered around the dining table, bathed in the soft glow of candlelight and the twinkling lights of the Christmas tree, Lani felt a sense of peace settled over her. The table was laden with food. The aroma of roasted turkey, savory stuffing, and sweet cranberry sauce filled the air, a comforting, festive perfume. Besides Julian, Lani felt a sense of rightness, a feeling that this was exactly where she was meant to be.

Naomi, nestled between Lani and Julian, chattered excitedly about her day, recounting the process of cookie-cutting and her fervent hopes for Santa's arrival.

Julian listened with genuine interest, occasionally interjecting with a question or a shared anecdote. Lani watched them, her heart swelling with a tenderness that was almost overwhelming.

This, she thought, *this was the beauty of family.*

Her parents also seemed to relax and open up as the evening progressed. By the time dinner plates were cleared and the last of the cider poured, the kitchen felt softer somehow, looser, lighter.

Her father leaned back in his chair with a satisfied sigh. "You know," he said, gesturing toward the plate of gingerbread men on the counter, "those turned out a lot better than the ones we tried to make when you were little, Lani."

Lani smiled, already knowing where this was headed. "You mean the ones that looked like they'd survived a house fire?"

Her mother laughed, covering her mouth with her hand. "Oh, those poor cookies. We couldn't tell if they were supposed to be men or, what did you call them, Thomas? Little brown ghosts?"

Julian chuckled, his eyes crinkling at the corners. "That bad, huh?"

Her father nodded solemnly. "Worse. I thought we'd have to throw the baking tray out with them. The smell alone could have emptied the house."

"I cried for an hour," Lani admitted, shaking her head. "I'd spent all morning decorating them. I think I gave one of them a mustache."

Julian leaned forward, laughing. "A mustache? On a gingerbread man?"

"I was very creative," Lani said with mock pride. "It was my artistic phase."

Her mother smiled fondly, her eyes softening. "You were so determined, even then. You wanted everything to be perfect." She took a sip of cider before adding, "That's why your father bought you that little baking set the next Christmas. You stayed up all night pretending to run your own bakery."

Julian glanced at Lani, warmth flickering in his gaze. "So, this place was destined to happen," he said softly. "Shepard's Sweets" has been waiting for you since you were five."

Lani felt a small smile tug at her lips. "Maybe it was," she said. "Though I had no idea back then that it would come with so many early mornings."

Her father chuckled. "She used to tell everyone she was going to own the biggest bakery in the world. I told her she'd better start saving her allowance."

Julian laughed, then shook his head. "You know, it's funny, listening to you all reminds me of my own family's Christmases."

"Oh?" her mother asked, leaning forward, curiosity bright in her eyes. "Tell us."

He smiled, a little wistful now. "We used to spend Christmas Eve at my grandparents' house in the mountains. It was always snowing. It never failed. My brother and I would wake up before dawn to see if Santa had come, even though my parents begged us to sleep in."

Her father grinned. "Ah, so you were one of those early risers, eh?"

"The worst," Julian admitted with a laugh. "One year, I snuck downstairs at three in the morning, tripped over the cat, and woke everyone up. My grandmother swore I'd scared Santa off."

Lani laughed softly, picturing it. The little boy version of Julian, tousle-haired and eager, wide-eyed at the magic of it all.

"What about your favorite gift?" her mother asked, clearly charmed.

He thought for a moment, then smiled. "A red sled. It wasn't new. It had been my dad's when he was a kid, but I thought it was the most incredible thing in the world. We spent the entire day on the hill behind the house, racing until it got dark."

There was something tender in his voice, something unguarded. Lani found herself leaning closer without meaning to.

Her father chuckled. "You sound like you miss it."

Julian hesitated, then nodded. "Sometimes," he admitted. "Those were... simpler days. Before everything got so loud." His eyes flicked toward Lani. "It's nice to be somewhere that still feels real. That still feels grounded."

"My grandfather used to say that stories were the glue that held families together," Julian explained, his voice thoughtful. "They were a way of passing down wisdom, of remembering who you were and where you came from. He believed that every family had its own unique mythology, its own collection of tales that defined its spirit."

He turned towards Lani, "I think that's what we're creating here, Lani. Something new. A chapter that includes your family, me, and maybe... the beginning of ours too."

Lani met his gaze, feeling that familiar warmth bloom in her chest, the quiet recognition of love.

Her mother smiled softly. "That's what Christmas is supposed to be," she said. "Family, good food, a warm fire. The rest of the world can wait."

Julian's eyes lingered on Lani for a moment longer. "I couldn't agree more," he said quietly.

And as the laughter and the soft hum of conversation carried on around the table, Lani felt something shift, a gentle, glowing sense of belonging, as if their separate stories had somehow, without effort, begun to weave together into one.

The conversation flowed effortlessly, shared laughter, quiet reflections, and a growing sense of camaraderie. It wasn't just about the food or the festive atmosphere; it was about the intangible yet powerful bonds being forged.

Lani felt a deep sense of gratitude for this moment, for the warmth and acceptance Julian had brought into her life and for the enduring love of her family which had always been her anchor.

The bakery, her new ventures with Julian, her future, were all exciting prospects. But tonight, the simple joy of sharing this moment with the people she loved most felt like the greatest gift of all.

Later, as the dishes were cleared and Naomi's excitement began to wane, a sense of quiet contentment settled over the house.

Naomi, her eyelids drooping, was curled up on the sofa, a half-read Christmas story in her lap, the promise of Santa's visit clearly weighing heavily on her sleepy mind. Lani found herself sitting beside Julian, their shoulders brushing, a comfortable silence enveloping them. The soft glow of the Christmas tree lights cast dancing shadows on the walls, creating an intimate, almost magical atmosphere.

"Thank you for tonight, Julian," Lani murmured, her voice barely above a whisper. "It means so much to me that you're here."

Julian turned to her, his expression soft and affectionate. "It means a lot to me, too, Lani," he replied, his thumb gently stroking the back of her hand. "This is...it's everything I'd hoped for. Being here with you, with your family. It feels like coming home."

The words settled into Lani's heart, warm and true.

Coming home.

She had felt adrift for so long, navigating life and their loss. But now, with Julian by her side, with her family's love a constant and unwavering presence, she felt the deep, settled peace of belonging. The future was beginning to reveal itself, not as a place to be feared, but as a space to be built, together.

As the night deepened and the final hours before Christmas dawned, Lani felt a sense of gratitude. The familiar rituals of Christmas Eve, the comforting presence of her family, and the promise of a shared future with Julian had settled like perfect joy in her chest. It was a reminder that even in the midst of change and uncertainty, the unwavering strength of love remained constant. And for that, Lani was eternally thankful.

Lani felt a warmth spread through her chest, a quiet joy blooming like a delicate flower. The word "family", spoken with such earnestness by Julian, resonated deeply within her. It was what she had clung to, nurtured, and fought for, and to hear him embrace it so wholeheartedly, to see him so comfortable and at ease in the heart of her world, was a profound gift.   "I remember one Christmas," Julian continued, his voice softer now, "when I was probably about ten. My father had always been a very practical man. He'd never really got into the spirit of things. But that year, he decided to surprise us. He'd been secretly learning to play the piano. On Christmas Eve, after dinner, he sat down at the old upright in our living room, and he played 'Silent

Night.' He wasn't perfect, his fingers fumbled a few times, but the effort, the sheer love behind it. It was shocked. I think that was the year I truly understood that love isn't always about grand gestures; it's often found in the quiet acts of trying, of putting yourself out there for the ones you love."

He looked at Lani, his gaze steady and filled with an emotion that made her breath catch. "And that's what I see in you, Lani. You're always trying, always putting yourself out there, not just for your business, but for everyone around you. You have that same quiet strength, that same willingness to put your heart into things."

Lani's mother sighed contentedly. "It's a beautiful thing, isn't it? To see two people who bring out the best in each other. Julian, you have a remarkable way of expressing what we've always felt about Lani, but perhaps couldn't quite put into words. You see her not just as our daughter, but as the remarkable woman she is."

"And you, " Lani's father added, his gaze fixed on Julian, "you are a man who understands the value of family, of tradition, of love. Those are qualities we cherish. We've seen how you look at Lani, how you interact with Naomi. You have a good heart, Julian. That much is clear."

The fire had dwindled to a bed of glowing embers, casting a soft, diffused light that seemed to permeate the room with a sense of peace.

Naomi stirred on the rug, a soft sigh escaping her lips, but she remained asleep, cradled in the warmth of the hearth.

The silence that fell between them was not an awkward one, but a comfortable, companionable hush, punctuated only by the gentle crackling of the fire and the quiet rhythm of their breathing. It was a silence filled with unspoken understanding, with a shared appreciation for the moment, and with the quiet promise of a future.

Lani shifted, resting her head on Julian's chest, listening to the steady beat of his heart. The shared stories, the playful teasing, and the heartfelt reflections had all served to deepen the already strong foundation of their relationship.

They had offered Julian a glimpse into her past, her family's history, and in return, he had shared pieces of his own, revealing vulnerabilities and strengths that further endeared him to her and her parents.

Their lives were no longer just Lani's and Julian's, or Lani's and her family's; it was becoming a single connection rich with shared experiences and mutual affection.

This was more than just Christmas Eve; it was a turning point —a moment when past, present, and future converged in a perfect, harmonious embrace.

Lani

The fire, now a gentle whisper of embers, cast a warm, intimate glow across the room, a stark contrast to the chill creeping in from the frosted windowpanes. The quiet hum of the night outside seemed to amplify the stillness within, a contented silence that had settled after the day's joyous excitement. Lani nestled beside Julian, as a sense of peace wrapped around her.

Naomi's chest rose and fell with soft breath as she slept soundly on the rug. The teddy bear was still clutched tight. She stirred as a tiny sigh escaped her lips, her brow furrowed for a fleeting moment before relaxing back into the peaceful slumber of childhood dreams.

Lani's heart ached with tenderness so powerful it felt physical. She traced the outline of Naomi's cheek with her gaze. She was so small, so innocent, and yet, in her young heart, carrying wisdom that often surpassed her years.

It was in these quiet moments when the world outside faded away and only the immediate, precious circle remained that the deepest desires often surfaced, unspoken by the adults but clearly felt.

As if sensing their thoughts, or perhaps nudged by the magic of the season, Naomi's eyelids fluttered open. Her wide eyes blinked slowly in the dim light. She pushed herself up, a sleepy yawn stretching her small frame, and then, with the uninhibited directness of a child, she looked from Lani to Julian.

"Mommy?" she whispered, her voice a soft thread of sound that cut through the quiet. "Is Santa coming soon?"

Lani smiled, her heart melting a little further. "Almost, sweet peas. He's probably getting his reindeer ready right now."

Naomi's gaze shifted to Julian, a thoughtful expression on her face. She reached out, her small hand tentatively touching his arm. Her fingers found the soft fabric of his sweater. Julian, who had been watching her with a gentle, attentive expression, met her gaze, his own eyes reflecting the warm glow of the dying fire.

"Julian?" Naomi asked, her voice a little clearer now, a hint of the day's earlier excitement returning. "Are you going to be here when I wake up?"

The question, so simple, so direct, hung in the air, weighed down by a force that surprised Lani. It wasn't simple curiosity. It was a quiet plea for reassurance. In her own way, Naomi was voicing what they all felt: she wanted Julian to stay, to be part of their lives, not just a visitor who would one day leave.

Julian's response was immediate, his hand covering Naomi's small one, his thumb stroking gently. A warmth bloomed in his eyes, a tenderness that Lani had come to cherish.

"You know what, Naomi," he began, his voice a low, comforting rumble, "Santa might be coming soon, but I'm not going anywhere. I'll be right here, just like I'll always be when you wake up."

He looked from Naomi to Lani, his gaze holding hers for a long moment as a silent promise passed between them. "I'm not going anywhere," he reiterated, his voice firm, his intent clear. "I'm going to be a part of your mornings, and your afternoons, and your evenings. I'm going to be here for both of you."

Lani felt a swell of emotion—a quiet, tender joy — that filled her chest like the slow, warm bloom of a mug of mulled wine. Hearing Julian say those words, seeing the honesty in his eyes as they met her daughter's, touched something deep within her. It wasn't just love he was offering; it was steadiness, belonging, a promise to both her and Naomi that they could build something lasting together.

Naomi, satisfied with his answer, snuggled closer, her head finding its familiar spot on Lani's lap.

"Will I call you Daddy?" She whispered. Her eyes, however, remained open, fixed on Julian with adoration that was both touching and a little overwhelming.

"When you are ready," he answered, swallowing back the lump in his throat.

"And...and will you help me make cookies with Mommy sometimes?" she asked, her voice barely above a whisper. "Like real ones, with sprinkles?"

Julian chuckled, "Absolutely, Naomi. We'll make so many cookies, with all the sprinkles you can imagine. And when you're older, maybe I can even teach you how to bake my grandmother's famous gingerbread. She used to say the secret ingredient was always a little bit of extra love."

He continued, his voice growing more serious, more heartfelt. "You know, Naomi," he said, his gaze holding hers, "I've always liked making things. I like building things, fixing things, and yes, I really like baking things. But the best thing I like making is... well, it's making you and your mom happy. That's the most important thing to me."

He paused, gathering his thoughts, and then looked directly at Lani. "And Lani," he said, his voice softening, "you know that too. You know that I want to be here, to be a part of your lives and build something real and lasting with you both. Your happiness, and Naomi's happiness, is my biggest wish. That's my wish."

Lani squeezed Julian's hand, a silent acknowledgment of his words, of his sincerity. She looked at Naomi, her sweet, sleepy daughter, and then back at Julian, the man who had so unexpectedly, so wonderfully, become such an integral part of their world.

"That's a beautiful wish, Julian," Lani said softly, her voice thick with emotion. "And I... I wish the same for us. For all of us."

Naomi, her mission accomplished, her fears soothed, let out another soft sigh, her eyelids drooping once more. She nestled deeper into Lani's embrace, her breathing evening out into the steady rhythm of sleep. The teddy bear, still clutched tightly, seemed to nod in agreement with the unspoken sentiment that now filled the room.

Julian's gaze lingered on Naomi for a moment longer, quiet protectiveness in his eyes, before he turned back to Lani. He gently brushed a stray strand of hair from her forehead, his touch tender, reverent.

"She's a remarkable little girl, Lani," he murmured, his voice full of admiration. "She knows what's important, doesn't she? The simple things, the things that truly matter."

Lani leaned her head against his shoulder, the familiar comfort of his presence a soothing balm. "She's learning that from you, you know," she whispered, her eyes tracing the soft glow of the embers. "She sees your kindness, your steadiness. She feels that you're a safe harbor."

Julian pulled her closer, his arm wrapping around her shoulders. "And you, Lani," he said, his voice barely audible, "you are my safe harbor. You and Naomi. You are my Christmas wish, come true."

The quiet hum of the night outside wrapped around them like a comforting shawl.

Julian's gaze drifted from Naomi's peaceful form to Lani, his eyes reflecting the warm, dying glow of the fireplace. A stillness settled between them. The air crackled with a quiet energy, a sense of anticipation, of something beautiful and fragile taking root.

Julian's thumb gently stroked the back of her hand, a silent affirmation of her words. He turned his head, his gaze meeting hers, and in the soft light, she saw a depth of emotion that made her heart swell.

"You know," he began, his voice laced with a sincerity, "I... I never expected this. This Christmas Eve, this... *us*." He paused, searching for the right words, his eyes holding hers with an intensity that stole her breath. "It's more than I could have ever wished for."

Lani felt a blush creep up her neck, a shy acknowledgment of the profound truth in his words.

"Me neither, Julian," she confessed, her voice barely above a whisper. "After... after everything, I thought that kind of happiness was just for other people. For fairy tales."

She chuckled softly. A sound tinged with a hint of disbelief. "And then you walked in and brought with you this... this light."

He squeezed her hand, a silent promise. "You always had the light, Lani. I just helped you remember where to find it again."

He gestured with his free hand towards the large picture window, where the snow had fallen the day before, transforming the familiar landscape into a hushed, magical expanse.

The moonlight, filtering through the thick, soft flakes, cast a ghostly glow on the oak tree's frosted branches, turning them into a spectacle of sparkling diamonds. The world outside was silent, serene, bathed in a celestial luminescence.

"Look at it," Julian said, his voice filled with a quiet awe. "It's like a world spun from pure magic. And here we are, in the middle of it, with Naomi sleeping soundly, and your parents resting. It feels like a secret, doesn't it? Like we are suspended in time."

Lani followed his gaze, her heart swelling with a quiet joy. The snow-covered world was indeed breathtaking, a pristine canvas of white, undisturbed and pure. It mirrored the new beginnings that seemed to blossom between them with each passing moment.

"It does," she agreed, her voice soft. "A beautiful, perfect secret." She turned back to him, her eyes tracing the strong lines of his profile, the gentle curve of his lips. "You brought that magic, Julian. You brought it into my life, into Naomi's life."

He turned fully towards her, his expression earnest. "It's not just me, Lani. It's you. It's Naomi. It's the way you opened your heart, the way you let me in, even when it must have been so hard." He lifted her hand, bringing it to his lips, his kiss feather-light against her skin. "I feel it, Lani. This... connection. This feeling that I've finally found where I belong."

His words settled over her like a warm embrace, chasing away any lingering shadows of doubt or past hurts. She had opened her heart, cautiously at first, then with increasing trust, to Julian. And he had responded with a tenderness, a steadfastness, that had chipped away at her defenses, revealing a vulnerability she hadn't known she still possessed.

"I feel it too," she admitted, her voice thick with emotion. "It's... it's like coming home. A home I didn't even realize I was searching for."

"I've done a lot of thinking today, Lani," Julian said, his voice dropping to a near whisper. "Watching you with Naomi, watching you navigate the day with such grace and love, it's inspiring." He met her eyes, his gaze unwavering. "And it made me realize, with absolute certainty, that I don't want to just be a part of your life. I want to build a life *with* you."

Lani's breath hitched. The words were so direct and profound. They hung in the air, shimmering with promise. This was it. The moment where their whispered wishes coalesced into a tangible future.

She saw in his eyes not just love, but a deep, abiding respect, a genuine desire to share in the everyday joys and challenges, to be a partner in the truest sense of the word.

"Julian," she began, her voice trembling slightly, "I… I don't know what to say."

He smiled, a warm, reassuring smile that reached his eyes. "You don't have to say anything, Lani. Just feel it. Feel what's between us. It's real. It's strong. And I want to be there for you, for Naomi, not just now, but always. Like a steady hand. Like a constant presence."

He released her hand for a moment, only to cup her face, his thumbs gently stroking her cheekbones. "You deserve all the happiness in the world, Lani. And if I can be a part of bringing that happiness to you, then that's all I'll ever need."

His gaze swept over her, a look of deep affection and profound gratitude. "You've brought so much joy back into my life. You've shown me what it means to love again, to truly care for someone and their child with all my heart."

Tears pricked at the corners of Lani's eyes, not tears of sadness, but of overwhelming joy. She had been so guarded for so long, so afraid of being hurt again, of opening herself up to disappointment. But Julian had approached her heart with such gentleness, such unwavering devotion, that her defenses had crumbled, replaced by a love that felt as natural as breathing.

"And you, Julian," she whispered, her voice choked with emotion, "you've reminded me that it's possible. That love can find you again, even when you least expect it. You've brought back a light I thought was gone forever." She reached up, her fingers tracing the strong line of his jaw. "You are... you are everything."

He leaned into her touch, closing his eyes for a brief moment as if savoring the simple intimacy. When he opened them again, they were filled with a quiet resolve.

"This Christmas Eve," he said, his voice firm, "feels like the beginning of everything for us. A true beginning. And I want to be able to look back on this night, years from now, and know that this was the moment we chose each other, fully and without reservation."

Lani felt a shiver of goosebumps run over her skin. The glow of the Christmas tree lights, now the primary source of illumination in the room, cast a warm, golden hue on their faces, illuminating the tender expressions shared between them. The air was full of unspoken promises, with the quiet certainty of a love that had found its footing.

"I choose you, Julian," Lani said, her voice clear and steady, each word carrying the weight of her heart. "I choose this. Us."

Julian's smile widened, a radiant expression of pure happiness. He pulled her closer, her body fitting against his as if it had always belonged there. He rested his forehead against hers, their breaths mingling in the hushed stillness.

"And I choose you. And Naomi," he reciprocated, his voice a low, reverent murmur. "Always."

In that moment, surrounded by the silent beauty of the snow-covered world and the gentle glow of the Christmas tree, their connection solidified. It wasn't a dramatic declaration yet, felt as steadfast and enduring as the ancient oak outside their window. The distant carols seemed to swell once more.

A heavenly chorus celebrating the birth of a love that was as pure and as hopeful as the first snowfall of the season. They sat there for a long time, simply holding each other. The comfortable silence filled the room as their two hearts beat as one. It was a testament to the magic of Christmas Eve and the enduring power of love to transform lives and create a future brighter than any imagined dream.

The gentle rise and fall of Naomi's breathing was a soft reminder of the precious life they were building, a life filled with love, laughter, and the unwavering promise of forever. The night outside was a silent wonder, and within, their own quiet, perfect world was just beginning to unfold.

{ **29** }

Julian

That word, *Daddy*, hit him right in the chest. He swallowed against the sudden rush of emotion, watching her wide-eyed excitement with a tenderness that surprised even him.

"He sure did," he said, his voice rough with affection. "Santa must know exactly what makes you happy."

Naomi beamed, and Lani knelt beside her, her expression glowing with quiet joy. The two of them together, mother and daughter, so full of light, it was almost too much to take in.

Julian joined them, crouching to help Naomi untangle a stubborn ribbon. Her small hands worked eagerly, her giggles filling the air. The sound of paper tearing and the scent of coffee brewing in the background created a sense of domesticity, simplicity, and perfection.

"Oh, look, Mommy! A doll!" Naomi held up her prize, eyes shining. "She's so pretty!"

"She's beautiful, sweetheart," Lani said, smiling. Then, catching Julian's eye, she added gently, "I think there's one more for you, honey." She paused. "From Daddy."

Naomi turned to the small, elegantly wrapped box Julian had tucked near the back of the tree. She tore into it, her excitement bubbling over, and then she went still. Inside lay a delicate silver locket engraved with a tiny unicorn catching the glow of the tree lights.

"For me?" she whispered, almost reverent.

Julian nodded, his heart full. "For you," he said softly. "It's for your special memories. Go on, open it."

Naomi unclasped it carefully, her little fingers trembling. Inside, two tiny photos gleamed, one of Lani and one of him, both smiling, side by side.

Her eyes lifted to his, wide and glistening. "It's you and Mommy," she breathed.

"It is," Julian said, his throat tightening. "So that you always remember, you are loved, Naomi. Always."

She threw her arms around his neck, her small frame squeezing with all her strength. He hugged her back, closing his eyes for a moment, feeling Lani's hand settle gently on his shoulder. When he opened them again, the three of them were wrapped together in the warm glow of the Christmas tree, not just a family in theory but something real and whole.

Later, as Naomi went back to unwrapping gifts, her delighted squeals bouncing through the room, Julian caught Lani's gaze. She was watching him, her eyes soft and her smile tinged with wonder. He reached for another box and grinned.

"Now," he said, his voice teasing, "I think Santa might have left a few things for your mom too."

Her laugh, quiet and disbelieving, was the best sound in the world. He handed her the first box, deep blue and perfectly wrapped. When she unwrapped it, her breath caught. The diamond earrings sparkled in the morning light.

"Julian," she whispered. "They're beautiful."

He brushed his thumb along her cheek. "They reminded me of you," he said softly. "Full of light."

She didn't answer right away, just smiled, eyes shining. Then came the bracelet, the tiny oak tree charm glinting with quiet symbolism. He saw her reaction instantly, that familiar well of emotion that always undid him.

"The oak tree," he said quietly, rubbing his thumb over the charm. "Strong roots. Something that lasts."

"Just like our initials," she murmured.

Her fingers trembled as she touched it, and for a moment, words failed them both. Then he handed her the last gift, the book she loved, beautifully bound and signed just for her.

She looked at him, eyes brimming. "Julian... this is too much."

He shook his head, his smile soft. "No. This is just the beginning." He leaned in, pressing his forehead to hers. "You and Naomi, you're my home now."

Their kiss was brief and gentle, not about passion but about peace.

The rest of the morning unfolded like a dream. Naomi chattered nonstop, bouncing between them as she showed off her treasures. Lani laughed, her smile coming easier than Julian had ever seen it. He helped Naomi build her first block tower, listening to her animated explanations, feeling her small hand tug at his arm as she called him Daddy again and again.

For the first time in a long time, Julian wasn't thinking about work or fame or what came next. He was simply here, surrounded by love and warmth, by a family he hadn't even realized he had been missing.

As the morning light poured through the windows, he looked at Lani, her hair glinting gold, her eyes shining with everything unspoken between them.

He had spent years searching for fulfillment in the noise of the world. But here, in this quiet living room, with a child laughing and the woman he loved watching him. He finally found it.

A place where he belonged.

The morning unfolded slowly, in that unhurried way that only happens on holidays. Naomi sat cross-legged on the rug, her new doll cradled carefully in her arms, while the unicorn box sat open beside her. Every few minutes she would giggle, or hum to herself, lost in her own little world.

Julian leaned back on the sofa, his coffee warm in his hands. Across the room, Lani was tidying stray ribbons, her robe slipping off one shoulder, her hair soft and a little wild. Every so often, their eyes would meet, and she'd smile. That kind of smile that said everything without a word.

He didn't think life could feel more complete than at this moment.

The sound of quiet footsteps came from the hallway, followed by the comforting murmur of familiar voices.

Thomas and Elenore appeared, bundled in sweaters, their faces glowing from the warmth of the house and the faint chill of morning.

"Well, look at this," Elenore said, her voice light and full of affection. "Seems someone had a visit from Santa after all."

Naomi jumped up, the doll still in her hand. "Grandma! Grandpa! Look what I got!"

She raced toward them, nearly tripping over the edge of the rug. Thomas caught her easily, laughing as he lifted her into his arms.

"My goodness, that's quite a haul," he said, pretending to study the doll. "I think Santa must have had extra help this year."

Naomi grinned and nodded eagerly. "Daddy helped him!" she announced, pointing straight at Julian.

For a second, Julian froze, coffee halfway to his lips. Then Thomas glanced his way, his eyes crinkling in quiet amusement.

"Did he now?" Thomas said. "Well, that explains why Santa's taste has improved."

The easy humor broke any lingering tension. Elenore crossed the room and pressed a quick kiss to Lani's cheek before turning to Julian with a warm smile.

"Merry Christmas, Julian," she said. "I hope you like cinnamon rolls, because we made plenty."

"Merry Christmas," Julian replied, returning her smile. "And I can promise you, I absolutely do."

Elenore laughed softly. "Good. Because I made enough for an army, and I don't take leftovers as a compliment."

The room glowed with the kind of warmth that didn't just come from the fire; it came from them, from this fragile, beautiful thing they were building together.

He felt it then, the weight of the moment pressing gently against his chest. There was still one more gift he hadn't given her. The one that mattered most.

He reached quietly for the package he'd tucked away earlier, hidden beneath the pile of brightly wrapped boxes. It wasn't much to look at, plain cream paper, a thin silver ribbon tied without any flourish. Simple, intentional. Just like what he hoped it represented.

"There's one more thing, Lani," he said, his voice low and steady. The words seemed to hum through the soft laughter and rustle of paper, drawing her attention instantly.

Her eyes lifted to meet his, curious and warm. He could feel the faint tremor of anticipation ripple through her, the same one running through him.

He offered her the gift, setting it carefully in her hands. "This one's a little different," he said, and for a moment his voice caught. He swallowed, then tried again, quieter now. "It's not just about today. It's about what comes next. About what we might build together."

Her fingers brushed the edge of the wrapping, delicate and hesitant, and Julian felt his heart stutter. Because this wasn't just another present. It was a promise. A glimpse of a future he finally dared to hope for.

The way she held it close to her heart, her thumb brushing absently across the embossed stitching, told him everything he needed to know. She understood what it meant.

He had not been sure she would. The idea had lived quietly inside him for months, growing roots while he watched her pour herself into every loaf of bread and every cookie Naomi decorated beside her. He had seen how her eyes softened when someone took that first bite of something she had made, how she found joy not in perfection but in connection. That was what this notebook represented. Not ambition, not profit, but purpose. A future that belonged to both of them.

Lani looked up then, her eyes bright and glassy.

"Julian," she whispered, "no one's ever believed in me like this."

He reached for her hand, threading his fingers through hers. "Then it's about time someone did." His voice came out rougher than he intended.

"Lani, I've spent years building things that didn't last. Projects, roles, deals… all of them temporary. But this," he gestured toward the notebook resting in her lap, "this is something that feels real. Something that matters."

Her thumb brushed over his knuckles, slow and thoughtful. "You really think I could do this?"

He smiled softly. "I don't think, Lani. I know. I've seen the way people light up when they taste your food. You have something special. That kind of heart can't be taught. It's already in you. I just want to help you build the space to let it shine."

She blinked back tears, laughing a little through the emotion. "You always know just what to say."

He chuckled quietly. "That's only because I mean every word."

The room had gone quiet around them. Naomi had curled up on the rug, her new doll tucked under her arm, half-asleep again in the aftermath of her excitement. Lani's parents in the kitchen preparing cinnamon rolls for breakfast. The faint hum of Christmas music drifted from the speaker, and the scent of cinnamon hung in the air. Julian felt something shift inside him, a soft, grounding certainty.

He had given her the notebook, but she had given him something far greater, a sense of belonging he had not realized he had been searching for.

Lani turned the pages again, pausing at a hand-drawn sketch of the bakery's front window. He had written two words above it in careful ink: *Shepard & Vance.* Her breath caught, and when she looked up at him, her expression was unreadable, awe, love, and disbelief all tangled together.

"Shepard and Vance?" she murmured.

Julian shrugged lightly, though his heart was pounding. "I thought it had a nice ring to it. But I'm open to negotiation."

Lani shook her head slowly, her lips curving into a smile that stole his breath. "No. It's perfect."

Her gaze softened, and something unspoken passed between them, a quiet understanding that this wasn't just a dream on paper anymore. It was a promise. One they were both ready to keep.

Julian leaned closer, his voice barely above a whisper. "You know, when I first came here, I thought the storm was an inconvenience. A delay. But maybe it was just life's way of stopping me long enough to find what really matters."

Lani's fingers brushed his cheek. "Maybe it was," she said gently.

He kissed her then, slow and lingering, full of the quiet certainty that this woman, this home, this messy, beautiful life, was exactly where he was meant to be.

Julian lingered in that moment, the quiet after their kiss stretching between them like a soft, sacred pause. The flickering light from the tree reflected in Lani's eyes, turning them into twin embers of warmth and wonder.

She still held the notebook close, as though afraid it might disappear if she loosened her grip, and the sight stirred something deep within him, a tenderness so fierce it almost hurt.

He had given her business plans, projections, and sketches, but what he had truly given her was belief. Belief that she could dream bigger, that she could step into something entirely her own. Watching her cradle that notebook, her expression a mix of awe and resolve, he knew he'd done the right thing.

Naomi's laughter carried across the room, bright and unrestrained, as she giggled in her sleep. The sound pulled Julian's gaze toward her, and a smile tugged at his lips. That little girl had changed everything for him. She wasn't his by blood, but by choice and by love. And he already knew he'd do anything to keep that light in her eyes.

He looked back at Lani, his chest tightening with quiet certainty. This, her, Naomi, the home they were creating was everything he hadn't known he was missing.

Lani turned slightly, her fingers brushing the edge of the notebook.

"You really think we can do this?" she asked softly, as if speaking the thought aloud might make it too real.

"I don't think," he said, his voice steady and sure. "I know." He reached for her hand, threading his fingers through hers. "You have the heart for it, Lani. The vision. And I have the drive to make sure it stands. Between the two of us, I'd say we've got more than a fighting chance."

Her lips curved into a small, genuine smile. That smile always managed to undo him.

"You make it sound so easy."

He chuckled under his breath. "It won't be easy. But it'll be worth it." He lifted her hand, pressing a kiss to her knuckles. "Everything worth having always is."

Lani exhaled slowly, leaning into him, her head resting against his shoulder. The warmth of her touch seeped through him, grounding him in a way nothing else ever had.

"I used to think life stopped when my marriage ended," she said quietly. "That I'd used up all my chances. But this..." Her gaze flicked to the notebook again. "This feels like a beginning."

Julian brushed his thumb along her hand, the motion instinctive, reverent. "That's because it is," he murmured. "The kind that doesn't come from running away from the past, but from walking straight into the future together."

When they finally pulled apart, Naomi stirred, blinking sleepily at them. "Mommy? Daddy?" she murmured, her voice soft and drowsy. "Can we eat now?"

Lani laughed through the shimmer of tears still clinging to her lashes. "Of course we can, sweetheart."

Julian grinned, brushing a kiss against Naomi's hair as she clambered into his lap. "Best idea I've heard all morning," he said.

Lani's eyes glistened as she met his gaze. It was fragile and infinite all at once. Julian didn't speak, didn't need to. Everything he felt, his love, his gratitude, his unspoken promise was there reflected right back at him.

And as the three of them rose, the notebook still resting on the coffee table, its pages glinting faintly in the firelight, Julian felt a calm settle over him. It wasn't the height of a grand gesture or the thrill of new love. It was steadier, deeper, the quiet joy of knowing that, at last, he was home.

{ 30 }

Julian

Within minutes, the kitchen filled with the scent of sweet rolls and freshly brewed coffee. Lani moved easily among them, her laughter floating through the air as she helped set the table.

Julian took it all in, the warmth of the light, the hum of small talk, Naomi's laughter echoing like a melody.

He had spent so many Christmas mornings in expensive houses and glamorous hotels, surrounded by glitter and perfection, but never belonging. This, the soft background chatter, the simple happiness. This was something entirely different.

As they sat down to eat, Elenore reached across the table and squeezed Lani's hand. "It's been a long time since this house felt this full," she said softly. "I think it's just what we needed."

Lani smiled, eyes shining. "Me too."

Thomas nodded, cutting into a roll. "You've done good, sweetheart," he said, glancing between her and Julian. "Real good."

Julian caught Lani's gaze again, his chest tightening with something deep and steady. Gratitude. Peace. The quiet realization that this home, this family, this love was everything he hadn't known he was missing.

Naomi was already halfway through her roll. A smudge of icing sat on her cheek. She leaned against Julian's arm, her voice soft and content.

"Daddy," she said, "this is my best Christmas ever."

Julian's throat tightened, but he smiled, brushing a crumb from her hair. "Mine too, sweetheart," he said quietly.

And for the first time in years, he truly meant it.

Cloves, roasted ham, and freshly brewed coffee filled his nose and wrapped around Julian like a familiar embrace, the kind of warmth that settled deep in his chest. The dining room glowed with morning light, soft and golden, catching the slow drift of dust motes above the table.

It was one of those rare moments that felt suspended in time, where laughter and comfort blended as naturally as the aromas in the air.

He had arrived early that morning, long before the rest of the house had stirred, and slipped into the quiet rhythm of the kitchen beside Lani's parents.

There had been easy conversation, the clatter of dishes, the hiss of the coffee maker. Now, as the table filled with plates and laughter, it all came together, a perfect Christmas lunch, the kind that lingered in memory long after the plates were cleared. His contribution, a platter of delicate smoked salmon blinis crowned with crème fraîche and dill, sat proudly among Lani's parents' dishes. It wasn't much, he thought, but it was his way of belonging.

Across the table, Lani looked radiant, relaxed in a way she rarely allowed herself to be. She laughed easily, her eyes bright, her hands moving gracefully as she passed a dish of her mother's famous apple-cranberry stuffing.

Naomi sat between them, her small legs swinging as she surveyed the spread with wide-eyed wonder. The chaos of gift opening had faded into a gentle hum of conversation, and Julian felt it then, the sense of home. Real, imperfect, alive.

"Julian, you've outdone yourself with these," Lani's father said, reaching for another blini. His tone was light, teasing. "Almost as good as Lani's baking."

Julian smiled, dipping his head slightly. "Thank you, sir, though I'm not sure anything can compete with Lani's cinnamon rolls."

"Call me Thomas," he replied, pointing at him with his fork.

Julian's grin widened. "Of course, Thomas."

Lani's mother laughed softly at the exchange, her eyes shining with amusement. "You fit in far too easily around here," she said.

He glanced at Lani, catching her faint, knowing smile. "I take that as the highest compliment," he said. And he meant it.

The conversation flowed easily after that, stories from old Christmases, the kind filled with small disasters and perfect moments.

Thomas shared one about their golden retriever, Pebbles, and a runaway garden gnome that had nearly caused a neighborhood scandal. Lani's mother countered with her memory of receiving a long-coveted doll as a child, her laughter filling the room as she described how she had refused to let anyone touch it for weeks.

Julian found himself swept into the rhythm of it all. He shared his own stories, his grandmother's gingerbread houses, his father's annual reading of A Christmas Carol, complete with booming voices and dramatic flair. The table erupted with laughter when he admitted that even as an adult, he still couldn't resist joining in on the carols far too loudly.

Lani's mother wiped a tear of laughter from her eye. "That sounds like a wonderful tradition," she said warmly.

"It was," Julian replied, his voice softening. "My dad always said Christmas was about the small things, the rituals, the effort, the time spent together. Even when things went wrong, that was part of the memory." He looked at Lani then, his gaze lingering. "That's what I want to build with this bakery. Something lasting. Something that feels like this."

Thomas, who had been carving the ham, looked up thoughtfully. "That's what family traditions are, aren't they? Something you build together, little by little. And this dream of yours, it sounds like it's built on that same foundation."

Julian nodded, feeling the truth of it settle inside him. "It is. It's not just about the pastries or the coffee. It's about creating a space that feels like home, where people can slow down and connect. Like this table."

Lani reached over, resting her hand on his. "Exactly," she said softly. "It's about sharing something real."

Julian squeezed her hand, warmth flooding through him. "And I couldn't imagine doing it with anyone else."

Across the table, Naomi giggled as she constructed a tower out of napkins and orange slices. Her small, contented sounds blended with the hum of conversation, and Julian's heart swelled with quiet gratitude. He hadn't just found love here, he had found belonging.

Thomas chuckled as he set down his fork. "You know, Julian, I've never actually written down my chili recipe. It's all in my head, measurements, timing, everything.

Maybe when the new bakery opens, you can help me turn it into something official. A family recipe worth preserving."

Julian's eyes lit up. "I'd love that," he said, leaning forward. "Imagine your chili spice blend, Lani's pastries, local honey, coffee from nearby roasters. A bakery that tells a story with every flavor."

Elenore smiled. "That's exactly it. Food should tell a story. And when it comes from the heart, people can taste that."

Julian nodded, feeling something shift inside him, small but certain. This was what he wanted. To build something with Lani that went beyond the surface, that connected people to something real, something rooted in care and food and love.

The conversation moved easily from there, talk of local farms, seasonal menus, and future plans blended seamlessly with laughter and second helpings. The sunlight grew warmer, spilling across the table, catching in Lani's hair, in Naomi's curious eyes, in the pages of the leather-bound notebook resting on the sideboard.

As Julian looked around the room, at the family, the food, the easy joy, he felt a quiet certainty take hold. This wasn't just brunch. It was the start of something that would last.

And when Lani glanced his way, her smile soft and knowing, he thought, yes. This was it. The life he hadn't even realized he had been waiting for.

The last remnants of the Christmas feast had been cleared, leaving the dining room bathed in the soft glow of the late afternoon sun filtering through the snow-laden trees. Lani found Julian's hand as it rested on her arm, her fingers intertwining with his.

The quiet hum of contentment that had settled over them after the joyous chaos of the day was a language of its own, a testament to the deep peace they had found in each other. The world outside had transformed into a pristine scene of white, the mountains serene and silent, mirroring the calm that had finally taken root in Lani's heart.

"It was perfect," Lani murmured, her voice a soft breath against the quiet. She turned her head, her eyes meeting Julian's, a profound tenderness blooming within her. "Everything. The way Naomi lit up with every gift, the easy laughter with my parents, it all felt so right. So *us*."

Julian's thumb traced circles on the back of her hand, his gaze unwavering. "It was, wasn't it? And your parents welcoming me, it means the world to me, Lani. More than I can express." He sighed, a sound of deep satisfaction. "I remember thinking, after everything with the firm, that my professional life was peaked. The relentless drive, the pressure, the endless pursuit of 'success' as I understood it then. I was so caught up in it, I didn't realize what I was missing."

He turned to face her fully, his arm tightening around her shoulders, pulling her close. "And then life happened. You happened. And I found a fulfillment I never knew existed. Building something real with you, Lani. Something that truly matters."

Lani leaned her head against his chest, the steady beat of his heart a comforting rhythm beneath her ear. "I understand," she admitted, her voice laced with a vulnerability she no longer felt the need to hide. "After the divorce, it felt like a door had slammed shut. Like the story I'd planned in my head had ended abruptly, leaving me with a blank page and no idea how to fill it. Mourning that lost future was a painful process. There were days I felt like a ghost in my own life, just going through the motions, a shadow of the woman I'd once been."

She shifted slightly, her gaze drifting back to the window, to the quiet beauty of the snow. "This town holds so many memories for me. The echoes of the past. It was where I'd envisioned building my forever, and then it became the place I had to rebuild myself from the ground up."

Julian's hand cupped her cheek, his touch gentle but firm, drawing her gaze back to his. "And you did, Lani. You rebuilt yourself into someone even more resilient, even more radiant. You took what felt like an ending and forged a new beginning. That takes an incredible amount of strength and courage."

He met her eyes, his own reflecting a depth of understanding that always seemed to calm the restless sea within her. "I used to believe that second chances were the stuff of fairy tales, or for those who had made truly catastrophic errors. But sometimes," he mused, his voice a low rumble of introspection, "sometimes they're just life's way of gently nudging us back onto the right path. Pushing us towards something we didn't even realize we were looking for."

"And sometimes," Lani added, a soft smile gracing her lips, her eyes sparkling, "they find you when you're too busy looking everywhere else. I certainly wasn't looking for love again. I was so focused on the bakery, on finding my own footing, on providing for Naomi, that the idea of sharing my life, of building a future with someone... it felt like a beautiful, but distant, fantasy."

She squeezed his hand, a surge of pure, unadulterated joy coursing through her. "And then you walked back into my life. It felt like a gift. Like the universe was saying, 'Here. You deserve this. You deserve to be happy.'"

"And you deserved it even when you didn't believe it yourself," Julian stated, his voice unwavering. "I am so grateful, Lani, that our paths crossed again. That we were given this second chance." He chuckled softly, a warm, rumbling sound.

"I still remember that first day back in town, seeing you in the café. My initial thought was, 'Is that really Lani?' You looked different. More at peace. And my second thought, almost immediate, was, 'I have to talk to her.' I couldn't let that moment slip away."

Lani laughed, a light, airy sound that filled the quiet room. "And I remember thinking, 'Julian? What is Julian doing back in town?' I was so surprised, and honestly, a little bit flustered. You always did have a way of making my heart do a little somersault, even back then."

She tilted her head back to look at him, her gaze tracing the familiar lines of his face. "It felt so surreal, didn't it? Like a gentle, perfect nudge in the right direction. We both found ourselves back in this town, this place that held so much of our shared history, and we found each other again."

Julian smiled, his gaze drifting to the window where the world outside seemed calm and bright, like a clean slate.

"Yeah," he said softly. "But I don't think it's just luck or timing. I think it's proof that we're tougher than we realize. That even after heartbreak, we can still heal and find our way back to love." He paused, his voice gentle but sure. "This town gave you space to heal. And for me, it brought a kind of clarity I didn't know I was missing."

He turned back to her then, his eyes warm and steady. "And now it's giving us something new. The bakery. It's not just a business, Lani. It's a fresh start. It's about taking what was broken and building something beautiful from it. To-gether."

"Exactly," Lani agreed, her voice resonating with a new-found certainty that thrilled her. " My passion for baking was always there, a constant in my life, but after the di-vorce, it felt like it was the only solid thing I could hold onto. It was my anchor. And now, to be able to share that passion with you, to build a future around it... it's every-thing I could have ever dreamed of and more."

She looked at him, her eyes shining with unshed, grate-ful tears. "And you... you've shown me that professional suc-cess isn't the sole measure of a life well-lived. You've found joy in something entirely different. And you're doing it with me."

"And I wouldn't trade it for anything," Julian stated, his voice firm and resolute. "The late nights at the restau-rants seem like a lifetime ago. The stress, the pressure, it's all faded into insignificance compared to the sheer joy I feel with you. Every early morning, every decision we make about the menu, about the decor, about our future... it's all with purpose and excitement that I never experienced be-fore in my life. It's a different kind of success, a much richer one."

He leaned down, his lips brushing against her forehead in a tender kiss. "This Lani, it's a second chance for both of us.

"A chance to rewrite our stories, " she added.

"Exactly, not by erasing the past, but by embracing it and learning from it."

This place, which had once held the bitter-sweet echoes of Lani's past sorrow, was now being imbued with the vibrant hues of their present happiness.

"You know," Lani said, her voice thoughtful, a gentle wonder in her tone, "when I first moved back here, I thought I'd be forever marked by what had happened. I thought this town would always feel like a reminder of failure. Of when my life had fallen apart. But you're right. It's become a place of healing. And now, with the new bakery, it's becoming a place of creation. It's truly beautiful, Julian."

Julian nodded, his gaze locked on hers, his eyes reflecting the soft, diffused light.

"It is. And it's all because we were brave enough to take that second chance. To open ourselves up to the possibility of something new. And then finding each other again, after all this time, after all the detours. It's like the universe was waiting for us. Waiting for us to be ready."

"And to believe in it," Lani added softly, her heart swelling with an overwhelming sense of gratitude. "To believe that we deserved this kind of happiness. That love, true, deep love, could find us again. It's a lesson I had to learn, a hard, painful lesson. But one, I'm so grateful I have you by my side, holding my hand through it all."

She squeezed his hand, the familiar contact grounding her, anchoring her in the beautiful reality of their present. "Thank you, Julian. Thank you for believing in me, for believing in us, and for giving me, giving us, this incredible second chance. It's more than I ever dared to hope for."

"Lani, no, thank you," he replied, his voice thick with emotion, a raw honesty that resonated deep within her soul. "For being my second chance," he said softly. "For reminding me that life's greatest rewards aren't found in accolades or Michelin stars, but in the warmth of shared moments, in love that feels steady and real, and in the promise of building something beautiful together."

Outside, snow drifted quietly, blessing their new beginning. The bakery stood as a symbol of everything they'd rebuilt—hope, love, and the sweetness of starting over.

***

Later that evening, as the stars began to pepper the inky sky, casting a soft, ethereal glow on the snow-covered landscape, Julian drew Lani onto the plush rug in front of the crackling fireplace. The scent of pine and burning wood filled the air, a comforting aroma that spoke of warmth and home. He took her hands, drawing Lani close, his gaze steady and earnest, a profound sincerity in his eyes that always managed to disarm her.

"Lani," he began softly, his voice a low rumble that seemed to blend with the crackle of the fire, "we've talked a lot about second chances. About finding healing, about rebuilding." He turned slightly so he could see her face, the firelight catching in her eyes. "And I'm so grateful for this life we've started to build, for you, for Naomi. You've both changed everything for me."

He took a deep breath, steadying himself. "But tonight, there's something I need to say. Something I've been carrying with me for a while."

Lani's brow furrowed gently, curiosity sparking in her gaze.

Julian reached into his pocket and pulled out a small box, simple but elegant, wrapped in deep green velvet. He held it between them, his thumb brushing the edge.

"I didn't want to make a grand spectacle of this," he said quietly. "No crowd, no elaborate plan. Just us, here, in the home that's come to mean everything to me."

Lani's breath caught as he opened the box, revealing a delicate ring, an oval-cut diamond set in a slender band of rose gold, understated yet breathtakingly beautiful.

"I love you, Lani," Julian said, his voice trembling slightly now. "More than I ever thought I could love anyone. You've brought light into every part of my life. You and Naomi have shown me what real happiness looks like. I want those quiet mornings, laughter at the table, the way love can feel both steady and new every day."

He took her hands in his, the ring glinting between them. "You once told me that life is about second chances. I believe that with all my heart. You're my second chance, Lani. My home, my peace, my greatest adventure. So..." He drew in a breath, emotion thickening his voice.

"Will you marry me?"

For a heartbeat, the world seemed to still. The only sound was the soft crackle of the fire and the faint whisper of snow falling outside. Then Lani's hand flew to her mouth, her eyes glistening with tears that caught the firelight.

"Julian," she breathed, her voice breaking on his name. "Yes. Yes, I will."

A laugh of relief and joy escaped him as he slipped the ring onto her finger, his hands shaking just enough to make her smile through her tears. The ring caught the glow of the fire, a perfect reflection of the warmth that surrounded them.

He cupped her face in his hands and kissed her, slow and tender, the kind of kiss that spoke of forever. When they finally pulled apart, she rested her forehead against his, tears slipping down her cheeks, her smile radiant.

"I meant every word," he murmured. "I want a life with you. A home filled with laughter, and love, and flour-dusted countertops. I want to wake up beside you every day, to build our dreams one step at a time."

Lani's eyes softened, full of love and certainty. "Then that's what we'll do," she whispered. "Together. Every day."

Julian ran a finger down her cheek. " I want you to know, with absolute certainty, that I am committed to this. To us. To our future. I want to be a constant in your life, and in Naomi's. I want to wake up every morning and know that I get to build another day with you by my side."

She looked at him, a newfound sense of security settled over her. "And I promise you this, Julian," she said, her voice firm with conviction. "I promise to cherish every moment we have, to nurture our love, and to continue building this beautiful future with you. We'll make this work together."

She leaned in, her lips brushing against his in a kiss that was soft, tender, and filled with the promise of all the tomorrows to come. It was a kiss of acceptance, of profound love, and of a shared future, as sweet and as comforting as the scent of freshly baked bread.

The fire continued to crackle burning bright and steady, a reflection of the promise they had just made. It was built not on grand gestures, but on love, trust, and the quiet beauty of forever.

{ 31 }

Lani

The fireworks burst overhead, scattering streaks of gold and red across the cold winter sky. Lani leaned into Julian, her head resting against his shoulder, feeling the steady rhythm of his heartbeat. The crisp air didn't feel cold, not with his arm wrapped around her and Naomi's mittened hand tucked safely in hers. The crowd's laughter and cheers felt like one big, joyful hug, wrapping them all in the warmth of shared celebration.

Thinking about the countdown?" he asked, his voice a gentle rumble as he came up behind her, wrapping his arms around her waist.

Lani leaned back into his embrace, a contented sigh escaping her lips. "Something like that," she murmured, her fingers finding his as they rested on her lap. "It feels... significant, doesn't it? This year. Not just the end of a chapter, but the beginning of something entirely new. Something we're building together."

He pressed a kiss to her temple. "It is. And I wouldn't want to be anywhere else, or with anyone else, to welcome it in."

Naomi, her cheeks rosy from the cold and excitement, clutched Julian's hand, her eyes wide with wonder.

"Look, Daddy! It's so sparkly!" she exclaimed, pointing at a particularly elaborate display of lights on the old clock tower that would soon mark the turning of the year.

Julian chuckled, squeezing her hand. "It is sweetie. It's the magic of New Year's Eve." He looked down at Lani, his gaze filled with a love that made her heart swell.

"And you," he whispered, his voice laced with a tenderness that always managed to surprise her with its depth, "are the most beautiful part of this magic."

Lani's breath hitched. "You say the sweetest things," she replied, her voice a little shaky. She squeezed his hand back, a silent acknowledgment of the profound connection that now bound them.

The crowd around them began to count down, their voices rising in unison, a unified chorus of anticipation.

"Ten! Nine! Eight!" The energy was electric, a wave of excitement washing over the square. Naomi, caught up in the fervor, started counting with them, her small voice adding to the joyous roar.

"Seven! Six! Five!"

Lani squeezed Julian's hand tighter, her gaze locked on the clock tower.

The years of loneliness, of self-doubt, of searching for a stable footing, seemed to recede with each passing second. They were being replaced by a sense of peace and gratitude for the unexpected blessings that had found their way into her life.

"Four! Three! Two!"

She looked at Julian, at the love etched in his eyes, at the way he held Naomi close. This was it. This was the moment. The culmination of so many quiet hopes, so many whispered prayers.

"ONE!"

A deafening roar erupted from the crowd as the clock struck midnight. Fireworks, brilliant and explosive, bloomed against the dark canvas of the sky. The town square was bathed in a dazzling rainbow of light. Cheers, whistles, and the popping of champagne corks filled the air.

Naomi squealed with delight, pointing at the sky. "Wow! It's like a rainbow!"

Julian held her up, letting her get a better view, and then turned to Lani, his eyes reflecting the fireworks. He didn't need grand gestures or speeches. In that moment, as the world around them exploded with light and sound, Lani saw everything she needed to see in his gaze: his love, his commitment, their shared future.

"Happy New Year, Lani," he murmured, his voice rough with emotion.

"Happy New Year, Julian," she whispered back, tears pricking at her eyes, as she placed a kiss on his lips.

As the last fireworks shimmered out, Lani looked up at the sky, still glowing faintly with smoke and color.

This is the beginning, she thought.

Their bakery, their dreams, their love, it was all taking shape, solid and sure. They'd walked through storms and somehow found their way back to each other. Now, standing here together at the start of a new year, she felt it deep in her bones: this was their fresh start, their next chapter.

"Beautiful, wasn't it?" she murmured, tilting her face toward Julian.

He smiled, his breath warm against her temple. "It was," he said, his voice soft but certain. "But not as beautiful as this."

He kissed her, just a gentle brush of lips, but enough to make her heart flutter like the fireworks all over again.

Naomi squirmed between them, rubbing her eyes. "Daddy, can we go home now? I'm sleepy."

Julian chuckled and lifted her up into his arms. "Home, it is sweet pea."

They walked through the quiet streets, the snow crunching softly beneath their boots. Faint pine and woodsmoke filled the air and for a moment Lani wished she could bottle the feeling, this warmth, this contentment.

By the time they reached the house, Naomi had fallen asleep in Julian's arms. Lani tucked her into bed, pressing a soft kiss on her daughter's forehead.

"Happy New Year, sweetheart," she whispered before slipping back into the living room.

Julian was waiting by the fireplace, his hands tucked into his pockets, that familiar spark in his eyes. The one that usually meant he'd been thinking, planning.

"You know," he began, his voice low, "I've been doing a lot of thinking about the bakery. About where we fit into all of this."

Lani smiled, curling up beside him on the couch. "That sounds serious."

He laughed softly. "Not serious. Just... right." He turned toward her, his gaze steady. "I think I've found the place for us to start fresh."

Lani's brow furrowed. "You mean for the bakery?"

"For the bakery," he said, then grinned. "And for us."

Her heart gave a little skip. "Julian..."

"I've been looking at spaces around town," he went on, his tone thoughtful. "And I keep coming back to Shepard's Bakery." He did his research. The building had been there so long that it was eligible for designation as a historic landmark.

"I know we would have to make a lot of changes. But the location is perfect. It's got history, charm, and good bones. We could keep the downstairs for the shop, and the upstairs..." He hesitated, a smile tugging at the corner of his mouth. "Well, it's not much right now. Your Dad showed it to me, and it's a little run-down. Dust everywhere. But it could be beautiful again. I can see it, Lani. A home — *our* home — right above the bakery."

She blinked, stunned. "You want to live there? Above the bakery?"

He nodded, his grin widening. "Think about it. It's large enough for several bedrooms. We'd be steps away from our dream. No commute, no separation between work and life, just... us, building something together.

Naomi could have her own little bedroom, maybe even a window seat where she can watch the snow fall. We'd wake up to the smell of fresh bread every morning."

Lani laughed softly, torn between doubt and excitement as she tried to picture it. The creaky old staircase, the peeling wallpaper, the wide windows that overlooked Main Street. It wasn't glamorous; in fact, it was a mess and had been used for storage for decades. But as she thought about it, potential began to outweigh hesitation. And the thought of creating a home there, in the heart of the town where they'd both found healing, stirred something deep inside her.

"Julian," she said slowly, "that place needs a lot of work."

"I know." His tone was full of quiet determination. "But so did we, once. And look at us now."

Her eyes softened. "You really think it could work?"

He reached for her hand, threading his fingers through hers. "I do. I think we could make it beautiful and full of life. A real home. And downstairs, the bakery could be everything we've dreamed of. I'm not just talking about a bakery. I'm talking about an experience. A place where people can come and taste the tradition of your baking, the kind that warms the heart and brings back memories. And then, we can add in my culinary flair. Innovative pastries, perhaps. Fusion dishes. We can create a menu that's both comfortingly familiar and excitingly new."

Lani's heart swelled as she imagined it. The scent of cinnamon and coffee drifting up the stairs. Naomi's laughter echoing through the halls. The hum of conversation from happy customers below. A life that wasn't just built around work, but around love, family, and shared purpose.

"Your baking, my food, our story. All in one place."

"But the permits, the cost," Lani began.

"I've looked into it," Julian said, as if reading her thoughts. "There are grants for historical building restoration. And I've spoken with some contacts... builders, designers. They're interested. They see the potential too. This isn't just about saving a historical building, it's about creating something that will remain a cornerstone of this community."

Lani's mind was already buzzing with possibilities. She pictured the bakery, its sturdy stone walls and wide windows, transformed. She saw the warmth of rustic wooden tables, the gleam of polished copper pots, the gentle hum of conversation. She saw herself, flour dusting her apron, her hands shaping dough, and Julian, with a mischievous glint in his eye, artfully arranging a complex dessert.

"We could knock out that wall like we talked about and have a small café area," she offered, her voice gaining confidence. "People could come in for a morning coffee and a pastry, or a light lunch.

"Yes," Julian added. "I could do my signature quiches, my hearty soups, and you could create some incredible salads, perhaps with ingredients sourced from local farms."

"Exactly!" Lani exclaimed.

His enthusiasm mirrored hers. "And we could source ingredients together. You know the best local suppliers for your flour and dairy. I have connections with farmers for specialty produce, herbs, even foraged ingredients. It would be a true farm-to-table, kitchen-to-counter experience. We could even have a small section selling local artisanal products. Maybe honey, jams, perhaps even handmade ceramics for our customers to take home."

He traced the line of her jaw with his fingertip. "My vision is for it to be more than just a place to buy food. It needs to be a place where people feel welcome and inspired. A place that celebrates craftsmanship and passion. Your passion, Lani. And mine."

He paused, his gaze serious. "I know this is a huge leap. And it will require a lot of hard work, long hours, and probably some sleepless nights. But I believe in us. And I believe that this town deserves something special, something that combines the best of its heritage with the future."

Lani's excitement grew with every idea he shared.

"I've even started sketching out some initial design ideas. Nothing concrete, just concepts," his enthusiasm grew. "We could even have an open kitchen concept, allowing customers to see the magic happening, to witness everything firsthand."

Lani's heart swelled with a mixture of awe and gratitude. He had taken her whispers of a dream and was making them a reality.

"Julian," she said, her voice thick with emotion. "This is... this is more than I could have ever imagined."

"I want you to be my partner in every sense of the word," he held her gaze. "Not just in baking, but in life. I want to build this with you, brick by brick, flavor by flavor. I want to see your traditional recipes and find a new home. I want our names above the door. People will see it and know inside is quality and a love for good food made with passion."

"You make it sound so simple," she whispered, smiling.

Julian chuckled. "Not simple. Just worth it." He leaned closer, brushing a kiss against her forehead. "So what do you say, Lani Shepard? Ready to move into a fixer-upper with a view of Main Street and a lifetime of potential?"

She laughed, the sound bright and sure. "You mean, am I ready to build a home above a bakery with the man I love and the daughter who will probably claim the best bedroom?"

"Exactly that."

She met his gaze, her heart full.

"Then yes," she said softly. "Let's do it. Let's make it ours."

"You mean it?" he murmured, the words barely a whisper, as if afraid to break the spell.

"I mean it, Julian," her voice was steady despite the tremor in her hands. "We'll be partners, truly," she replied. She had conditions. "Not just in the bakery, but in everything. But just know, my time with Naomi and our time together it has to be protected. No late nights at the bakery every single night. We need balance, Julian. Real balance." She had seen a flicker of understanding, a nod of agreement in his eyes, and it had eased a knot of tension she hadn't realized she was carrying.

"It's a big leap, I know," Julian said, his voice still low, imbued with a seriousness that Lani found deeply reassuring. "And your conditions I wholeheartedly agree with. We're building this together, Lani. Not just a business, but a life." He offered a small, wry smile, and Lani couldn't help but return it.

"And you promise," she continued, needing that final reassurance, "that we won't forget why we're doing this? That it won't just become about profit margins and deadlines, but about the joy we talked about? The joy Naomi feels when she imagines it?"

His gaze softened, his eyes holding a depth of sincerity that melted away with the last of her doubt.

"Lani," he said, his voice firm, "I promise. This isn't just a business venture for me. It's about creating something lasting. It's about building a legacy, for us and for Naomi. For the community."

He gently tilted her chin up, his eyes locking with hers. "And Naomi," he added, a warmth spreading through his voice, "she's going to be our biggest inspiration. Her excitement and joy... that's what we need to hold onto."

Julian pulled her into his arms, holding her close as the fire crackled beside them. Outside, the snow kept falling, quiet, steady, full of promise. And for the first time in a long time, Lani felt that same steady peace settling deep inside her.

The fireworks might have faded, but the new beginning was just getting started right there, in the little town that had brought them back together, and in the old bakery that was about to become the heart of their forever.

***

Naomi had been listening from the doorway, her little form framed by the soft glow of the firelight. Lani hadn't even noticed her at first, the way her daughter's eyes had grown round with wonder as Julian spoke about their plans, her small fingers curled around the doorframe.

The talk of old brickwork, renovations, and business permits meant nothing to her. But the moment Julian mentioned filling the space with the smell of fresh bread and laughter, Naomi's face lit up. She didn't hear logistics; she heard magic.

She took a hesitant step forward, her voice soft but bright. "Mommy? Is Daddy talking about a new bakery? Like a really big one?"

Lani turned, smiling. "That's right, sweetheart. A bakery."

Julian's expression softened the moment he saw her. He knelt down so they were eye level. "We're dreaming up something special," he said warmly. "We want to fix up the bakery and make it shine again. Fill it with the best cakes, cookies, and bread you can imagine."

Naomi's whole face came alive. "With cupcakes too? And maybe tarts with strawberries on top?"

Julian laughed, his voice rich and gentle. "Definitely cupcakes. And plenty of strawberries."

Naomi clapped her hands together, her excitement bubbling over.

"And Mommy can bake all her best things! Remember your cinnamon rolls, Mommy? Those were the bestest ever!"

She spun toward Julian, eyes wide with hope. "And maybe you can help! You make things fancy. We could have sparkles on the cakes! And sprinkles! Oh, and bread, lots of bread that smells warm and happy."

Lani felt her throat tighten with affection. Leave it to Naomi to capture the dream so simply, to see it not as a business plan but as something joyful.

Julian's smile softened. "That's exactly the idea," he said. "A place that smells like happiness."

Naomi threw her arms around her mother's legs. "It's gonna be the best bakery ever!"

Julian met Lani's eyes over Naomi's head, and for a heartbeat, everything else fell away, the worries, the risks, the unknowns. In that quiet look, she saw the same certainty that Naomi carried, that this wasn't just a dream. It was the start of something real.

Naomi's excitement carried her back toward Julian. But this time her tone shifted, quieter, unsure. She fidgeted with the edge of her pajama sleeve.

"Daddy?" she asked softly.

He tilted his head, giving her his full attention. "Yes, sweet pea?"

Her big brown eyes lifted to his. "Are you gonna stay? After the bakery's finished, I mean. You're not gonna go away, right? My first daddy left. Mommy said he didn't want to stay, not even for me." Her little voice trembled. "You're not gonna do that, are you?"

The words hit Lani like a blow to the chest. She opened her mouth to say something, to soothe, to protect, but Julian was already moving.

He lowered himself so he was sitting on the floor, right in front of Naomi, his eyes level with hers. There was no hesitation, no flicker of discomfort, only quiet certainty.

"Hey," he said softly, reaching out to gently take her small hand in his. "Look at me, Naomi."

She did.

"I'm not going anywhere. Not when the bakery's finished. Not ever. You and your mom are my home now. Okay?"

Naomi blinked, her bottom lip wobbling. "Forever?"

Julian smiled, his voice tender but sure. "Forever. Cross my heart."

Naomi studied him, searching his face the way only a child could. Then, as if satisfied by what she saw, she leaned forward and wrapped her arms around his neck. "

Okay," she whispered. "Forever sounds good."

Lani pressed a hand to her chest as emotion swelled so thick and full she could hardly breathe. Watching them, Naomi's tiny frame tucked into Julian's arms, his face buried in her curls, she felt something deep inside her settle. The ache of old wounds, of loss and betrayal, softened. This moment, this connection, was something real.

Julian glanced up, his eyes meeting hers. There was a quiet promise there, one that didn't need words.

Naomi pulled back slightly, wiping her eyes with the back of her hand. Then, as if the heaviness had never been, she grinned. "So, can I still have a cupcake corner in the bakery? With sprinkles?"

Julian chuckled, brushing a stray curl from her forehead. "Absolutely. Your very own cupcake corner. You'll be the official sprinkle supervisor."

Naomi giggled, her earlier worry already dissolving into excitement. "Then it's settled! We're gonna make the best bakery ever!"

Lani smiled through her tears. "I think we will, sweetheart."

Julian stood, scooping Naomi up and settling her on his hip. "Come on," he said. "How about we draw it out? We can plan the counters, the ovens, and of course, the sprinkle station."

Naomi gasped. "Yes! I'll get my crayons!" She wriggled down and ran off toward her room, her laughter echoing down the hall.

When she was gone, Julian turned to Lani. He reached out, brushing his thumb gently along her cheek. "She's amazing," he said quietly. "So are you."

Lani swallowed, her eyes glistening. "You handled that perfectly. Thank you for saying what she needed to hear."

Julian's hand slid down to clasp hers. "I didn't just say it, Lani. I meant it."

And standing there in the warm glow of the fire, surrounded by sketches of dreams and the scent of cinnamon still lingering in the air, Lani believed him. For the first time in a long while, the future didn't feel

{ 32 }

Julian

The days following the vibrant celebrations of New Year's Eve settled into a rhythm of quiet intensity. Julian watched the soft transformation of their lives, from fireworks and champagne to flour dust on Lani's apron and the comforting scent of morning coffee.

The dream of their bakery, *Shepard and Vance,'* was no longer a shimmering idea. It was becoming real, and that meant structure, strategy, and sometimes a little fear.

Julian had commandeered Lani's dining room. Whiteboards took over, once reserved for Naomi's doodles, now covered with flowcharts, bullet points, and calculations.

Evening chats about weekend plans shifted into planning sessions, each one focused on turning what they felt into what they could build.

One crisp January morning, Julian tapped a heavy binder filled with recipes and Market research.

"Menu development," he said. "This is where our heart meets the market. What are the absolute must-haves, Lani?"

She looked up from her sketch of a sourdough boule, her eyes lighting up.

"Sourdough, of course. That'll be our signature. But we also need croissants, flaky, buttery, melt-in-your-mouth. And celebration cakes, something customizable for every occasion. We can have a 'Naomi's Imagination' tier, where kids design their own cake."

Julian nodded, scribbling. "Celebration cakes, excellent. Breakfast pastries, lunch options, too. We want to be a destination, not just a place to grab a loaf."

"How about the 'Artisan Sampler'," Julian suggested, pointing to a section on the whiteboard. "A curated selection of our best sellers, perfect for weekend brunch for two. It will be a higher price point, but it offers a tasting experience. We can market it as 'a journey through 'Shepard and Vance'. What do you think?"

"Absolutely," Lani agreed. "And we should have a signature coffee blend. Something locally sourced, perhaps, to tie into our community focus. We can partner with a local roaster."

"And we need to think about dietary needs," she added, flipping through her worn recipe notebook. "Gluten-free options, vegan pastries. We don't want anyone to feel left out."

Lani spoke of texture, crumb, and balance, while Julian layered in ingredient costs, labor hours, and shelf life. They made spreadsheets, crunched numbers, debated artisanal versus scalable, and always circled back to what felt right.

Then one afternoon, Lani's parents, Thomas and Elenore, came in. Her cheeks were flushed with curiosity and warmth.

"You two have been at it all week," she said, setting down a tray of warm cider in the makeshift office. "How's the dream going?"

Thomas leaned forward, eyes bright. "Your excitement is contagious, Julian. It sounds like something special."

Julian smiled, feeling the warmth in the room. "Thank you, Thomas. It really is our vision. Lani's talent, my logistics. And now we're building the place."

Elenore put a hand on Lani's shoulder. "That's wonderful. And we're here for whatever you need."

Their support made something in Julian settle. It wasn't just about business anymore. It was about family.

What do you think of this?" He presented a design featuring a gracefully unfurling wheat stalk with subtle shading. "Our Logo."

Lani studied it, a thoughtful expression on her face. "It's beautiful, Julian. It's sophisticated. But does it also show... warmth? Maybe we could soften the lines slightly, or add a touch of color that feels more earthy, like a warm terracotta or a muted olive green?"

She then pulled out a small sketchbook she kept for creative inspiration, quickly sketching a few variations Julian watched her, a quiet admiration in his eyes, recognizing the intuitive artistry that fueled her vision.

Thomas and Elenore offered ideas, told stories of local traditions, and became a living bridge between the past and what they were creating.

And when it all felt big, and real, and a little scary, Julian looked at those two women, Lani with flour on her fingers, Naomi with sparkles of imagination in her eyes and knew they were ready.

The business plan, the loans, the grants, they mattered. But what mattered more was the warmth, the shared laughter, the flour-dusted mornings, and the promise of something lasting.

***

A few days later, Julian led Lani and Naomi upstairs in the bakery. The space was dusty, the wallpaper peeling, the windows cold. Thomas and Julian had cleared out boxes and crates. The sunlight streamed through wide panes, the hum of potential, and a chance for them.

Lani's breath caught. "Julian... this is huge."

"It is," he said. "But it's ours. A place where you bake your heart out, and where Naomi can play and have friends over. It will be our sanctuary. And I'll be there day in, day out. Not just in the mornings or weekends."

Naomi tugged his sleeve. "Daddy, are you staying? After the bakery's done? You're not going away, right?"

Julian's heart stopped. He knelt and took her hand. "No," he said softly but firmly. "I told you I'm staying. You and your mom are my home now, every day."

Her face broke into a grin.

Lani's eyes filled with tears. In that moment, the vision transformed into the home they were building together.

Design sessions with their architect became less about obstacles and more about possibilities. Earthy tones, reclaimed wood tables, soft lighting, and windows that invited in the mountain breeze all became strands of their story.

The air in Lani's cozy living room, usually filled with the comforting scent of baked goods and the warmth of shared laughter, took on a slightly different hue that Sunday afternoon.

Elenore, her hands habitually busy arranging the cushions on the sofa, spoke first, her voice soft but carrying the weight of maternal concern.

"Lani, darling, it's all so exciting, truly it is. This bakery… Julian is so clearly passionate, and your baking is simply divine. But we've seen you when you've been… stretched. Remember that period after college when you tried to do freelance design work and take night classes? You barely slept. This venture sounds… big. Really big."

She looked at Lani, her eyes a mirror of genuine worry. "We just don't want you to take on too much, sweetie. We've seen you find your peace again, and we cherish that for you."

Thomas, seated beside her, nodded his agreement, his gaze steady and kind. He was a man of quiet wisdom, his support a bedrock for Lani. "Your mother's right, Lani. It's a wonderful dream, and Julian seems like a very capable young man. We can see how happy he makes you. But running a business, especially a food business, it's a marathon, not a sprint. There will be long hours, unexpected problems, and a great deal of pressure. We're just... concerned about you. About your energy and your well-being." He reached out and gently squeezed Lani's hand.

"You've worked so hard to find this balance, and we don't want to see it disrupted."

Lani's heart ached slightly at their worry. She understood their concern. The years of watching her navigate life's challenges and the moments they had worried about her. This was their way of protecting her.

She turned to Julian, who had been listening intently, his expression one of understanding and quiet reassurance. He met her gaze, a subtle nod passing between them, a silent promise to address her parents' concerns with care and respect.

Julian stepped forward slightly, his calm presence grounding the room. He understood that Elenore and Thomas's worries didn't come from doubt, but from love. A love that wanted to protect their daughter from being overwhelmed again. When he spoke, his voice carried a warmth that immediately softened the air.

"Elenore, Thomas," he began gently, "I understand your concerns completely, and I appreciate you sharing them with me and with Lani. It's natural to worry. Lani has faced so many challenges and shown resilience. She is so much stronger than you think."

He turned toward Lani then; his gaze filled with such sincerity that it brought a faint blush to her cheeks. "My partnership with Lani is built on more than just a shared business idea. We have respect, shared dreams, and a commitment to each other's well-being. When we talk about *'Shepard and Vance,'* we're not just talking about expansion plans. We're talking about building something beautiful together. Lani's happiness and peace of mind are important to me. I don't want to add stress to her life. This is about Lani using her talent and passion and shining more than ever.

He paused for a moment, ensuring his words sank in before continuing. "I've been involved in the planning every step of the way, and I can assure you, Lani won't be carrying this burden alone. My role is to manage the operational and financial aspects. To smooth out the rough edges and anticipate potential obstacles so she can focus on what she does best: create. We have a clear vision of the workload and a strong financial foundation.

"We can hire skilled staff when needed rather than me getting overloaded," Lani quickly added.

"I'm committed to Lani. We're building a team." He smiled softly. "And you know Lani. If she ever feels overwhelmed, she'll be the first to say so."

Elenore listened intently, her hands folded in her lap, the crease in her brow slowly softening as Julian spoke. She studied his face and the way he spoke of Lani with such tenderness and conviction. When she finally responded, her voice carried a hint of emotion beneath practicality.

"It's just... the passion can be so consuming, Julian. We've seen it before with Lani. When she gets an idea, she pours her entire being into it. We've seen her burn the candle at both ends. We don't want to see that sparkle in her eyes dim under the weight of responsibility."

Julian nodded, his tone steady and compassionate. "I understand that concern, Elenore. And I agree, passion is powerful, but it has to be channeled properly. That's why we're putting systems in place from the start to prevent burnout.

"We're setting realistic schedules, delegating tasks, and, most importantly, maintaining boundaries, "Lani added.

"We'll have policies around hours, regular breaks, time off, everything designed to keep our team thriving. Lani and I will adhere to those policies. Our goal is to create an environment where passion drives creativity, not exhaustion."

Thomas, who had been quiet until now, leaned forward, his expression thoughtful. "We've seen how you've helped Lani find her footing, Julian. She seems... lighter, more grounded. This bakery feels like it's going to add to that, rather than take away from it."

Julian met his gaze without hesitation. "That's precisely the aim, Thomas. When Lani first shared her vision for the bakery, I didn't just see a business opportunity, I saw a reflection of who she is. We've talked at length about what this means for her, and we've built everything around ensuring Naomi and Lani's happiness is at the center.

"My promise to you, as Lani's parents, is that I'll do everything in my power to make sure this business remains a positive, empowering force in her life."

Lani's heart swelled with pride as she listened. When she finally spoke, her voice was steady but full of feeling. She reached out, threading her fingers through Julian's.

"Mom, Dad," she began softly, "I know you worry, and I love you for it. But Julian's right. This isn't just a business to me; this bakery is a space for me to express myself. To take 'Shepard's Sweets' and build it into something secure for Naomi. And Julian... he's not just my partner in this; he's my partner in everything. He's my rock, and I trust him completely." She looked between them, her expression bright and sure.

Elenors' eyes glistened as she reached for Lani's hand. Her voice was softer now, the worry in it laced with love. "Seeing you so happy, Lani, it's everything. And knowing that Julian cares so deeply about that happiness... that means the world to us. We trust you both. Just promise us you'll always talk to us if things ever get too heavy, alright?"

"Always, Mom," Lani said, her smile tender.

Thomas nodded, a trace of pride in his expression. "It sounds like you've thought this through, both of you. That's all a parent can hope for. We're proud of you, Lani and very happy for you, Julian. Just... pace yourselves."

Julian's answering smile was warm and genuine. "We will, Thomas. We're building this carefully and thoughtfully. And when we open, the first celebratory loaf will be yours."

The tension that had once filled the room melted into something lighter and warmer. Lani poured tea, after setting out a plate of her latest cookies.

Soon, the conversation drifted to the upcoming community fair and Naomi's latest artistic masterpiece. Laughter returned easily. The room felt full again, of love, of hope, of possibility.

Julian watched the easy rhythm of Lani's family, the way her mother laughed at something Naomi had said, the way her father's smile softened. And he knew, with quiet certainty, that this—*all of this*—was what they were building toward. Not just a bakery, but a life grounded in love, care, and connection.

{ **33** }

Lani

The dawn broke with a gentle, hesitant light, brushing the winter sky with strokes of rose and gold. It was the kind of morning that whispered of new beginnings—a perfect prelude to the day Lani and Julian had poured their hearts into.

"Shepard and Vance" stood gleaming in the early light, its polished wood and gleaming glass restored to life after years of neglect. The old bakery now shined.

Every shelf, every polished surface, every carefully placed detail spoke of love and labor. It was the result of months of sleepless nights, anxious planning, and joyful creation.

The quiet, forgotten upstairs was once empty and echoing with the ghosts of the past. Now, it was the center of their love and their family home.

Lani smoothed the front of her emerald dress, the same shade as the rosemary sprigs Julian had tucked into her hair that morning. Her reflection in the glass display caught her off guard: the same woman yet somehow transformed. Her hands trembled slightly, betraying the swirl of emotions within with nervousness, exhilaration, and disbelief. The dream she had had for so long was finally real.

Julian stood beside her, solid and steady. His dark shirt was rolled at the sleeves, his expression calm, though she could see the fatigue in the corners of his eyes. When he met her gaze, his smile was quiet but full of warmth. His smile anchored her.

"Ready?" he murmured, his voice low and steady.

Lani took a slow breath. "As I'll ever be."

Naomi's bright laughter filled the air as she skipped from table to table, her pink apron slightly too big and tied in a lopsided bow. She stood on tiptoe to straighten a napkin, then carefully nudged a vase of winter flowers into place, mimicking her mother's careful touch.

"It's so pretty!" she declared, her voice full of pride. "It smells like happiness in here. You and Daddy made it perfect!"

Lani's heart swelled at the words. Naomi had been their constant cheerleader, pouring as much love into this bakery as they had. Together, they had built not just a business, but something that felt alive. A place of warmth and belonging.

The scent of freshly baked sourdough hung heavy in the air, mingled with the sweetness of croissants dusted in sugar and the delicate perfume of lemon and elderflower financiers cooling on the racks. The aroma alone could have drawn a crowd.

Julian checked the coffee machine and polished it to a mirror shine. "The espresso's ready," he said with a wink. "First pot's on."

Lani smiled. "I think excitement will be enough caffeine for today."

Outside, the town was waking. The people who had watched the bakery's transformation from the street. Many who had lingered by the windows, peeking through to glimpse progress, were gathering now, their breath fogging in the cold air.

Julian reached for her hand, his thumb tracing lazy circles across her palm. "We did it," he said softly. "After everything... we really did it."

She met his eyes. "We did."

Naomi glanced at the clock. "Almost time! The whole town is here," she exclaimed

Lani's pulse quickened. Months of dreaming and planning had led to this single moment, the opening of the doors. Shepard and Vance was no longer an idea or a hope.

Julian's voice broke through her thoughts. "No matter what happens today, Lani," he said, "I'm proud of you. So proud of us."

She leaned into him for just a heartbeat. "And I of you."

Then the clock struck the hour.

Julian turned the brass handles and opened the doors. A breath of cold air swept in, carrying the hum of voices. The crowd outside was filled with familiar faces, curious strangers, and neighbors who had once known her family stepped forward. The warm light from the bakery spilled out onto the street, and the first few visitors crossed the threshold.

The sound of laughter followed them in.

Within minutes, Shepard and Vance was alive with conversation and the morning rush, the hiss of steam from the espresso machine, the gentle thud of loaves on the counter, the soft clink of cups. Lani moved from guest to guest, her nerves dissolving with each smile she met.

"This sourdough," said an older man holding a round loaf, "tastes like your grandmother's."

Lani's heart caught. "It's her starter," she said softly. "She passed it down to me. I think she'd be happy to see it alive again."

A woman nearby smiled as she tasted one of the financiers. "And this? Lemon and elderflower? It's so delicate."

"That was Julian's idea," Lani said, glancing toward him. "He always finds the perfect balance."

Julian, ever gracious, was already chatting with a group of customers at the counter, his laughter blending easily into the hum of voices. Naomi, wearing braids with pink ribbons, handed out samples, her cheerfulness filling the space like music.

The bakery was exactly what they had hoped for, a place where people lingered, shared stories, and left a little lighter than when they came in.

And then, through the bustle, Lani saw her parents near the entrance.

Her father stood tall, pride softening his usually stern features. Her mother's eyes shimmered with tears. Her hand pressed gently to her heart as she took in the sight.

"You've done it, darling," she said when Lani approached. "Your grandmother would have been so proud. We are so proud of you. You've brought the heart of this town back to life."

Her father nodded. "This bakery isn't just a business. It's a legacy—and you've made it your own."

Emotion welled in Lani's chest. "Thank you," she whispered. "That means everything."

The day unfolded in a golden blur. The steady rhythm of baking and serving continued until the afternoon sun streamed through the windows, casting honey-colored light across the floor. The crowd began to thin, replaced by a few lingering customers savoring the final cups of coffee.

Naomi attempted to tidy up with her usual awkward grace, and Julian wiped down the counter with unhurried precision.

Lani leaned against the counter, exhaustion and happiness blending in her chest. The air smelled of sugar and coffee and warmth. When she looked up, Julian was watching her. His smile was quiet, knowing, and full of love.

"This," he said softly, "feels like home."

She crossed to him, resting her head briefly against his shoulder. "It is home."

As twilight settled outside, they climbed the narrow stairs to the renovated space above the bakery, the place Julian had chosen for them months ago. Once an empty attic full of dust and cobwebs, it now glowed with soft light. The scent of bread still drifted upward through the floorboards.

Lani stood by the window, looking down at the warmly lit bakery below. Snow had begun to fall again, the flakes swirling in the streetlamps like slow-motion confetti.

Julian came up behind her and wrapped his arms around her waist.

"First day down," he murmured.

She smiled. "And a lifetime to go."

Below them, Shepard and Vance stood proud against the night, its windows glowing like a hearth at the heart of the town. It was all theirs.

Lani exhaled softly, the tension of months melting away. The bakery had begun as a dream —a tribute to her past —but had become something more: a life, a love, a promise made real.

Julian bent down and kissed her temple. "To us," he whispered.

Lani smiled, her eyes lifting to the sky. "To us," she echoed, her voice soft but sure.

Lani knew with quiet certainty that this was only the beginning.

The sweetest one yet.

Author Biography

Renee McCorry began her writing career as a small-town reporter, where she discovered her love of storytelling and simple living. A passionate suburban homesteader and lifelong advocate for self-sufficiency, Renee is the author of *Urban Homesteading for Beginners*, *6 Ways to Live a More Self-Sufficient Life*, and *The Farm Girl's Journal*

After years of writing nonfiction Renee has returned to her first love—fiction—bringing with her the warmth, humor, and heart of a life well-lived. When she's not dreaming up new stories or wrestling unruly squash plants, you can find her strolling through Scottish Highland Games with her husband, spending time with her friends, children, and grandchild, or doting on her "well cared for" dog.

Renee lives in the Southeast with her husband and fur baby, where she continues to embrace the joys and challenges of a not-so-ordinary life.

For more information about Renee and her books, please visit:

www.leafandlores.com
or follow her on Facebook@leafandlores
or Instagram @leafandlores

Please consider leaving a review on Amazon, Barnes & Noble, and Good Reads.

Your feedback helps others discover this book, and supports indie authors like myself.